ANDRÉ MALRAUX

Born in 1901, coming of age amid the crises and conflicts of a troubled century, André Malraux has lived a life that has about it the aura of a legend. As an archeologist, he has hunted for forgotten temples in the jungles of Cambodia and for lost cities in the Sahara. He has participated in revolutionary movements in China and Southeast Asia. He has fought in the air in Spain, and in the French tank corps and the French Resistance. Once a leading Communist sympathizer, now one of Charles de Gaulle's most active supporters, he is currently Minister for Cultural Affairs in the Fifth French Republic. All this, however, remains secondary to his writings. The Voices of Silence *stands as a monumental work of art history and aesthetic theory. His novels—chief among them* Man's Fate *and* Man's Hope*—are among the very few works of fiction that have succeeded in giving true voice to the violent realities and moral complexities of our age.*

BANTAM MODERN CLASSICS

ALL THE KING'S MEN
by Robert Penn Warren

APE AND ESSENCE
by Aldous Huxley

DEMIAN
by Hermann Hesse

THE DESERT OF LOVE
by François Mauriac

GOODBYE, COLUMBUS
by Philip Roth

THE LAST TEMPTATION OF CHRIST
by Nikos Kazantzakis

MADELEINE
by André Gide

MAN'S HOPE
by André Malraux

MAN'S HOPE

ANDRÉ MALRAUX

*Translated from the French
by Stuart Gilbert
and Alastair Macdonald*

*This low-priced Bantam Book
has been completely reset in a type face
designed for easy reading, and was printed
from new plates. It contains the complete
text of the original hard-cover edition.*
NOT ONE WORD HAS BEEN OMITTED.

MAN'S HOPE
*A Bantam Book / published by arrangement with
Random House, Inc.*

PRINTING HISTORY
*Random House edition published September 1938
2nd printing . . . November 1938
3rd printing . . . December 1938
4th printing . . . December 1938
Bantam Modern Classic edition published January 1968*

*Bantam Books are published by Bantam Books, Inc., a subsidiary
of Grosset & Dunlap, Inc. Its trade-mark, consisting of the words
"Bantam Books" and the portrayal of a bantam, is registered in the
United States Patent Office and in other countries. Marca Registrada.
Bantam Books, Inc., 271 Madison Avenue, New York, N.Y. 10016.*

PRINTED IN THE UNITED STATES OF AMERICA

Contents

Part One

"CARELESS RAPTURE"

I. "Careless Rapture"

1

ALL Madrid was astir in the warm summer night, loud with the rumble of lorries stacked with rifles. For some days the workers' organizations had been announcing that a fascist rising might take place at any moment, that the soldiers in the barracks had been "got at," and munitions were pouring in. At one o'clock in the morning the Government had decided to arm the people, and from three o'clock the production of a union-card gave every member the right to bear arms. It was high time, for the reports telephoned in from the provinces, which had sounded hopeful between midnight and two o'clock, were beginning to strike a different note.

The Central Exchange at the Northern Railway Terminus rang up the various stations along the line. Ramos, the Secretary of the Railroad Workers' Union, and Manuel, assigned to help him that night, were in charge. With the exception of Navarre—the line from which had been cut—the replies had been uniform. Either the Government had the situation well in hand, or a Workers' Committee had taken charge of the city, pending instructions from the central authority. But now a change was coming over the dialogues.

"Is that Huesca?"

"Who's speaking?"

"The Workers' Committee, Madrid."

"Not for long, you swine! *Arriba España!*"

Fixed to the wall by thumb-tacks, the special late edition of the *Claridad* flaunted a caption six columns wide: *Comrades to Arms.*

"Hullo, Avila? How's things at your end? North Madrid Station speaking."

"The hell it is, you bastards! *Viva el Cristo Rey!*"

"See you soon. *Salud!*"

An urgent message came through to Ramos.

The Northern lines, it seemed, were converging on Saragossa, Burgos and Valladolid.

"Is that Saragossa? Put me through to the Workers' Committee at the station."

"We've shot them. Your turn next. *Arriba España!*"

"Hullo, Tablada! Madrid North here, union delegate."

"Call the jail, you son of a bitch. That's where your friends are. And we'll be coming for you very soon; we want to have a word with you."

"*Bueno!* Let's meet on the Alcala, second bar on the left. Got it?"

"Hullo, is that Burgos?"

"*Commandante,* Burgos, speaking."

Ramos hung up.

A telephone-bell rang.

"Hullo, Madrid! Who's there?"

"Railway Workers' Union."

"Miranda speaking. We hold the station and the town. *Arriba España!*"

"But *we* hold Madrid. *Salud!*"

So there was no counting on help from the North, except by way of Valladolid. Remained the Asturias.

"Is that Oviedo? Yes? Who's speaking?" Ramos was getting wary.

"Workers' Delegate. Railway Station."

"Ramos here, the Union Secretary. How are things at your end?"

"Aranda's loyal to the Government. It's touch and go at Valladolid. We're entraining three thousand armed miners to reinforce our lot."

"When?" A clash of rifle-butts drowned the answer. Ramos repeated the question.

"At once."

"*Salud!*"

Ramos turned to Manuel. "Keep in touch with that train, by telephone." He called Valladolid.

"Is that Valladolid?"

"Who's speaking?"

"Station Delegate."

"How's it going?"

"Our fellows hold the barracks. We're expecting a rein-forcement from Oviedo. Do your best to get them here as soon as possible. But don't you worry; here it'll all go well. What about you?"

They were singing outside the station; Ramos could not hear himself speak.

"What?" Valladolid repeated.

"Going well! Going well!"

"Have the troops revolted?"

"Not yet."

Valladolid hung up.

All reinforcements from the North could be diverted in that direction.

The air was thick with engine-smoke, the reek of hot metal —the door stood open on the summer night—and a faint odour of cardboard files came from the office shelves. Manuel noted down, among official messages concerning points and sidings—of which he could make little—the calls coming in from the various Spanish towns. From outside came bursts of song, a clatter of rifle-butts. Time and again he had to have the messages repeated. The fascists merely rang off. He made a note of the various positions on the railway-map. Navarre was cut off; all the east of the Bay of Biscay—Bilbao, Santander and San Sebastian—was loyal: communications were cut at Miranda. The Asturias and Valladolid, however, were with the Government. The telephone rang ceaselessly.

"Hullo! Segovia speaking. Who are you?"

"Representative of the Union." Manuel looked at Ramos doubtfully. After all, what was his real position here?

"We're coming along to bite 'em off you."

"We won't even notice it. *Salud!*"

Now it was the turn of the fascist stations to start ringing up: Sarracin, Lerma, Aranda del Duero, Sepulveda, Burgos again. From Burgos to the Sierra, threats came pouring in faster than the reinforcement trains.

"Ministry of the Interior speaking. Is that the North Station Exchange? Inform all stations that the Civil Guard and the Assault Guard are with the Government."

"Madrid South speaking. Is that Ramos? How's it going in the North?"

"They seem to be holding Miranda and a good many places further South. Three thousand miners are going to Valladolid. That district looks pretty good for us. How's things your way?"

"They've occupied the stations at Seville and Granada. The rest are holding out."

"Cordova?"

"We don't know. There's fighting going on in the suburbs of the towns where they hold the stations. We're in rather a jam at Triana. At Pennaroya, too. Look here, what you say about Valladolid's hard to swallow; sure they haven't taken it?"

Ramos changed over to another telephone.

"Hullo, Valladolid! Who's speaking?"

"The Station Delegate."

"Oh! We'd heard the fascists were in."

"You heard wrong. All's well. What about you? Have the troops revolted?"

"No."

"Hullo, Madrid North. Who's speaking?"

"In charge of transportation."

"Tablada here. Didn't you ring us up?"

"We heard you were all shot, or in jail, or something of the sort."

"We made a getaway. It's the fascists who're in jail. *Salud!*"

"*Casa del Pueblo* speaking. Inform all loyal stations that the Government, supported by the popular militia, is master of Barcelona, Murcia, Valencia, and Malaga, all Estremadura and the Mediterranean coast."

"Hullo! Tordesillas here. Who's speaking?"

"Workers' Council, Madrid."

"Ah! Bastards of your sort are shot! *Arriba España!*"

Medina del Campo; same dialogue. The Valladolid line was the only main line of communication with the South still open.

"Hullo, Leon! Who's speaking?"

"Union delegate. *Salud!*"

"Madrid North here. Has the miners' train from Oviedo passed?"

"Yes."

"Do you know where it is?"

"Somewhere near Mayorga, I guess."

Outside, the Madrid streets were alive with songs and the clash of rifle-butts.

"Is that Mayorga? Madrid this end. Who's speaking?"

"Who are you?"

"Workers' Council, Madrid."

The receiver clicked dead. What had become of the train?

"Is that Valladolid? Are you sure of holding till the miners arrive?"

"Dead sure."

"Mayorga doesn't answer."

"It doesn't matter."

"Hullo, Madrid? Oviedo speaking, Aranda's just revolted. Fighting going on."

"Where's the miners' train?"

"Between Leon and Mayorga."

"Hold on a moment!" Manuel rang up, Ramos beside him. "That Mayorga? Madrid here."

"Who's that?"

"Workers' Council. Who are you?"

"Company Commander, Spanish Falangists. Your train's gone by, you fools. We hold all the stations up to Valladolid. We're waiting for your miners with machine-guns. Aranda's been cleaned up. See you soon!"

"The sooner the better!"

Manuel rang up all the stations between Mayorga and Valladolid, one after the other.

"That Sepulveda? Madrid North this end; Workers' Committee."

"Yes, your train's gone through, you god-damned fools. And we're coming this week to castrate you, you silly bitches."

"A slight physiological mistake, my lad. Salud!"

The calls continued.

"Hullo, Madrid! Is that Madrid? Navalperal de Pinares here. Railway Station. We've rushed the town again. Yes, we disarmed the fascists; they're in irons. Pass the good news along. Their people telephone us every few minutes to know if the town is still theirs. Hullo! Hullo!"

"We must send false news out everywhere," Ramos said.

"They'll check up on it."

"Still, it'll always give them something to scratch their heads over."

"Hullo, Madrid North? U.G.T. here. Who's speaking?"

"Ramos."

"We're told a train-load of fascists is on its way, with up-to-date armament. Coming from Burgos, they say. Have you any news of it?"

"We should know about it here; all the stations up to the Sierra are in our hands. Still we'd better take precautions. Hold the line a moment."

"Manuel, call the Sierra."

Manuel called one station after another, sawing the air with a ruler as if he were beating time. The whole Sierra was loyal. He called up the General Post Office Exchange. The same answer. Obviously, on the near side of the Sierra, either the fascists were lying low, or they'd been crushed.

Still, they were holding half the North. In Navarre, Mola, the former Chief of Police at Madrid, was in command; three-quarters of the regular army, as usual, was against the Government. On the Government side were the populace, the Assault Guards, and possibly the Civil Guards as well.

"The U.G.T. here. Is that Ramos?"

"Yes."

"What about that train?"

Ramos passed on the news. "And how's things generally?" he asked.

"*Bueno!* Excellent. Except at the War Ministry. At six they said that all was over but the shouting. We told them they were barking up the wrong tree. But they claim that the militia's sure to scuttle. Anyhow, we don't give a damn for their opinion. . . . The men here are making such a racket, singing, I can hardly hear you."

In the receiver Ramos could hear the songs across the noises of the railway station.

Though the attack had obviously been launched almost everywhere at the same moment, it seemed as if an army on the march were sweeping down; the railway stations held by the fascists were getting nearer and nearer Madrid. And yet there had been such tension in the air for several weeks, the dread of an attack which they might have to face, unarmed, had weighed so heavily on all the populace that tonight's warfare came as an immense relief.

"Got your winter-sports bus handy?" Ramos asked Manuel. "Yes."

He deputed one of the railway officials to take over the Central Exchange. Some months before, Manuel had bought a second-hand car for his skiing expeditions in the Sierra. Every Sunday Ramos used it for propaganda work. That night Manuel had put it once again at the disposal of the Communist Party. The Party was overwhelmed with work, and Manuel had chosen to co-operate once again with his old friend, Ramos.

"We mustn't have 1934 all over again!" Ramos said. "Let's get off to Tetuan de las Victorias."

"Where's that?"

"Cuatro Caminos."

When they had gone three hundred yards, they were challenged by the first *guardia*.

"Your papers, *Compañeros*."

"Your papers" meant his union-card. Manuel rarely had with him his Communist Party card. He earned his living in the film industry as a sound-man. A vaguely Montparnassian style of dressing enabled him to fancy that he had escaped, anyhow sartorially speaking, from the influence of the bourgeoisie. In his dark, rather thick-set features, only the bushy eyebrows struck a proletarian note. But no sooner had the *milicianos* glanced in his direction than they saw and recognized the jovial, solid-looking jowl of their friend, Ramos, and his shock of curly hair. So the car moved off again amid back-slappings, uplifted fists, and cries of *Salud;* and the darkness was all fraternity.

And yet the conflict between Right- and Left-Wing Socialists —Caballero's antagonism to any idea of a Prieto cabinet—had been violent enough during these last few weeks. . . .

At the second sentry-post some F.A.I. men were handing over a suspect to a group of U.G.T. workers, their former adversaries. Good work! thought Ramos. The distribution of arms was still going on.

A lorry, piled with rifles, had just arrived.

"They look like shoe-soles, don't they?" Ramos said. All that could be seen of the stacked rifles was the steel socket at the bottom of each butt.

"That's so," Manuel said. "Like tholes."

"What the hell are you lisping for?"

"Broke a tooth at breakfast. That's all my tongue can think about; it doesn't care a hoot for anti-fascism today."

"What were you eating?"

"A fork."

In the dim light, shadowy forms were embracing the rifles that had just been given them. They were greeted by the envious curses of others, who stood packed like matches in a box, waiting for their turn. Women went by, with baskets full of ammunition.

"And none too soon," some one was grumbling. "Considering all the time we've been expecting them to launch their bloody rising!"

"I quite believed the Government was going to leave us in the lurch."

"Don't you fret; we'll show 'em mighty soon where they get off, the dirty swine."

"The people of Madrid are *sereno* tonight."

Every five hundred yards came another sentry-post. Fascist cars were scouring Madrid with machine-guns. And everywhere were the same clenched fists, the same fraternity. Everywhere, too, the quaintly sheepish gestures of sentries handling a rifle for the first time. The first time in a hundred years.

When they arrived, Ramos dropped his cigarette and stamped it out. "No more smoking," he said.

He ran off and came back ten minutes later, followed by three of his comrades, each carrying parcels wrapped in newspaper and tied up with string.

Manuel had placidly lit another cigarette.

"Better not smoke," Ramos smiled. "It's dynamite."

The three men stowed away the parcels, half in front and half in the back of the car, and disappeared. Manuel had left his seat to stamp out his cigarette on the ground. When he looked up at Ramos, there was consternation in his face.

"Hullo? What's come over you?" Ramos exclaimed.

"Can't you leave a fellow in peace?" Manuel retorted.

"All right. . . . Now let's get a move on."

"Look here! Couldn't we find some other car? I could drive another one, you know."

"Listen! There's bridges to be blown up, Avila bridge to start with. We're bringing the dynamite; it'll be sent off right away where it's wanted, see? To Peguerinos, and so forth. You don't want us to wait two hours, do you? This car runs all right anyhow—we know that much."

"Very well," Manuel gloomily agreed.

It was not so much to his car that he clung as to its wonderful gadgets. They set out again with Manuel at the wheel and Ramos behind, holding on his lap a bundle of hand-grenades.

Quite suddenly, Manuel discovered he had lost all interest in his car. It had ceased to be: nothing remained but this memorable night, fraught with a vague and boundless hope, this crowded night when every man had his appointed task on earth. And he heard, like the beating of his heart, a distant drum.

Every five minutes the car was held up by a sentry.

The *milicianos,* many of whom could not read, patted the occupants of the car on the shoulder as soon as they recognized

Ramos. No sooner did they hear him shout, "Stop smoking, damn you!" and see the parcels in the car than they began capering with delight. Dynamite it was—the good old romantic weapon of the Asturianos!

The car moved on again. From his right an F.A.I. camion, packed with armed workers, suddenly swerved to the left. All vehicles that night were doing a good fifty miles an hour. Manuel tried to dodge the camion, felt his light car lifted clear off the ground, and thought to himself: "This is the end!"

Suddenly he found himself lying on his belly among packets of dynamite rolling over and over like chestnuts—on the pavement, as luck would have it. Under his eyes lay a small black patch; a pool of his own blood glistening in the light of a streetlamp. He felt little or no pain, but his bleeding nose gave him the semblance of a wounded hero. What was Ramos bellowing over there? "No smoking, *compañeros!*" He followed suit, swung round and saw his friend, his legs crossed, still nursing the bundle of hand-grenades, while armed civilians swarmed round him, fussing over the packages they did not dare to touch. There right in the middle, a cigarette butt—Ramos had taken advantage of the fact that he was in the back of the car to light yet another cigarette—smouldered in solitary state. Manuel crushed it out with his foot. His friend began to stack the packages along the wall. As for the little sports car, the less said about it the better.

A radio was announcing: *The insurgent troops are marching on the centre of Barcelona. The Government has the situation well in hand.*

Manuel helped to stack the dynamite. Ramos, usually so active, did not move.

"Why in hell don't you lend a hand?"

The insurgent troops are marching on the centre of Barcelona.

"Haven't got over the shock. Can't move my arm. But it'll come back. Let's stop the first empty car that comes by, and get going."

2

THE first faint light of a summer dawn was rising over Barcelona, silvering the cool, newly watered streets. The little tavern looking out on the huge, deserted Avenida, had remained open all night, and in it Sils, known as "the Negus," and a member of the Iberian Anarchist Association and the Railroad Workers' Union, was handing out revolvers to his "pals."

The insurgent troops were entering the suburbs of the city. Everyone was talking at the same time.

"What are the troops going to do here?"

"Clean us up, you can bet your boots on that."

"But yesterday the officers took the oath of allegiance to Companys."

"There's your answer—Listen to the radio!"

The little radio set at the back of the narrow room was repeating every five minutes: *The insurgent troops are advancing on the centre.*

"Has the Government handed out rifles?"

"No."

"Yesterday two of my pals from the F.A.I. were thrown into jail for going armed. We couldn't get them out till Durruti and Oliver lent a hand."

"That's bad."

"What do they think at the *Tranquillidad* café?" one of them asked, referring to a meeting-place for anarchists. "Will they be given guns or not?"

"More likely not."

"How about revolvers?"

The Negus went on doling out his stock. "Those worthy gentlemen, the fascist officers, were kind enough to place these little fellows at my disposal. My beard inspires confidence, I guess."

With two friends and some accomplices he had rifled the armouries on two warships that night. He was still wearing the workman's suit of blue overalls which he had put on to get himself admitted on board the ships.

"And now," he said, as he handed out the last revolver, "let's pool our cash. We have to buy ammunition at the first gunsmith's shop that opens. We've only twenty-five rounds each, and that's not enough."

The insurgent troops are advancing on the centre.

"The gunsmiths won't open today. It's Sunday."

"Don't worry. We'll have them open all right. Now each of you's got to go and collect his pals, and bring 'em along."

Six men remained behind. The others went off at once.

The insurgent troops . . .

The Negus was in command. Not by virtue of his position in the Union, but because he had done five years in prison, and because one night when the Barcelona tramways, after a strike, had dismissed four hundred of their men, the Negus with a dozen friends had set fire to the trams in the Tibidabo depot and launched them down the hill, brakeless and in flames, amid panic-stricken hootings from the automobiles along the road, into the heart of Barcelona. And, after that, his campaign of less spectacular sabotage had prospered for two years.

As they stepped out into the mist-blue radiance of daybreak, each of them was wondering what the next dawn would bring. The men who had been the first to leave the tavern had done their work well, and the friends they had enlisted were gathering in groups at every street corner. When they reached the Diagonal, they saw the troops advancing towards them, from the sunrise. The regiments from the Pedralbes barracks, headed by their officers, were moving up the long, straight avenue, the largest street in Barcelona, towards the centre of the city.

The tramp of marching feet stopped suddenly and a volley raked the boulevard.

The anarchists took cover in the nearest side-street; the Negus and two of his companions went back to the avenue. This was not the first time they set eyes on those officers. They were the very men who had rounded up the thirty thousand captives in the Asturias, the men who had played a ruthless part in 1933 at Saragossa, who had connived at the repression of the agrarian revolt; thanks to whom the confiscation of the Jesuits' wealth, ordered for the sixth time in a century, had remained a dead letter. And these were the men who had dispossessed the Negus' parents. According to Catalonian law a wine-grower is evicted when the vineyard he is working becomes fallow. During the phylloxera epidemic all infected areas were declared fallow, and the growers were evicted from vineyards they had planted and been cultivating for twenty to fifty years. The men who took their places, having no claim on the vineyards, were paid lower wages by the owners—among whom were, perhaps, those very officers.

The main body moving along the centre of the avenue was preceded by an advance-guard patrolling the pavement on each side. Whenever they came to a side-street, the patrols halted, and scoured it with a volley before continuing on their way. The street-lamps had not yet been switched off; neon-signs wove traceries of light more vivid than the dawn. The Negus went back to his friends.

"They must have spotted us. We'd better cut round and have a go at them higher up."

They ran noiselessly—almost all were wearing canvas shoes —and took cover in the doorways of a street at right angles to the Diagonal. A street of rich people's houses with wide, deep porticos. The trees along the boulevard were alive with birds. Each man saw in front of him, across the way, a comrade, revolver in hand, motionless as a statue.

Little by little the empty street began to echo with the tramp of the advancing troops. And now the column was only fifty yards away. An anarchist fell; someone had shot him from a window. Each doorway was in full view of the windows across the street. In the porches of the deserted avenue, that throbbed to the measured footfalls of the column, the anarchists stood motionless, waiting to be mowed down, like tin rabbits in a shooting gallery.

The patrol fired a volley. Bullets zipped past like a swarm of dragon-flies. The patrol moved on. As the main body crossed the end of the street, from every doorway a revolver barked. . . . Anarchists are good shots.

The officers shouted "Forward!" and led their men not up the side-street, but towards the centre of the city; each thing in its time. Through the intricate stone-work of the portico under which he was hidden, the Negus had only a partial view of the soldiers, from the belt down. He could not see the rifles, shoulder high, aiming along the side-street. But he noticed a good many civilian trousers under the tunics; the fascist fighting wing had joined the troops. The rearguard marched by, the sound of marching feet receded. The Negus assembled his men, took them down another street, and halted. What they were doing now was mere waste of time. Obviously the real fight would take place in the Plaza de Cataluña. Their best plan was to take the enemy in the rear—but how?

A detachment of soldiers had been left behind at the first square—rather rashly, perhaps—but the soldiers had a sub-machine-gun with them.

A worker ran past, revolver in hand.

"They're giving out arms to the people."

"To us as well?" the Negus asked.

"I tell you, they're arming everybody."

"Including the anarchists?"

The man did not stop to answer.

Entering a café, the Negus telephoned to the anarchist news-paper. Yes, arms were being issued to the people, but so far all the anarchists had got was sixty revolvers. "Simpler to go and help oneself to them on the warships," he grinned.

A factory whistle shrilled through the morning air. As on the days when only trivial destinies are in the making; as on the work-days when the Negus and his friends had heard the whistles calling and hurried to their work, along grey and yellow walls, walls without end; in the same flush of dawn, with the same street-lamps still alight, seeming to dangle from the trolley-wires. . . . Another siren hooted. Ten, twenty sirens.

A hundred!

All stopped dead in the middle of the road, struck dumb with wonder. Never had any of them heard more than five sirens going at once. As in Spanish cities of old all the belfries jangled a summons to the townsfolk in the hour of peril, so now the proletariat of Barcelona answered the volleys with the tocsin of their factory whistles.

"Puig is at the Plaza de Cataluña." The man who spoke was running towards the centre, followed by two other men armed with rifles.

"I thought he was still in hospital," one of the Negus' companions remarked.

Shrilling all together, the sirens had no longer the funereal accent of a liner putting out to sea; rather they seemed to voice the jubilation of a revolting fleet.

"Rifles!" the Negus exclaimed, staring at the detachment with the submachine-gun. "We'll fix that up ourselves!"

His lips became fixed in a hard smile, his teeth protruding slightly between the black beard and heavy moustache. From all the factories occupied by workers the strident sirens throbbed in long-drawn howls or short, staccato blasts, through streets and houses, over the bay up to the sunlit hills.

The troops in the Park Barracks, like the others, were marching on the centre of the city. Puig, a short squat figure in a black sweater, had occupied a square with three hundred men. All were not anarchists; more than a hundred of them had been furnished with arms by the Government. Some, who had little experience with rifles, were being taught how to handle them. "No question of private ownership today," Puig grinned, as he transferred the rifles to the best marksmen, amid general approval.

The soldiers were coming up the main avenue. Puig posted his men at various points in the streets at right angles to it. The Negus had just arrived with his men and the submachine-gun, which only the Negus knew how to operate. There was not a sound; the *milicianos* moved noiselessly on their canvas shoes, the trams were silent, and the soldiers were still too far off to be audible. And now that the factory whistles, too, had fallen silent, an ominous tranquillity pervaded Barcelona.

The troops moved forward, rifles in hand, under the huge publicity posters of a hotel and a scent manufacturer. All the anarchists brought their rifles up to their shoulders.

The front rank of the column—they were in civilian trousers —fired down a side-street and deployed under a rising cloud of pigeons, several of which dropped back into the street. The second rank fired down another street, and also scattered. Puig's companions opened fire from concealed firing-points; not as the men with the Negus had done, merely across a section of the street, but sweeping all the square from different angles.

The front rank of soldiers broke into a run, came against the Negus' submachine-gun, and streamed back into the avenue under a hail of bullets, leaving behind them a straggling line of bodies, fallen full-length or huddled, like jetsam dropped by a wave along the foreshore.

Some foreign sportsmen, visiting Barcelona for the Olympic games, appeared at the windows of their hotel, in their shirt-sleeves, and started applauding—whether the soldiery or the anarchists there was no knowing. Again a factory hooter bayed like a fog-bound ship. The workers darted forward, at the soldiers' heels.

"Back to your posts!" Puig bellowed, waving his stumpy arms. No one heard him.

In less than a minute a third of the pursuers had fallen; but now the troops had taken cover in the porticos along the avenue, and the tables had been turned upon the workers. At the far end of the square lay dead and wounded men in khaki, in the foreground, dead or wounded in blue or black; and, between the two groups, lay dead pigeons. Again the mingled blasts of twenty sirens jarred the sunlit air. More and more workers were flocking up and, despite their losses in the square, Puig's men were plugging away at the enemy. Across the fading note of the sirens ripped the brisk sounds of rifle-fire. The soldiers were retiring at the double. Otherwise the forces of the Popular Front might have run round the side-streets parallel to the avenue, attacked them under cover of a barricade, and cut off their retreat.

The barrack doors clanged to. . . .

"Where's Puig?"

"I'm Puig. What you want?"

Fresh recruits were steadily pouring in. As the Civil Police and Assault Guards were engaged in the centre of the city and communists were few in Barcelona, the command automatically devolved on the anarchist leaders. Puig was relatively little known; he did not contribute to the workers' newspapers. But it was common knowledge that he had organized the evacuation of the children from Saragossa, and non-anarchists preferred to deal with him rather than with the leaders of the F.A.I. In the spring of 1934, for five weeks, the workers at Saragossa, led by Durruti, had put through the biggest strike that Spain had so far known. They had turned down all financial aid, and all they had asked of the proletariat was to show their sympathy by doing their utmost for the children. Over half a million persons had contributed money and provisions to the *Solidaridad*. Puig had seen to their distribution, and got together a fleet of lorries which had conveyed the children of the Saragossa workers to Barcelona. As the anarchists paid no contributions to a common fund, Puig, like Durruti and all the group of Solidarists, had on occasion attacked and captured vans carrying gold to the Bank of Spain. The proceeds were used to assist strikers and the Anarchist Library. Those who had heard of his romantic career were always taken aback when they set eyes on this dwarf-like but sturdy little man, with the predatory face, hook nose and twinkling eyes. The only thing that fitted in with his reputation was the black sweater. . . . All that eventful morning the little man had never ceased grinning.

He left on the spot a third of his rapidly increasing force, and the submachine-gun, which one of the newcomers knew how to handle. The men he set to work building barricades. A number of soldiers who had come over to the People's Front swelled their ranks: they were in their shirt-sleeves, to prevent mistakes, but had kept their helmets on. Each man had been issued with two tots of rum that morning, so they said, and told he was wanted to put down a communist rising.

Puig went with the others to the Plaza de Cataluña. The first thing was to crush the rebels in the heart of the city; after that, they could deal with the barracks.

They approached it by the Paseo de Cataluña. Opposite them the Colon Hotel with its pineapple tower and nests of machine-guns loomed above the square. Troops from the Pedralbes Barracks in separate detachments occupied the three main buildings on the Square: the hotel at the far end, on the left the Eldorado, on the right the Central Telephone Exchange. The troops were doing little in the way of fighting, but the machine-guns enabled the officers, the fascists disguised as regulars from the waist up, and those who had "turned soldier" during the past fortnight to keep command of the square.

Some thirty workers made a rush across the central portion of the square, which stands above the level of the roadway, taking what cover they could behind the trees that border it. The machine-guns chattered, and they fell in bunches. Shadows of the pigeons wheeling above at no great height glided across the fallen bodies, over a man who still was staggering, waving his gun at arm's length above his head.

Round Puig were grouped the leaders of all Left-Wing parties; thousands of men behind them. For the first time, Liberals, members of the U.G.T. and C.N.T., anarchists, Republicans, trade-unionists, and socialists joined in an attack on their common foe and his machine-guns. For the first time the anarchists had voted, so as to ensure the liberation of the prisoners in the Asturias. Mingling at last today, all the various strains of the Asturian blood had brought about the unity of Barcelona, quickening Puig's hope that now at last he would see unfurled and triumphant the red-and-black banner which had hitherto rarely known the light of day.

"The troops from the Park have gone back to their barracks!" shouted a bearded man who was running past, a cock under his arm.

"Goded's just landed from the Balearic Islands." (Goded was one of the best fascist generals.)

A car sped by, with "U.G.T." in white paint on the hood. "*Our* shop-sign," Puig smiled to himself, remembering the posters on the little square.

Other attacking parties were trying to slip by along the walls, under what little cover they could get from porches and balconies. But always they were under fire from at least two machine-guns. Watching the men drop one after the other, Puig felt his throat grow parched and hot as if he had just smoked three packets of cigarettes.

They were acting thus, he knew, because frontal attacks were in the revolutionary tradition. Once halted in front of the hotel, on the sunlit pavement cluttered with round café tables, they would be shot down from the windows. Heroism which is only an imitation of heroism leads to nothing. Puig had a liking for tough men; he liked the men who now were falling —and he was appalled. A brush with Civil Guards in a successful raid on Government gold was a different matter from storming the Colon Hotel. But, however scanty, his experience told him unco-ordinated tactics such as he now was watching were doomed from the outset.

Over the smooth asphalt of the wide boulevard around the Square, bullets were capering like crickets. . . . So many windows! Counting those of the hotel—over a hundred—he saw, or seemed to see, a machine-gun peering through each big "O" of the huge neon sign, C O L O N.

"I say, Puig!"

"What?"

He answered the little bald man with the grey moustache who had accosted him almost vindictively. They were going to ask him for orders. And all that lay deepest in his heart forbade him to give orders.

"Shall we have a shot at it?"

"Wait a bit!"

Small groups of men were still trying to get across the Plaza. Puig had told his men to wait a bit; they had confidence in him and had waited. . . . Now what?

Another wave of attackers had swept forward—white-collar workers, some with hats on. They started at the double from the Calle de Cortes; crumpled up at the corner of the Paseo de Gracia, mowed down by the machine-guns posted in the Eldorado and in the Colon Tower. . . . More bodies, more blood, calm in the calm sunshine.

Puig heard the boom of the first cannon. If the artillery was in the workers' hands, the hotel was lost. But if the troops were marching up from the barracks with field-guns supporting them, things would go with the people just as in '33, and in '34.

Puig ran to a telephone. There were only two guns, and the fascists had them.

He collected his men, entered the first garage on their way, piled his men into two lorries, and started out. Along the road sparrows flew up from all the sunlit trees.

Two eighteen-pounders were in position on either side of a wide avenue, sweeping it from end to end. In front of them was a group of soldiers, all in mufti trousers, with rifles and a machine-gun. Behind them were about a hundred more, without machine-guns, so far as Puig could make out. The avenue ended two hundred yards away, where another avenue crossed it at right angles. In the centre of the T was a portico, from which a light field-gun was firing.

Puig sent a small party of his men to reconnoitre the defences of the gunners in the cross-bars of the T, and posted the rest in a side-street leading off the avenue.

Suddenly, with a syncopated stridence of horns and klaxons, two Cadillacs tore up the road behind them, wildly zigzagging like cars in gangster films. The driver of the front car, the bald man with the small moustache, drove headlong through a barrage from rifles and machine-guns, under shells which hurtled harmlessly above him. Like a snow-plough, the car scattered the soldiers on either side, and raced between the two seventy-fives, crashing against the wall just beside the field gun, which presumably had been it objective. Black, blood-spattered wreckage—a squashed fly on a wall.

The gunners went on firing at the second car. With its klaxon in full blast, it screamed past the two eighteen-pounders and dived into the portico at seventy miles an hour.

The field-gun ceased fire. From all the side-streets, workers were staring at the black maw of the portico; the klaxon was silent; all was silent. Waiting for the men in the car to reappear. None of them reappeared.

Again the sirens blared across the silence. It was as if the roar of the klaxons had swelled prodigiously, soaring up into the high air, till the whole city echoed with a dirge for the first glorious victims of the revolution. A cloud of pigeons, used to the daily hubbub of the city, circled above the avenue. Puig felt envious of his dead comrades' fate, yet at the same time eager to see the days that were at hand; for today Barcelona was pregnant with his whole life's dreams.

"No point in getting sentimental about it," said the Negus. "A smart piece of work—but there are more important jobs at hand."

The men Puig had sent on reconnaissance came back. "Over

there, on the right, there are ten or a dozen fellows just behind the guns."

Obviously the fascists hadn't enough men to cover all the streets around them; Barcelona is laid out like a chess-board.

"Take command," said Puig to the Negus. "I'll try to get round the other way and nab them from behind. Bring your men up as close as you can to the eighteen pounders, and try to rush 'em once we've got through."

He hurried off with five of his men. The Negus and his companions advanced.

Barely ten minutes had elapsed. Taken by surprise, the soldiers turned their heads; the gunners tried to swing their guns round. Puig's car had broken through the little barrier, was charging down on the gunners, the muzzle of his sub-machine-gun peering between the panels of the wind-shield, while the butt jerked from side to side like a pendulum gone mad. Puig watched the gun crews, unsheltered by their bullet-shields, looming large and larger, like close-ups on a screen. A machine-gun, firing, loomed closer. Four bullet holes in the triplex glass. Handicapped by the shortness of his legs, Puig leaned well forward and stamped with all his might on the accelerator—as if he were trying to break his way through the floor-boards so as to reach his pals on the far side of the gun. Two more holes starred the triplex. A cramp in his left foot, his fingers knotted on the wheel . . . rifle barrels jabbing the wind-shield . . . the submachine-gun roaring down his ears . . . houses and trees turning a somersault . . . veering, the pigeons all changing colour . . . the Negus shouted something. . . .

Puig recovered consciousness to find the Revolution in full swing, the eighteen-pounders captured. When the car turned turtle his neck had had a nasty jar, nothing worse. Two of the men with him were dead. The Negus was bandaging his wound.

"There's a turban for you, Puig. You look fine as an Arab."

At the far end of the street some Civil and Assault Guards were marching past. Officers and fascist volunteers in tunics and civilian trousers were being escorted to Police Head-quarters, and the disarmed soldiers to the barracks. The latter chatted with the workmen who had taken over their rifles and were now accompanying them. Everyone else was moving up towards the Plaza de Cataluña.

There the position was unchanged, except that more corpses

were strewn about the square. This time Puig entered it from the Paseo de Gracia. At the corner stands the Colon Hotel. A loud-speaker was announcing: *The Prat airmen have joined the defenders of the people's freedom.* So far, so good. . . . But where were they?

Once again there was a general rush forward, from all the streets facing the hotel—anarchists, socialists, some bourgeois in starched collars, and a few groups of peasants—for, as the morning wore on, the peasants were beginning to flock into the city. Puig halted his men. The assaulting wave, raked by the three nests of machine-guns, receded, leaving behind its festoon of the dead.

Like a flight of pigeons, the papers of a fascist league, flung from the windows, fluttered slowly down, or settled on the trees.

For the first time, Puig had an impression that he was witnessing, not a hopeless struggle like that of '34—like every other he had seen so far—but quite possibly a victory in the making. Though he had studied Bakunin—perhaps he was the only member of the group who had read that author between the lines—he had always looked on the Spanish revolution as another *Jacquerie.* Since he saw no hope for the world, exemplary revolts were the utmost he could hope from anarchism. And so for him every political crisis resolved itself into a test of character and courage.

He remembered Lenin dancing in the snow the day when the duration of the Soviet State had outlasted that of the Paris Commune by twenty-four hours. Today the task for him and for his friends was not to give examples, but to achieve a victory. If his men rushed blindly forward like those others, they would fall like them, and the hotel would not be captured. Along the two boulevards which converge across the square in a large inverted V pointing towards the Colon, and the Calle de las Cortes which runs along the frontage of the hotel, three brigades of Civil Guards came into view at exactly the same moment. Puig watched the cocked hats of his traditional enemies glinting in the sunlight. The loud cheers which greeted their approach showed they were on the Government side. Such was the hush which fell upon the square that the flapping of the pigeons' wings was clearly audible.

Even the fascists withheld their fire, in the shock of finding the police standing by the Government. And, as they knew, the Barcelona Civil Police are all crack shots.

Colonel Ximenes limped up the steps, on to the central precinct of the square, and walked straight towards the hotel. He was unarmed. Till he was a third of the way across no one fired. Then on three sides machine-gun fire broke out. Puig ran up to the second floor of the nearest house. Of all their enemies, it was the police whom the anarchists detested most. Colonel Ximenes was a devout Catholic. And today they were actually fighting side by side, allied in an incredible fraternity!

Ximenes was carrying the baton of his rank, as Chief of the Civil Guard. He turned and raised it, and the men in the cocked hats began to charge up the three streets. Ximenes was walking on with a curious waddling gait—Puig remembered that his men called Ximenes "Old Quack-Quack"—alone in the midst of the enormous square under a hail of bullets. The police on the left were now advancing alongside the Telephone Building, the defenders of which could not fire down vertically on them; the posse on the right, along the Eldorado. The gunners in the latter building should have fired at the men approaching from the left. But, now they were up against the civil police, each fascist group fought only for itself, without troubling about the others.

The machine-guns in the Colon were hard put to it, having to aim right and left alternately. The police were advancing not on a long front but in a thin column of attack, skilfully taking advantage of the cover afforded by the trees. Anarchists came swarming out of all the streets, and followed them. Then, with a rapid thud of heavy boots, the detachment from the Calle de Cortes doubled past under Puig's eyes. The fascists had ceased firing at them. In the centre of the square the Colonel limped on, straight ahead.

Ten minutes later the Colon Hotel had been captured.

The civil police were occupying the Plaza de Cataluña. All that night Barcelona resounded with shouts and songs and gunshots. Armed civilians, workers and members of the middle class, soldiers and Assault Guards streamed under the lights of the great beer-house on the Plaza, where police-officers sat drinking at all the tables.

Colonel Ximenes, too, was drinking in a little room on the second floor, taken over for his Staff Headquarters. He was in charge of the whole district, and for the last few hours the heads of the local organizations had been coming to get instructions from him.

Puig entered. Wearing a leather windbreaker and carrying an enormous revolver, he cut a romantic figure under the grimy, blood-stained turban.

"Where can we be of the most use?" he asked. "I've a thousand men."

"Nowhere; all's well for the moment. But they'll be trying to get out of the barracks—from Atarazaña anyhow. You'd better stay around for half an hour; your men may come in very handy any moment. It seems they've got the upper hand at Seville, Burgos, Segovia and Palma—not to mention Morocco. But we'll beat them here."

They might have been fighting side by side for a month, judging by the free-and-easy manner of the anarchist, whose attitude conveyed discreetly that he had come here for suggestions, not for orders. Ximenes had often studied his dossier in the police records but, familiar though he was with the man's appearance, he now was struck by his extreme shortness and sturdiness. "A pocket pirate," he smiled to himself. Though Puig was not one of the "big shots," he interested Ximenes more than the others because of the part he had played in rescuing the Saragossa children.

"The Government has given orders that the soldiers are to be disarmed and set at liberty," the Colonel replied. "The officers will be court-martialed. By the way, you were in that Cadillac, weren't you? The one to which we owe the capture of the field-guns?"

"Yes." Puig remembered having noticed the cocked hats of the Civil Guards flash past the end of the street, at the critical moment.

"A good piece of work. If they'd brought those guns up here, things might have been very different."

"You had luck, too, when you crossed the Plaza."

Fanatic in his love for Spain, the Colonel was grateful to the anarchist, not for the compliment, but for a form of speech so characteristically Spanish; for speaking as might have spoken one of King Charles the Fifth's captains. For it was obvious that by "luck" he had meant "courage."

"I was scared," Puig said, "scared stiff, of not being able to get up to that gun. Living or dead, I *had* to get there. . . . And what were *you* thinking of?"

Ximenes smiled. His head was bare, and his white, close-cropped hair, like the down on a duckling's neck, suited the nickname his beady eyes and shovel nose had helped to earn him.

"At such times my legs say: 'Stop it, you blinking idiot! What are you up to?' Especially my game leg." Shutting one eye, he raised an admonitory finger. "But my heart says: 'Go on!' Never before had I seen bullets bouncing along like hailstones. Of course, firing from above, one mistakes a man's shadow for his body, and it's hard to aim correctly."

"That attack was well carried out." There was a note of envy in Puig's voice.

"Yes. Your men are good in a scrap, but they're no soldiers."

Below them on the pavement, stretchers were being carried by, empty but blood-stained.

"Yes, they're good fighters," Puig agreed.

Flower-sellers had strewn carnations on the stretchers; white flowers lay on the straps, beside the blood-stains.

"When I was in prison," Puig said, "I never dreamt that such fraternity was possible."

The word "prison" reminded Ximenes that he, a colonel commanding the Barcelona civil police, was now hob-nobbing with one of the anarchist leaders; and he smiled again. All the leaders of the extremist groups had shown courage; many had fallen, or been wounded. For Ximenes, as for Puig, courage was a second fatherland. Anarchist militants went past, the unshaven cheeks showing black under the restaurant lamps. There had been no time to shave before the fighting started. Another stretcher passed, with a lily hung on one of the slings.

A ruddy glow spread up the sky beyond the square; another kindled in the distance on a hillside. Then, on every hand, wisps of bright red fire began to flicker above the house-tops. That morning Barcelona had summoned the whole city with the shriek of her sirens. Now by night she was sending her churches up in flame. Through the windows, open on the summer night, came a reek of burning. Ximenes watched the lurid smoke-clouds, lit from below, billowing above the Plaza de Cataluña. Rising, he made the sign of the cross. Not overtly, as though wishing to advertise his faith; but for himself, as if alone.

"Ever studied theosophy?" Puig enquired.

In front of the hotel some foreign journalists were chatter-

ing excitedly about the neutrality of the Spanish clergy, about
the monks of Saragossa who laid out Napoleon's veterans with
crucifixes. The speakers were out of sight, but their voices
rang clear across the darkness, across the thudding explosions
and the shouting in the distance.

"No," Ximenes muttered, watching the smoke-clouds rolling
overhead. "God should not be dragged into man's family
squabbles, like a communion-cup looted by a thief."

"What chance have the Barcelona workers had of learning
about God? Through the lips of those men who in His name
declared the terror inflicted upon the Asturians was just and
proper—eh?"

"No, but they could have learned about Him through those
few things that *tell* in a man's life—childhood and death and
courage. Not from the lips of preachers. Let's assume the
Church in Spain has fallen short of its duty to our country-
men. But why should the ruffians who pretend to share your
views—and heaven knows there's any number of them!—why
need they prevent you from carrying out yours? It's a mistake
appraising men by what is lowest in them."

"When you condemn folk to low living, you can't expect
high thinking of them. During the last four centuries who's had
the 'cure of souls' as you would call it? If they'd not been
taught so well to hate, perhaps they could learn better how to
love—eh, Colonel?"

Ximenes stared at the distant flames.

"Have you ever noticed something about the portraits of
men who've championed the noblest causes? They should look
cheerful, shouldn't they? Or, anyhow, serene. Well, the first
thing you notice is their sadness. . . ."

"Priests are one thing, the heart's another; that's sure. But
I can't explain to you how I feel about it. I'm used to speaking
and I'm not an ignoramus—I'm a printer. But there's always
something. . . . It's just the same when I talk to writers at
my press. I can talk to you about priests, and you'll speak of
Saint Teresa. I can talk to you about the catechism, and you'll
quote—what's his name?—Thomas Aquinas."

"The catechism is more important to me than Saint
Thomas."

"Your catechism is not the same as mine; our lives are too
different. I read the catechism again when I was twenty-five.
I picked it up near here in a gutter—sounds like the beginning
of a moral tale, doesn't it? It's no use telling people who've

been having their cheeks slapped for the last two thousand years to 'turn the other cheek.' "

Puig was a puzzle to Ximenes. In his personality, intelligence and stupidity were compounded otherwise than in the men the Colonel was accustomed to.

The last men to be released from cellars, garrets, closets and store-rooms where the fascists had interned them were coming out into the open—bewildered faces lit up by the ruddy glow from the burning buildings. The smoke-clouds were steadily thickening and the smell of burning was as pungent as if the hotel itself were on fire.

"About the clergy . . . Listen! For one thing, I don't care for people who talk a lot and do nothing. I belong to another species. But the trouble is I'm of their species, too; that's what makes me hate them. To teach poor people, workers, to accept what happened in the Asturias—why, it can't be done! And to do so in the name of love—I ask you! Could anything be more disgusting? Some of my comrades say we're acting like fools, we'd do better to burn down the banks. I tell them: 'No! Leave that to the bourgeoisie; it's in their line. The priests, that's another matter. Those churches, where they've gloated over having thirty thousand men arrested and tortured, and the rest of it—let 'em all burn, and a good thing too! Except for the works of art—that's why the Cathedral must not burn.' "

"And . . . Christ?"

"He was an anarchist who succeeded. The only one. Oh, and, speaking about priests, I'll tell you something—only you won't understand; you've never been poor. It's this. I hate a man who says that he forgives me for doing the best thing I've ever done. *I don't want to be forgiven.*"

A radio blared across the darkness. *The troops of Madrid are still undecided. The Government has the situation in hand. All is quiet in Spain. General Franco has been arrested in Seville. At Barcelona the victory of the people over the fascists and the Army is now complete.*

Waving his arms, the Negus burst in. He shouted to Puig: "The soldiers have come out again. They've built a barricade."

Puig turned to Ximenes. *"Salud!"*

"Au revoir," the Colonel replied.

In a peremptorily chartered car Puig and the Negus drove top-speed across the glowing darkness of the clamorous night. In the Caracoles quarter, from the windows of the brothels, *milicianos* were tossing down mattresses into lorries waiting below, which made off at once for the barricades. Everywhere in the city barricades were springing up, built with mattresses, paving-stones and furniture. One of the oddest was made of confessionals; another, in front of which a number of horses had fallen, showed in the fleeting radiance of the headlights like a fresco of dead horses' heads.

Puig could not make out the purpose of the barricade set up by the fascists, for they were now fighting a lone hand, the soldiers having turned against them. They were firing from under cover of a shapeless mound of débris bristling with the legs of chairs, in almost complete darkness, for the street-lamps had been extinguished by rifle-shots. No sooner was Puig's turban recognized than the street echoed with gleeful shouts. The people were getting a taste for leaders, as always happens when a struggle lasts long. With the Negus at his side, Puig entered the first garage they came to and commandeered a lorry.

In the flame-lit night the trees flanking the avenue showed as patches of dark blue. The fascists, who had a machine-gun—always and everywhere the fascists had machine-guns—were invisible.

Puig changed into high speed, and, as he had done in the morning, pressed with all his might on the accelerator. As the rattle of the changing gears died out, between two bursts of firing, the Negus heard a single shot. Suddenly Puig straightened up, his fists flattened on the steering-wheel as if it were a table; from his mouth came the rattling gasp of a man whose teeth have just been shattered by a bullet.

A mirror-wardrobe flashed up into the headlamps, crashed into them like a fisticuff. Raked by the shrill tattoo of the Negus' submachine-gun, the mound of furniture burst open like a crashed-in door.

The *milicianos* poured in through the breach, past the lorry jammed among the wreckage. The fascists fled to the nearest barracks. Still firing, the Negus glanced round at Puig. His face was hidden by the turban; he lay crumpled up across the steering-wheel, dead.

3

July 20

THE Civil Police and the Assault Guards were vainly trying to impart order to the crowd—among men in their shirt-sleeves or naked from the waist up, among women no sooner ordered off than hurrying back. Scattered in front, it formed a solid mass behind, loud with the deep, incessant hum of voices. An officer was taking to a café a soldier who had just escaped from the Montaña Barracks. Jaime Alvear had noticed them on their way and entered the café just in front of them. Like heart-beats of the serried crowd, there came at regular intervals the boom of cannon, drowning the thin patter of shots from doors and windows, reverberating through the tumult of voices and the heavy fumes of heated stone and tar pouring up from Madrid.

The heads of all the people in the café gathered like flies around the soldier.

"The Colonel told us," he panted, "you got to save . . . to save the Republic."

"The Republic?"

"Sure! Seeing as it is . . . going to fall into the hands of the bolsheviks . . . Jews and anarchists and what not."

"What had the soldiers to say to that?"

" 'Bravo!' they said."

" 'Bravo?' "

"Sure! They didn't give a damn one way or the other. Of course, they were mostly rookies, the ones who said it. For the last week, the whole place was stiff with rookies."

"What about the left-wingers?" someone asked.

In the motionless glasses the brandy and manzanilla quivered in rhythm with the gun-fire. The soldier took a drink. Gradually he was getting his breath back.

"The only ones left are the men they didn't know about. All the others were shifted—a fortnight ago. There must have been about fifty leftists, all told. But they weren't there; they've been stowed away in some corner, I heard."

The rebels had never dreamed the Government would give arms to the people. They had been waiting for the Madrid fascists, who so far had made no move.

Suddenly all fell silent. The loud-speaker was beginning an

announcement. As newspapers came out only once a day, it was the radio that made known the destinies of Spain.

The Barcelona barracks are continuing to surrender. The Atarazanas Barracks have been taken by the trade-unionists, led by Ascaso and Durruti. Ascaso fell in an attack on the barracks. Fort Montjuich has surrendered to the people without a fight.

Cries of jubilation filled the café. Even in the Asturias no name had more sinister associations than that of Montjuich.

The garrison refused to obey their officers, when informed by radio, in the name of the lawful government of Spain, that they were under no duty to obey the insurgent officers.

"Who is keeping up the fight at your barracks?" the officer enquired.

"Only the officers and rookies. Our fellows are beating it as fast as they can. But the cellars must be crawling with them. Once your big guns started in, we saw how the land lay, and we weren't taking any, not us! We knew the 'anars' and bolshies hadn't any artillery. 'That speech of the Colonel's,' says I, 'that was just another piece of fascist ballyhoo.' Nothing doing, when he wanted us to fire on the people. Not me! So I beat it over to you."

The man's shoulders still heaved uncontrollably. The punctual boom of cannon continued, followed like an echo by the shell-burst. Jaime had seen the gun that was in action. It was manned by a captain from the Assault Guards who had so far discovered only how to fire it; training it was beyond him. Lopez, a sculptor and *comandante* in the socialist militia, to which Jaime belonged, was helping the captain, strenuously if ineffectively. The first shell went high and burst somewhere in the suburbs; the second exploded in a cloud of yellow dust on the brick wall. The gun, not being fixed in any way, recoiled savagely at every shot and Lopez' men, their arms straining on the spokes—like the gunners in old prints of the French Revolution—trundled it back into position as best they could. One shell went through a window and burst inside the building.

"You'll take care, won't you, when you're inside?" the soldier said. "Seeing as how the fellows haven't fired a shot at you. On purpose, they didn't."

"How can we tell which are the new recruits?"

"Right away like that? Well I can't hardly say. But later on it'll be simple enough. They haven't any families."

What he meant was that the fascists who had lately joined the army to facilitate the rising kept their wives out of the way—they were too obviously "ladies"; whereas the neighbouring streets were full of soldiers' wives, waiting in suspense, the only silent members of the excited crowd.

Suddenly the rattle of rifle-fire intensified, accompanied by a rumble of heavy vehicles. Another detachment of Assault Guards was coming into action. One of the armoured cars was already in position. The cannon was still firing, making the wine in glasses tremble at each round. Men with rifles under their arms were drifting in, bringing the latest news, like the film actors who drop into a studio bar, in costume, between two takes. But here on the white-tiled floor were tracks of blood-stained shoes.

"There's another battering-ram."

A gigantic beam was gliding forward, flanked by men in parallel lines on either side—like some strange geometrical monster. The men were straining forward like boat-haulers; some wore collars, some not; but each had a rifle across his back. It moved across the wreckage on the roadway, the débris of railings, and rubble of bricks and plaster, hit the barracks entrance with the clang of a tremendous gong, and recoiled. Full as it was of shouts and swirling smoke and gun-fire, the whole place rang hollow like a convent, and quaked behind the massive door. Three of the men carrying the battering-ram fell, hit by shots from the fascists. Jaime stepped into the place of one. Just as the ram was starting forward again, a tall man with shaggy eyebrows—one of the trade-unionists—suddenly clasped his head between his hands as if to shut his ears, and slumped across the moving beam, arms dangling on one side, legs on the other. Few of his companions noticed him; the battering-ram continued lumbering slowly forward, with the dead body riding it. To Jaime, who was twenty-six, the Popular Front meant fraternity in life and death. The hope he set on the workers' organizations was intensified because of his despair of all the rulers of Spain during the last few centuries. Those he knew best in left-wing groups were certain obscure, uncompromising militants, always out to tackle any job, embodiments of the spirit of devotion in modern Spain. So now, out of the fulness of his heart, he helped them push the massive beam, straddled by their dead comrade, towards the doorway, under the brilliant sunlight and the fascist bullets. Again the battering-ram

clanged on the door; the corpse astride it lunged forward. The
two men beside him, one of whom was Ramos, caught it and
began carrying it away. The beam swung back more slowly.
Five more men fell. The track the ram had followed, flanked
on each side by dead and wounded, once more shone white
and empty.

The July morning was growing warmer; faces were beginning to glisten with sweat. Listening to the boom of the gun
and the crashes of the ram that dinned their rhythm on all the
other sounds of conflict, a crowd of workers and small shop-
keepers stood waiting for the final rush, along the sloping
streets and at the foot of the flights of steps leading up to the
barracks. All were staring up at the great door, rifles in hand—
the Government had omitted to issue slings, and loops of cord
were dangling from each weapon—their cartridge-pouches
hung across their chests on straps that were too short.

The battering-ram slowed down; the guns ceased firing. Even
the fascists held their fire. The deep drone of a plane was
throbbing overhead.

"What's up?"

Eyes squinted in Jaime's direction. All his comrades in the
socialist militia knew that the big fellow, with the ruddy skin
and the tousled black hair, was an engineer in the Hispano
factory. The machine, Jaime said, was one of the old Spanish
Army Bréguets—but there were fascists in the air force, too.
Over the dense silence of the crowd the machine planed down
in a wide sweep. Two bombs exploded in the barracks square,
and some pamphlets fluttered slowly down, like confetti,
lingering in the sky above the cheering crowds.

Up flights of steps, from all the neighbouring streets, there
was a general rush towards the barracks. Once more the ram
clanged against the door; it was greeted by a half-hearted burst
of firing. As it recoiled, a sheet fluttered out from a window,
loosely knotted at one end to make it easier to launch. Not
noticing the signal, the battering-ram team charged once
more. The gate gave way at once. The fascists had just un-
bolted it.

The inner court was absolutely empty. Beyond the empty
space, behind the windows, beyond the closed doors of the
patio, the prisoners began to appear.

The soldiers came out first, waving their union-cards; many
were half-naked. One of the men in front was staggering; as

the crowd pressed him with questions, he flung himself on all fours and began lapping the water in the gutter. The officers came next, their arms uplifted. Some were unconcerned or trying to appear so, one man hid his face in his forage cap, another was smiling as if the whole performance struck him as a farce. Holding his hands only shoulder high, he looked as if he were going up to the *milicianos* to embrace them.

Above them, the last remaining shutter at one of the central windows, which a shell had grazed, came clattering down. Suddenly a young man burst through the opening on to the balcony, half of which had been blown away; he was roaring with laughter, he had three rifles across his back and was trailing two others behind him by the barrels, like dogs on a leash. Crying *"Salud!"* he flung them all down into the street.

The wives of the soldiers, of the battering-ram team and Civil Police, rushed forward into the barracks. Their voices echoed down the long, monastic corridors on which, now that the firing had ceased, an eerie silence had descended. Shouldering their rifles, Jaime and his friend climbed to the second storey. Other *milicianos* had entered through a breach in the wall. A gay crowd of civilians in their work clothes—collars and ready-made suits—with cartridge-pouches dangling on their chests, gathered round the officers who were coming out.

Obviously the breach was a wide one, for the *milicianos* were pouring in by hundreds. A roar of cheers from the huge crowd massed outside crashed against the walls. Jaime looked out of the window; a thousand bare arms, a thousand clenched fists shot up all together from the seething mass, like a concerted movement at an athletic tournament. The distribution of the captured rifles was beginning.

The wall, in front of which the ceremonial swords and modern rifles were being stacked, hid from the crowd a large courtyard into which Jaime could see. At the back of the yard, was a cycle shop. While the *milicianos* were fighting, looters had been at work; the yard was littered with sheets of packing-paper, wheels and handle-bars. And suddenly Jaime remembered the crumpled body sagging across the battering-ram.

In the first room he entered, an officer was seated, his head propped on his hand, above a pool of blood, his own, still spreading over the table. Two other officers lay on the ground, each with a revolver beside his hand.

In the next room, which was rather dark, some soldiers were

lying on the floor, yelling *"Salud! Hey! Salud!"* They did not move; they were tied hand and foot. These were men the fascists had suspected of loyalty to the Republic, or sympathy with the workers' movement. Their bonds did not prevent them from tapping their heels in jubilation. Jaime and his companions, as they set them free, embraced the prisoners in characteristic Spanish style.

"There's some more of the mates down there," one of them remarked. They ran down an inner staircase, and, in a still darker room, found another batch of comrades shackled in the same way; them, too, Jaime and his companions kissed. They had been shot the day before.

4

July 21

"HELLO, there!" Rising from his seat at the Granja café, Slade held out a friendly hand to a black cat. It eyed him suspiciously, hesitated, then ran back into the crowd. "Since the revolution," Slade observed, "the cats, too, are free; but they're still down on me. I'm always one of the down-trodden."

"Oh, come back to your chair, you owl," Lopez said. "Cats —they're unfriendly little brutes; fascists, for all I know. And dogs and horses are restless; a sculptor can't make anything of them. The only animal that's the friend of man is the Pyrenean eagle. During my 'birds-of-prey' period I used to keep one. The only food they eat is snakes, and snakes cost a lot of money. I'd thought of scrounging 'em from the Zoo, but nothing doing. So I bought hunks of meat and cut them into strips. I shook them in front of my eagle and, like the nice chap he was, he pretended to be fooled and gulped them down."

Radio Barcelona here, the loud-speaker blared. *The guns captured by the people are trained on the Capitanía where the rebel leaders have taken refuge.*

As he watched the Alcala, Slade was jotting down his notes for next day's article. It flashed on him how—the shock of hair and thick lips notwithstanding—the sculptor's Bourbon nose recalled a portrait of George Washington. But, above all, the head of a macaw. All the more so that just then Lopez was flapping his arms like wings.

"Hi there! On the set, everyone!" he yelled. "We're shoot-ing."

Bathed in the bright glare of its street-lamps, disguised in its revolutionary dress, Madrid looked like an enormous night scene in a film studio. Suddenly Lopez calmed down; some *milicianos* were coming to shake hands with him. His popularity with the artists who frequented the Granja café was due less to his exploit with the field-gun—in the best sixteenth-century manner—during the previous day's attack on the Montaña Barracks, or even to his talent, than to a famous retort he once had made. One day an embassy attaché had asked him to make a bust of the Duchess of Alba. "Certainly," he had replied with a smile, "but only if she'll sit for me as the female hip-po-po-ta-mus." He spent all his time at the Zoo, and was on even friendlier terms with all the animals than Saint Francis ever was. He declared that the hippopotamus came up when he whistled, held the pose quietly, and trotted off when no longer wanted. The Duchess, as a matter of fact, was well out of her rash project. Lopez carved in diorite, and his model, after hearing his hammer clanging away like a blacksmith's for hours on end, was apt to find that the bust had progressed by a mere quarter-inch.

Soldiers were passing, in their shirt-sleeves, greeted by cheers and followed by swarms of children. They were the troops from Alcala de Henares who had turned against their fascist officers and gone over to the people.

"Look at all those kids going by," Slade remarked. "They're crazy with pride. And I must say I like the way the men here are just like kids. There's always a touch of the child, more or less, in everything I like. You look at a man, somehow you get a glimpse of the child in him, and you fall for him! Do the same thing with a woman, and you're sunk! Yes, look at them! They usually try to disguise their childishness—now it's coming out. The boys here are revelling in a perfect orgy, while out there on the Sierra their pals are dying; and it's all the same thing. In America they see the revolution as an outburst of blind fury—whereas what hits you in the eye here is the good humour of it all."

"Good humour's not all there is to it."

Only when he was discoursing about art did Lopez' wits work nimbly; now he could not find the words he wanted.

"Listen!" was all he said.

Cars were racing past in both directions, placarded with

huge white inscriptions indicating one or another of the various unions, or the U.H.P. The men in them waved their fists by way of greeting, shouting *"Salud!"* And the triumphant crowd seemed united by the cry, which rose in a never-ending chorus of fraternity. Slade closed his eyes.

"There's a spark of poetry," he said, "in every man, and one day he has to come out with it."

"Guernico said the driving force of revolution is—hope."

"Garcia said the same thing. Everybody says it. Guernico's a bore; all Christians bore me stiff. . . . Go on!"

Slade was rather like a Breton curé; that, Lopez reflected, might, in the last analysis, explain his hatred of the Church.

"But it's true, you owl! Look at me, for instance. What have I been crying for these last fifteen years? A renaissance of art. See? Everything here is ready for it. That wall over there, for instance. All those fools go trotting their shadows over it, and never give it a look. We have such a mob of painters, they sprout between the paving stones. Why, I ran up against one the other day in an attic at the Escorial—asleep he was. You've got to give them walls to work on. You can always find one when you need it; white, yellow or burnt sienna. Well, you just rub it down with whitewash, and give it over to a painter."

Smoking his clay pipe with the elegance of an Indian chief, Slade was listening attentively; he knew that just now Lopez was in earnest. The madman apes the artist, and the artist resembles the madman.

Slade mistrusted the theorizing about art which is the bane of every revolution, but he knew the work of the Mexican artists, and the huge, barbaric frescos, so typically Spanish, bristling with claws and horns, that Lopez painted—vivid symbols of the spirit of man engaged in mortal conflict.

Two buses, packed with *milicianos* and bristling with guns, left for Toledo. There, the rebellion was not finished.

"Yes, sir, we'll give our painters bare white walls. 'Get to work! Draw! Paint! The people who're going to pass this way want you to *tell* them something—see? You can't fake an art that means something to the masses when you've nothing to say to them. But we're all fighting the same fight, to create a new life together, so we've plenty to say to each other. The cathedrals helped in the fight, all for all, against the devil— who, by the way, has rather Franco's mug. Well, we . . .'"

"Oh, the cathedrals make me sick! There's more 'brother-

hood of man' right here in this street, than in any old cathedral
on the other side. . . . Sorry! Go on!"

"Art isn't a matter of subjects. There's no great revolutionary
art, and why? Because they're always wrangling about its tend-
encies, rather than its function. So we've got to say to our
artists: 'Have you anything to tell the man at the front? (It's
got to be something definite, not a vague abstraction like "the
masses.") No? Well then, do something else. Yes? Then,
there's your wall. That wall's yours to play with, old chap.
Two thousand people will go past it every day. You know
them. You want to speak to them, don't you? Fix it up your
own way; you have the right and the need to use it. All right.
We may not turn out masterpieces; masterpieces aren't made
to order; but we'll create a *style*.' "

Looming on high across the shadows, the palatial Spanish
banks and insurance companies—and, a little lower down, the
Government offices with their exotic pomp and splendour—
seemed to set forth into the darkness upon the tide of time,
with all their pageantry of gorgeous hearses, the glow and
glitter of clubs, the chandeliers, and the banners of old-world
galleons drooping into the Admiralty courtyard, still in the
airless night.

An old man was leaving the café; he had been listening. He
laid his hand on Lopez' shoulder.

"I'll paint a picture of an old man toddling off and a young
fellow having a bath. The nincompoop who bathes, and goes
in for sports, who can't keep quiet for a moment—that's a
fascist."

Lopez looked up; the man who spoke was an excellent
Spanish painter. Obviously he had half a mind to add: "Or
else, a communist."

". . . as I say, a fascist. And the old chap toddling off, he's
—Old Spain. Now, my dear Lopez, I'll wish you a good
evening."

As he hobbled away a sound of cheering surged across the
darkness. The Assault Guards and loyal regiments who had
defeated the insurgents at Alcala were re-entering Madrid.
Clenched fists shot up at every table along the crowded pavements. And the Assault Guards marching past raised their
clenched fists in answer.

"It's unthinkable," Lopez broke out, "that, given people
who have something to say and people who are willing to
listen, we won't create a style. Just give them a free hand,

give 'em all the air-brushes and spray-guns, all the modern
contraptions they can want and, after that, a chunk of model-
ling-clay—and then you will see!"

"What pleases me in your idea," Slade murmured pensively,
fingering the ends of his bow tie, "is that you're such a born
idiot. The only people I like are idiots—innocents, as they
used to be called. Most people have the big head, and they
can't do a thing with it. But all those folks there are idiots—
like us."

Above the grinding of changing gears the street was shrill
with voices, snatches of the *International* rising above the din
of tramping feet. A woman walked past the café with a
sewing-machine in her arms, hugging it to her breast, like a
sick animal. Slade flicked back his little soft hat with the up-
turned brim, and sat motionless, grasping the stem of his pipe.
An officer with a brass star on his blue one-piece uniform
came by; he shook hands with Lopez.

"How are things going in the Sierra?" Lopez asked.

"They won't get through. The *milicianos* are pouring in."

"Good!" said Lopez as the officer went on his way. "One
day that new style of ours will catch on in the whole of Spain,
just as the cathedral style spread over Europe, and their painters have given Mexico a revolutionary fresco style."

"Very well for your new style—if you'll kindly undertake
to shut your damned trap about those cathedrals."

All the cars in the city, commandeered for the war or for
the service of a dream, were roaring down the streets amid
fraternal shouts. The photographs taken at the Montaña Barracks by photographers formerly employed by the fascist press
—which had been nationalized that morning—were passing
from hand to hand along the café tables. *Milicianos* were
examining them eagerly. "That's us!" "That's me!"

Slade felt inclined to devote that night's article to Lopez'
scheme, to the glamour of the Granja, to the hope that tri-
umphed in the street. Why not to all these things? Behind him
an American woman was waving her arms. She had the
Stars-and-Stripes, eighteen inches wide, pinned across her
chest—the reason being, so he had just learned, that she was
deaf and dumb. Yes, a style might well spring up from all
these empty walls, and the men who walked by them; the
very men who just now were streaming past him, exulting in
their carnival of liberty. They shared with their painters in the
dark, underground communion that Christianity had once pro-

vided, that today the Revolution gave them; they had chosen the same way of life, and were dying the same deaths. . . .

"Either it's a loony idea," Slade observed, "or it's something that should be taken in hand by you, or by the Government, or by the League of Revolutionary Artists, or—how about the Worshipful Company of Eagles and Hippos?"

Some of the people going by carried bundles of linen or neatly folded squares of sheets, like lawyers' portfolios, under their arms. A man who looked like a small shopkeeper was pressing to his chest a quilt—scarlet in the bright glow from the tavern—just as the woman who had just gone past had hugged her sewing-machine. Some passers-by carried chairs piled upside-down upon their heads.

"It'll be done," Lopez said. "Not by me, anyhow at present. My company's ordered off to the Sierra. But we shall bring it off, don't you worry!"

Slade blew into thin air a little cloud of pipe-smoke. "My dear Lopez, if you only knew how sick to death I am of the whole human race . . . !"

"It's hardly the right moment . . . !"

"Wait! Day before yesterday I was at Burgos, don't forget. And it was just the same as here. Absolutely. The poor fools are fraternizing with the troops."

"Well, and here, you owl, it's the other way round. The troops are fraternizing with the poor fools."

"And in the swell hotels I saw bare-backed countesses drinking with royalist peasants in berets and woollen blankets."

"And the peasants getting themselves shot for the said countesses, who certainly weren't getting themselves shot for the peasants. But, of course, that's as it should be!"

"When such words as 'Republic' or 'Trade Union' were spoken, they spat, the poor fatheads! I saw a priest with a rifle; he obviously thought he was defending his faith. And in another quarter of the town I came across a blind man with a brand-new bandage over his eyes. On it was written in violet ink: *Viva el Cristo Rey!* I'll bet he thought he was a volunteer like the rest of them."

"He was blind. . . ."

Once more, as always happened when the loud-speakers bawled "Hullo!" a deep hush followed.

Radio Barcelona speaking. General Goded is about to address you.

No one present but knew that Goded was the fascist leader

at Barcelona, and the officer commanding the rebellion there. Silence seemed spreading like a tide up to the furthest limits of Madrid.

The voice sounded listless, indifferent, but not without dignity. *General Goded is speaking. I want to let everybody know that the day has gone against me; I am a prisoner. I make this known so that those who do not wish to keep up the struggle may understand they are absolved from any obligation towards me.*

It was the same declaration Companys had made in 1934 when he was defeated. A wave of cheering broke over the night-bound city.

"That bears out what I was just going to say," Lopez went on, tossing off the contents of his glass at a gulp, in token of his joy. "When I was making those bas-reliefs which you call my 'Scythian dinguses,' I hadn't any stone to work with. Good stone costs a heap, you know; but the cemeteries are stiff with it, that's all you find in 'em. So I looted the graveyards, nights, and all the stuff I turned out in those days was carved in 'Eternal Peace.' That's how I came to give up using diorite. Now we're going to do things on a bigger scale. Spain's a graveyard full of tombstones, and we're going to turn them into works of art—got it, you owl?"

Men and women were passing, laden with bundles wrapped in black sateen. One old woman had a clock; a child carried a handbag; another, a pair of shoes. All were singing. A little behind them a man was dragging a hand-cart loaded, it seemed, with the stock-in-trade of a curiosity-shop; he was singing, too, but lagging a beat or two behind the others. An agitated young man started waving his arms to stop them. It was a newspaper-man who wanted to take a snapshot by the light of his flash-bulb.

"Is this moving day, or what's the big idea?" Slade jerked his little hat back over his forehead. "Afraid of a bombardment?"

Lopez raised his eyes. For the first time their gaze was simple and sincere.

"You know the whole country's overrun with pawn-shops, don't you? This afternoon the Government ordered them to open up and hand back all the pledges right off. All the down-and-outs in Madrid rolled up, you bet. They took their time; they didn't hurry. (I guess they didn't quite believe the news.) Now they're on their way home with their quilts and watch-chains and sewing-machines and what-not. This night belongs to the poor!"

Slade was fifty. He had travelled a good deal and life had given him some nasty knocks—among others, a taste of utter destitution in the States, and the lingering, mortal illness of having loved a woman. And the only things to which he attached any importance he called idiotic or bestial; elemental things like pain and love, humiliation, innocence.

People were moving down the avenue in groups, some behind wheelbarrows bristling with chair legs; others carrying wall-clocks. The idea of the Madrid pawn-shops kept open all night for the benefit of the poor—now on top—and the sight of the crowd scattering across the city to the slums with their rescued pledges, gave Slade his first notion of what the word, revolution, can mean for men.

Above the rumble of patrol-waggons, requisitioned to combat the fascist cars that were scouring the darker streets with submachine-guns, sounded incessantly the cries of *Salud,* fading away and roaring up again, rapped out in measured beats and dying away. Men and darkness seemed united in a fraternal pact—all the stronger for the fight that was impending. The fascists were entering the Sierra.

5

WITH the exception of the men in workmen's overalls with zippers—the garment known as the *mono* and adopted as the militia uniform—all the volunteers in the International Air Force were in cheerful mood. The August sun was hot; their shirts were open at the neck; they might have just come home from a morning's hunting or a bathing party. Only the professional pilots and the machine-gunners from China or Morocco were at the moment in action; but the turn of the others, the new recruits arriving daily for their baptism of fire, would come in the course of the day.

In the centre of the aerodrome a sleek, bright form of aluminum shone in the sun; it was a three-engined Junker whose pilot, hearing the Seville wireless announce the capture of Madrid, had trustingly come down.

At least twenty cigarettes lit up at once. Camuccini, the squadron clerk, had just remarked:

"Two and a quarter hours in all, for the B."

In other words, the large war plane lettered B had fuel for that time and no longer. And everyone—from Leclerc squatting monkey-wise on the bar-counter to the more serious spirits poring over their machine-gun manuals—everyone knew that the plane manned by their comrades, that had left for a flight over the Sierra, had been away just two hours and five minutes.

The cigarette smoke ascended, not in long, lazy spirals, but in quick, short puffs. All eyes were focussed, parallel, across the panes upon the crest-line of the hills.

Now or tomorrow, anyhow quite soon, one of the planes would fail to return. And each man knew that his own death would mean, for those awaiting him in vain, just those quick puffs of smoke from nervously lit cigarettes, in which hope seemed gasping to survive, like a man who is being throttled.

Polsky (known as Pol) and Gardet walked out of the bar, without once taking their eyes off the hills.

"The Boss is in the B, you know."

"Sure about it?"

"Oh, don't play the idiot! You saw him start."

The "Boss" was liked by all—and he was in the missing plane.

"Two hours, ten minutes."

"Wait a bit! Your watch is out of order, isn't it? It was barely one when they took off; that makes only five minutes over the two hours."

"No, Raymond, old chap, there's no getting out of it. It's ten good minutes over the two hours. Look at little Scali up there—see how he's hanging on to his phone!"

"That chap Scali, what is he exactly? An Italian?"

"I believe so."

"He might be Spanish."

Scali's face had the somewhat mulatto cast characteristic of the peoples of the western Mediterranean.

"You've only got to see the state he's in!"

"Things look pretty bad, I'm telling you."

The conversation went on in undertones, as if both men were fearing death might overhear them.

The Ministry had just advised Scali that two Spanish pursuit planes and two adapted bombing planes of the International Flight had been knocked out by a squadron of seven Fiats. One of the bombers had crashed behind the republican lines; the other was only slightly damaged, and trying to return. Scali raced downstairs to Sembrano's office, his fuzzy hair blowing in all directions.

Magnin, the "Boss," was in command of the International Air Force. Sembrano was in charge of the civil aerodrome and the airline machines converted into war planes. He resembled a younger and more amiable edition of Voltaire. Reinforced by old army planes from the Madrid aerodromes, the new Douglases bought by the Government from the Spanish air-lines could, if necessary, tackle the Italian war planes. For the present, anyhow. . . .

The hum of conversation ceased abruptly. No siren could be heard, nor the droning of an engine, but all the "Pelicans" were pointing at some object in the distance. One of the bombing planes, both engines shut off, was skimming a hilltop, coming down to the landing-ground. In the harsh light of early afternoon the sallow-coloured expanse looked as lifeless as the surface of a dead planet. Close above it, the plane, with its freight of dead or living comrades, was gliding silent as a dream.

"The ridge!" Sembrano shouted. "The ridge!"

"Darras is an air-line pilot," Scali replied, cocking his nose-tip with his forefinger.

"The ridge!" Sembrano cried again.

But the plane had just bucked over it, like a horse, and was beginning to circle the field. Down in the bar, everyone held his breath, listening for a shout; not a scrap of ice tinkled in the wine-glasses.

"Look, his tires are cut to shreds!" Scali exclaimed. "He'll turn turtle." He was waving his stumpy arms, as if trying to help the plane to land. Then it touched earth, tilted, scraped a wing-tip, and halted at a slant, but without turning over.

All the Pelicans rushed up, shouting, round the hermetically closed cockpit.

Pol, a lump of candy sticking in his throat, stared at the hatch, which showed no sign of rising. Behind it, in the cabin, were six of his mates. Gardet, his cropped hair bristling forward, was vainly tugging at the handle. All eyes were riveted on the hand battling so furiously with the hatch, which obviously had jammed. At last it rose half open. Some feet showed in the opening; then the trouser-legs of a blood-stained suit of overalls. The slowness of the man's movements made it clear that he was wounded. As Pol stared, half suffocated by the lump of candy, at the blood—whose was it?—and the limb feeling its way gingerly out of the cabin, Pol realized that everyone knew the meaning of solidarity with his whole being.

Little by little the pilot worked his leg out of the doorway; drops of blood, scarlet in the dazzling sunlight, were dripping from it. At last his head emerged—the blotched face of an old winegrower from the Loire, crowned by a gardener's wide-brimmed hat, his mascot.

"So you brought the bus back after all!" Sembrano's timid voice was loud with admiration.

"What about Magnin?" Scali cried.

"Safe and sound," Darras replied, as he tried to get a purchase on the door to wriggle out.

As Sembrano rushed forward and kissed him, the hats of both men fell to the ground. Darras' hair was white. The Pelicans giggled nervously.

Once Darras had got clear, Magnin sprang out. He was in flying kit; his drooping, greyish-blonde moustache and the crash-helmet gave him the look of a bewildered Viking—the bewilderment being imparted by his horn-rimmed glasses.

"And the 'S'?" he shouted to Scali.

"In our lines. Damaged. The crew's only slightly hurt."

"Look after the wounded men. I'm off to the telephone to make my report."

The men who were uninjured jumped out, greeted their pals excitedly, then tried to climb back into the cabin to help the wounded out. Gardet and Pol had already entered it.

Among red splashes and the prints of blood-stained shoe-soles, a very young man was lying. His name was House, "Captain House," and he had not yet been given his *mono*. He had been gunner in the lower turret, and this, his first flight, had brought him five bullets in his legs. He spoke only English—and perhaps one or two classical languages. A little copy of Plato, in Greek, filched that morning from Scali (who had raised hell about it) jutted from the blood-stained pocket of his red-and-blue blazer. Propped against the observer's seat, the bomber, who had two bullets in his thigh, sat waiting. Once a Breton sailor, he had enlisted as a bomber in the Morocco air-force, and set up to be a tough one. He was gritting his teeth, but, despite his wounds, his rubicund, bloated face kept its normal jovial expression, while Gardet cautiously extracted him from the cockpit.

"Take it easy, pals!" Pol cried officiously, his eyes bulging like marbles. "I'll go and fetch a stretcher. That's the only way to fix it without messing the poor chap up worse than he is." Leaning on the arm of Seruzier, his chum (known as the "Flying Wonder" because of his constant look of puzzlement), Leclerc, a lean, monkey-like little scallawag in overalls and an incongruous grey hat, launched out on a tall tale.

"Got to wait a bit, old boy, before they ship you for the torture truck. To pass the time away, I'm going to spin you a yarn. My last brush with the petty bourjoys in gay Paree. It all happened because of a chum. Like this. His concierge, the silly old bastard who opens the door o' nights, couldn't bear the sight of him. Always licking the boots of the tenants with the money-bags, and treating us poor bloody proletarians like so much dirt. That's the sort of swine he was. One night when my pal came home, the concierge fairly tore the poor fellow to pieces just because he'd forgotten to sing out his name when he was passing the cubby-hole. 'Well,' says I. 'Just you wait a bit.' So one night at two in the morning, I unharness an old hack that's standing in the street. And I lead him just inside the hallway in front of the concierge's door and I bawl out in a sort of hollow voice: *'Monsieur le Horse!'* Then, by your leave, I make a quiet getaway. . . ."

The bomber stared at Leclerc and Seruzier without moving a muscle; then, casting a lordly look on the young Pelicans, commanded:

"Get me a copy of *L'Humanité*."

Then he relapsed into silence till the stretcher came.

6

A PUFF of smoke drifted up from the crest of the Sierra. The glasses shivered, the tinkle of the tea-spoons in them following the crash of the explosion by the tenth of a second. The first shell had fallen, at the far end of the street. A tile came slithering down the roof onto a table, the glasses tumbled off, a pit-a-pat of running feet drummed on the bright air of noon. Evidently the second shell had landed half way down the street. All the peasants crowded into the café, rifle in hand, chattering volubly, but with steady, watchful eyes.

At the third shell—only ten yards away—all the window-panes crashed, volleying splintered glass at the men wearing cartridge belts. They were glued to the wall, paralysed.

A sliver of glass impaled the cinema poster spattered with tiny wine-drops.

Another crash. Then another, much farther off, on the left this time. Now everyone in the village seemed to be shouting at once. Manuel had a walnut in his hand; he held it up above his head, between two fingers. Another bomb exploded, nearer.

"Thanks," Manuel said, and exhibited his walnut, broken in pieces. (He had cracked it with his fingers.)

A peasant asked in a low tone: "Eh, but what may a man do to keep them shells from coming his way?"

No one replied. Ramos was with the armoured train. All stayed on, sometimes moving away from the wall, but always coming back to it, waiting for the next shell.

"There's no sense in what we're doing here." Old Barca's jerky voice broke the silence. "If we stay in here, we'll all go crazy. Better go and have a whack at them."

Manuel looked at him intently, wondering if the man were in earnest.

"Well, there are lorries on the square," he said.

"Know how to drive 'em?"

"Yes."

"Big lorries?"

"Yes."

"Oh, boys!" Barca yelled.

Such was the shock of the explosion that all the peasants flung themselves on the ground. When they rose, the house opposite the café had lost its front wall, and the rafters were tumbling down belatedly, like matches. Forlornly, a telephone was tinkling above the void.

"There's lorries yonder," Barca continued. "Let's climb in and have a whack at the bastards."

All began speaking at once. "Good for you!" "We got no orders." "You sons of bitches!" "Want orders, do you? Well, the orders are: 'Shut your traps and get into them damned lorries.'"

Manuel and Barca had run outside. Most of the others followed them. Anything was better than staying where they were. More shells were falling. A little behind them were the laggards—the look-before-you-leap men.

Thirty peasants clambered into a lorry. Shells were falling thick all round the village. It struck Barca that while the fascist artillery could see the village, they could not see what was going on in it. For the moment, no planes were up. Laden with villagers singing the *International* and brandishing their rifles above the racket of the changing gears, the lorry gathered speed.

Since Ramos' propaganda campaign in the Sierras, the peasants had come to feel a certain, if somewhat diffident, regard for Manuel. It had steadily intensified as he grew more and more ill-shaven, and the face with the pale green eyes under the jet-black lashes, which brought to mind that of a rather heavy-jowled Roman emperor, became more and more like a Mediterranean fisherman's.

Shells were sweeping overhead through the bright sunlight, with a rustling swish like the sound of pigeons' wings, and dropping in the village. With Manuel at the wheel, the lorry rumbled ahead along the road. His nerves tense, he was singing, of all things, the song from *Manon*, at the top of his voice.

Adieu, nôtre peti-te table. . . .

Equally tense, the others were breaking in with the *International*. They stared at two dead men, past whom the car was speeding, with the uneasy thrill of comradeship that men going up into the line feel for the first to fall. Barca was wondering exactly where the field-guns were stationed. "The smoke, that ain't enough to tell you."

"Hi! One of the boys has fallen off."

"Stop!"

"No!" yelled Barca. "No stopping! Let's get at those guns!"

The other men gave in. Barca had taken charge of the situation. Changing gear, the lorry emitted a harsh screech that shrilled above the crash of the shell-bursts. More dead men were lying on the roadside.

"There's three more lorries just behind!"

Everyone, even Manuel at the wheel, looked round, shouting "Hurrah!"

All began to sing in Spanish, stamping their feet, in unison with Manuel.

Adieu, nôtre peti-te table. . . .

At the opening of a tunnel from which a long, inquisitive snout—the locomotive of the armoured train—protruded,

Ramos was gazing down on the lorries across four hundred yards of pine-clad slopes.

"It's a ten to one chance, my boy," he said to Salazar, "against their bringing it off."

Ramos had replaced the commander of the armoured train, who had gone over to the fascists—or was it merely for a "binge" in Madrid?

Against the vastness of the mountain-side the lorries looked absurdly small. But their hoods were catching the sunlight, and the fascists could hardly help seeing them.

"Why not give them a hand?" Salazar suggested, stroking his handsome moustache the wrong way. He had served as a sergeant in Morocco.

"Our orders were not to fire. There's no getting them changed. Your home-made telephone is working fine; only there's no one at the other end of the line."

Three *milicianos* in *monos* were setting out two chasubles and a priest's stole on the rails some yards in front of the loco-motive. But their eyes were fixed on the lorries moving along the pale blue ribbon of road across which two dead bodies lay.

"Shall we get a move on?" one of them shouted.

"No," Ramos replied. "The orders are to stay here."

The lorries were still advancing; the hum of their engines was clearly audible between the anvil-clangs of gun-fire. A *miliciano*, one of those Castilian peasants whose elongated faces give them a family likeness to their horses, climbed down from the tender, picked up the chasubles and began folding them. Ramos went up to him.

"What are you up to, Ricardo?"

"We been talking it over, me and the boys," he muttered.

He unrolled a short length of the stole, with a puzzled air; the brocade glittered in the sunlight.

The lorries were still climbing. The engine-driver's head, peering out of the cab, showed bright against the dark mouth of the tunnel. He was grinning.

"It's like this," Ricardo said. "We got to be mighty careful. How can we tell these filthy contraptions won't bring bad luck to our mates in the lorries, or heave the old locomotive off the rails? I don't trust 'em, that's sure."

"Give them to your wife," Ramos suggested. "She'll find some use for them."

The big, good-humoured young man with the curly hair inspired the peasants with confidence. But, just now—how could they be sure he wasn't joking?

"My wife wear that there thing?" Disgustedly the peasant flung the glittering roll of fabric into the ravine.

The enemy machine-guns opened fire, in punctual, measured cadence.

The lorry in front skidded, swung round and toppled over, spilling its human freight like apples from a basket. Such as were not killed or wounded took cover behind it and began firing. All that the men in the armoured train could make out of Ramos was his curly hair and bulky field-glasses. On their radio, someone was singing an Andalusian song. A coffin-like scent of resin from the uprooted pines filled the warm air, which throbbed as if it were being churned up by the machine-guns.

There were olive-trees on each side of the wrecked lorry. Some *milicianos* ran out from behind it towards the trees; they fell one after the other. The road being blocked, the lorries behind halted.

"If only the boys would lie down!" Salazar exclaimed. "There's cover if they knew how to use it."

"To hell with orders! Get back to the train and open fire."

Salazar ran back, a martial figure, somewhat hampered by his gorgeous riding boots.

As the *milicianos* could no longer advance, Ramos ran the risk of firing on them. But he had only one chance in a hundred of hitting the enemy machine-guns, for he had no idea of their location.

On a siding were some freight-trucks still bearing the inscription: *Good Luck to the Strikers*.

The armoured train crept out of the tunnel, menacing but blind. Once again Ramos was conscious that all an armoured train amounts to is one field-gun and a few machine-guns.

The men behind the lorry were aiming at the place from which the noise of firing came. They were learning that the most important and hardest thing in warfare is not so much man-to-man attack as cold-blooded slaughter.

Just now it was they who were being slaughtered.

"Hold your fire," Barca shouted, "until you see something. Else we'll have used up all our ammunition when the bastards attack."

Nothing would have suited them better than an attack from

the fascists; a straight fight rather than this sick suspense—like the ordeal of a doctor's waiting-room.

A man ran forward towards the batteries; at his seventh step he was shot down, as the men who had tried to run to cover behind the olive-trees had been shot down.

"If they turn their field-guns on us . . ." Manuel remarked to Barca.

Obviously, this was impracticable; otherwise they'd have done it already.

"Comrades . . . !" A woman's voice!

Almost everyone looked round in amazement. A girl in the militia uniform stood behind them.

"You've no business here." Barca spoke without severity; all were grateful to the girl for having come to join them.

She carried a fat, squat hand-bag, bulging with tinned provisions.

"Say," Barca asked, "how did she get here?"

Her parents, it seemed, were peasants living in the village; she knew all the foot-paths about the hills. Barca's eyes followed the pointing finger; forty yards without cover.

"Well? Can we get round that way?" A *miliciano* asked.

"Sure," said the girl. She was about seventeen, and pretty.

"No," Barca said. "See that open patch we'd have to cross? They'd mow us down."

"She came that way. Why shouldn't we . . . ?"

"Listen! Isn't it possible they let her through purposely? We're in a tight corner sure enough; no need to make it worse."

"Seems to me, we might get through to the village."

"You're not thinking of turning back?" the girl exclaimed, in a shocked tone. "The people's army never retreats from its positions; the radio said it again, only an hour ago."

Her voice had the theatrical intonation which comes so readily to Spanish women, but, quite unconsciously, she was wringing her hands. "We'll bring you anything you want." She sounded like a kind lady offering toys to a group of children, to get them to behave.

Barca was pondering. "Comrades," he said at last, "that's not the point. That kid says . . ."

"I'm not a kid!"

"Very well. Our comrade says we can get away, but it's up to us to stay here. What I say is: It's up to us to clear, but we can't do it nohow. Got to get things straight, ain't we?"

"You've pretty hair," Manuel whispered to the militia-girl. "Give me—just one."

"Comrade, I haven't come here for—for silliness."

"All right, keep your hair, stingy."

While chatting with the girl—without much real interest— he had been keeping his ears open. Now he cried:

"Listen! What's that?"

They listened. Only the vast, birdless silence. And the distant machine-guns reeling off band after band. One out of action? No, only jammed; off again at once. But no more shots were coming near the lorry.

Suddenly someone shouted, "Look there!"

"Keep your head down, you bloody fool!"

He lowered his head. In the direction where the man was pointing, tiny blue-clad forms were moving up towards the fascist batteries along a line parallel to the road, taking advantage of the cover of the wood. It was the Assault Guard.

"That's the stuff!" Barca exclaimed. "If we'd gone about it that way . . ."

"Good work!" a *miliciano* exclaimed. "Say, boys, shall we lend a hand?"

"Just a minute!" Manuel said. "Mustn't bungle it up again this time. Number off by tens, all of you. Got it? Right! The first man of each section is in command. You'll advance by sections ten yards apart—four sections. You've got to get there, all of you, at the same moment. The leading section will be ahead, but that won't make much difference, as they've got to spread out wider than the others. Got it?"

"No, I ain't got it," said Barca. "Sounds sort of muddled up to me."

Yet everyone had listened as closely as if it were a lecture on first aid to the wounded.

"Now then! Number off by tens."

They did so. The section leaders came up to Manuel. From the hill-top the guns still pounded the village with shells, but the machine-guns fired only at the Assault Guard, which continued its advance. Manuel was used to handling the men of his Party; unfortunately there were few of them here.

"You take command of the first group of ten. We'll deploy on the right of the road, all of us; no use getting cut in two if those swine come down the road in an armoured car or God knows what. And it will bring us nearer the Assault Guard.

. . . Ten comrades, over a hundred yards. Now, number one, get a move on with your ten men. When you've gone three hundred yards, leave one man behind every ten yards. When you see the section on your left advancing, you'll advance. If anything goes wrong, hand over the command to the next man, and run back. You'll find, behind you . . ." Whom would he find? Manuel had thought of sending Barca back to give instructions to the men from the other lorries. As for himself, it was up to him to be in the front line. So much the worse. ". . . You'll find Barca."

Someone else could be sent to the men in the other lorries.

"When I whistle, everyone falls back on Barca. Got it?"

"Yes."

"No, say it again."

All was going well.

"Look, boys—the armoured train!"

All felt like kissing each other for sheer joy. The train was firing at the presumed emplacements of the batteries and machine-guns—firing blind. But the *milicianos,* now they heard their guns answering the fascist guns, no longer felt trapped. They greeted the second boom with an ovation.

Manuel dispatched a communist to Ramos to tell him how things were; a U.G.T. man to the Assault Guards; and the oldest of the anarchists to inform the men in the lorries of his plan of campaign.

"Take something to eat with you," said the militia-girl. "You never can tell!"

"Go to it, lads!"

"Well, I'll bring you some food later on," she said determinedly.

While the others went ahead, Barca ran back to the lorries. The enemy was still plugging away at them, but now with rifles only. The second section started off, the third and then the last, with Manuel in command.

The view between the rows of olive-trees was unobstructed. Up one of the spacious, tranquil avenues, Barca saw a *miliciano* advancing, then ten men, then a long file. He could not see beyond five hundred yards, and the long procession covered all his field of view; the whole grove seemed full of men advancing to the thunderous rhythm of the guns. The Assault Guards were firing on the adjoining hillside, but, now that he was hidden by the trees, Barca could see them no longer. Evidently they had a submachine-gun, for a mechanical purring linked the ragged rifle-shots and merged with the incessant stutter of the fascist machine-guns. The line of *milicianos* kept advancing, under a rather ineffective rifle-fire from the fascists. Manuel broke into a double, and all the line followed suit, like a cable dragged along a river-bed. Now Barca, too, was galloping uphill carried along by the confused fervour of an ideal which he called "The People," a ferment of emotions worked up by the chaos and confusion of the day, the bombardment of the village, the wreckage of the lorry, the gunshots from the armoured train—and now embodied in the little band that like one man was charging the fascists.

As they ran they trampled fallen branches underfoot; before the advance of the Assault Guards the machine-guns had been trained across the olive grove. Here the tang of resin gave place to the warm fumes of sun-baked soil. On branches grazed by bullets the foliage drooped and faltered, falling leaf by leaf as in an autumn wind. And, to the incessant rhythm of the guns, the little group raced upward, upward, appeared and disappeared, now flashing through tracts of sunlight, now all but invisible in shadows of the grove. The firing from the armoured train and the submachine-gun sounded in Barca's ears the promise of a new world; never again would the vineyards be wrested from the men who planted them.

They had twenty yards of open ground to cross. The moment they came out of the olive grove, the fascists turned one of their machine-guns on them. Round Barca the air was alive with bullets buzzing like angry wasps; he ran towards the rifles through the shrill steely swarm—invulnerable! Suddenly his legs crumpled up; he rolled over. Despite the searing pain, he went on looking straight ahead. Half his men had fallen, and lay where they fell; the other half had got through. Beside him lay the village grocer, dead, the shadow of a butterfly flickering on his face. The front line of the men from the other lorries stood hesitating on the edge of the olive grove. A distant drone of aeroplanes came to Barca's ears. Whose? Theirs or ours? he wondered. Then, from beside the place where the submachine-gun was firing, a rocket soared up into the sunlit air. The armoured train ceased fire.

Salazar turned to Ramos. "Have the Assault Guards reached the field-guns?"

They had sent a runner to the train to say they would release a rocket when they reached the battery. They must be very near it now. So Ramos had ceased fire.

"Looks like it," he said.

"How are our men getting on?"

"They're out of sight. They can't have got through, as the heavies and machine-guns are still firing."

"Shall I go and have a look?"

"Manuel seems to be putting up a damned good show, with Barca's help. He's just sent a message through to me."

The field-glasses gave Ramos a close-up of all the false serenity of rocks and pines and olives, festering now with wounds. But it was impossible to make out what was happening. He could only listen.

"What's so sickening," he said, "is that it's always the enemy who puts up the real show, not our people."

The fascists began by a bombardment, cleaned up an area, then marched their men into it. The people, leaderless and all but unarmed, could merely fight. . . .

"By the look of things just now, those poor chaps below must be getting butchered like sheep. Still, as they've risked an attack, there's always the chance the Assault Guards may rush the battery." Ramos' voice was tremulous with excitement, his sensual lips were thin and anguished, his smile was gone; even his wayward hair looked like a wig.

"Anyhow the fascists won't get through."

"The battery on the left has ceased fire."

The foreheads of both men were tingling with the strain of listening to each sound.

A plane approached, golden in the sunlit sky; a light, fairly speedy machine. It dropped a bomb five hundred yards from the train. Probably it had no bomb-sights, and not being fitted for dropping bombs, had launched it through a window. Ramos had given instructions to the engine-driver, who now took his train quietly under cover of the near-by tunnel. After dropping all its bombs into the pine wood, the plane went off, satisfied. The smell of resin grew still more pungent.

From the armoured train, they could see nothing. Between the thuds of clanging steel that shook the train from end to end, Pepe, an Asturian, naked to the waist, was explaining to his mates how the train had been fixed up.

"We used cement instead of steel plate. It ain't much to look at, but it's tough, you can bet your boots on that. This train looks like it was built of cardboard, but it'll stand up against most anything. In thirty-four, in the Asturias, we armoured the trains real fine—a good job that was, my lads. But this time, seems as if everyone was absent-minded—that's how the revolution is. The boys forgot all about the locomotive! What do you make of that—an armoured train charging full steam through the Tercio lines with an ordinary, unarmoured engine pulling it? Thirty miles out, you couldn't count the bullets that had gone through her guts—and through the driver's, too. Riddled like a sieve. Well, we managed to slip past at night with another train and engine—armoured this time—and we had the boys entrained before the Tercio had time to bring their guns up."

"Say, Pepe!"

"What?"

"That battery's still not firing."

Ramos had come out of the tunnel to see how things were going with the rebels; he was switching his field-glasses in all directions, like a blind man groping for something with his hands.

"Our men are beating it for the village," he said at last.

The *milicianos* were falling back, firing—rather ineffecitvely —as they did so. They vanished into a cutting. The fascists following them had three hundred yards of open ground to cross.

Ramos leapt into the engine-cab, brought the train forward to a point where it had the treeless patch in range—though it could not be seen from the fascist batteries, which were still pounding away.

Compared to the disorder of the militia, the fascists advanced with mechanical precision.

Now the machine-guns on the train went into play.

From left to right the fascists began falling, limply, their arms in air or fists clenched upon their bellies. The second wave hesitated at the edge of the clearing, took heart, dashed forward at the double; the hail of bullets mowed them down from right to left. The gunners in the train might be poor soldiers, but they were good shots. For the first time that day Ramos saw, again and again, that curious caper of a man who is shot while he is running—one arm upraised and his legs doubled under him, as if he were jumping to catch death on the wing. The fascists who had not been hit ran back into the wood, from which such as had escaped the machine-guns on the train had opened fire.

Shots rang out on the right, where a group of *milicianos* were posted. The fascists retreated through the wood, firing as they fell back.

"They have officers, and equipment," Ramos murmured, running his fingers through his curls, "but I'm damned if they'll get through. No, they won't get through."

7

UNDER the tranquil summer sky pilots were still being put through their trial flight.

A volunteer, wearing a sweater despite the heat, came up to Magnin.

He gave his name. "Captain Schreiner." A wolfish little man with steely eyes and a pointed nose, one time second-in-command of Richthofen's famous "flying circus." Magnin peered benevolently over his moustache upon the little man.

"How long since you last flew a plane?"

"Since the War."

"Ah, the devil! And how long would it take to get in shape again?"

"A few hours, I suppose."

Magnin looked at him without replying.

Schreiner repeated: "Yes, an hour or two should do."

"Had a job in aviation?"

"No, I've been working in the Alès mines." Schreiner did not look at Magnin as he answered; his eyes were intent on the whirling propeller-blades of the practice plane. The fingers of his right hand were twitching.

"The money-order came too late," he said. "I had to come by lorry as far as Toulouse."

Closing his narrow eyes, he listened to the engine, while his fingers, still twitching, plucked at the creases of his sweater. Magnin's own passion for flying was such that the sight of the fingers twitching the rough fabric warmed his heart towards the German. Without opening his eyes, Schreiner was sniffing the vibrant air eagerly. "Like a prisoner," Magnin thought, "who's just been set free." Yes, that chap might make a useful officer. Magnin was short of assistants and Schreiner's voice had the clean-cut intonation common to professional soldiers and many communist leaders.

Towards them, across the shimmering sunlight, came Sibirsky, the chief instructor. Another instructor called Schreiner, who walked off to the practice plane, unhurrying but with his fingers still twitching.

Standing in the bar or on the tarmac, all the pilots were watching. Several of them had served in the Great War, and Magnin felt a little ill at ease. But, confronted with this man, who had brought down twenty-two allied machines, the only sentiment felt by all, even the mercenaries, was that of purely professional rivalry.

Near the bar, Scali, Marcelino and Jaime Alvear were taking turns with the field-glasses. Jaime Alvear, who had spent his student years in France, had been appointed combatant interpreter to the International Air Force. He was a tall, swarthy young man with the look of an Indian chief; a rugged face and black hair always flapping on his forehead. Beside him stood a smaller man with wine-red cheeks: Vegas—to his pals, Saint Anthony—who, in the name of the U.G.T., showered cigarettes and gramophone records on his friends, the Pelicans. Scali's black basset, "Raplati," was poking his long nose between the two men. Raplati was by way of being the squadron mascot. Jaime's father was, like Scali, an art-historian.

Some gusts of firing came from the far end of the landing-ground where Karlitch was putting the machine-gunners through their paces. Schreiner's machine took off, fairly well.

"Those volunteers will be a problem," Sibirsky said to Magnin. Magnin, too, was aware that it might be troublesome getting the mercenaries to work under the orders of volunteers, when the latter were, professionally speaking, well below their standards. "I'm grateful for the confidence you've shown in me, Monsieur Magnin, by appointing me instructor," Sibirsky continued.

They took some steps side by side, without looking at each other; both were gazing up at the plane, now in full flight.

"Know anything about me?" Sibirsky asked abruptly.

"Why, of course." As he spoke, chewing his long moustache, Magnin reflected that really he knew nothing about the man. He liked Sibirsky; despite his rather foppish look—golden curls, diminutive moustache—the sadness in his voice suggested, if not intelligence, at least experience. All Magnin really knew of him was his value as a technician; there was no questioning that.

"I want to tell you, Monsieur Magnin. Here they all think

I'm a Red. That has its uses, I suppose. It's just as well. But I'd like you to know I'm not a White, either. They don't know much about life, these airmen of yours, even those who are getting on in years." Uncomfortably, Sibirsky stared at his shoes. Then, raising his eyes, he watched the plane in flight for nearly a minute. "Well, he can fly it—but that's the most one can say." There was no irony in his voice. Schreiner was one of their oldest pilots. Every aviator on the field dreaded what could happen to a great flyer, forty-six years old, who had spent ten years in the mines.

"We'll need at least five machines tomorrow, for the Sierra." Magnin sounded anxious.

"I hated the life I was leading with my uncle in Siberia. People talked of nothing but fighting. Then I went away to college. When the Whites came, I joined them. Afterwards, I went to Paris. I was a chauffeur for a bit, then a mechanic; then I took to flying again. I'm a lieutenant in the French Army."

"I know. You'd like to go back to Russia, eh?"

Many Russians who had been White were now serving in Spain, hoping thus to prove their loyalty and be permitted to return to Russia.

Another burst of machine-gun fire rattled across the sunlight from the far end of the flying-ground.

"Yes. But not as a communist. As a partyless man. I'm here on a contract; but even for twice the money I wouldn't have joined the others. I'm what you call a liberal. Karlitch, now, believed in order; he used to be a White. Now that order reigns in Russia—and there's force behind it—he's gone Red. Personally, I'm all for democracy—the United States, France, England . . . Only—Russia's my country."

He looked up at the plane again; this time to avoid meeting Magnin's eyes.

"There's just one thing," he said, "I hope you'll let me ask you. I don't want to have to bomb objectives within a city—not under any circumstances. I expect I'm rather too old for pursuit work. But for reconnaissance or bombing at the front. . . ."

"The Spanish Government doesn't countenance bombing open towns."

"You see, I was detailed once to bomb the enemies' headquarters. The bombs fell on a school."

Magnin did not dare to ask whether the headquarters and

the school had been German or bolshevik. Schreiner's machine was getting into position to land.

"Undershooting," Magnin grunted, steadying his binoculars. "Perhaps he'll give her the gun."

As Sibirsky expected, the pilot opened his throttle again. Both men had stopped and were following every movement of the plane. The field was enormous and for a pilot to muff a first landing like that . . . ! Magnin was familiar with practice flights; he had been a chief pilot for the French air-lines.

The plane returned, landed a trifle short. The pilot pulled his stick back and the machine leapt like a stone skipping off a ripple, then plumped down with a rending crash. It's lucky, Magnin thought, that machine has no military value.

Sibirsky, who had run towards the damaged plane, came back, followed by Schreiner and the assistant instructor.

"Forgive me," Schreiner said, in such a tone that Magnin dared not look him in the face. "I told you I needed two hours. Two days wouldn't be enough. It's all those years spent in the mines; I've lost my reflexes."

Sibirsky and his assistant moved away.

"We'll talk about that later," Magnin said.

"No use. But, thank you. I never want to see a plane again. I'm through with flying. Put me down for the militia, please."

To the clatter of machine-guns, drumming nearer and nearer, the *milicianos* were dragging another machine across the runway; a sporting plane once the pride of some young *señorito*.

Schreiner walked off the grounds, with unseeing eyes, staring into emptiness. Like men shrinking from the sight of a child's agony, or of a disaster where all human words are futile, the pilots moved aside to let him pass. The war assimilated mercenaries and volunteers alike in a romantic venture; but aviation united them as maternity makes all women one. Even those incorrigible gossips, Leclerc and Seruzier, had for once dried up; each man knew that the experience he had just witnessed would be his own one day. No one dared meet the German's gaze—which shrank from the eyes of all.

But one pair of eyes was fixed on Magnin; the eyes of the pilot whose turn came after Schreiner's: Marcelino.

"Five machines are needed for the Sierra tomorrow," Magnin repeated mechanically.

The machine-gun rapped out five shots, ten shots, and

stopped. When Karlitch, the machine-gun instructor, saw
Magnin coming, he went up to him, saluted, and drew him
aside. Without saying anything, he produced three cartridges
from his pocket; the caps showed the marks of the striker, but
the bullets had not gone off.

"Made in Toledo," Karlitch said, tapping the inscription
with his finger-nail.

"Sabotage?"

"No, bad workmanship. And if a gun stalls while we're up,
in the middle of a fight, and we've got to start it going again,
you know what that means."

Karlitch had gone to England, a broken man, and the
privations he then endured had shattered what he had taken
hitherto for his convictions. After some desultory years the
former champion machine-gunner of Wrangel's army had
joined the "Back-to-Our-Country" movement sympathetic to
the U.S.S.R. which was developing among the émigrés. He was
perhaps the only volunteer who hated the enemy simply because he was the enemy.

"What about the ground guns?" Magnin asked. "We need
some for the Sierra right away."

The *milicianos* had no experience in handling any kind of
machine-gun whatever, still less in restarting it when it
jammed. Magnin had converted his best machine-gunners into
instructors under Karlitch's direction. The ground force machine-gunners were being given a course in air gunnery and a
group of picked *milicianos* was being trained in the use and
upkeep of field machine-guns. Magnin also hoped to organize
a motorcycle corps of machine-gunners.

"Those men in the militia," Karlitch said, "are good.
They've been well picked. They're disciplined, they take pains
and they listen. So far, so good. But that fellow, Wurtz, Comrade Magnin—he's a wash-out. Always at Party meetings,
never on his job. The only help I get is from Gardet. Our men
have learned all about handling machine-guns in the air, but
I can't say how they'll do when they're actually up. I've nothing to test them with; no towed targets, no camera guns, no
doped gasoline. And there's precious little ammunition, and
bad at that. They know how to work their turrets. At the after-
guns I'll post only men with air experience—we can't have 'em
putting bullets through the tail! For training, I guess, they'll
have to practise on the enemy!"

Karlitch gave a high-pitched cackle of delight, his cocks-

comb hair and eyebrows lifting, his nostrils quivering with joy.
He had returned to his beloved machine-guns, as Schreiner
to his planes. And it struck Scali, who had just come up for
the end of their conversation, that war has its physiological
side as well.

All the revolutionary pilots who, on pacifist grounds, had
abandoned their military training, had now to be put through
a course of instruction, or be eliminated. But there was no
question of waiting till next year to tackle Franco. And for the
moment, the only men Magnin could count on were the professional civil pilots and those who had kept up their annual
courses.

He had cashiered several pilots from Morocco, used to old-
fashioned aircraft and bombing a defenceless foe. The sight of
their first casualties had stirred them to noble sentiments.
"After all, those chaps haven't done us any harm. Why'd we
want to start scrapping with 'em?" But without definitely giving
up their contracts. To France with the whole useless lot of
them!

A Frenchman called Dugay was the first of the volunteers
who had asked for a private interview with him. He was fifty
years old; his grey moustache was paler than his cheeks.

"Comrade Magnin," he began, "this idea of packing me off
to France—it ain't fair, you shouldn't do it. I served as an instructor in the War. Seems I'm too old to go up again. Very
well. That's all right. But just give me a scrap of cotton waste
and a job as a mechanic's mate. With a bus to look after—any
old bus."

Sembrano dashed up, waving his arms.

"Listen, Magnin. We want a machine for San Benito right
away. They're marching on Badajoz."

"Ah . . . yes, of course. But all the fighters are in the air,
you know. And without fighters, what can we do?"

"Just got the orders. We're to send three machines; I've only
two Douglases left."

"Very well! What is it? A motor column?"

"Yes."

"Right."

He went to the telephone. Sembrano hurried off, his underlip protruding.

"Well, Comrade Magnin"—Dugay's voice again—"what
about me?"

"What? . . . Oh, all right, you can stay. Now what—what am I forgetting?"

He was forgetting nothing; but that flustered air—like the phrase he had just used—had become a mannerism with him. As a matter of fact his actions were always cool and calculating.

No sooner was Dugay gone than he was pestered by a group of newcomers. "We've all got our tickets for light planes, and we're quite willing to learn." Next a mercenary group, men who were out merely for the pay, and would malinger at the least pretext. Magnin shipped the whole lot back, "unserviceable goods," to the far side of the Pyrenees.

Jaime came in, Raplati trotting between his legs. Magnin was not expecting him.

"Comrade Magnin, I wanted to tell you . . . I know you don't need me as interpreter just now, but—well, it's like this. Marcelino's got to go through his trial flight, of course. Only I thought, Comrade Magnin, in case you haven't heard about it, you ought to know that Marcelino's been two years in prison, under the fascist régime."

Listening, Magnin felt drawn to the tall young Spaniard in the tight-fitting overalls, with the prominent chin and brow and aquiline nose. Friendship, it seemed, could get no hold on those rugged, strongly moulded features, and showed only in the changed expression of his eyes.

"He used to be a professional hydroplane pilot. Then, after Lauro de Bosis' death, he dropped pamphlets on Milan. Balbo's planes brought him down, of course; he was in a light plane. He was sentenced to six years' imprisonment, but he managed to escape from the Lipari Islands. He hasn't flow any sort of plane since the trial. Or a pursuit plane since he left the Italian army. He's . . . a broken man. What I mean to say, Comrade Magnin, not that I want to bias your decision in any way, and of course there's no question of giving him a pilot's job—I'd like to suggest that something should be done for him; the Spanish comrades who're here would be awfully glad if you could . . ."

"I'll be glad, too," Magnin replied. Jaime went away. Captain Mercery came up. He, too, was nearly fifty. A grey moustache straddled his upper lip; he had the hard-bitten look of an old pirate chief—a look which he deliberately accentuated —and he wore cavalry boots outside civilian trousers.

"See here, Monsieur Magnin, it's all a question of technical knowledge; there's no getting away from it. It's experience that tells . . ."

"Are you going back to France?"

Mercery raised his arms excitedly. "Monsieur Magnin, my wife was in Spain on the sixteenth. For the Stamp-Collectors' Congress, you know. Well, on the twentieth, she writes to me: 'What's happening here is too foul for words. No man would submit to it.' A woman, mind you; a woman wrote that. But I'd started off already! I'm at the service of Spain. In any capacity—but serving Spain. We've got to smash fascism. As I said to the reactionaries back there in Noisy-le-Sec, 'No, gentlemen, it's not the mummies that keep Egypt going, it's Egypt keeps the mummies.' "

"Just so. Exactly. You're a captain. Would you like me to place you at the disposal of the Ministry of War?"

"Yes. Well, I mean. . . . I'm a captain, as you just said. I might be in the Officers' Reserve, only I've always refused to do my periods of service, on account of my convictions."

Magnin had been told that Mercery served in the War as company sergeant-major, and that he was "captain" of—a fire-brigade! Then, he had taken it for a joke.

"Why . . . yes . . . of course."

"Hold on. I know what a trench looks like. I went through the War."

For all his exaggerations, obviously the man meant well; and, thought Magnin, a competent sergeant-major can be quite as useful to us as a captain.

It was Marcelino's turn. Wearing a loose, beltless flying-suit, he was staring at his boots with a woe-begone air. He raised his eyes and said gloomily: "Prison life, you know . . . doesn't do the reflexes any good."

A gust of gunfire cut him short; Karlitch was on his job at the far end of the ground.

"I used to be quite a hand at bombing," Marcelino went on, "and I guess I'm still pretty good."

A fortnight earlier, while Magnin, in the intervals of re-cruiting volunteers and hiring mercenaries, was trying to buy for the Spanish Government all the aircraft available on the European market, he had found one morning, when he came home, a young man with a drooping moustache, misted eye-glasses and a hat set well back on his head, waiting on the landing between the two doors of his flat. When they entered, all the telephones were buzzing and several visitors, strangers to each other, were pacing up and down the various rooms. He had installed Marcelino on his little boy's bed, with his back to an open cupboard, and had completely forgotten about him. Returning at about two in the afternoon, he had found the Italian pilot still seated on the bed, surrounded by a number of dolls which he had unearthed from the cupboard, and telling stories to himself about them.

"If you send me up as a bomber, I might be able to do a bit of dual control as well. I'm sure I'd get my hand in pretty quickly."

Magnin looked hard at the spare figure in the flapping overalls, the head with its sleek curls like the head on a Venetian medal. "We'll give you a bombing test tomorrow, with cement bombs."

Sembrano's Douglases and one of Magnin's transport planes were being brought to the far end of the landing-ground.

After the events in Algeria, when the Italian war planes flying in battle formation had crashed, several governments had put their older war planes out of commission and sold them off. The machines which were now being brought on to the tarmac would have short shrift against the new Savoias, if the Italian pilots put up a good fight.

Looking round, Magnin noticed that Schreiner had stepped into Marcelino's place. The German's silence contrasted both with the young Italian's timid insistence and Dugay's bewilderment; it was an animal silence.

At last he spoke. "Comrade Magnin, I've been thinking. I said I was through with flying, and that's so—I am no longer good for it. But I am still a good marksman. I know it; haven't I practised at the village fairs, and with my revolver?"

His face was expressionless, but his voice was vibrant with an undertone of hatred. His narrow eyes were fixed on Magnin, his head sunken between his shoulders like a vulture's. Magnin was watching an anarchist car moving past the hangars; it was the first time he had set eyes on the black flag.

"Seems the planes don't want me any longer," Schreiner said. "Right. Give me an anti-aircraft job." Again, two or three gusts of gunfire. "I beg of you."

Is there a pattern common to revolutions? The figures of the volunteers passing in the dusk behind the Le Corbusier buildings on the field suggested the men of the Mexican revolutions and those of the Paris Commune. All the planes had been grounded for the night. Magnin, Sembrano and his friend Vallado were drinking tepid beer. Since the war, ice was no longer to be had at the airport.

"Things are in a bad way at the military aerodrome," Sembrano remarked. "The army of the revolution needs organization from beginning to end. Otherwise Franco'll fill the graveyards with the victims of *his* law and order. How do you think they managed in Russia?" Seen in profile against the lights in the mess, with his protruding underlip, he looked still more like Voltaire—an amiable Voltaire in a white flying-suit.

"They had rifles. Plus four years' discipline and active service. And the communists—they were the embodiment of discipline."

"Tell me, Magnin, why are you a revolutionary?" Vallado asked.

"I wonder! Well, I've run several factories; people like us, men who've always been interested in our work, can hardly realize what it means to spend one's whole life—giving eight hours a day. . . . But I want men to know *why* they're working."

Sembrano's view was that as a rule the owners of industrial Spain were incapable of running their enterprises and left them in the hands of experts. As an expert, he preferred to work for the collectivity, rather than for a private owner. His view was shared by Jaime Alvear and most of the leftist technicians.

Vallado saw things from another angle; what he wanted was a Spanish Renaissance and he saw no hope of it from the Spanish Right. Vallado belonged to the upper middle class; it was he who had dropped the pamphlets on the Montaña Barracks. But for the absence of the small moustache, which he had shaved off at the outbreak of the rebellion, his was a typical *señorito's* face.

Magnin admired the intelligence with which these men supported their passions.

"Personally, I rather think," he said, "I'm Left because that's the way I'm built. And there are all sorts of links and loyalties, between me and the leftists. I've seen what they are aiming at, I've helped them to achieve it, and I've been drawn nearer and nearer them each time there's been another effort to block them."

"When one's merely wedded to a political belief," Sembrano smiled, "that's no great matter. But when one has children by it . . ."

"By the way, what used you to be? A communist?"

"No, a right-wing socialist. Were you a communist?"

"No," Magnin said, pulling his moustache with little nervous jerks. "I, too, was a socialist. But of the revolutionary left wing."

"Personally," replied Sembrano, with a sad smile that was like the gathering darkness, "I was, above all, a pacifist."

"Ideas change," Vallado remarked.

"The people for whom I'm fighting haven't changed. And that's the only thing that matters."

In the warm shadows of the summer nightfall mosquitoes circled round them. And as they talked on, the advancing night flooded the flying-field with a grave, unfathomable gloom.

8

August

TWENTY *milicianos* in *monos* were coming down from the Sierra for lunch. No officers were among them; presumably, as there was no depending on the outposts in the mountain-passes staying on duty at meal-times, the officers had thought it better to assume that task themselves. Fortunately, Manuel reflected, things were much the same with the enemy.

Five of the young men wore women's hats, saucer-shaped, in sentimental shades of green and blue—in the 1935 fashion —above a three days' growth of beard. Wild roses, the summer's last on the Sierra, were stuck into the crowns.

"From now on," Manuel said, "only the comrades detailed for that duty by the Workers' and Peasants' Unions will be authorized to doll up as mannequins. Preferably, elderly men with written references from at least two unions. Get that into your thick heads, my lads!"

"The sun was in our eyes when we attacked, and we couldn't see a darned thing. There was a hat-shop near by—closed, of course, but we helped ourselves. Afterwards, we hung onto the hats."

Their headquarters that day (it was also the base of the armoured train) was a village some six hundred yards distant. The market square was surrounded by a wooden balcony, like the courtyard of a farmhouse; there were some shops painted red and orange—one of them adorned with an enormous mirror—for the benefit of summer visitors, and a sugar-loaf tower in the Escurial style.

"They're not so bad," a young man grinned.

They sat down at the café tables, their rifles slung across their backs, the flowered hats still on their heads. Behind them, on the slopes of the Sierra that stretched away for fifteen miles and more, last patches of the bluebells, which two months earlier had clothed the hillsides, were turning brown and sere, above the yellow cornfields of the plain. The hum of a car driven full speed came nearer and suddenly a brown Ford loomed across the portico and three arms shot up parallel, in the fascist salute. Below the raised arms were the Napoleonic cocked hats and the green, yellow-braided uniform of the Civil Guards. They had not noticed the *milicianos*, who were having their meal on the left of the portico, and evidently imagined they were in a fascist village. The armed peasants in another, adjoining café rose slowly from their seats.

"Friends!" shouted the new-comers, stopping the car with a jerk. "We are on your side!"

The peasants brought their rifles up. The *milicianos* had opened fire already. Though many members of the Civil Guard had come in from the enemy lines, none so far had given the fascist salute. At least thirty shots were fired. Above the rifle-shots Manuel heard the duller explosions of bursting tires. Most of the peasants had aimed at the car. One of the guards, however, was wounded. A gust of wind filled the little square with the fragrance of sun-scorched flowers.

Manuel had the guards disarmed and searched, and dispatched them to the mayor's office under an escort of *milicianos*—the peasants had a particular animosity towards the Civil Guard—and telephoned to Colonel Mangada's headquarters.

"Is it urgent?" an orderly officer enquired. "Any special danger?"

"No."

"Then, no 'summary justice,' please. We'll send an officer for the court martial. They'll be tried in an hour's time."

"Right. There's something else. Their coming like this shows that we're within reach of a fascist locality, I've posted a sentry at the entrance of the village and another man in the road. But that's not enough. . . ."

The court martial took place at the mayor's office. In the

large, whitewashed room, behind the accused men, stood the peasants in their black and grey smocks, and the *milicianos*. In the front row were the wives of peasants who had been killed by the fascists. Each man and woman watched in silence, with the grim aloofness of an Islamic warrior.

Two of the Civil Guards made statements. Yes, they had given the fascist salute; that was because they believed the village to be fascist, they had been passing through it on their way to the republican lines. A story as pitiful in the hearing as in the telling—like all obvious falsehoods. The guards seemed struggling to extricate themselves from their predicament, gasping for breath in their stiff trappings, like men in uniform being slowly strangled. A peasant woman went up to the presiding officer. The fascists had occupied her village, a neighbouring village that the republicans had recaptured. She had seen the guards drive up in their car.

"When they asked me to come for my son, I thought 'twas to bury him. No, that wasn't it—seems they wanted to question me, the filthy scum!" She moved back a pace, as though to have a better view. "That fellow there, he was one of 'em. If it was his son who had been killed, what would he have to say about that, eh? What would *you* say, you brute, you?"

It was the wounded man she was accusing. He tried to defend himself, puffing and blowing like a fish out of its element. Quite likely, Manuel thought, the man was innocent. The woman's son had been shot before she was questioned, and she was seeing his murderers everywhere. Now the accused was speaking of his loyalty to the Republic. Beads of sweat were forming on the shaved cheeks of the man beside him, trickling down on both sides of his waxed moustache. It was as if fear had turned his blood to water and his very life were ebbing away in the stillness of the courtroom.

"You say you came here to join us," the presiding officer observed. "How is it you have no information to give us?"

He turned to the third prisoner, who had said nothing so far. The man looked him straight in the eyes, making it clear that he was addressing the president alone.

"Listen. You are an officer—though you've gone over to these people. I've heard quite enough talk from those two fellows. I have my identity card with me, Number 17 in the Segovia Falangists. You are going to have me shot. Well and good. I suppose you'll have it done today. Only, before I die, I'd like to have the satisfaction of seeing those two filthy bastards shot first. Their cards are Numbers 6 and 11. They make me vomit! Now, as soldier to soldier, will you oblige me by making them shut up, or else, put me outside the courtroom?"

"What airs he's putting on, the baby-killer!" the old woman muttered.

"I'm on your side!" the wounded man screamed to the tribunal.

The presiding judge was looking at the officer who had been speaking. With his very flat nose, thick lips, curly hair and short moustache, he might have stepped out of a Mexican film. For a moment he seemed about to strike the wounded man; but nothing happened. His hands were not a policeman's hands. Had the fascists disseminated agents in the Civil Guard, as they had done in the Montaña Barracks?

"When did you join the Civil Guard?"

The man made no reply; the proceedings had ceased to interest him.

"I'm on your side! On your side, I tell you!" For the first time, there was a note of sincerity in the wounded man's voice. "I'm on your side! . . ."

Manuel did not enter the square until the volley had been fired. The three men had been shot in a neighbouring street; they had fallen forward onto their faces, their heads in sunlight, feet in shadow. A very small kitten was sniffing the warm blood of the flat-nosed man. A boy came up, pushed the cat away, dipped his forefinger in the blood, and began scrawling on the wall. Manuel watched the moving finger with a tightening of his throat. *Death to the Fascists*. Rolling up his sleeves, the young man went to the fountain and began washing his hands.

Manuel stared at the dead body and the cocked hat in the shadow beside it; then he looked up at the writing on the wall, still almost crimson, and the peasant bending over the fountain. "When we are building the new Spain," he thought, "we shall have both alike to contend with. And one will be no easier to handle than the other."

The sun struck the yellow walls with its full force.

9

RAMOS and Manuel were walking on the embankment, and the evening was like any summer evening without sound of guns. Fragrant with the scent of pines and rock-plants, and bathed in a grey-green twilight like the backgrounds of old equestrian portraits, the Sierra rolled its decorative foothills down to the great plain of Madrid. In the tide of darkness flooding the plain, only one thing looked new or strange, the armoured train crouching in its tunnel; and it, too, seemed like the relic of some bygone war that had receded with the failing light.

"I've just been having a hell of a time with our men," said Ramos. "Half an hour ago! Ten of them wanted to go home to dinner; one man actually wanted to trot back to Madrid!"

"It's the hunting season now; they can't tell the difference. And how did it all turn out?"

"Five are staying, seven leaving. If they were communists, every man would stay."

Some desultory gunshots and a distant boom of cannon made the great silence of the mountains deeper still.

"What made you become a communist, Ramos?"

Ramos pondered for a while, then said:

"Growing old, I think. Oh, I know at forty-two one's not so very ancient. But in my anarchist days I was much fonder of mankind in general. Anarchism, for me, meant the 'Syndicate'—but above all, human relations, human contacts. The political shaping of a worker, is, to start with, a matter of outside influences; it only becomes a personal affair later on." He glanced up at the sky; the night promised to be fine. "There's one thing, Manuel, I do wish you'd explain to me— if you can make any sense of it. There, against us, is the Spanish Army. Oh, I grant you it's mostly the officers. Well, in the Philippines, they took it in the neck, didn't they? In Cuba, too. Because they were up against the Americans? Let's say that was it; superior equipment, *plus* first-class organization. In Morocco, too, they took a nasty knock—but Abd-el-Krim wasn't the Americans, not by a long shot! Why should our little gentlemen with the tooth-brush moustaches cut and run before the Krim, and not now? A 'comic-opera army,' that's

what we always called them. Why the hell don't they hop it
now, like they did in Melilla?"

The relations between Manuel and Ramos were changing.
Till now they had been such as an experienced trade-unionist
might have with a thirty-year-old man. For all his frivolous
air, Manuel was fundamentally serious. He applied himself
to analyzing the world on which he had set his hope and drawing a clear line between romantic fancies and verified realities
—but lacking political experience. Now he was beginning to
acquire that experience, and Ramos knew that Manuel's knowledge covered a much wider field than his own. As on that
first night at the Telephone Exchange Manuel had kept on
waving a ruler, so tonight he had a pine-branch in his hand—
with its tuft of pine needles still on it—which he kept on waving like a feather-duster. He could not bear to feel his right
hand empty.

"No, Ramos old chap, there aren't any comic-opera armies
—only comic operas about the army. What they call a comic-
opera army is an army fighting a civil war. Why, in ours—the
Spanish Army—there's an officer for every half a dozen men,
do you think, in the innocence of your heart, that the army
budget is meant to pay for war? Not a bit of it; it's to pay the
officers—who belong to the owning class or serve its interests
—and to buy automatic arms quite inadequate for actual warfare (too much goes in graft) but adequate to police the
country. Our machine-guns, for instance, are of the 1913
type, our planes are over ten years old; worthless in real war,
but good enough to crush a rising. Our armament's not up to
the standard of a colonial war, let alone an international one.
No one ever hears of the Spanish Army except in connection
with defeat or rackets. And repressions. It's not a comic-opera
army, it's a poor imitation of the Reichswehr."

Sounds of distant gunshots drifted up from the valleys.
Some wounded men were carried past on sheets held at the
four corners.

"Every day," Manuel said, gazing towards the hill-tops
behind which were the fascists coming from Segovia, "the
people save Madrid."

"Yes, and after that they go to bed!"

"But start again next day."

"You're doing well, Manuel. I'm glad of it. You did a
damned good job in that attack on the battery."

"Perhaps something has changed in me, and for the rest of

my life. But it doesn't date from that attack on the battery the day before yesterday. No, the change came today when I saw that fellow writing on the wall with the blood of the dead fascist. I hadn't any more sense of responsibility when I was giving orders in the olive grove than when I drove the lorry or, in the old days, when I used to drive my winter sports car."

" 'In the old days!' " Ramos sounded amused. The "old days" were—a month ago!

"The past isn't a matter of mere time. But when I saw that writing on the wall—well, I realized a duty lay on us. Yes, Ramos old chap, for me it was the birth of responsibility."

Within the region under Government control, a shepherd's or a peasant's fire burned, smokeless. The night-mist converged in the flames. The earth disappeared. The flames illuminated the dark hillside. The spirit of peace, hounded down from the mountains and driven to earth, like the armoured train within the tunnel, seemed leaping joyfully to life amid the dancing flames. Another fire lit up, much farther away on the right.

"Who's looking after the wounded?" Manuel asked.

"The head physician of the sanatorium. A very painstaking fellow."

"A Republican leftist?"

"Right-wing socialist, I think. The militia-girls are very helpful, too."

Manuel told him about the young girl who had so unexpectedly turned up behind the lorries.

Running his fingers through his curls, Ramos smiled. "What's your impression of the militia-girls, Manuel?"

"In an offensive, useless; all they're good for is to rattle the men's nerves. In a defensive action, excellent. Their courage works by fits and starts (so does a good many men's for that matter) but they're magnificent at times."

"Do you know, there's one thing pleases me in this war. In every village Franco takes, everybody gets more servile than ever; not only our people—that's inevitable—but even the children, who're sent back to the padre, like the women to their kitchens. That's why all the underdogs, in every walk of life, have joined our side."

Strange is the power of fire. The flames rose and fell in the rhythm of a forge. They seemed a beacon for the bodies of the fallen and they brought quiet to the frenzies of the living with the night.

Ramos felt the smile dying from his lips. He watched the second fire a while. Then put up his field-glasses again. Those were not shepherds' fires, but signals.

Was he, like the *milicianos*, getting to see spies everywhere? But such fire signals were nothing new; moreover—he had been counting—yes, those swine were using Morse, but unluckily the message was in code.

The other fire, too, was flashing a message; the fascists had made their preparations well. How many similar fires were lighting up tonight behind the Republican lines? On all those hillsides, as far as eye could reach, comrades in arms were lying, sleeping. All was silent but for the faint hum of cicadas. Those who had fallen in the day's fighting, stretched full length on asphalt roads or sprawling in the brushwood of the hillside, were entering now on their first night of death. Under the tranquil afterglow brooding above the Sierra, only the soundless speech of treachery floated up from the rising tide of darkness.

10

MANUEL began to realize that to make war successfully you must riddle the living flesh with fragments of steel.

Agonizing screams—they might have been either a man's or a woman's, for at the extremest pitch of pain there is no difference—echoed down the ward of the San Carlos Hospital, and died away.

It was a high room, lit from above by small round airholes almost entirely blocked by luxuriant foliage, through which the rays of the high summer sun were filtering. The greenish light and vast, blank walls in which no window was to be seen except high overhead, the twisted bodies in pyjamas hobbling back and forth on crutches in the uneasy silence of the hospital, and the spectral forms, like masquers in a carnival, shrouded in their bandages—all gave an impression that pain had set up its kingdom here for all eternity, beyond time and the world.

Next to this cavern of sea-green gloom was the ward for

serious cases, whence the screams originated; a room of normal height, with real windows and eight beds. All that Manuel saw as he went in was a line of box-shaped mosquito-nets, and a nurse sitting by the door. In the full light of day the ward looked strangely empty, Manuel thought, comparing this sunny room with the dim torture-chamber haunted with white-swathed ghosts, which he had just left. But the sounds he heard were enough to dispel any illusions as to the nature of the place.

From a bed in the centre of the room came endless moans of pain, pain so intense as to transcend all human speech, the suffering that wrings from the sufferer those cries of wordless agony which are common to both man and beast; that succession of hoarse screams, rising and falling with the breath, which gives the impression that they can only end when the breath itself gives out. And when at last they did stop, they were followed by a grinding of the teeth, a relief for the sufferer, like the shrieks of a woman in childbirth, but appalling to listen to. Manuel felt the screams would start again once the man got back his breath.

"What's the matter with him?" he whispered to the nurse.

"A flying accident. He was brought down with all his bombs. They exploded when they hit the ground. Five machine-gun bullets, twenty-seven splinters."

The muslin of the mosquito-net bulged, as if the wounded man were sitting on the edge of his bed.

"It's his mother," said the nurse. "He's twenty-two."

"Of course you're used to this sort of thing." There was bitterness in his voice.

"We haven't enough nurses. I'm a surgeon, really."

The screams began again, even shriller than before, as though the man were trying to intensify his agony to the point of swooning; then stopped abruptly. Now Manuel could not hear even the grinding of teeth. But he dared not approach the bed.

An almost imperceptible sound made him aware that the wounded man's fingers were plucking at the bed-sheets. Then he heard another sound, so soft at first that he was puzzled what it could be; at last it grew distinct . . . a sound of lips. When the whole body is a quivering mass of pain, what use are words? During this brief respite from agony, his mother was doing the only thing she could—kissing him.

Manuel could hear the kisses distinctly. Given with feverish haste, knowing the pain was on the point of coming back, she hoped to stave it off with her caresses.

A hand seized the mosquito-net and wrung it convulsively; Manuel felt as if the agony he seemed to see poised in empty air were throbbing in his own arm. Suddenly the clenched fist opened and the screams began again.

"How long has . . . has this been going on?" Manuel asked.

"Since the day before yesterday."

Now for the first time he noticed the nurse. She was small, very young. She was not wearing a veil. Her hair was black and glossy. "We nurses . . ." she began. "Well, one gets used to hearing the patients' screams; but when their people start shrieking, it's different. We simply have to send them away or we could never do an operation."

"Is Barca still here?" asked Manuel, between two spasms of cries. To him it seemed that the cries would be part of this room for eternity.

"No, next door."

Manuel was relieved; he was sensitive to the suffering of others, but incapable of expressing the sympathy he felt. Only too aware of his awkwardness in such cases as this, he resented it bitterly.

Barca's ward was just beyond and communicated with the green-lit cavern which he had passed through first. Manuel opened the door, then hesitated a moment, feeling that to close it behind him would have been too much like shutting down the lid of a coffin upon the wounded man. Finally, he left it ajar.

Barca was sitting up in bed. Yes, he had everything he wanted. He had plenty of oranges and illustrated newspapers. And many friends. Only—the trouble was that they refused to give him morphine. If they were afraid that he would become a drug-fiend at his age, they'd better leave him alone. As it was, they'd put a great weight on the end of his leg—it was broken in two different places—and the result was he couldn't sleep. If only they could get him to sleep, it would not be so bad.

"You could manage to sleep with all that—?"

Manuel was thinking of the screams from the adjoining ward, which reached him, only slightly muffled, through the half open door.

"Well, I couldn't bear it in the same room. I couldn't explain why, but that's the way it is. In another room, I can manage. Of course, they ought to put the quiet ones together. Shut the door; we're a quiet lot in this ward, anyhow."

"What was he, that chap?" Manuel felt as though by speaking of the man he were somehow reopening the door he had just closed on him.

"A mechanic. He was in the militia first; then in the air force. Bomber."

"Was he militant?"

"What do you think!"

"Why was he on our side?"

"Which side would you expect him to be on—him, a mechanic? With the fascists?"

"Well, he might have stayed out."

"Stayed out? Hm . . ."

Barca knitted his brows and raised his head, as a fresh twinge shot up his leg. He rested his head on the pillow, and once more the pain he was enduring showed in the worn old face, deepening the hollows of his eyes and giving his features that strange fluidity, that grave, disconsolate air of a sick child, which we so often see when suffering brings forth the nobility latent in a face. Already, at the Sierra, Manuel had been struck by Barca's eyes. The entire expression of his face, with its common-place features, with its coloring darker than his hair, darker even than his clear eyes, came from the heavy eyelids, weary with all the bitterness of a long life resentfully endured. Covered with a network of tiny wrinkles, like a piece of crackle china, they gave his face its air of rustic humour; whenever the eyes closed, he seemed to be smiling.

"How's the armoured train getting on?"

"Pretty well, I think," Manuel replied. "But I don't really know; I'm not on it any longer. I've been appointed company commander in the Fifth Regiment."

"Like it?"

"I've lots to learn."

In spite of the closed door they heard again the sound of groans.

"That young chap was with us because—well, that's how he was."

"What about you, Barca?"

"There are no end of reasons. . . ."

His face twitched, he tried to move, then turned towards Manuel, as though waiting for him to explain himself.

"You weren't really obliged to join up," Manuel remarked.

"I was a trade-unionist, mind you."

"Yes. But not a militant; you weren't really in any immediate danger."

"See here, lad, I'd like to know how you'd have taken it, that phylloxera racket."

Barca had formerly been a tenant wine-grower in Catalonia, as his father and grandfather had been before him. The phylloxera epidemic had given his landlord a pretext to rob him of the fruits of over half a century's toil.

"But you'd made a fresh start, you had enough to live on."

From the tone of his voice Barca realized that Manuel was out to get to the bottom of his motives, not to question them.

"You mean to say: why wasn't I neutral?"

"Yes."

Barca smiled, and to his smile it seemed that pain had lent a curious depth of experience.

"There are some that never can stay neutral. When was I ever neutral, I'd like to know?"

Manuel had a glimpse of men on crutches in the greenish twilight of the next room gliding past the open doorway, one following the other.

"All the same it's no laughing matter," Barca went on. "It's serious business. It's bad enough to be a fascist—but, believe me, it's worse to be dead." He closed his eyes. "And I tell you this: my leg bothers me more than these fascist questions." He tried to raise his hand, but weakness cut short the gesture. "No, that isn't so either. No, come to that, I'd do the same thing all over again. Well, then?"

Another burst of screaming came from the next room. Would *that* man do the same thing over again? That question was no doubt in Barca's mind.

"Mind you, what you ask just now," he went on, "that's no new idea with me. That day in the pinewood, well, I thought it all over. Just as any man thinks things over now and then. Not as you do, perhaps. In my own way. When I don't know something, I can pick it up, often enough, when I set my mind to it. But as far as understanding what I am . . . It's the words that get me down. See what I mean?"

"Quite."

"That's because you've got the brains. Well, the long and the short of it is this: I won't have people looking down on me. Listen, lad." He did not raise his voice, only he spoke

more slowly, in the sort of tone he might have used had he
been sitting with others at a table, and raised an admonishing
finger. "That's how it is. All the rest's beside the point. You're
right about the money; I could have fixed it up with them
maybe. But those people want to be looked up to, and I'm
damned if I'll look up to them. They're not worth it. There's
some I can respect, but not them. I can respect a man of
learning like Professor Garcia, sure! Not them."

Garcia was one of the leading Spanish ethnologists. He
used to spend his summers in San Rafael, and Manuel had
been impressed by the regard in which he was held by the
militants in that part of the Sierra.

"And there's something else," Barca continued. "I'm going
to tell you a thing I once heard. Perhaps there's nothing in it,
perhaps there is. When I was still a peasant—before I went
to Perpignan—the Marquis came once to have a look at us.
I heard him talking to the people who'd come with him—
talking about *us*. This is what he said; I remember it word
for word. 'Did you ever see such people!' says he. 'Why, they
think more about humanity at large than they do about their
own families!' His voice was scornful. I couldn't have argued
the point but it set me thinking. Yes, that time too, I thought
it over. And this is how I see things: when we, our people I
mean, try to do something for humanity we're working for
our own families as well. It's one and the same thing. But
those others, they pick and choose—see what I mean? They
sort folk out." After a moment's silence, he continued. "Señor
Garcia came and saw me here the other day. We've known
each other quite a while. He's a man who's always interested
in things. Now that he's in the Intelligence, as they call it,
he wants to know what's happening in the villages. 'What
about "equality?" ' he asks me. See here, Manuel, there's
something mighty important you don't know, neither of you.
That's because you and he are . . . eh, let's say things always went too easy for you. A man like Garcia, he doesn't
hardly know what it means to be badgered. And let me tell
you, the opposite of that—humiliation, as he calls it—isn't
equality. You know that bellyaching motto the French put
up on all their buildings, *Liberté, Égalité, Fraternité*. Well,
those chaps weren't such fools as you'd think. Seeing that's
just what 'fraternity' means: the opposite of being badgered."

In the main ward, beyond the open door, men could be
seen walking about with their arms set in plaster, swathed in

cocoons of bandages. Sometimes an arm, held by the splints in an unnatural position far from the body or at right angles to it, gave its owner the look of a strolling fiddler in the act of playing on his violin. There was something particularly eerie in the scene; those monstrous, rigid arms paralysed into fixed gestures, and the phantom violinists gliding like waxwork figures trundled to and fro in the green twilight, in a spectral silence murmurous with the low, incessant drone of flies.

11

August 14

AMIDST general enthusiasm, and in the sweltering heat, six planes of the latest type were lined up for the take-off. A column of Moors engaged in the Estremadura offensive was marching from Merida on Medellin. A strong motorized force, it was believed to contain the pick of the fascist army. Staff Headquarters had just sent through a telephone message to Sembrano and Magnin, informing them that Franco in person was commanding the column.

Without leaders, without arms, the militia in the Estremadura tried to put up some resistance. A conglomerate force of field-labourers, potboys, innkeepers, saddlers and the like, some thousands of the most down-trodden people in Spain were sallying forth from Medellin with shot-guns to face the submachine-guns of the African brigade.

Three Douglases and three multi-seaters armed with 1913 machine-guns occupied half the width of the aerodrome. (There were no fighters, all had been sent to the Sierra.) Round them stood Sembrano and his friend Vallado; the Spanish Air Line pilots Magnin, Sibirsky, Darras, Karlitch, Gardet, Jaime, Scali, and some novices. In front of the hangars were old Dugay and all the mechanics—with them, Jaime's dog, Raplati. The whole ground staff had turned out in force for the occasion. Jaime was singing a Flamenco folksong.

The squadron took off and soared south-west in two V-shaped groups.

Though up in the planes the air was cool enough, the world below was blanketed in a heat-haze like the quivering air above a furnace. Here and there a peasant in a wide-brimmed straw hat appeared among the corn. From the Toledo mountains to the hills of Estremadura, up to the limit of the battle area, the harvest-coloured earth drowsed in its afternoon siesta, wrapped in peace from one horizon to the other. Dust-clouds welling up across the light made spurs and foothills stand out flat against the plain. Badajoz, Merida (taken by the fascists on the 8th) and Medellin were still almost invisible—tiny specks upon the vastness of the shimmering fields.

Gradually the countryside became more rugged, and at last Badajoz, with its Alcazar and deserted bull-rings, came into view, gaunt as the land of treeless crags around it, with its roofs of weathered tiles grey in the sunlight—like Berber skeletons stretched on an African desert. The pilots studied their maps, bombers glanced down their bomb-sights, machine-gunners looked at their foresights, tiny whirligigs that fluttered in the rushing air outside the cockpit. Now below them lay the time-scarred Spanish city with its dusky women at the windows, olives and aniseed put out to cool in buckets of well-water, children strumming the piano with one finger and lean cats listening for each note to trickle out and die upon the heat-mist. Everything looked so parched and desiccated that one could imagine tiles and stones, houses and streets crumbling into dust at the first bomb, in a brittle din of bones and rubble. Above the central square Karlitch and Jaime waved their handkerchiefs in greeting, and the Spanish bombers let fall scarves patterned in the Republican colours. Next came a fascist town; the observers identified the ancient theatre and ruins of Merida—though it might as well have been Badajoz, or any other country town in Estremadura. At last they reached Medellin.

Along which road was the column advancing? The treeless roads were yellow under the sun, only a little paler than the countryside, and all were empty as far as the eye could reach.

The squadron flew over the open square of Medellin and began following the road that led towards the enemy lines but also towards the sun. Against the blinding glare they saw the road as little more than a ribbon of incandescent light. The two Douglases behind Sembrano's plane began to slow down, then moved behind in line; the enemy column was approaching.

Darras, who had just handed back the controls to the first pilot, leaned sideways, his whole body bent across the cockpit in a poise of tense expectancy. During the World War his quarry had been merely this or that German plane. But now his quarry was what he had been fighting for so many active years—in his mayoralty, in workers' organizations laboriously built up, defeated, resurrected—the enemy he fought today was fascism. After Russia, Italy, Germany and China, now it was Spain's turn. The hope which Darras was fostering in the world had hardly been given a chance. Yet here in Spain was fascism once more—almost under his wings. The only indication of its presence for the moment was the movement of his squadron moving into battle formation.

To get into position again, the machine in which he was (Magnin's, the leader of the Internationals) began to turn, and now Darras could see the straight road in front studded with little red dots at regular intervals. Then, as the plane took the straight again, the sun came back and all he saw was an empty white road.

The road swerved round, the sun slipped to one side, and the red dots reappeared. They were too small to be cars, yet moving too mechanically to be men. It looked as if the roadway itself was in motion. Suddenly Darras understood. It was as if he had just acquired a gift of second sight; seeing things in his mind, not through his eyes. The road was a solid mass of lorries covered with drab tarpaulins, yellow with dust, and the red dots were the hoods painted in red oxide; there had been no attempt at camouflage. Spanned by the silence of the far horizons round the three cities, the land lay bathed in tranquil light, threaded with roads that forked out like the imprint of some huge bird's claws. And among all those quiet ways, one road there was that throbbed and thundered—the road of fascism.

On both sides of the roadway bombs were exploding; twenty-pounders that spurted spear-heads of red flame and veiled the fields in smoke. There was nothing to show that the fascist column had put on speed, except that the road was throbbing still more violently. Lorries and planes were advancing on each other. Against the sunlight Darras could not discern the falling bombs; he could only see them as they burst —in bunches now, but still along the fields. His wounded foot was beginning to hurt again. One of the Douglases, he knew, was not equipped with bomb-dropping apparatus; the latrine vent had been enlarged to take its place. Suddenly one section of the road stopped vibrating. The column had halted. Un-

noticed by Darras, a bomb had hit one of the lorries, overturn-
ing it across the road.

Like the head of a cut worm crawling off by itself, about a
third of the column, its vanguard, pressed steadily on towards
Medellin, while the rain of bombs continued to sweep the
road. Darras' plane came just above the moving segment. But
a second pilot cannot see the ground below.

Meanwhile Scali, the bomber on the second International
machine, had been watching the bombs falling nearer and
nearer the road. He had a thorough training in the Italian
Army behind him, and, till he left his country, had put in a
yearly reserves course. Three raids on the Sierra had restored
his skill. During the fifteen seconds while Sibirsky, his pilot,
had been directly above the road, he had been watching the
explosions draw nearer and nearer the lorries. It was too late
to aim at the leading section. The lorries behind were trying to
squeeze round on either side of a vehicle lying across the road,
which had, it seemed, been smashed by a bomb. Seen from
the plane, the lorries seemed stuck to the road like flies on a
strip of flypaper.

From his vantage-point above, Scali saw them in imagination, buzzing up into the air, or darting across the fields. But
most likely the road was flanked by embankments. The line,
so compact only a few minutes ago, was trying to spread out
round the obstacle, like a river flowing round a rock. Scali
could distinctly make out the white tips of the Moors' turbans.
In a flash of memory he pictured the poor devils at Medellin
with their shot-guns and, just as the swarm of lorries glided
across his bomb-sights, he loosed off his two racks of light
bombs. Then, leaning above the opening in the floor, he waited
for the bombs to strike; nine fateful seconds intervened between those men and himself. Two, three . . . impossible,
looking through the trap, to see back far enough. He ran back
and looked through the machine-gun slit in the tail. Down
below people were running, their arms above their heads,
scuttling over the embankment. Five, six . . . A battery of
machine-guns below was opening fire on the planes. Seven,
eight . . . "See how they run!" Nine . . . Under twenty
simultaneous bursts of scarlet flame they all stopped running.
The plane sailed on, as if all that were none of its concern.

The squadron circled, to launch another attack. Magnin's
machine came over the road just after Scali's bombs had burst,
and Darras had a glimpse of a welter of lorries sprawling bot-

tom upmost under the thinning smoke-clouds. Only at the actual moment when the bombs flared red did death seem to play any part in the affair. Darras saw only little specks of khaki dotted with the white turbans flying for their lives, like panicked ants carrying away their eggs.

Sembrano had the clearest view of what was happening, for the leader of the Douglases came back behind the Internationals, closing the circle. Sembrano realized, far better than Scali, the plight of the Estremadura militia—that they were helpless, and only the air-force could save them. He circled the road again; if any light bombs were left, they might knock out some more lorries. Motor transport, as he knew, was the fascists' most powerful weapon. But now the important thing was to catch up the vanguard of the column on its way to Medellin, before the enemy aviation came to its rescue.

More lorries were slithering down into the fields, their wheels in the air. Now they were no longer head-on to the sun; long shadows trailed behind them, cast by the declining rays; like dead fish rising to the surface of a dynamited pool they became visible only when derelict. The pilots had had time to adjust their course exactly above the road, and shadows of the disabled lorries began to pile up in front of the column and behind it, like barricades.

"It'll take Franco more than five minutes to straighten that out," thought Sembrano, thrusting forward his lower lip. Then, falling in line, he flew towards Medellin.

Now as ever pacifist at heart, Sembrano was, however, a far more competent bomber than any Spanish pilot; only, to appease his conscience, whenever he flew solo he came down very low to drop his bombs. Somehow the sense of danger, the risks he was going out of his way to run, solved, for him, the ethical problem. Like Marcelino, like most diffident men, he was brave by nature. And now he was saying to himself: "Either the lorries are inside the town, in which case we've got to bomb them all to hell, or else they're outside it and, if we're to save the militia from being butchered, well, in that case also we must bomb them all to hell." So now he set his course towards Medellin at a hundred and seventy miles an hour.

The lorries which had formed the head of the column were massed in the shadows of the city square. As the populace was hostile they had not dared to scatter. Sembrano came down as low as he could, followed by the five other machines.

The afternoon sun had lined the streets with shadows, yet from a thousand feet up they could just distinguish the various colours of the houses—salmon pink, pale blue, pistachio green —and the outlines of the lorries.

Some of the vehicles were hidden away in by-streets. Instead of following him, a Douglas was heading towards Sembrano; the pilot, he supposed, had fallen out of formation.

The planes began to circle at a tangent to the square. His first air-raid came back to Sembrano's mind, the one he had taken part in with Vargas, now director of field operations, and he remembered how the workers at Pennaroya, hemmed in by the fascists, had hung at windows and in courtyards their most colourful possessions—curtains and counter-panes—to greet the Republican airmen.

The falling bombs flickered across a belt of sunlight, vanished, and sped on with the free movement of torpedoes. The square began to fill with smoke, and bursts of sudden orange-coloured flame exploded everywhere like mines. Upon the highest flame, in a swirl of dense brown smoke, a plume of white shot up; then, suddenly, above it, a tiny black lorry turned a fantastic somersault and fell back into the murk below. As he waited for the smoke-cloud to clear off, Sembrano glanced ahead and saw once again the Douglas that had fallen out of line, and two more with it. Now only two Douglases, including his own machine, were taking part in the attack. How account for the three facing him? He waggled his plane to indicate the squadron was to take up its fighting formation.

So preoccupied had he been with what was going on below that he had failed to notice anything else. But now he knew; those unaccountable machines were not Douglases, but Junkers.

That was the moment Scali had come to the conclusion that military aviation was a disgusting business. Indeed, from the moment he had seen the Moors running to cover he had been wanting to quit. But this did not prevent him now from keeping his eyes fixed on the bomb-sights, like a cat at a mouse-hole, waiting for the square to flash across them (he had still two hundred-pounders left). Machine-guns were firing up at him from below, but he paid no attention; he felt as if he were at once a judge and a murderer—and of the two rôles the former struck him as by far the fouler. Those six Junkers, three facing him (the ones Sembrano had seen) and three below, swept his mind clear of introspection.

Yet now the sole resource was flight; with its one wretched machine-gun placed beside the pilot, it was folly for a Douglas to engage a German war plane with its three emplacements and its modern machine-guns. Sembrano had always looked on speed as the best means of defence for bombing machines. So now the Douglases swerved away at full throttle, while the large International machines plunged down on the three Junkers below them. They were three against six Junkers in all; but luckily the latter had no fighter escort. Now the Douglases had attained their object, there was no question of fighting; only of getting away. Magnin decided to attack the lower group; in a moment they would show up against the sky; whereas Magnin's machines, thanks to their camouflage, would be almost invisible against the fields at this hour of the evening. The other three Junkers hardly had time to come into line for the battle. So he, too, flicked his throttle wide open.

Hermetically closed like submarines, their "dust-bins" dangling like pendulums between the spats on their under-carriage wheels, the Junkers approached from below. One of them was still banking, and the Internationals could clearly see its aerial, and the form of the rear gunner showing above the cockpit. Gardet stood waiting in the forward turret, a small rifle slung across his back. Too far to make himself heard by the crew, he was pointing towards the enemy planes, gesturing frantically with his left arm. Standing beside Darras, Magnin watched the Junkers looming larger and larger as if air were being pumped into them. Suddenly all on board realized that a plane can crash. Gardet spun around his turret and the planes swept past each other with a fantastically accelerated rattle, all their machine-guns drumming in the cockpits. Few shots—only those fired by the under-turret machine-guns— had touched the Internationals. The Junkers fell away behind; one of them began to come down, without, however, crashing. All of a sudden a dozen shots zipped through the cockpit of Magnin's machine. The distance separating them increased. Under fire from the rear guns of the Internationals the five Junkers turned back to their lines, while the sixth went floundering down across the fields.

Back at the landing-ground, Magnin telephoned his report; then asked for Gardet.

"He's in the Junker; the one that landed here under the impression that Madrid had fallen!" Camuccini said.

"All the more reason for me to see him."

To his surprise, Magnin found a man from the Secret Service Bureau awaiting him.

"Comrade Magnin," the man said after casting a shrewd exploring glance round the white-painted office, "the chief of police has asked me to inform you that three of your German volunteers"—he took a piece of paper from his pocket—"Krefeld, Wurtz and er . . . Schrei . . . Schreiner, that's it, Schreiner, are Hitler's spies."

Magnin's first reaction was to answer, "You're mistaken." Then he remembered that in such cases one's first idea is always that. As a matter of fact, Karlitch had warned him that Krefeld was always taking photographs (but would a spy take photographs?), and Magnin had been surprised one day to hear him mention the name of an official in the French Intelligence Department.

"Right. Krefeld . . . you're sure, eh? Well, that's your business, of course. Still I must say I'm very much surprised about Schreiner. Wurtz and Schreiner are communists—have been communists for quite a while, I believe. And their Party vouches for them."

"Parties are like people, Comrade Magnin, they trust their friends. *We* trust our information."

"What does your Chief want of me?"

"He wants you to see that those three men don't set foot again on an aerodrome."

"And what then?"

"He'll see to that himself."

Tugging at his moustache, Magnin thought it over. "This business about Schreiner—it's really appalling. And . . . well, the long and the short of it is, I don't believe he is guilty. Can't you have further enquiries made?"

"Oh, there's no violent hurry. The Chief will ring you up presently; but only to confirm my information."

Gardet arrived. His little rifle had been stowed away with his equipment; his tousled hair fell over his forehead; there was a twinkle in his eye.

The police-officer left the room. Gardet's unruly mane and pointed cheek-bones brought to mind the head of a tiny kitten; but when he smiled the little teeth, set well apart, gave the triangular face a look of keen alertness.

"What the hell have you been up to in that machine?" Magnin asked. "Sampling the gunners' seats?"

"I know a thing or two," Gardet grinned. "I'd been round one of 'em before, of course, but it struck me there was something I didn't quite understand. Well, I got it straight this time, and it's not so hot! Now they've fired at us I know just how things are with them; those buses are good as blind in front. That's why they couldn't hit us once with the first round, but got us fair and square when we were on their tails."

"I suspected as much," Magnin said. He had studied their structure in the technical magazines. The third engine on the Junker takes the place of the forward turret in two-engined machines, and Magnin had suspected that a submachine-gunner posted low down in the cockpit, firing between the wheels, and another at the tail, would be inadequate to defend the forepart of a plane against attack. That was why he had launched a frontal attack, single-handed, on the two enemy planes.

"Say, Magnin, do you think they gave it everything when they came after us?"

"I'm sure of it."

"How those Fritzes must have been laughing up their sleeves these last two years! A good twenty m.p.h. less than we make with our old buses! So that's all there is to it—Goering's famous air-force!" He paused, then added ruefully: "Still, there's no two ways about it, their machine-guns can knock spots off ours, the home-made Spanish brand. Didn't jam once, did they? I was listening. . . . Ah, if only the Russians or those lousy fellow-countrymen of ours would get a move on with some new ones . . . !"

Magnin went off to General Headquarters, perplexed. Yes, he must visit the hospital first.

His features drawn with pain, the British bomber was arguing listlessly with his neighbour, a Spanish anarchist. His bed was strewn with copies of *L'Humanité* and Courteline's stories. House, however, had a room to himself on the floor above—a questionable privilege.

When Magnin opened the door the Englishman saluted him smilingly with a clenched fist—but his eyes were unsmiling. The clenched fist seemed as childishly pathetic as his smile.

"How are you getting on?" Magnin asked.

"How can I tell? Nobody here knows English."

The "Captain's" answer was given less to his friend's question than to his obsession. What he couldn't tell was whether or not there would have to be an amputation.

With his silky blonde moustache under the pointed nose, House looked like a schoolboy tucked up in his dormitory bed. That clenched fist had been irrelevant, a heedless gesture. Surely far truer to the youngster's personality were the hands that now lay quietly on the sheets, or that face which, in some far-away cottage, a Mrs. House was picturing most likely just as it looked now, at rest on a white pillow. But there was another truth, of which the good lady had certainly no idea; the two legs with five bullets in them under the carefully drawn sheets. And, the lad's not twenty-five yet! Magnin mused. What can I say? Words are so futile, when a boy's got to have his legs off.

"Well . . . er . . . is that so?" Magnin said, tugging at his moustache. "Wait a bit, I've got some oranges for you downstairs."

He went out. To Magnin infirmity seemed more horrible than death; he hated lies, and had not known what to say. Well, the great thing now was to *know*. He went upstairs to see the medical officer.

"No," the doctor told him. "That English pilot was lucky, no bones were touched. There isn't the least necessity for an amputation."

As Magnin dashed down the stairs a silvery chime of spoons came tinkling up them, and seemed to echo in his heart.

"No bones were touched," he exclaimed as he entered the room; his story about the oranges had gone clean out of his head.

House raised his fist again. As no one in the hospital knew English, he had got into the way of making the gesture automatically; he had no other way of conveying friendliness or gratitude.

"There's not the slightest question of—er—an amputation." Magnin stumbled over the words, embarrassed at having to repeat in English what the doctor had just said in Spanish.

Torn between hope and apprehension of a charitable lie, House stared down at the sheets. Then, mastering his breath again, he asked point blank:

"When'll I be able to walk?"

"I'll go and ask the doctor right away."

As Magnin once again dashed up the white-enamelled staircase, he was thinking: That doctor'll take me for an awful idiot!

"Excuse me," he said. "The young Englishman wants to know when he'll be able to walk again. . . . I'd hate to lie to him."

"In a couple of months."

Magnin returned to the bedroom. No sooner had he uttered the words "two months" than he grew conscious of a resistless tide of joy surging up from the bed, the joy of a prisoner set free, mysterious in its immobility. House could not move a limb; his arms lay motionless on the sheets, his head upon the pillow. Only his fingers twitched and his rather prominent. Adam's apple rose and fell convulsively—outward signs of a vast delight, oddly identical with those of terror.

In the suburbs of Madrid fewer *milicianos* were visible brandishing rifles in fewer cars, and the cars flaunted fewer placards. Near the Toledo gate young men were practising foot-drill. Magnin thought of France. Until this war the Junkers had constituted the bulk of Germany's air force. They were commercial machines converted into war planes, and such had been the general belief in German efficiency that they had been regarded as a formidable weapon of offence. But their armament though good, was inadequate, and ordinary American commercial planes such as the Douglases could outdistance them easily. True, they were more than a match for the ramshackle buses Magnin had bought on various European markets; but they could not have held their own against the modern types of French machines, nor against the Russian air force. But now all that would be changed; the gory army manoeuvres of the Western world had tragically opened here. For two years Europe had quailed before the constant menace of a war which Hitler was not equipped to wage.

12

WHEN Magnin entered the Ministry he found Vargas, the Officer Commanding Field Operations, listening to Garcia, who was reading a report.

"Evening, Magnin!"

Vargas rose, but remained where he was at the edge of the sofa. His *mono,* slipped off from the waist up because of the heat, but still clinging to his legs—was it mere laziness or to be readier for an emergency?—hampered his movements. (Magnin was amused to find himself recalling the skinned rabbits sold in France with their pelts clinging to their legs.) Vargas sat down again, stretching his long legs cased in the close-fitting trousers, a glow of friendliness on his thin, bony face —the face of a beardless Don Quixote. He was one of the officers with whom Magnin had collaborated in reorganizing the Spanish air lines, before the rebellion; it was with his aid and Sembrano's that Magnin had blown up the line between Seville and Cordova. After introducing Garcia and Magnin to each other, he called for drinks and cigarettes.

"Good work!" Garcia said to Magnin. "You've pulled off our first victory in the war."

"Really? I'm glad to hear you say so. I'll pass on your congratulations. Sembrano was our Squadron Leader."

The two men exchanged looks of cordial scrutiny; this was Magnin's first direct contact with a chief of the Spanish Intelligence Service. Garcia, of course, had heard Magnin's name mentioned every day.

Garcia was far from being as Magnin had pictured him. His corpulence and big tip-tilted nose came as a surprise, as did his general likeness to some great landowner of Normandy or England. Nor had Magnin expected this eminent intellectual to have that genial, humorous air, any more than those pointed ears; nor that the anthropologist who had spent arduous years in Peru and the Philippines should seem so physically robust. And somehow he had always pictured Garcia as wearing glasses.

"It wasn't a big show, of course," Magnin continued, "more like a frontier raid. Six machines. Still we managed to do in some of their lorries on the road."

"It wasn't the bombs you dropped on the road that did them the most damage, but the ones in Medellin itself. Several heavies landed plumb in the market square. Don't forget it's the first taste the Moors have had of what a serious air-attack can mean. The column had gone back to its base. Our first victory. . . . Unfortunately, Badajoz has fallen. Which means that Franco's army has joined up with Mola's."

Magnin looked up at him questioningly. Garcia's attitude, too, was a surprise to him. Where he had expected reticence was expansiveness, almost exuberance.

"And Badajoz adjoins the Portuguese frontier," Garcia continued.

"On the sixth," Vargas said, "the *Montesarmiento* brought fourteen German machines and a hundred and fifty trained men to Lisbon. On the eighth, eighteen bombing planes left Italy. The day before yesterday twenty arrived at Seville."

"Savoias?"

"That I can't say. And twenty more Italian machines are on their way."

"Including the eighteen you mentioned?"

"No. Within a fortnight we'll have a hundred up-to-date machines against us."

The Junkers might be inefficient, but the Savoias were in another class. For bombing purposes they were far superior to any aircraft at the Republicans' disposal.

Through an open window the Republican anthem floated in, diffused from twenty radios, and with it a smell of sun-burnt leaves.

"I'll go on reading," Garcia said, picking up his report again. "This morning's news from Badajoz," he added, for Magnin's benefit.

5 A.M. The Moors have just entered Fort San Cristobal, which has been practically wiped out by the bombardment.

7 A.M. The enemy artillery, posted in Fort San Cristobal, is bombarding the town continuously. The militia are holding out. The dispensary at the Provincial Hospital has been demolished by an air-attack.

9 A.M. The ramparts on the east are wrecked. On the south the barracks are in flames. We have only two machine-guns left. The guns in San Cristobal are still firing. The militia are still holding out.

11 A.M. Enemy tanks are arriving.

He let fall a page of typescript and picked up another.
"The second report is short," he said bitterly.

12 noon. The tanks have reached the Cathedral, followed by the infantry. We have repulsed it.

"How ever did they manage that?" he mused aloud. "With only four machine-guns all told at Badajoz!"

4 P.M. The enemy troops are entering the town.
4:30. House-to-house fighting in progress.

"At four?" Magnin sounded surprised. "But we were told at five that we were still holding Badajoz!"

"The news has just come in."

A picture rose before Magnin's eyes of the tranquil city of the crags aglow in the long rays of the evening sun. He had served in the artillery at the beginning of the World War. Then he had always been conscious of his ignorance of the battle in progress, for the good reason that he saw nothing of it. But he couldn't stop thinking of the calm and friendly town, now drenched in blood. Well, he had seen it from too high up— like God! *The tanks have reached the Cathedral* . . . the old Cathedral with long shadows flowing from it, the narrow streets, the arenas. . . .

"When did the fighting end?" he asked.

"An hour before you passed over it," Vargas replied. "Except for the hand-to-hand fighting in the houses."

"Here's the latest news," Garcia said. "Timed about 8 o'clock. Perhaps earlier. Dispatched from our lines—if so be that we have any left!"

"The fascist prisoners have been released, safe and sound. All *milicianos* and doubtful characters are being court-martialled and shot. Twelve hundred have been dealt with so far. The charge is: 'armed resistance.' Two *milicianos* shot in the Cathedral, on the high-altar steps. The Moors are wearing scapulars and emblems of the Sacred Heart. Firing squads have been busy all afternoon. We can still hear the volleys."

Magnin recalled the handkerchiefs that Karlitch and Jaime had waved in friendly greeting to the men who were now being shot.

The night life of Madrid, the Republican hymn blaring from all the radios, songs of all kinds, cries of *Salud,* shrill when near and low-pitched in the distance, mingled like the notes of a piano—sounds of hope and exaltation filled the night.

"It's good for them to sing." Vargas nodded approvingly; then, in a lower voice, "This is going to be a long war." After a pause, he continued. "Yes, the man in the street's an optimist. So are the political leaders. Major Garcia and I should be temperamentally inclined that way. . . ." He raised his eyebrows, worried. The little movement gave him an air of curious naïveté; for a moment he looked quite boyish. And it struck Magnin that he had never thought of Don Quixote as having been young. "Just think what happened today, Magnin. You held up that column with six machines—in what you likened to a frontier skirmish. The column turned its machine-guns on the militia and Badajoz has fallen. And, mark you, they were anything but cowards, our militia. Yes, this war's going to be a war of mechanized equipment—and we're running it as if noble emotions were all that mattered. . . ."

"Still, you can't deny it was the people's army that held the Sierra."

Garcia looked attentively at Magnin. Like Vargas he was convinced that this would be a technicians' war, and did not believe that foremen become experts merely by the grace of God. And the destinies of the Popular Front, he suspected, lay to a great extent with its experts. Everything about Magnin struck him as significant: his lack of ease in company, his seeming absent-mindedness, his "jumpy" mannerisms, his look of a factory superintendent (as a matter of fact he had taken an Engineering Degree at the *École Centrale*), and, above all, the energy, disciplined but unmistakable, that shone out, puzzled, behind his round eye-glasses. Perhaps it was his moustache that gave Magnin something of the look of an old-school Parisian cabinet-maker; artist and artisan at once. But there was also something in his drooping lips—they brought to mind a seal's—which betrayed his age; as, in his eyes (when he removed his glasses), as in his smile and gestures, one glimpsed subtle evidences of the intellectual. Magnin, he knew, had been director of one of the leading French air-lines, but Garcia, who made a point of stripping men of the glamour of their functions, was trying to see down into the nature of the man himself.

"The people are magnificent," Vargas exclaimed. "Absolutely magnificent, Magnin—but helpless!"

"Let's get things straight," Garcia said, aiming his pipe-stem at Magnin. "I was in the Sierra. Well, it took the fascists by surprise. The positions were particularly suited for guerrilla warfare, of course, The people have a striking power that can be terrific—only it doesn't last.

"My dear Monsieur Magnin," he continued, "we're aided but no less handicapped by two or three rather pernicious

superstitions. The French superstition, to begin with. The
People—with a capital P—brought off the French Revolution,
I grant you that. But the fact that a hundred pikes can knock
out some inefficient muskets doesn't prove that a hundred shot-
guns can beat the modern war plane. Then the Russian Revolution—it's made confusion more confounded! Politically
speaking, it's the first revolution of the twentieth century; but
don't forget that, militarily speaking, it was the last of the
nineteenth. The Czarists had neither tanks nor planes; the
revolutionaries used barricades. What was the idea behind
these barricades? To resist the imperial cavalry, for the people
never had horses. Today Spain is littered with barricades—to
resist Franco's war planes!

"No sooner had his cabinet fallen than that fine fellow, our
President, dashed off to the Sierra, gun in hand. Perhaps, Monsieur Magnin, you don't know Spain quite well enough. Gil,
the one competent aircraft manufacturer we had, has been
killed at the front, fighting in the ranks."

"But surely . . . the revolution . . ."

"We are not the revolution. Ask Vargas there what he thinks
about it! We are the people, I grant, but not the revolution—
though we used to talk of nothing else. By revolution I mean
the change of system that follows a revolt; a change that's
organized by political and expert groups formed during the
conflict and capable of promptly replacing the régime that
they've destroyed."

"And, above all, Magnin," Vargas said, hitching up his
mono, "don't forget it isn't we who started the present conflict. We haven't any organization. Franco hasn't any either,
except the army *cadres,* but he has with him the two nations
you know of. No militia will ever defeat a modern army.
Wrangel was beaten by the Red Army, not by enthusiastic
partisans."

"From now on no social change, still less a revolution, can
make good without war; and no war without organization on
the technical side." Garcia emphasized each point with a jab
of his pipe-stem.

Vargas agreed, nodding in rhythm with the movement of
Garcia's pipe.

"Organization, discipline—I don't see men giving their lives
for that!" Magnin exclaimed.

"In times like the present," Garcia said, "I'm less interested
in the reasons men may have for giving up their lives than in

the means they have for killing off their enemies. And make no mistake: when I speak of 'discipline' I don't mean that cast-iron authoritarianism we hear too much of nowadays. Anything but that. What I mean is an organization of the factors which give an army in the field its maximum efficiency." (Garcia's taste for definition was notorious.) "It's just a method like any other. Needless to say, I don't care a damn about the military salute and so forth."

"You hear those sounds coming in through the window? Well, to me they're something real, concrete. Something which —you know it as well as I do—we're far from using to the best advantage. You say, we're not the revolution. Well, I say: let's be it! And don't you think it likely the democratic nations may come to your aid?"

"Don't be too sure about that, Magnin," Vargas said.

Garcia pointed his pipe-stem, like a revolver, at each man in turn.

"I've seen the democracies come in against pretty well everything—except fascism. Apart from Mexico, the only country which might help us is Russia. And Russia's too far away. . . . As to those sounds coming in through the window, Monsieur Magnin—I might define them as an Apocalypse of fraternity. They work on your emotions, I can well understand it. They stand for one of the most moving things on earth, and one of the rarest. But all of that's got to be transformed—or perish!"

"Well, you may be right. Only, mind you, for my part I don't countenance, and I won't countenance, any conflict between all that revolutionary discipline stands for and those who still are blind to its necessity. Even the wildest dreams of absolute liberty, of power given to the worthiest and the rest of it —all these things, as I see them, are part of what I'm here to implement. I want each individual man to have a life that isn't classified in terms of what he can exact from others. See what I mean?"

"I'm afraid you don't quite grasp the actual situation, my dear Monsieur Magnin. We have to deal with two separate, but simultaneous *coups d'état*. The first is nothing more nor less than our old friend, the *pronunciamento* of the 'families'! Burgos, Valladolid, Pamplona, and the Sierra. On the first day the fascists had all the garrisons in Spain with them. Now, they've only a third of them. In a word, that famous *pronunciamento* is beaten, knocked out by the Apocalypse.

"But the fascist states, who are no fools, allowed for that

possibility in their plans. Hence, what I may call the problem
of the South. And that, mind you, is of a quite different order.
To get things clear, let's drop that word: fascism. Franco
doesn't give a damn for fascism; he's a playboy dictator on
South American lines. Secondly, Mussolini doesn't personally
give a damn if fascism is set up in Spain or not. Moral problems are one thing, foreign policy's another. What Mussolini
wants here is a government which he can control. That's why
he is using Morocco as the base of his campaign. An up-to-
date army with modern armaments has been sent out from
that base. As they can't depend on the Spanish troops—they've
seen what's happened to Madrid and Barcelona—they're rely-
ing on a small, but highly efficient army composed of the Foreign Legion, the Moors and . . ."

"But Garcia," Vargas broke in, "there are only twelve thousand Moors in Morocco."

"Let me set you right, Vargas. Forty thousand. No one over
here has devoted the least study to the relations between the
spiritual chiefs of Islam and Mussolini. But wait a bit! France
and England will have some nasty surprises. If the Moors can't
see it through, there'll be Italians sent over here, my good
friend."

"What do you think Italy's after?" Magnin asked.

"Impossible to be sure. But I suspect their idea is to get a
hold on Gibraltar; in other words, to be able to convert, automatically, an Anglo-Italian war into a European war, by forcing England to operate across the territory of a European ally.
While the British were more or less disarmed Mussolini would
have preferred to tackle them single-handed; now that they're
rearming, Italian policy has to make a fresh start. . . . But
all that's mere guess-work—café gossip. We are up against one
solid fact: that Franco's army, backed by the two fascist
states, firmly supported by Portugal, and equipped with motor
transport, submachine-guns, Italo-German aircraft and organization, is going to have a shot at taking Madrid. To protect
his rear Franco will have to practise large-scale terrorization;
he's begun it at Badajoz. The question is: how are we going
to tackle this new phase of the war, which has nothing whatever to do with what's been happening in the Sierra?" Garcia
rose from his chair and moved towards Magnin; his peaked
ears showed sharply against the glow of an electric lamp standing on the desk.

"For me, Monsieur Magnin, the whole problem is just this:

a popular movement, or a revolution, or even a rebellion, can hold on to its victory only by methods directly opposed to those which gave it victory. Sometimes opposed even to the sentiments from which it started out. Just think it over—in the light of your own experience. For I doubt if you expect to keep your aviation corps up to the mark on a basis of mere fraternity.

"The apocalyptic mood clamours for everything right away. Tenacity of purpose wins through bit by bit; slowly, laboriously. That apocalyptic fervour is ingrained in every one of us; and there's the danger. For that fervour spells certain defeat, after a relatively short period, and for a very simple reason: it's in the very nature of an apocalypse to have no future. . . . Even when it professes to have one."

Putting his pipe back in his pocket, he added sadly: "Our humble task, Monsieur Magnin, is to *organize* the apocalypse."

13

THE staff headquarters at Toledo into which Garcia was just turning, his long nose and pipe well to the fore as usual, had been a modest bootshop. On the right of the door was posted a large photograph, cut from an illustrated magazine, showing the hostages who had been interned by the fascists in the Alcazar and were to be spared when the Republican army stormed the subterranean vaults. Under each picture was a name. As if the storming party, in the heat of battle, were likely to remember all—or any—of those faces! After the garish sunlight of the street with its bare torsos and Mexican sombreros, Garcia had an impression that the room was in complete darkness.

"That battery's firing at us!" a voice was shouting.

"What battery, Negus?"

"Our own!"

"I rang them up and told them they were firing short. What d'you think the officer replied? 'I've had enough of firing on my pals. So we're blasting you for a change.'"

"It's an outrage against the highest principles of civilization." A shrill, affected voice, with a strong French accent.

"So another traitor's shown his hand!" A lower voice, languid but charged with bitterness. The Captain, whose face Garcia was just beginning to make out in the faint light, had spoken. To a lieutenant he added: "Take twenty men and a machine-gun and rout them out." And to a secretary: "Inform the Commanding Officer about it."

"As to that man at the battery, . . ." the Negus said, "I've sent three fellows to settle him."

"I've cashiered him once, damn it! If the F.A.I. hadn't gone and reinstated him . . ."

Garcia could not hear the end of the sentence. Yet, as compared with the din outside, it was fairly quiet in the room. Sporadic explosions, like thunder underfoot, punctuated the "Ride of the Valkyries" that was blaring from the radio in the Square. Now that Garcia's eyes were used to the dimness, he recognized Captain Hernandez. Hernandez resembled the

Spanish Kings of the well-known royal portraits, all of which resemble Charles the Fifth as a young man. The gilt stars on his *mono* glimmered palely in the gloom. Behind him, on the wall, a series of oval patches disposed in formal patterns was slowly growing visible, framing his body as a fringe of rays surrounds the bodies of certain Spanish saints—the cobblers' lasts and soles, which had been left behind when the little shop was taken over. Beside the Captain was Sils, a leading anarchist from Barcelona.

At last Hernandez' eyes fell on Garcia, his pipe stuck in the corner of a smile.

"Major Garcia, isn't it? Intelligence has just phoned me." He shook hands with Garcia and led him out into the street.

"What can I do for you, Major?"

"I should like to spend a few hours in your company, having a look round . . ."

"Just now I'm off to Santa Cruz. We're going to try using dynamite against the Government Military Buildings."

"Right. Let's go there."

The Negus, behind them, was appraising Garcia with a friendly eye; for once Madrid had sent them someone who seemed all right. Funny ears, a husky fellow, with not too much of the bourgeois about him (Garcia was wearing a leather windbreaker). Beside the Negus another man, in an alpaca coat, riding-breeches and boots, was waving his arms excitedly; a man who seemed all bones and sinews, with grey hair curling across his head. It was Captain Mercery who had been sent by Magnin to the War Ministry and was now posted to Toledo staff-headquarters.

"Comrade Hernandez," a voice cried from within the shop, "Lieutenant Larreta's just phoned to say the officer in charge of the battery has decamped."

"Get someone to take his place." Hernandez shrugged his shoulders disgustedly, and stepped over a sewing machine lying on the road. An escort was following them.

"Who's in command here?" There was a shade of irony in Garcia's voice.

"Whom would you expect to be in command? Anybody and everybody, of course. Ah, you're smiling . . ."

"I'm always smiling. It's a habit—a cheerful one, anyhow. Who gives orders here?"

"Officers, lunatics, delegates of political groups and God knows how many more." Hernandez spoke without bitterness;

only a flicker of the black moustache on his thin upper lip seemed to suggest his profound discouragement.

"How do your professional officers get on with the political groups?" Garcia enquired.

Hernandez looked at him in silence, as though no words could possibly express how appallingly bad things were in that respect. Cocks were crowing in the bright sunlight.

"And why?" Garcia continued. "Because every god-damned fool assumes authority? In the beginning the revolution is always a vast scramble for authority."

"That's one thing. And then, confound it, we're up against the colossal ignorance of all the people who start telling us how to run the war. An army of two thousand men who really knew their job could wipe out our militia. Why, even the *real* leaders seem to believe in the people as an effective military force."

"*I* don't. Not for the present anyhow. Well, what's to be done?"

In the streets, divided equally in light and shade, life was going on as usual. But rifles were lying across the baskets of tomatoes. A Flamenco folksong rose after the tumult of the "Ride of the Valkyries" was ended. Guttural, throbbing with emotion, it had at once the accent of a dirge and the desolate clamour of a caravan lost in the desert. Tentacles of sound seemed tightening around the city and the stench of horses, as dead men's fingers clench the dust.

"Well, Major, for one thing, when a man wants to join the Socialist or Communist Parties, or any of the liberal organizations, he has to produce a minimum of guarantees; but anyone at all can join the C.N.T. No questions asked! Of course it's no news to you; but for us it's a damned serious matter. Every time we nab a falangist he's got a C.N.T. card on him. There are some anarchists who are dependable—the comrade behind us, for example. But so long as the policy of the 'open door' exists, it's the door open to every sort of disaster. That trouble with the officer commanding the battery, for instance."

"The regular army officers who are on our side—what were their motives for joining us, do you think?"

"Some of them think that because Franco hasn't pulled it off right away he'll be beaten in the end. Some are attached to one or another of the senior officers who are on bad terms with Franco, Mola, Queipo, or some other leader of the revolt. Then there are the officers who haven't budged because they couldn't make up their minds or hadn't the guts to take a line; they chanced to be with us, and they've stayed with us. But, now that the political committees have taken to cursing them, they wish they hadn't!"

In the Sierra, Garcia had come across officers professing to be Republican, who approved of the silliest things done by the *milicianos*, then spat when they were out of sight. And he had seen the staff officers at a military aerodrome moving away the chairs and tables in their mess when badly dressed foreign volunteers turned up. And other regular officers correcting the *milicianos'* mistakes with unvarying patience, teaching them their duties, training them. And he had been told of the tragedy of the Republican officer commanding the XIIIth Lancers, one of the regiments which had revolted at Valencia. He had gone to the barracks to take up his command fully knowing the risk he was running. The door had closed behind him and a volley had been heard.

"Can't *any* of your officers get on with the anarchists?"

"Yes. The worst get on very well with them. The only man whose orders the anarchists—or, rather, those who profess to be anarchists—obey to any extent is that French captain. They don't take him very seriously, but they like him." Garcia gestured a question with his pipe. "He gives me the most ridiculous advice about how to run the war—and very sound advice on practical matters."

All the streets converged on the city square, the no-man's land between the Alcazar and its besiegers. Unable to cross it, Garcia and Hernandez made a circuit round it, Hernandez' footsteps dragging, Garcia's ringing on the ancient cobblestones. At the far end of each street spanned by a barricade of mattresses, and at the end of every alley, beyond a perilously low line of sandbags, they caught sight of it again. The men were firing lying down, in badly placed groups, and offered an easy target for the enemy marksmen.

"What do you think of these barricades?" Garcia watched his companion from the corner of an eye.

"I think as you do. And now I'm going to show you something. . . ."

Hernandez went up to the man apparently in charge of the barricade. He had the jovial face of an old-time cabby, a swashbuckling moustache, a huge Mexican hat, and was lavishly tattooed. Strapped to his left arm was a death's head in aluminum.

"You should raise that barricade eighteen inches, spread out your men, and post some at the windows on both flanks."

"Pa . . . pers," growled the "Mexican" amid a series of detonations fairly close at hand.

"What?"

"Yer papers, blast you, yer i-dentity papers!"

"I'm Captain Hernandez in charge of the Zocodover sector."

"Then you don't belong to the C.N.T. and my barricade is none of your damned business. See?"

The man's gorgeous headgear fascinated Garcia; round the crown was a garland of paper roses, and below it a ribbon inscribed: *The Terror of Pancho Villa.*

"What's that mean?" he asked. " 'The Terror of Pancho Villa'?"

"It's plain enough, isn't it?"

"I suppose so," Garcia smiled.

Hernandez looked at him without speaking. The two men moved on. On the radio, the marvellous Flamenco song had ceased. Down a side street, in front of a dairy, was a row of milk-jugs on each of which rested a card with a name written on it. As the women disliked waiting in queue, they had left their jugs there; the milkman filled them and they came to fetch them later—unless. . . .

The firing died down. For a moment, there was no sound above the footfalls of the escort drumming on the silence. Then Garcia heard a voice. "As Mrs. Mercery wrote to me, and she's a very intelligent woman, comrades: *They're greatly mistaken if they think they'll wash out their defeats in Africa with the workers' blood!*" From a back street came the tinkle of a child's scooter.

Rifle-fire again. More streets, sheltered from the guns of the Alcazar and, like the others, halved by light and shade. Along the shady side people were chatting on their doorsteps; some seated, others standing, leaning on their shot-guns. At the corner of a by-street they had a back view of a man standing by himself, in a soft hat and, though the day was hot, with his coat on, firing shot after shot.

The little street abutted on a lofty wall, the back of one of the Alcazar outbuildings. No loopholes or windows, not an enemy in sight. Surrounded by a swarm of flies, the man was deliberately firing again and again at the blank wall. When one cartridge-clip was empty, he slammed in another. Hearing steps behind him, he turned. He was a man in his forties, with a serious face.

"I'm shooting."

"At the wall?"

"At anything I can hit."

He looked at Garcia gravely. "You don't happen to have a child inside there, do you?" Garcia returned his gaze, but said nothing. "Then you can't understand."

The man swung round and starting firing again at the huge blocks of stone.

They went on.

"Why don't we take the Alcazar?" Garcia emphasized the question with a brisk tap of his pipe on the back of his left hand.

"How should we take it?" After they had walked a few paces Hernandez continued: "Firing at the windows of a fortress has never led to its capture. This is a siege, yes; not an attack. So what do you expect?" Both men gazed up at the towers. "Have you noticed how the air smells, Major?" Hernandez asked. "There's been a curious change. It doesn't smell of the enemy any longer. This Alcazar business is—just play-acting! We used to get his smell at first, but nowadays—not a whiff, confound it! In fact, if we took drastic steps just now, we'd feel like murderers. Ever been on the Saragossa front?"

"Not yet. But I know Huesca."

"Why you fly over Saragossa, you see the country all around pitted with shell-holes. The strategic points—barracks and so forth—are hit ten times less than the open country. Why? It isn't just bad aiming or cowardice. But it's quicker work getting a civil war afoot than getting men to hate each other all the time. Duty is duty, I grant you, and those shell-craters round Saragossa don't give me any pleasure to see. Only . . . I'm Spanish—and I can understand."

His explanations were cut short by loud bursts of cheering that died away upon the sunlight. They were passing a rather squalid music-hall gaudy with posters. Once again Hernandez shrugged his shoulders; then went on in a slower voice.

"It's not only the Toledo militia who're attacking the Alcazar; many of the ordinary townsfolk are taking part and the youngsters the fascists have with them in the Alcazar are the Toledo *milicianos'* children."

"How many hostages are there?"

"Haven't a notion. Trying to make enquiries here is—beating the wind, confound it! There must be a good many, with quite a large proportion of women and children. They made as big a haul as they could in those first days. What holds us up isn't so much the hostages as the legend about the hostages. Quite likely there aren't so many of them as we fear. . . ."

"So it's impossible to get any definite figures?"

Like the Captain, Garcia had seen at the Jefatura the photographs of the women and children who were definitely known to have been taken as hostages; and, in addition, other photographs—of empty rooms, abandoned toys. . . .

"We've tried four times."

They were half blinded by the dust of a cavalcade of mounted peasants, who looked like a tribe of Mongol nomads, as they entered Santa Cruz. Beyond it were enemy windows, those of the Government Military Building; and Alcazar loomed above it.

"Is this where you propose to try dynamite?"

"Yes."

They walked across a chaos of scorched gardens, cool halls and flights of steps to the Museum. The windows were barricaded with sandbags and broken statuary. In the atmosphere of a stokehold, streaming with sweat, *milicianos* were firing through the loopholes, their naked torsos mottled like pantherskins with flecks of sunlight. Enemy rifle-fire had riddled the brickwork of the upper portions of the wall till it was like a sieve. Behind Garcia, on the outstretched arm of an Apostle, machine-gun loading-belts were hung out to dry like washing. He hooked his leather waistcoat on the pointing finger-tip.

For the first time, Mercery approached him. "I'd have you know, sir," he said, bringing his heels together, "that the best statues here have been stored in a safe place."

Let's hope so, Garcia thought, clasping a saint's hand in his.

After passing through a series of passages and dimly lit rooms they came out on a roof. Sunlight drained the colour from the roof-tiles, but beyond them the Castilian harvest-fields glowed to the pale horizon in a motley of sunburnt flowers. The vibrant frenzy of the air throbbed in Garcia's body; the intense glare and heat almost made him vomit. Then, as his eyes fell on the graveyard, suddenly, strangely, he was humbled; it was as if those stones and monuments, ghastly white against the yellow-brown expanse of fields, made all human conflict seem futile and ridiculous. Bullets sped past them with a wasp-like drone and hit the splintered tiles with a harsh, brittle crack.

Hernandez moved forward, stooping, revolver in hand; Garcia, Mercery, and the men with the dynamite followed him. They felt the sunlight blistering their backs and the heat accumulated in the roof roasting their bellies. The fascists were firing at ten yards' range. A *miliciano* flung a dynamite cartridge; as it burst on a roof, splinters of slate rattled on the wall behind which Garcia, Hernandez, and the rest were crouching. A steady stream of bullets flowed diagonally above them.

"Bad work," Mercery remarked.

A machine-gun joined in. What if a bomb should land in all that dynamite? Garcia thought. Mercery stood up, half his body above the wall. Now that he was visible from the waist up, the fascists started plugging away at the grotesque figure in the alpaca coat and red tie, ears plugged with wadding, that was launching a charge of dynamite with the gesture of a Discobolus.

The whole roof burst in fragments with a terrific crash; tiles flew high into the air and rained down upon the watchers, who were shouting with excitement. Mercery squatted down behind the wall, beside Hernandez.

"That's the way!" he shouted to the men who, dynamite in hand, were taking cover behind the wall. His face was a foot away from the Captain's.

"What was the Great War like?" Hernandez asked.

"Living—not living—waiting—carrying on—knowing fear!"

Just now Mercery felt he was "knowing fear" because he wasn't doing anything. He grasped his revolver, aimed, and fired, his whole head visible above the wall. Now he was doing something, fear had left him. The third charge of dynamite exploded.

The tassel of Hernandez' cap was just in front of a crack in the wall. A rush of air flicked it violently aside; the cap dropped. Hernandez was bald. He replaced the cap, became a younger man.

Some shots tore across the wall, and whizzed through a loop-hole, almost under Garcia's nose. At last he brought himself to tap out his pipe and put it in his pocket. The fore part of the fascist stronghold blew out, as if a mine had been touched off behind it. A man on Garcia's right sank to the ground, blood spurting from his head, his arms still lifted in the gesture he had made to fling the dynamite. Across the space where his neck, now smeared with blood, had been, Garcia saw on a terrace of the Alcazar, in front of the graveyard, a motor-car drawn up full in the line of fire. In the harsh light it looked undamaged; five people were seated in it, motionless, two in front and three behind. Ten yards below a woman lay on the slope, one arm extended and the other clasping her head; he could clearly see the crisp, dark curls. She might have been asleep (but her head was pointing towards the bottom of the valley), were not the body under the flimsy dress flatter than any living woman's, and welded to the soil by the peculiar earthward impulse of the dead. And all those phantoms of the flaming light seemed corpses only by their odour.

"You don't happen to know of any experts in explosives, at Madrid?" Hernandez asked.

"No."

Garcia's eyes were still fixed on the graveyard; in all those cypresses and stones was something unnerving, an intimation of eternity, which gripped his bowels. The stench of rotting flesh seemed to be flooding his senses wave on wave, and throbbing with the beating of his heart under the dazzling effulgence that merged living and dead together in a holocaust of light. The last charge of dynamite burst in the last surviving fragment of the fascist building.

In the hall of the Museum the heat was intense as ever, so was the din. The dynamite-throwers exchanged congratulations with the men on duty in the vaults and, above ground, in the Museum. As Garcia slipped his waistcoat off the saintly finger, the lining stuck; the saint refused to let it go. Some *milicianos*, naked from the waist up, emerged from a flight of steps leading down to a cellar. They carried chasubles in bundles, glimmering rolls of pale pink silk and greenish gold; another man, with a sixteenth-century cap set on the back of his head, and a bare tattooed arm, noted them down in a register.

"What's the point of what we've just been doing?" Garcia asked.

"By blowing up those buildings we'll make it impossible for the rebels to try a sortie. No more than that; but it's the least silly thing to do. . . . Till now we used bombs containing sulphuric acid and gasoline with an outer case of wadding steeped in potassium chlorate and sugar. Poor stuff!"

"Are the Cadets still trying to make a sortie?"

Mercery, who was beside him, raised both arms in protest.

"It's the biggest fake in history!" Seeing Garcia's puzzled look, he continued; "I will submit a full report to you, sir, if you desire it."

But Hernandez had laid his hand on Garcia's arm and, in deference to his superior officer, Mercery drew back. On Hernandez' face was the "it's-beyond-everything" look he had worn when describing the relations between the anarchist organizations and the officers—with some astonishment thrown in. An aeroplane droned overhead.

"You too!" he exclaimed. "The Intelligence Department!"

Garcia waited, nose in air, his squirrel eye alert and twinkling.

"The Cadets of the Alcazar," Hernandez said, "are just a myth, but a marvellous piece of propaganda. There aren't twenty Cadets in the place; all the students of the Military Academy were on holiday when the rising occurred. The Alcazar is being defended by the Civil Guard, under the command of the officers of the Military Academy; Moscardo and the rest."

A group of *milicianos* ran up, the Negus amongst them.

"They're out again—with a flame-thrower!"

Through dark, narrow staircases Hernandez, Garcia, the Negus, Mercery, and the *milicianos* rushed down into a high-roofed cellar. It was full of smoke, echoing with gun-shots. Before them loomed a large tunnel-like corridor in which the smoke glowed red. *Milicianos* ran by with buckets of water held by the handle or hugged between their arms. The din of the battle going on outside was hardly audible here and the fumes of burning gasoline had effectively dispelled the stench of carrion. The fascists were in the corridor.

The nozzle of the flame-thrower, phosphorescent in the darkness, roved to and fro, spraying roof, floor, and wall opposite. The slowness of its movements suggested that the man behind it had to cope with an unwieldy length of hose. Hampered by the narrow doorway, the jet of liquid flame could not reach the walls to right and left of the entrance. Despite the ardour which his men showed in sousing the walls and hissing flames with the water from their buckets, Hernandez felt that all were anxiously awaiting the moment the fascists would burst in, and the way some of them were hugging the walls gave him an impression they did not mean to put up much resistance. It had nothing to do with warfare, this fight against an element of nature. As the spray crept slowly forward the move-

ments of the *milicianos* drenching the walls with water grew
more and more frenzied. The hiss of steam mingled with nerve-
racking coughs from throats rasped by the pungent fumes of
petrol and the rancid sweat forming upon the nozzle. Sizzling,
the shaft of fire gained foot by foot, and sudden, sputtering
bursts of bluish flame chequered the walls with a fantastic
rout of dancing shadows as the *milicianos* turned and twisted
in their frantic saraband; it was as though a horde of phantoms
were capering with glee around the madness of the living men.
And somehow the living forms seemed more spectral than
those wildly capering shadows, less palpable than the stifling
fog across which solid shapes showed flat as stencils, less real
than the angry hiss of fire and water and the weak, whimper-
ing cries of a burnt man.

"I've gone blind!" The cries came from the floor. "I've lost
my sight. Get me out of this!"

Hernandez and Mercery had grasped his shoulders and
begun dragging him away, but the man went on shouting. "Get
me out of this—take me away!"

Now the flame-thrower had reached the threshold. Revolver in hand, the Negus was standing near the door, flatten-
ing himself against the wall. As the brass nozzle peeped round
the corner, he snatched at it, but let go at once; his skin was
peeling off. His flowing silky hair glimmered like a blue aureole
in the vivid flamelight; bullets were crackling all around him.
The fascist swerved aside so as to bring his projector to bear
on the Negus, whose hand was pressing on his chest. The
Negus fired. The projector clanged on the stone floor, flung all
the shadows up on to the roof. The fascist, an elderly officer,
stood tottering above it for a moment, his face lit up from
below, bathed in the livid sheen of the dancing flames. Then
with the unnatural languor of a slow-motion picture, he fell
alongside the Negus, his head bumping against the nozzle,
which spluttered and flung it off, like a foot kicking aside an
obstacle. The Negus picked up the projector and pointed it in
the other direction. At once the room was plunged in darkness,
and the tunnel filled with clouds of glowing smoke traversed
by flying shadows. The *milicianos* thronged excitedly into the
tunnel, following the blue flames, in a wild hubbub of shouts
and gun-shots. Suddenly everything went dim. The only lights
remaining were an electric torch and a single hurricane-lamp.

"They turned off the gas once they saw we'd got hold of the
projector," a voice called in the darkness. Then, after a mo-

ment, added: "I know what I'm talking about. I'm an officer in the fire brigade."

"Halt!" Hernandez shouted from the tunnel. "They've a barricade across the exit."

"One can't become a savage by command!" the Negus exclaimed to Hernandez. (The *milicianos* were relighting the other hurricane-lamp.) "It was touch and go," the Negus went on. "He had just time enough to turn the jet on me before I fired. But I was looking him in the eyes, you know. It's queer the way men are. Yes, it must be hard to bring yourself to burn a man who's looking right at you!"

The corridor by which they returned was in darkness, but for a glimmer of light from the door at the far end. The Negus lit a cigarette; as one man the others followed his example—their return to life. Each man's face showed up for a second in the brief, brisk glow of match or lighter; then the gloom closed in again.

When they entered the hall of the Museum, they were greeted by shouts. "There's a plane up there, above the clouds."

"The hardest thing," the Negus went on, "is not to hesitate. It's a question of seconds. Two days ago the Frenchman turned a projector around like that—the same one, most likely. He didn't get burnt himself, but all the same he did no harm to the other chap. That Frenchman said he knew what it was; when a fellow looks at you, you just can't turn the flame on him. You just can't bring yourself to do it."

14

EVERY day one of the officers in the International Air Force reported at staff headquarters; sometimes at the Special Police Bureau as well. Usually, it was Scali whom Magnin detailed for this duty. Because of his intelligence and his reputation he got on excellently with the air force general staff, composed for the most part of regular army officers. (Sembrano and his pilots formed a group apart.) Scali was a thick-set man, who would certainly tend to grow fat as he grew older; his tact and cordiality made a good impression on everyone, including the functionaries of the Special Police. He was hail-fellow-well-met with all the other Italians in the aviation corps who had elected him as their spokesman, and with nearly all the other airmen. Last but not least, he spoke Spanish fluently. He had just received an urgent summons to police headquarters.

The entrance gates were guarded by machine-guns. The building, before being taken over as an annex of the Special Police Bureau, had been a private mansion, and the furniture had not been changed. The sorry company of nondescripts that a war always brings to the surface hovered around the ornately scalloped chairs, majestic and empty. In a small dining-room, he found Seruzier, Leclerc's pal, gesticulating between two sentries, looking more bewildered than ever.

"Ah, Scali, so it's you, Scali!" Scali listened with half an ear, waiting for a lull. "Yes, I thought I was going to get it in the neck, straight in the neck, old boy!"

As a police official was accompanying Scali, the *milicianos* round Seruzier moved away from him a little, but he did not dare as yet to feel at liberty.

"Those bloody whores!" he exclaimed. "Why—it beats everything!"

Even when he was seated, the restless movements of the little beady eyes under the hairless eyebrows made him look like a panicked butterfly beating its wings in a closed room.

"Just a minute!" Scali raised a peremptory forefinger. "Begin at the beginning."

"All right, I'll begin at the beginning. Well, that bloody tart picks me up in the Gran Via. I couldn't make out all she said, but it meant she knew . . . well, she knew all sorts of ways of doing it. See? So I says to her: 'Know the "Italian" way?' 'Sure,' says she. I go upstairs to her room, and when I start getting down to the job, she wants to have it in the ordinary way. Nothing doing! 'Ho!' says I. 'Cut it out! That's not what we agreed on. Like the Italians do it, that's what I'm here for. Not that way.' She wouldn't listen. I tell her it's a bloody swindle, and I start dressing. She goes to the phone and says something in Spanish. A great fat tart comes in, but she don't understand me either. The fat dame keeps on pointing to the little one. Stark naked she was and a nice little piece, I'll say that. Looked like the fat dame meant: 'Get on with it!' Only I knew better; the little one, she wasn't taking any. So I explained to the fat dame how it was, how the little one wouldn't do what I wanted, but she thought I was kidding. It's not that I'm so mighty keen on that Italian stunt; don't get that idea. Only I don't like being made a fool of—I won't stand for that. See what I mean?"

"Yes, but what's brought you here? Don't tell me you've been run in for . . . for lewdness?"

"Well, the fat dame, once she sees I'm not going to be bluffed, she too ups and goes to the phone. So then . . ."

"A still fatter tart romped in, eh?"

Seruzier was vastly relieved; Scali was taking it as a joke. Then all was well. When Scali smiled, he seemed to be laughing outright; merriment puckered his eyes and brought out the Creole cast of his face.

"What happened? Six F.A.I. men came in, guns and all! 'What's biting you?' I asks, and then I starts explaining how things stood; how it wasn't me who'd asked the girl to do it, it was her own idea. Of course, I knew they were against prostitution, tarts and the rest of it. And, seeing they're a respectable lot, they'd be down on doing it in the Italian way—or make out to be, anyhow, like all vegetarians. The hell of it was my not knowing Spanish; because when you're in a jam like that you can often fix things up by talking man to man. But the more I explained, the more the bastards scowled at me. Yes, and to make things worse, one of them fetched out his revolver. The more I bawled, that I didn't do Italiano the tougher they got. Then the two tarts started raising hell. 'Italiano! Italiano!' they kept on shouting. You couldn't hear yourself speak. After a while I got fed up with their bloody noise, and no wonder. Then I had an idea, I showed the F.A.I. men my squadron card; it's in Spanish of course. Then they brought me here. And then I put a call through to the flying field."

"What's he charged with?" Scali asked the clerk in Spanish.

The clerk looked at the charge-sheet. "There's not much to it. The only witnesses are prostitutes, you know. Wait . . . here it is. 'Espionage on behalf of Italy.' "

Five minutes later Seruzier was released amid general laughter.

"We've something more important for you," the police clerk said. "Two fascist airmen, Italians, have crashed behind our lines south of Toledo. One is dead; the other's here. The Intelligence Department wants you to have a look at their papers."

Scali flicked the papers over with his stubby little finger—the task rather disgusted him. There were letters, visiting-cards, photographs and club membership cards in a pocket-book, as

well as maps found in the cockpit. It was the first time Scali
met an enemy Italian with an illusion of intimacy; and the man
whom he met now was dead. One sheet especially held his
attention.

A long rectangle, like a folded air-map, it looked as if it
had once been pinned to the pilot's chart. A sort of log-book,
judging by its aspect. There were two columns. *Course. From
. . . To . . .* with a space for the date of each journey. *July
16* (before Franco's rising) *Spezia;* then *Melilla, July 18, 19,
20;* then *Seville,* and *Salamanca.* In the margin the purpose of
the flight was noted: Observation, bombing, escort, and protection. The last entry—the record of the day before—read:
From Segovia to . . . The destination, *Death,* was blank.

But below it, written some days earlier with a different pen,
were large block letters covering both columns: TOLEDO,
with a date, the next day but one. Obviously an important
flight over Toledo was impending.

In the next room someone was bawling into the telephone.
"Yes, President, yes, of course, I'm aware our personnel is
under strength. But I'd have you know that under no circumstances, none whatever, will I take men for the Assault Guards
who aren't vouched for by a political organization."

" . . ."

"And what about the day when we've got to smash a fascist
mutiny with regiments that have been tampered with? As long
as I'm responsible, not a man who isn't vouched for! There
were quite enough falangists in the Montaña Barracks; I won't
have any in the Special Police."

From the start Scali had recognized the voice as that of the
Chief of Special Police.

"His grand-daughter's a prisoner, at Cadiz," a clerk observed.

A door banged and they heard no more. Then the dining-
room door opened and the clerk who had first spoken to Scali
came back.

"There are some more papers with the Intelligence Department. Major Garcia says they're important. He wants you to
sort out the ones you have there—to separate the dead pilot's
papers from the observer's. You're to turn the whole lot over to
me and I'll take it to him at once. You'll send in your report
to Colonel Magnin."

"A great many of these things," Scali observed, "are printed
forms or maps; how can I possibly say to whom they belong?"

"The observer's here; you've only got to question him."

"Very well." There was no enthusiasm in Scali's voice. His feelings towards the prisoner were as mixed as those he had had when given the documents. Still his curiosity was aroused. Two days before a German pilot who had crashed in the Sierra near staff headquarters—where two inspecting officers had chanced to be present—had been taken before them to be questioned. When the interpreter told him the names of those confronting him, he was evidently amazed to find himself in the presence of generals; he had imagined that the "Reds" had no such officers. "Good God!" the German had exclaimed. "I never dreamt of it! Why, I flew over this shack three times without dropping a single bomb!"

"One moment, please," Scali said to the clerk. "Tell the Major I've just seen something here which may have its importance."

He had in mind the pilot's log with the dates proving he had left Italy before Franco's rising.

He went to the office where the observer was in custody. Sitting at a table, his elbows propped on the green tablecloth, the prisoner had his back to the door by which Scali entered. All Scali could see at first was a hunched-up form clad half in mufti and half in uniform, a leather windbreaker and blue trousers. At the sound of the opening door the fascist airman rose to his feet and glanced towards it; the movements of his legs and long emaciated arms, and his back, still bent when he was standing, gave the impression of a rather neurotic consumptive.

"Wounded?" Scali enquired.

"No, only bruised a bit."

Scali laid his revolver and the documents on the table beside him, sat down and signed to the two sentries to leave the room. The fascist sat down opposite him. He had the sparrow face—tiny eyes and a perky nose—which is common among airmen; it was accentuated by his shock of hair and prominent cheekbones. Though he did not resemble House, one could see he came of the same family. Why was the man looking so puzzled? Scali glanced round; behind him, under Azaña's portrait, was a yard-high heap of silverware; dishes, plates, tea-pots, ewers, Arab trays, clocks, vases, knives and forks, the harvest of recent house-to-house requisitions.

"Is that what's puzzling you?"

The prisoner hesitated. "That? You—you mean . . . ?" He

pointed to the glittering profusion of an Aladdin's hoard. "No
—of course not!" he stammered, like a man at bay.

What surprised him most, perhaps, was Scali himself. Looking at him, one thought at once of an American film comedian.
This was due less to his face—there was really nothing very
odd about it, despite the thick lips and horn-rimmed glasses—
than to the disproportionate shortness of his legs (which gave
him a "Charlie-Chaplin" walk), the buckskin waistcoat (so
unexpected on a "Red"), and the pencil tucked behind his ear.

"Look here!" Scali addressed him in Italian. "I'm not a member of the Secret Police. Just an air-force volunteer, posted
here as technical adviser. I've been told to sort out your papers
from those of the . . . of your dead companion. That's all."

"That's all right with me."

"Put your own stuff on the right and the other fellow's on
the left."

The observer began to sort out the papers into two heaps.
He hardly glanced at them. His eyes seemed held by the broken
gleams that faceted the pile of silver under the brilliant ceiling-
lights.

"Did your engine fail," Scali asked, "or were you shot
down?"

"We were on a scouting flight, the pilot and I. A Russian
machine downed us."

Scali shrugged his shoulders. "Have it your own way! The
pity is—there aren't any Russian machines over here. But let's
hope we'll have some soon."

The pilot's log, however, showed clearly that they were on a
bombing raid, not scouting. And suddenly Scali was conscious
of that rather frightful sense of superiority which comes from
knowing that another man is lying. Still, he hadn't heard of any
Italian two-seater bombing machines in service on the Spanish
front. Well, that was a problem for the Intelligence, not his
affair. Just the same, he made a note of it. On the right-hand
pile the observer laid a receipt, some Spanish bank-notes and a
small photograph. Scali, who was long-sighted, peered through
his glasses at the photograph; it showed a detail of a fresco by
Piero della Francesca.

"Is that yours or his?" he asked.

"You told me: my things on the right."

"Very well. Continue."

Piero della Francesca, Scali glanced at the passport. *"Student. Florence."* But for fascism this man might very likely

have been one of his pupils. Scali had imagined for a moment that the photograph had belonged to the dead man and felt a vague fraternity towards him. In the old days he had published a study of the Piero della Francesca frescos. During the previous week a similar examination of a prisoner, conducted by an airman, not by the police, had wound up in a heated argument about flying records.

"Did you jump?"

"The machine didn't catch fire. We made a landing in open country, that's all."

"You cracked up?"

"Yes."

"And then?"

The observer hesitated before replying. Scali glanced through the report. The pilot had climbed out first; the observer—the man whom he was questioning now—had been trapped in the wreckage. A peasant had come up; the pilot had drawn his revolver. The peasant had continued to approach. When he was three paces off, the pilot had taken from his left-hand pocket a wad of notes, large white thousand-peseta notes. The peasant had approached nearer, while the pilot added a handful of dollars, which doubtless he had kept ready for such an emergency—doing all this with his left hand, his right still grasping the revolver. When the peasant was near the pilot, almost touching him, he had levelled his shot-gun at him and shot him dead.

"Why didn't your companion shoot first?"

"I can't say."

Scali remembered the parallel columns in the log: *Point of Departure; Destination.* That man's destination had been the peasant's gun.

"Right. What did you do then?"

"I waited. A number of peasants gathered round, they took me to the mayor's office first, then brought me here." He paused, then added: "Shall I be tried?"

"What for?"

"Without a trial!" the man exclaimed. "So they'll shoot me without a trial!" An exclamation less of horror than of acquiescence. Obviously, ever since he had crashed, the young man had been convinced that the most he could hope for would be to be shot without a trial. He was standing up, clasping the back of the chair with both hands as if determined not to be wrenched away from it.

Scali pushed back his spectacles and shrugged his shoulders with a gesture of profound hopelessness. That notion, so prevalent among the fascists, that their enemies were as a matter of course a lower race, despicable and subhuman—that impulse to disdain, so typical of fools—had not been least among the reasons for which he had left his country.

"You are not going to be shot at all," he replied gruffly, using once more the tone of a school-teacher scolding an idle pupil.

But the prisoner did not believe him. And the fact that his disbelief made him suffer gave a bitter satisfaction to Scali's sense of justice.

"One moment," he said. Opening the door, he called to the clerk. "Bring me that photo of Captain Vallado, please."

The clerk handed him a photograph which he passed on to the observer.

"You're an airman, aren't you? And you can tell whether a cabin is in one of your machines or ours?"

Sembrano's friend, after shooting down two Fiats, had been himself brought down in a transport plane on the Sierra. The militia had occupied the village next day and found the airmen still at their places in the cockpit. Their eyes had been torn out. The mutilated bomber was the Assault Guard Captain who had trained the field-gun on the Montaña Barracks, though he had never handled such a gun before.

The observer stared at the face with the eyes plucked out. His teeth were clenched and his cheeks were quivering.

"I've seen several Red pilots who'd been taken prisoners . . . none of them had been tortured."

"You've yet to learn that neither you nor I know much about this war. We're fighting in it, but that's another story."

The observer's gaze strayed back to the photograph, fascinated. In his expression there was something youthful, which went with his little gnome-like ears; the faces on the photograph were expressionless.

"What's there to prove," he asked, "that the photograph isn't . . . I mean, wasn't sent to you after being faked?"

"Very well, that explains it," Scali replied. "We pluck out the eyes of our best pilots just to make these photographs! We use Chinese torturers, communists, you know, for the job!"

Scali himself used to suspect, when shown the photographs entitled "Anarchist Atrocities," that they were faked. It is always hard for a man to credit the vileness of those beside whom he is fighting.

The observer had gone back to his task with the papers, as if he found in it a refuge from his thoughts.

"Are you so very sure," Scali asked, "that if I were placed as you are at this moment, your people . . . ?"

He stopped. From the mound of silverware there stole out, like mice, one, two, three, four little silvery chimes. It was as if the treasure-hoard itself were striking; not a clock buried in a jumble of pathetic bric-a-brac. That chiming clock breaking into their conversation (how long, he wondered, before it would run down?), that little clock so far from those who once had owned it, striking now its desultory hour, gave him a feeling of the utter indifference of things, a sense of eternity so poignant that whatever he might say seemed futile; he no longer had any wish to speak. He and the man before him, each had *chosen*.

Scali was glancing absent-mindedly at the dead pilot's map and tracing over the criss-cross lines with the pencil which he had dislodged from behind his ear. Beside him, the prisoner had just turned Vallado's photograph face downwards. Suddenly Scali adjusted his glasses, stared first at the observer, then back at the map.

The flying log showed that the pilot had taken off from Caceres, south-west of Toledo. Now the Caceres aerodrome, which was inspected daily by Republican scouting planes, was known to be unused. The map was a Spanish aviation chart; all details were clearly shown and the aerodromes indicated by small rectangular blocks of violet ink. Some twenty-five miles from Caceres was another rectangle, a mere indentation on the map and hardly perceptible; the outlines had been traced in pencil and, as the graphite would not take on the glossy surface, all that could be seen was a faint grooved line. There was a similar rectangle near Salamanca, and there were others south of the Estremadura, in the Sierra. All the secret air-bases of the fascists had been marked thus—including those of the Tagus region, from which their machines took off for the Toledo front.

Scali's face had grown tense, and he was conscious of the change. His eyes met enemy eyes; each man knew the other had understood. The fascist did not stir, did not say a word. But his head sagged between his shoulders and his cheeks twitched, as when he had been shown Vallado's photograph.

Quietly Scali folded up the map. . . .

The landing ground was sweltering under the blaze of a

Spanish summer afternoon as the battered plane, piloted by
Darras, bumped on the turf with its flat, bullet-scarred tires.
On the road behind the olive-trees, a peasant was singing an
Andalusian folk-song.

Magnin, who had just returned from the Ministry, had gathered all his personnel round the bar.

"I want a volunteer crew for the Alcazar."

There was a longish silence, filled by the hum of flies. Every
day now planes were coming back with wounded crews and
tanks ablaze; under the blinding sunlight or in the dusk, silently, their engines cut off, they limped home—if they returned at all. The hundred machines whose coming Vargas
had predicted had reached the fascists, and many more as well.
Not a single Republican pursuit plane was left, and the enemy's
pursuit planes were operating in full strength along the Tagus.

"A volunteer crew for the Alcazar," Magnin repeated.

15

MARCELINO shared Magnin's view that as they had no pursuit
planes the best thing they could do was to operate from behind
clouds. Often he flew back from an engagement on the South
Tagus front when the sun had almost set and Toledo lay like a
gigantic garland flung on the harvest-fields, with the Alcazar
looming up at the river's bend. Here and there a ribbon of
smoke from a burning house slanted across the pale expanse
of yellow stone, trailing off into tenuous wisps sparkling with
motes of light like sun-glints in a pool of shadow. In the spacious calm of one of war's "off hours," under the evening
glow, the smoke rose from each smouldering house as placidly
as from a cottage chimney. Marcelino, still an expert pilot,
could foresee each reflex of the flyers on board; yet he had not
returned as a pilot. He was, however, the best bomber in the
squadron and an excellent commander. And now, he knew,
somewhere under the cloud-bank, the battle was raging round
Toledo, and the enemy planes were not far away.

Above the clouds the air was marvellously clear. An infinite
peace brooded upon the white sea of clouds under the plane,
and there was as yet no sign of enemy air-patrols moving
towards the city. According to the pilot's reckoning, they were

quite near Toledo. The plane accelerated to its maximum speed. Jaime was singing, the other straining to see ahead, with the fixed stare of absent-mindedness. In the distance some isolated mountain peaks pierced the level whiteness of the cloud-floor, and sometimes through a rift they had a glimpse of corn-fields.

By now the machine was presumably above Toledo. But there was no instrument to record the drift due to a wind blowing directly at right angles to their course. Once the plane came down through the clouds it was almost certain to be spotted from the town and, if they were too far from it, the enemy pursuit planes would be on them before they had had time to drop their bombs. The plane swooped down.

Expecting every moment to catch sight of the earth below, of the guns of the Alcazar, the enemy pursuit planes and his lines of defense, Marcelino and the pilot watched the height-gauge more passionately than they had ever scanned a human face. 2500. . . . 1800. . . . 1200 feet. . . . But still they were immersed in clouds. There was no choice but to climb back, and wait till a hole appeared below them.

They zoomed into the upper air poised motionless above the clouds that seemed to stream away beneath them, following the earth's movement. The wind was driving the cloud-bank from east to west, and here it was pocked with numerous holes. They began to circle, with the immutable precision of a star, in the empty firmament. Jaime, who was in charge of the forward machine-gun, waved his hand to Marcelino.

For the first time both men grew conscious of the earth's rotation. An unheeded atom in the vast cosmic movement, the aeroplane gyrated like a tiny planet, waiting till the old city, the rebel Alcazar and its besiegers came into view below, rolled round in the incessant rhythm of earthbound things.

But at the first rift in the clouds—too small for observation —the instinct of the bird of prey came uppermost again. Like a circling hawk the plane swung round and round, prospecting for a larger opening, the gaze of all on board set vigilantly earthward. It seemed to them that they themselves were stationary and the clouds and peaks were wheeling slowly round them on a far-flung orbit. Suddenly, at the fringe of a cloud-rift, the earth came into view, and two hundred yards or so away a little puff-ball floated past; the Alcazar had opened fire. The machine swooped again.

Space seemed to contract and the bright air faded out as the plane dived below the clouds. Here was man's little world. The Alcazar.

Toledo was on the left and, at the angle of their descent, the gorge above the Tagus loomed larger than the city, than the Alcazar itself, which was still firing up at them. The gun-layers were officers in the Artillery School, but the real danger for the crew lay in the enemy's pursuit planes rather than in gunfire from below.

Slanting at first, Toledo was swinging slowly back to the horizontal. Even at this strange moment it had not lost its quaintly decorative air, and the expanse of roofs was striped with ribbons of smoke from burning houses. The plane began to circle, at a tangent to the Alcazar. This hawk-like circling above their quarry was imperative. The besieging troops were so close to the Alcazar that each bomb had to be dropped with absolute accuracy on the target. But each successive circle gave the enemy more time to bring up their pursuit planes. Marcelino's machine had come down to nine hundred feet and now he saw below him ant-like forms with round white hats, moving in front of the Alcazar.

The first time over, Marcelino opened the trap, took his sight without loosing off the bomb, and checked up on it. The sight was a good one, as he could judge. The Alcazar was a small target and fearing the scatter effect of light bombs, he decided to use heavy ones only. He had withheld the signal and the rest of the crew stood by, waiting. A second time the cockpit telegraph told the pilot to turn. The puff-balls of smoke were coming closer.

"Stand by!" Marcelino shouted.

Standing up in the cabin, with his beltless overalls flopping all round him as usual, Marcelino was an ungainly figure. He never let the Alcazar out of his sight. He pulled the trap-hatch wide open and squatted down. A gust of cold air swept up the cabin and all of them knew the fight was going to begin.

The Alcazar veered again, approached. Now Marcelino was lying flat on his stomach, his wrist in air, counting the seconds. Then his arm fell as if he were ripping down a curtain. The Alcazar swept underneath, with a few ill-aimed shells circling it like satellites, spun round and sheered off to the right.

A tenuous puff of smoke appeared in the main courtyard; was it the bomb? The pilot continued to wheel round, taking the Alcazar again at a tangent. The bomb had fallen in the middle of the courtyard. Followed by bursts of shrapnel, the plane dropped a second bomb, swerved off, returned. Marcelino raised his hand again, but this time did not let it fall. In the courtyard white sheets had been hastily spread out; the Alcazar was surrendering!

Jaime and Pol were shadow-boxing out of sheer joy. The entire crew were capering with glee.

Level with the clouds, the enemy's pursuit planes came into view.

16

AT THE Jefatura, a college now converted into barracks, Lopez with his genial, Bourbon air was concluding his examination of a group of fugitives from the Alcazar; a woman hostage who had been smuggled out under a false permit given her by the chief armourer (who, too, had fled), and ten soldiers who had been incarcerated on the first day but had managed to escape by jumping into a ravine.

The woman was a dark, robust matron in the forties, with a snub nose and keenly alert eyes; but privation had left its mark on her.

"How many were there of you?" Lopez asked.

"That I'm afraid I can't tell you, sir. We weren't all kept together; the prisoners were scattered about here and there, in different places. In the cellar where we were there must have been a good twenty-five of us, but that was only one roomful seemingly. . . ."

"Had you enough to eat?"

The woman looked Lopez in the eyes. "More than enough."

Some peasants walked past the Jefatura with enormous wooden pitchforks shaped like candelabras on their shoulders and a gun tucked under each right arm. Behind them an abundant harvest was entering Toledo, carted by oxen whose horns were wreathed with sprigs of broom. The woman went on speaking.

"There are some people here who say they've nothing to eat in the Alcazar. Don't you believe it, sir. It's only horseflesh and a poor sort of bread, but starving they are not. I've eyes in my head and I keep an inn, and I guess I know more about cooking then menfolk do. Yes, sir, they've enough to eat."

"And what about the planes that drop sardines and ham?"

exclaimed one of the escaped soldiers. "Of course, the ham's kept for the officers. We didn't get a smell of it, not once in all those cruel weeks. A mean shame, I call it. And to think the Guards are standing by those chaps!"

"What else did you expect the Guards to do, my lad?" the woman asked.

"The same thing we did."

"Oh, that's your idea, is it?" she said slowly. "But you haven't killed anyone in Toledo, have you?"

The remark confirmed what Lopez had suspected. When the Right was in power the Civil Guards had carried out "punitive measures" in the Toledo district. So now they were afraid to move, for they realized that the terms of their surrender might not be respected, once their faces were recognized.

"What about the fascists' wives?"

"They!" There was scorn in her voice. Her expression—respectful, while she had been addressing Lopez—had changed. "What's come over you men, I'd like to know, that you're so afraid of touching those women? They're not all your mothers, are they? Why, they treated us worse than the men did! Eh, if it's the women you're afraid of, just hand those bombs over to us!"

"You wouldn't know how to throw them." Lopez was smiling, but somehow he felt ill at ease.

He turned to some journalists who had just strolled up, notebook in hand. "We've made a proposal that all non-combatants should be evacuated, but the rebels have turned it down. They say their wives wish to stay with them."

"That's a good one!" the woman broke in. "That woman up there who's just had a baby, does she want to stay? And the one who started firing a revolver at her husband, does *she* want to stay? Or maybe she'd like to have another shot at him! And that other creature who keeps howling at the moon, hour after hour—for all that she's crazy, does *she* want to stay?"

"Yes, and you can't help hearing them—all the time!" one of the soldiers said. Then he burst out hysterically, pressing his fists against his ears. "And you keep on hearing them, you keep on hearing them!"

A voice outside made itself heard. "Comrade Lopez, Madrid wants you on the phone."

Lopez left the room, his nerves on edge. The picturesque was all very well; human suffering another matter. The thought of all the hatreds festering up there in the Alcazar where men

were being shot down in courtyards, and children born, was
beginning to prey on his mind. One morning he had heard cries
in the Alcazar: "We want to surrender! We want . . . !" A
gun-shot, and then nothing more.

Over the telephone he summarized what he had just learned
—little enough.

"One thing's sure," he concluded, "somehow we've got to
save those people."

"The fascists have taken hostages all over Spain."

Lopez could hardly hear what was being said. Out in the
courtyard an officer was strumming on a piano, a phonograph
was playing an old rhumba, a loud-speaker bawling raucous
lies.

The voice from Madrid grew stronger. "I quite agree we
must do our best for them. But we've got to clean up the Alcazar and shift the militia to the Talavera front. You'd better
give those bastards up there another chance. Fix up a parley as
soon as you possibly can. We can deal with them ourselves,
through the diplomatic corps."

"They've asked for a priest. You have priests at Madrid,
eh?"

"Right—through the Church then. We'll ring up the commanding officer at once. Thanks."

Lopez went back to the room. One of the soldiers was speaking.

"The women are kept underground, because of air-raids. If
they're our women, they're put near the stables—where they
had us cooped, you know. Their own women are elsewhere.
Round the stables the stench is something awful. There's thirty
bodies buried there, in the riding-school, only an inch or two
deep, not to speak of the skeletons of horses lying about with
bits of skin left on them. The bodies—those are the people who
wanted to surrender. So you see how we were—between the
devil and the deep sea, as they say; with the stiffs under foot
and those chaps upstairs who hung out sheets when the plane
came over. That plane of yours gave us the jitters when it was
laying eggs on us, but we were mighty glad to see it all the
same. That's when they hung out the sheets."

"Who did that? The Civil Guards?"

"No, the soldiers. The others—let them do it. But when the
plane had gone they got busy with their machine-guns. The
fellows began toppling over, here, there, on top of their sheets,
everywhere. When the Guards came and gathered up the

sheets, they weren't white any longer. They hauled them away by the corners, like handkerchiefs. Well, we put our heads together; looked like we'd be mopped up next. So we took a chance, and jumped. . . ."

"Know if they killed a chap called Morales, a Corporal?" someone asked. "That's my brother. Something of a socialist in his way."

The soldier made no answer.

"Of course," the woman said resignedly, "those folks up there kill everyone!"

When Lopez left the Jefatura, children, satchels in hand, were coming home from school. As he walked along, his arms swinging loosely, with unseeing eyes, he all but stepped into a black puddle on the road; an anarchist drew him aside, as if he were about to tread on a wounded animal.

"Take care, old man. That's blood." And added reverently: "Comrades' blood."

17

HALF the Pelicans lay dozing on the benches in the airport bar. Only half. The ground staff, however, were all at their posts. About a quarter of the pilots and machine-gunners were away —heaven knew where! Magnin was puzzled how to institute some sort of discipline, without using coercion. For all their unruliness, their horse-play, their boasting and irresponsibility, any Pelican was good to win in a "dog fight," one against seven. The same applied to Sembrano's Spaniards and to the Bréguets from Cuatros-Vientos and Gétafé. All had lost more than half their war strength. Several mercenaries, including Sibirsky, had asked to be allowed to serve one month out of two without pay; thus securing a little money and—better still —comradeship. Daily Saint-Antoine came back, with his freight of cigarettes, field-glasses, and gramophone records, in still more melancholy mood. The machines, which had set out to cross the Sierra without an escort of pursuit planes (where were they to come from?), hoping that the early hour, their wariness or a fight elsewhere in progress would see them through, as often as not failed to return and, when they did return, had been cut to tatters. The consumption of alcohol at the bar was going up.

Scali and the other men lying on the benches rose and began roaming up and down the terrace; they looked like prisoners at exercise. Even if the trolley-man with the bomb-racks had not reminded them of the time, every man would have known that Marcelino's machine was overdue. By now he had only fifteen minutes' fuel left at most.

Enrique, a commissar attached to the Fifth Regiment (formed by the communists in the early stages of the war as the nucleus of a regular army), who claimed—perhaps with truth—to be a Mexican, was walking with Magnin on the field. The sunset was behind them and the Pelicans saw Magnin's limp moustache glinting in a last ray above the sharp-cut, totem-like profile of the Commissar.

"Actually, how many many machines have you left?" the Commissar asked.

"I'd rather not talk about it. As a regular air force, we have ceased to exist. And we're still waiting to get decent machine-guns. What the hell are they up to, the Russians?"

"And what are the French up to?"

"Oh, forget that. The point is what can be done about it. Apart from an occasional stroke of luck, I'm going in for night raids; and playing hide-and-seek among the clouds. Fortunately the autumn's coming on." He raised his eyes; the night promised to be fine. "It's the weather that interests me most just now. We're no more than a guerrilla air force nowadays. If we don't get some more machines sent us from abroad, all that's left us is to die—in the best way possible. . . . By the way, what's behind that damn-fool story of Russian planes arriving at Barcelona?"

"I was in Barcelona the day before yesterday. I saw a fine machine in an open hangar; it was covered all over with red stars. There was a hammer-and-sickle on the tail, and inscriptions on all sides. And in front the word LENIN. Only the Russian 'I' "—his finger traced it in the air—"was upside down, like the Spanish 'N.' Well, I went up close to have a squint at it, and I recognized your old 'Negus' plane."

Magnin had picked up in the English market the Emperor Haile Selassie's private aeroplane. A fairly fast machine, with capacious tanks, but tricky to handle, it had been damaged by a pilot and shipped to Barcelona for repairs.

"Can't be helped! But why the camouflage?"

"Some childish nonsense, I dare say—to conjure up the real Russian planes or, more likely, just a provocative gesture."

"Very likely. . . . Anyhow, how are things with you?"

"Going quite well—but slowly." Enrique halted, drew from his pocket a reorganization plan and switched on his flashlight, for the night was getting dark. "From now on you may take this plan as final."

His scheme was practically the same as that of the "Shock-Battalion" organization. Magnin remembered how at Saragossa the militia had gone out to fight without ammunition; how field telephones were non-existent on almost the whole Aragon front; and how at Toledo alcohol and iodine were all they had for first aid.

"Have you succeeded in restoring discipline?"

"Yes."

"Had to use coercion?"

"No."

"How did you manage?"

"The communists are disciplined already. They obey their group secretaries and military delegates—often, you know, the same men hold both posts. Any number of people who want to take part in the war joined the Party, just because it's decently organized, and that appeals to them. Formerly, our people were disciplined because they were communists; now plenty of people become communists because the Party stands for discipline. In each army unit we have a good many communists, who themselves keep discipline and make a point of seeing that the others observe it too. Each group is a solid nucleus round which the new recruits gravitate, so to speak—till these in turn split off into another nucleus. When all's said and done, ten times more men than we can cope with are joining up, men who realize that by joining us they're doing good work against fascism. Oh, and by the way, I'd like to have a word with you about the Germans."

This was not the first time Magnin had been tackled on the subject, and it was getting on his nerves.

Enrique took his arm; the gesture, coming from the hard-boiled warrior he believed Enrique to be, took Magnin by surprise. He had always divided communist leaders into two categories: the soldierly type and the priestly type. Having to place this fellow, as big and bulky as Garcia himself, a man who had fought in five civil wars, in the second category, disconcerted him. Just then he noticed that, for all their likeness with those of a Mexican idol, Enrique's lips pursed at moments like a carpet-hawker's.

What had the Secret Police demanded? That the three Germans must never again be allowed to set foot on an aerodrome. Magnin regarded Krefeld as a suspicious character, and incompetent as well; he had posed as an instructor but did not know how to handle a machine-gun, and he was always at meetings of the Communist Party just when Karlitch needed him; in fact Karlitch had to do everything single-handed. The Schreiner affair had been most regrettable; the man was certainly innocent. In any case, however, he was best out of the Anti-Aircraft Corps.

"You see, Enrique," he said, "the whole business is lamentable from the humane point of view, but I can't put forward any valid reason for turning down what the Police are asking for—and have the power to insist on. I'm not a communist, and, under the circumstances, I can't profess to be obeying a mandate of my Party. Good relations between the Air Force, the Police, and the Intelligence Service, are too vitally essential to us just now, when we have to play into each other's hands to get things done, for me to risk upsetting them over this affair. They'd simply think I was being pig-headed. You see how I'm placed?"

"They've got to stay," Enrique said. "The Party vouches for them. You must see that if they're compelled to go, all their comrades will take it to mean that they've fallen under suspicion. Really, you can't treat people who have been good militants for years like that."

The machine-gunner belonged to the Party; Magnin did not.

"Personally," Magnin said, "I'm convinced that Schreiner's innocent; but that's not the question. You've had a report on him from the German section of the Party at Paris; you accept it. Well and good; make the Government realize you take full responsibility. For myself, I've no means of making enquiries and I can't decide off-handed on an issue which may have very serious consequences. All the more so since, as you know, they're perfect duds as airmen."

"We might fix up a dinner at which I'd convey to you the welcome of the Spanish comrades, and you could say a word of welcome to the German comrades. I've been told that in the Squadron there's some bad feeling against the Germans—a touch of nationalist prejudice."

"I haven't the slightest desire to drink the health of people who have such queer methods of imparting information." The high esteem in which Magnin held Enrique's work, if not the man himself (he knew him very slightly), merely intensified his annoyance. He had watched the battalions of the Fifth Regiment being trained; they were the best militia battalions, by and large. The whole army of the Popular Front might well be organized on the same lines. They, anyhow, had solved the crucial problem, the problem of revolutionary discipline. So Magnin regarded Enrique as one of the ablest organizers of the Spanish popular field force. But he was convinced that the shrewd and conscientious man beside him, for all his geniality, had he been in his, Magnin's, place, would never have assented to such a request as that which he had just made.

"The Party has looked into the question," Enrique said, "and considers that the men should be kept."

Magnin recalled the anxiety he had felt in the days of the conflict between the socialists and communists.

"Sorry; for me the Revolution counts for more than the Communist Party."

"Comrade Magnin, I'm no fanatic. And I was once a Trotskyite. Nowadays fascism goes in for the export industry. It exports finished articles: armies and aeroplanes. That being so, I maintain that in the fight we're putting up our first line of defence isn't so much the world proletariat, as Soviet Russia and the Communist Party. A hundred Russian planes would help us more than fifty thousand volunteers with no war experience. But if you want the co-operation of the Party, you must take it as it is, without reserve."

"Very true. But those Russian planes—they aren't here. As for your three . . . comrades, if the Communist Party vouches for them let it vouch for them to the police, or take them on its strength. I've nothing against that."

"So that's your last word. You're determined they shall go."

"Yes."

Enrique dropped Magnin's arm.

They were standing now in the glow that issued from the airport buildings. Enrique had moved from the shadow into a ray of light and now that he had dropped Magnin's arm and was standing at a certain distance, Magnin had a good view of the man's exotic face. One of Enrique's sayings—he had heard it quoted but it had slipped his memory—came to his mind. "For me a Party comrade counts more than all the Garcias and Magnins in the world."

"Don't forget," Magnin continued, "I know what a party means; I belong to a weak one, the left socialist revolutionary.

But when one turns the switch, all the lights have got to go on at once. It can't be helped if some of the bulbs are a bit weak and, anyhow, big bulbs so often light up badly. So—party first . . . !"

"You'll keep them, then?" Enrique spoke with studied tonelessness, less to feign indifference than to show he was not trying to bias his companion.

"No."

The Commissar was more interested in decisions than in mental processes.

"Salud!" he said.

There was nothing to be done about it. True, Magnin had built up the air force, had found the men, had risked his life unsparingly, and had a dozen times engaged the squadrons he directed in adventures which he had no right to authorize. But he was not a member of the Party, and that settled it. His word weighed less than that of a gunner incapable even of taking down a machine-gun; and here was a man whom he esteemed for his worth and work, trying to force on him a fatuous line of conduct, just to gratify the least worthy whim of a Party comrade. Of course all that could be defended. And, there was no denying it, to Enrique's organizing ability they owed the best Spanish troops. After all, hadn't he himself acquiesced in Schreiner's dismissal? Action, he mused, always involves injustice.

Now the aerodrome was in almost complete darkness.

No, it was not in the cause of injustice that he had come to Spain.

Some distant gun-shots rattled across the flying-ground. How trivial all that was compared with the realities: villages going up in flames, the peasants streaming forth into the darkness from their blazing homes!

For the first time he was profoundly conscious of the loneliness of war, as he trudged across the flying-field, through the dry grass, walking towards the hangar where men were busy patching up old machines; men united in a spirit of fraternity.

Darkness, it seemed, would steal a march on Marcelino's homing plane—and night landings are not recommended for wounded pilots. The ground staff seemed lost in contemplation of the nightfall; but what they were watching in hushed suspense, under the tranquil menace of the dusk, was the unseen race between the airmen and the advancing night.

Attignies walked up, his eyes fixed on the crest-line of the hills.

"My dear Siegfried," Magnin said, "the communists are getting on my nerves."

The Spaniards and all his friends always referred to handsome, fair-haired young Attignies as Siegfried—but only among themselves. It was probably the first time he heard his nickname. He took no notice of it.

"Each time," he said, "I hear there's friction between the Party and a man like you—whose aims are ours—it distresses me profoundly."

Of all the communists in the squadron Attignies was the one whom Magnin held in highest esteem. He knew that Attignies was against Krefeld and Kurtz. He felt a need to speak out. And he knew that Attignies was fond of Marcelino, and, like himself, was on tenterhooks, waiting for his friend's return.

"I quite admit the Party is taking a wrong line about that matter," Attignies replied. "But are you quite sure you aren't a bit in the wrong as well?"

"An impulsive man, my son, is always a bit in the wrong." Magnin's tone was not patronizing but paternal. "There's something to be said for both sides, of course." He had no wish to air his grievances, but could not help adding: "Do you think I'm not aware how the communists have been attacking me ever since Kurtz has been busy on his dirty job of police-dog for the Party?"

"Kurtz isn't a policeman. He has been campaigning in Hitler's Germany. I shouldn't be at all surprised if the men who are putting up a fight in the Reich just now aren't the best of our bunch! The whole business is absurd, I grant you; but there's no help for it. Look here, as a revolutionary and a man of experience, can't you . . . well, can't you take it in your stride?"

Magnin reflected before answering. "If the men on whose side I'm fighting don't trust me, why go on fighting, my son? I might as well throw up the sponge."

"If your son is in the wrong, do you cast him off for that?"

It was Magnin's first experience of the deep, almost physical bond between the best communists and their Party.

"Jaime's in the plane, isn't he?" Attignies asked.

"Yes. He's the forward gunner."

Swiftly the dusk was deepening into night.

"Our personal feelings," the young man said, "even our lives are things of little importance in this war."

"Quite so. But if your father's in the wrong . . ."

"I didn't say, 'your father,' I said, 'your son.' "

"Have you a son, Attignies?"

"No, you have, haven't you?"

"Yes."

They took some steps side by side, watching the horizon. Would Marcelino never come? Magnin felt that his companion was about to speak.

"You know who my father is, Comrade Magnin?"

"Yes. I suppose that's why. . . ."

All the squadron knew what Attignies—the name was not his real one—believed a secret: that his father was one of the fascist leaders in his country.

"Friendship," he said, "doesn't mean being with one's friends only when they're right, but with them right or wrong."

Together they went up to Sembrano's quarters.

The beacon was ready and all available cars had been posted round the landing-ground with orders to switch on their headlamps the moment a signal was given.

"Better light up at once," Magnin suggested.

Sembrano looked dubious. "I'd rather wait, if you don't mind. If the fascists come this way, there's no point in having the ground lit up for them. Yes, I'd rather wait."

Magnin knew that it was merely superstition that made Sembrano prefer not to light up. Nowadays almost all the airmen had grown superstitious.

Every window was open; this was the hour when, before the war, the Superintendent of the airport used to call for his first whiskey. From the earth was rising the darkness of a late summer night.

Suddenly there was a general cry: "Lights on!" They had heard the sound of the plane signalling its approach.

Sembrano had turned on the alarm whistle at once, though neither he nor Magnin had yet caught sight of the plane. Judging by the sound it was on the far side of the buildings.

Midway between the short rays of the motor headlights the station beacon laid its long, pale beam across the field. Magnin raced down the stairs, followed by Attignies.

Below, all heads turned in the same direction told him whence the machine was coming. No one had actually observed its approach but now, guided by the sound, all caught sight of it as it turned to make its landing. The slate-grey sky was steadily darkening and the plane glided below it clean-cut as a paper silhouette; framed in a pale blue halo, it stood out like a building seen against the glare of floodlights.

"An outboard engine is on fire," someone said.

The plane grew larger and, ceasing to turn about, began gliding earthwards in their direction. The wings dwindled to straight lines and merged into the shadows massing upon the surface of the field. But now all eyes were gazing only at the shapeless mass of the fuselage on which the fierce blue flame of a steel-welder's blow-pipe seemed battening like some bird of prey. The landing was interminably protracted; planes freighted with the dead are slow to take the earth.

Magnin's fingers were nervously gripping the rims of his glasses. "The bombs!" he muttered.

Just as the machine touched earth, fuselage and flames interlocked in the last furious round of a struggle to the death. The body of the plane crashed down on to the flame which writhed and flattened out, then leapt up again with a hissing roar. Then the machine turned turtle.

Alert as death itself, the ambulance flashed by. Magnin jumped into it. The moment they saw how the plane would land, the Pelicans had started running towards it; the pilots followed, cursing. Now they were racing round the huge straight pillar of fire, their shadows veering from them like the spokes of a wheel. Once more the flames had spread out from the body of the plane, swathing it in a pale sheen of broken lights. The cockpit had snapped in two like a cracked egg. With the deft gestures of a doctor stripping a bandage off a wound, the Pelicans fell to rescuing the men within, peeling them off the wreckage with infinite precaution as if their blood had glued them to it. Carefully they worked but in feverish haste, alarmed by the ominous reek of gasoline. While extinguishers sprayed the flames, dead and wounded were carried to a safe distance. Their comrades huddled round them in a chequerwork of shadows; under the spectral glare the watchers moved like unquiet corpses guarding the quiet dead.

Three wounded and three dead, among them Marcelino. Six accounted for. Where was the seventh, Jaime? He emerged long after the others, clawing the air with shaky fingers, a comrade leading him. A tracer bullet had burst before his eyes. Blind.

By the feet and shoulders the airmen carried their dead to the mess. The van would come for them later.

Marcelino had been shot in the nape of his neck and there was little blood on his body. There still was beauty in the face, though the eyes had been left open and a ghastly light was playing on them.

One of the waitresses scanned his features.

"It takes an hour at least for the soul to begin to show," she said.

Magnin had seen death often enough to know the peace it engraves on many faces. When thoughts and cares vanish, wrinkles and crow's feet are smoothed away. Gazing at that face washed clean of life, but to which the open eyes and leather helmet still gave the illusion of the will to live, Magnin recalled the words he had just overheard, an opinion he had often encountered under many forms in Spain: only an hour after death does a man's true face show across the mask of life.

18

THE fascists were occupying a group of three farms; yellow roofs and stone fields nestling in a gully of white rocks. The first thing was to drive them out. There was nothing complicated in the task. The rocky nature of the ground along the Tagus, between Toledo and Talavera, enabled the militia to approach them from under cover all the way, provided they went about it methodically and carefully.

During the night Ximenes had asked for hand-grenades. The officer in charge of munitions was a German émigré, and at dawn Ximenes, all admiration for his promptitude, had seen the lorries rolling up, laden with—pomegranates! In German, as in Spanish, the same word serves for pomegranates and for grenades.

A little later, duly requisitioned for a second time, the grenades he wanted arrived.

One of Ximenes' companies was composed of *milicianos* with only a few days' service who had not yet had their baptism of fire. Ximenes had put his best non-commissioned officers in charge of them, and today was personally taking them in hand.

He began by putting them through a course of bomb-throwing. The Third Company—the company composed of the new recruits—betrayed its inexperience. One of the men, after lighting his bomb, kept it in his hands. "Throw it, you fool!" the sergeant yelled. It was just going to explode, blowing the poor devil to smithereens, when Ximenes' fist crashed against his elbow. The bomb exploded in the air and the man fell. Blood streamed down Ximenes' face.

The recruit had had luck; he was wounded in the shoulder only. After he had been bandaged and led off, those round began preparing bandages for Ximenes. He waved them away. "Let's leave turbans to the Moors. Get me some adhesive plaster." The effect was far less heroic; his face looked as if it had been patched up with postage-stamps. He took his stand beside the man whose turn for bomb-practice came next. There were no further accidents. Twenty incompetents were weeded out.

Under orders from Ximenes, Manuel had been exploring the terrain. His Party had been wise enough to attach him to one of the officers from whom he could learn most. The officer had taken a fancy to Manuel, who was amenable to discipline, not because obedience—or its counterpart, authority—appealed to him, but because it was natural to him and he liked efficiency. Moreover, he was a man of culture, and Ximenes appreciated him as such. The Colonel, whose ideas of communists were mainly based on lurid hearsay, was amazed to discover in the sound engineer (who was also a gifted musician) a born officer. He had not realized that the duties of a militant communist of the front rank demand strict discipline and great powers of persuasion. Manuel's experience as organizer, propagandist and man of action gave him the qualifications of a first-rate military leader.

The attack on the first farm began. The morning air was still; the leaves hung motionless as stone, save when now and again there came a breath of chill wind, an unexpected presage of the autumn. The *milicianos* carrying hand-grenades moved ahead in open formation, sheltering behind rocks and covered by their sharpshooters. The fascist position was rapidly becoming untenable. Suddenly, a band of thirty *milicianos* jumped onto the rocks and dashed forward in the open, yelling, with the reckless frenzy of a savage tribe.

"They've done it!" Ximenes crashed his fist down on the window-ledge of his car.

Already twenty men were sprawling on the rocks, huddled up or with their arms spread out. Some had their fists pressed against their faces as if to shield them. A pool of blood beside a fallen man spread slowly, glistening in the sun, over a flat rock that sparkled white and crystalline as a sugar-loaf.

Fortunately the other attacking parties on each side of the farm had already reached the rocks abutting on it. They had not seen their comrades falling. Under a hail of bombs the roof-tiles began spouting up like geysers, and the farm was taken within a quarter of an hour.

The new recruits had been detailed to attack the second farm. They had seen everything that happened.

Ximenes climbed onto the hood of his Ford.

"Listen, my lads," he said, "we've taken that farm. The men who disobeyed orders and left cover are dismissed from the column, whether they reached the farm or not. Don't forget that we're under observation. History is watching us, is judging and will judge us, and it calls for the sort of courage that goes in and wins, not the courage that consoles. . . .

"If you follow the line of advance we've shown you, you're in no danger up to two hundred yards' distance from the farmhouse. I'll prove it to you by going that far with you, in this car. We shouldn't have a single casualty before that.

"Then we'll start fighting, boys, and capture the farm. May Prov . . . luck be with us. May He who watches over everything . . . the Spanish people, I mean, see us through, since we're all fighting in a cause that we believe to be just."

He had selected the best shots in the regiment to accompany and cover the advance of the young bomb-throwers.

Before they reached the farms, they saw the fascists evacuating them.

During the previous week some fascist soldiers had come over to them; fifteen had been assigned to Manuel's company. A man named Alba was acting as their leader, though not elected to that post. His courage was undoubted, but he had a way of always finding fault; many suspected him of being a spy. Manuel sent for him.

They started walking among the rocks, Manuel leading the way, in the direction of the fascist lines. There were no definite front lines, but the enemy after retreating from the farms was known to have taken up a new position some two miles away.

Manuel asked: "Have you a revolver?"

"No."

Alba was lying—the way the man's trousers dragged at the belt was enough to tell Manuel that.

"Then here's one for you."

He took a revolver from his pocket and handed it to Alba, but kept at his waist his long automatic pistol, in its holster.

"Why don't you join the F.A.I.?"

"Don't want to."

Manuel scanned his face. The features looked puffed out rather than mature or manly, the nose was rounded and the mouth thick-lipped; there was a slight wave in the long hair clumsily plastered over the low-set forehead. Doubtless a "mother's darling" in his youth, Manuel surmised.

"You're a great grouser, aren't you?" Manuel said.

"There's lots to grouse about."

"There's lots to be done. If you, or I for that matter, were in Ximenes' shoes, things wouldn't be any better; no, they'd be worse. So we've got to help him at his job. After, we'll see."

"They might be a good deal worse, but at least we wouldn't have one of our class enemies bossing us—and that would suit me better."

"I don't care a damn what a man is; it's what he does that counts with me. Why, Lenin himself wasn't a worker. . . . But what I wanted to say was this: you can be very useful, and we must see that you pull your weight. Doing something, and not just grousing. Think it over, and then tell me which of them suits you. The F.A.I., the C.N.T., or the P.O.U.M.— whichever you like. We'll call a meeting of the comrades in your group, and you'll be given a responsible post. We're short of lieutenants. Have you been wounded?"

"No."

"I have—in a dynamite attack and a damn silly stunt it was. Catch hold, will you? This darned thing makes my hips ache." He took off his belt. "Every man has some hobby. Mine is fooling about with a piece of stick."

He moved to the roadside, snapped off a branch, came back to Alba. Unarmed now. For all he knew, the fascists were almost within earshot. And anyhow Alba was at his side. "Do you know, I rather doubt if you really belong here. Perhaps you never will. But *I* say: Give every man a chance!"

"Even if he's been excluded from the Party?"

Manuel halted, flabbergasted; he hadn't thought of that!

"If and when the Party issues formal orders on this point, I'll carry them out to the letter. But till then I say: Even a man excluded from the Party. In these times it's every able-bodied man's duty to fight for the Republic."

"You won't stay in it—in the Party."

Manuel turned to his companion with a smile. "I shall." He had a boyish laugh, but when he smiled the corners of his lips went down, giving a look of harshness to his rather heavy lower jaw. "Do you know what they say about you?" He kept on walking as if to show the question had little importance.

"Maybe . . ." Alba was still carrying Manuel's belt, and the holster rapped his calves at every step. And in this stony waste they were utterly alone. "Tell me"—a faint grin flickered on his lips—"what's your idea about it, what they're saying about me?"

"It's impossible to command men unless one trusts them." Manuel walked steadily on, flicking the pebbles from the pathway with his stick. "Fascists may manage it. We can't. If we can't trust our men, there's no point in what we're doing. The cynical outlook *plus* a taste for action makes a man a fascist, or a potential fascist—unless there's loyalty behind him."

"The communists always call the people who are against them fascists."

"I'm a communist."

"What about it?"

"And I don't hand over my revolver to fascists."

"Are you so sure?" There was a rather uncomfortable look on Alba's face.

"Yes."

There was no mistaking the man's embarrassment and Manuel's conviction that he was in no immediate danger left him. Obviously, he reflected ironically, one *would* feel embarrassed, talking to a man one's just going to shoot. So death was walking at his side, in the form of this self-opinionated youth with the plump, babyish cheeks.

"I've no use for those who like to command," Alba said.

"Very likely. But they're no worse than those who shirk taking it."

They were returning to the village. Though his every sinew was keyed up, Manuel was conscious of a feeling that was almost trust growing up between him and the man beside him; somehow it reminded him of the sudden gusts of affection or sensuality that came and went between his mistress and himself. "Must be like this one feels," he thought, "when one sleeps with a woman spy."

"The hatred of all authority as such," he said, "is a disease. A legacy from childhood. Something to get over."

"If that's so, what difference do you see between us and the fascists?"

"Well, for one thing, the idea of seventy-five per cent of our fascists isn't authority but—having a good time. Then, too, it's second nature with the fascists to look up to their leaders as beings of a superior race. The Germans don't believe in 'Race' because they're fascist; they're fascist because they believe in 'Race.' A fascist commands by divine right. That's why the question of trust doesn't trouble him as it does us."

Alba drew the belt tighter round his waist and said to Manuel, but without looking at him: "Look here, supposing you found you were all wrong about a fellow . . . ?"

"Spain's a country where just now dying is all in the day's work."

Alba's hand dropped on the hoster, opened it, half withdrew the revolver—slowly, but without concealment.

I've landed myself in a damn-fool situation, Manuel thought. Then, at the same moment: Still, it's not such a bad way to die. . . . Alba thrust back the revolver.

" 'All in the day's work!' You're right."

It struck Manuel that after all Alba might have drawn the revolver—to shoot *himself*. And, perhaps, there had been a touch of play-acting in the gesture.

"Think it over," he said. "I'll give you three days for it. Join up with any group you like. Or else do without Party support and take command of the men who don't belong to any party. I can guarantee you'll find it interesting, but that's your concern . . ."

"Why?"

"Because if you want to lead men, all sorts of men, you've got to know exactly what your own beliefs are. I don't know much about mine, but I'm learning. . . . Well, as I said, that's your own business. Mine's this: You've assumed a sort of moral responsibility among us, and now you must make it into a practical responsibility. And, needless to say, I shall check up on you. See?"

Had Alba said "No," Manuel would have sent him packing at once. But he said nothing. Did he acquiesce? He still seemed hostile.

In the village Manuel took back his belt and hitched it round his waist; then he laid his hand on Alba's arm and looked him in the eyes. "Have you understood?"

"Perhaps." Frowning, he walked away.

The sun was setting. The three captured farms had been fortified in a rough-and-ready way, and the *milicianos* who had broken cover in the first attack sent back to Toledo. Ximenes had issued his orders and, with a neat cross of adhesive plaster adorning his close-cropped temples, was walking with Manuel towards San Isidro, where the column was billeted for the night. Tessellated with loose pebbles, the road had the colour of a stone pavement, and up to the horizon everything was stone; the spiked branches of the prickly shrubs were hardly distinguishable from the yellow-fanged rocks.

Manuel was thinking over what Ximenes had just been saying in his address to the officers of the column. "In a general way, the personal courage of the leader is all the greater for the qualms he feels about his leadership. And remember it's far more important to get definite results than to set an example." Manuel walked slowly so as not to outpace the Colonel who was trailing his game leg. His waddling gait was another reason for his nickname of "Old Quack-Quack."

"The new men did very well, didn't they?" Manuel said.

"Not too badly."

"Well, the fascists cleared off without putting up a fight."

"They'll come back."

Ximenes, who was rather hard of hearing, had a habit of talking, almost to himself, as he walked.

"Yes, my boy, things are as bad as they can be; at Talavera they're using Italian tanks . . .

"Courage is a thing that has to be *organized;* something that lives and dies; you've got to keep it in condition, like a rifle. Personal courage is no more than the raw material of the courage of an army. Only one man in twenty is, through and through, a coward. Two men in twenty are naturally brave. One builds up a regiment by getting rid of number one, using the other two to the best advantage and training the remaining seventeen. . . ."

Manuel recalled an incident which had become legendary. Standing on the hood of his Ford in a village square, Ximenes had given a lecture to his men on the procedure to adopt when attacked from the air. An enemy squadron, newly arrived from Italy, had left Talavera for Toledo. "Think of the nozzle of a watering-can; that's how a bomb sprays when it explodes." The men were in a terrible state of nerves; seven enemy bombers, escorted by pursuit planes, were taking up formation before flying above the village square. Now, if the Colonel was deaf, the regiment could hear the engines only too distinctly. "I'd have you know that at such moments fear and rashness are equally absurd. Nothing less than a yard above the ground is hit. When a company lies flat, an air bomb wounds only the man directly underneath it." So that's how it is, his hearers thought, watching the sky and listening to the deep drone of the engines coming nearer every second. Even Ximenes' vast prestige could hardly keep them from dropping on their faces. (All of them knew how he had captured the Colon Hotel.) Then, suddenly, unblushingly, every nose jerked up at once; Manuel, without moving, was pointing skywards with his thumb. "On your bellies, everyone!" Ximenes roared out. Having already learned the movement, they scattered and were down in a trice, and the leading enemy bomber, now that the group had vanished from its bomb-sights, dropped its "pills" at random on the village. The others reserved their stock for Toledo. There had been only one casualty. Since that day, Ximenes' men had ceased being afraid of air-attacks. . . . The Colonel was still talking—almost to himself.

"War's a queer thing. For even the most callous general killing's a problem in economy; he expends the maximum of powder and shot so as to save up his human material as far as possible. But we're short of powder and shot. . . ."

Manuel knew that—from the incomprehensible Spanish Infantry Manual to Clausewitz and the technical French reviews—all that he had read had taught him merely the syntax of warfare, whereas Ximenes was its living tongue. Behind the village, campfires were lighting up. Ximenes gazed at them with an affection that was half bitterness.

"It's sheer waste of time discussing their shortcomings. Once an army has to take the field, something wrong with the troops always means something wrong with the staff-work. I've served in Morocco. When the Moors turn up at the barracks, do you imagine they're so magnificent? I grant you it's far easier to build up an army under military discipline; and I grant you we'll have to impose a 'republican discipline' on our men—or be wiped out, if we fail. But even at this stage—make no mistake about it, my boy—it's our defective staff-work that's at the root of our troubles. Well, our task is harder than our adversaries'; that's all there is to it.

"What your worthy friends, the communists—who'd ever have believed a year ago that one day I'd be taking a friendly walk with a Bolshevik?—what your friends are organizing, that

Fifth Regiment, even if it isn't up to the Reichswehr standard, is a damn good job. But when they're made into an Army Corps, where will they get their arms from?"

"That Mexican boat has reached Barcelona, I hear."

"Twenty thousand rifles . . . we've hardly any aeroplanes left. Hardly any field-guns. As for machine-guns—you've seen for yourself, on our right wing there's one for every three companies. When they're attacked, they pass it round. The fight isn't between Franco's Moors and our army (we haven't any) but between Franco and the organization of our new army. All the militia, poor chaps, can do just now is to get themselves killed so as to gain time for us. But where's the new army to get rifles, artillery, planes? It's quicker fixing up an army than a factory."

"Sooner or later"—Manuel spoke with conviction—"the Soviets will give us help."

Ximenes nodded, and took some paces without speaking. Russian help—that was something more serious than taking a stroll with a Bolshevik. He had expected everything from France; now he had lost that hope. But Russia? Were the Russians to be the salvation—or the ruin—of his country? A last ray of sunlight played on his close-cropped hair starred with the plaster cross. Manuel watched the lines of campfires spreading out. Slowly night was descending on the world of men, making their never-ending struggles seem infinitely vain, lost in the spate of darkness, the massive indifference of the earth.

At last the Colonel spoke. "Russia's a long way off."

The countryside along the road had been lavishly bombed by fascist planes, but many of the bombs were duds. Manuel picked one up, unscrewed the cap, and took out a small type-written note. He passed it to Ximenes who read, in Portuguese: *Comrades, this bomb won't burst. That's all for the present.*

It was not the first of its kind.

"Well, that's fine!" Manuel exclaimed.

Ximenes did not care to show his emotions. "What have you done about Alba?" he asked abruptly.

Manuel described their conversation.

The stony waste seemed sinking back into the abject desolation from which daylight had temporarily rescued it. And whenever a certain aspect of the rocks brought back to Ximenes' mind his childhood, he thought of his youth. "Soon," he said, "you'll have to start training young officers. They want to be beloved. That's only human. And it's an excellent thing, my boy, provided you get them to grasp this: an officer should be liked for the way he uses his authority—because he's more competent, more just, better than the average—not for his personal charm. Do you see what I mean when I say an officer ought never to play up to his men?"

Manuel called to mind the revolutionary leader's task: it struck him that to make oneself loved without courting popularity is one of the finest careers a man can hope for.

They were near the village; the flat, greyish houses seemed clamped upon a hollow in the cliffs, like thumb-tacks along a fissure in a tree.

"Yes, it's a most dangerous foible, wanting to be loved." Ximenes sounded half in earnest, half in his "quack-quack" mood. The heel of his game leg crunched heavily on the pebbles at regular intervals. For a while they walked on in silence; the hum of insects had died out of the air. "It takes more nobility to be a leader of men," the Colonel added, "than to be oneself; and it's far harder . . ."

They had reached the village.

"Good day to you, my children," Ximenes called in answer to the cries of welcome. The troops were encamped east of the village, which was practically empty and which they had not occupied. A crenellated château faced the village church.

"Tell me, Colonel, why do you call them 'my children'?"

"You mean I ought to have called them 'comrades'. I can't do it. I'm sixty; it's beyond me, I'd feel I was play-acting. So I call them 'boys' or 'my children'; and it does just as well, you know."

They were walking past the church. It had been set afire; this was the Tagus front. From the open porch came a musty, cavernous smell mixed with an odour of dead ashes. The Colonel entered. Manuel stared at the façade.

It was one of those Spanish churches, in a style at once baroque and popular, to which the use of stone instead of Italian stucco gives an almost Gothic aspect. The flames had burst forth from the interior and great black tongues of smoke gone writhing up the walls from every lintel, to flatten out under the feet of the topmost statues, charred and tottering above the void.

Manuel went in. The whole interior of the church was

black and littered with scraps of twisted iron-work; the shattered pavement was a mass of sooty wreckage. Peeled to a chalky whiteness by the flames, the plaster statues in the aisles loomed tall and pallid at the foot of the smoke-grimed pillars; on the frantic gesturings of the saints hovered the mist-blue evening light that streamed in from the Tagus through the broken porch. Deeply impressed, Manuel felt himself an artist once again. What savage grandeur was in those convulsed statues, that somehow had outlived the holocaust! It was as if the flames had set them dancing in the church and their agony had given birth to a new school of art, the school of fire.

The Colonel seemed to have vanished. Manuel's eyes were seeking him too high; he was kneeling among the embers, in prayer. Though Manuel knew that Ximenes was a Catholic, he was none the less dumbfounded. He left the church and waited for his friend outside. For a while they walked in silence.

"Will you allow me to ask a question, Colonel? How do you come to be with us?"

"You know I was at Barcelona. Well, I got a letter from General Goded summoning me to join in the rebellion. I thought it over for five minutes. True, I'd never taken an oath of loyalty, but I knew that in my heart I'd pledged myself to serve the Government. So I had no trouble in making my decision; still I didn't want to be left with an impression later on of having acted on a sudden impulse. After those five minutes' thought, I went to Companys and said: 'President, the XIIIth Tercio and its Colonel are at your disposal.' "

He gazed once more at the church. In the quiet evening, fragrant with the scent of hay, it seemed fantastically incongruous with its torn façade and charred statues outlined against the sky.

"Why," he murmured, "oh, why must people always confound the sacred cause of Him who at this moment watches us, with that of His unworthy ministers . . . Of those among His ministers who are unworthy?"

"But, Colonel, who but those unworthy ministers you speak of have made Him known to them?"

Silently, with a slow gesture, Ximenes led his eyes towards the peaceful countryside around them.

"Here's a case in point," Manuel continued. "Once in my life I fell in love. Head over heels—in dead earnest, I mean. Well, it was as if I were up against a brick wall. I might have been that woman's lover, but it wouldn't have made an atom of difference—there was a barrier between us, the Spanish Church. I loved her, yes, and when I think about it now I feel as if I'd been in love with a madwoman, a sweet and childish cretin! Look, Colonel, just look at this country. What has the Church reduced it to? A sort of beastly second childhood! What has the Church taught our women? Two things only: To obey and to procreate . . ."

Ximenes stopped short on his wounded leg and, puckering his eyes, gripped Manuel's arm.

"My boy, if you'd made that girl your mistress, very likely she'd have developed brains! And, I suppose, the nobler a cause is the more scope it offers to hypocrisy and lies."

Manuel went up to a group of peasants, gaunt black forms against a wall that glimmered whitely in the twilight.

"Look here, comrades,"—his voice was cordial—"that schoolhouse of yours isn't much to look at. Why didn't you convert the church into a school as they did in Murcia, instead of burning it?"

The peasants did not answer. In the growing darkness the statues on the church were disappearing. The two officers saw before them a row of unmoving forms, black smocks and wide-brimmed hats along the wall; the peasants' faces were invisible.

"The Colonel would like to know exactly why you burnt down the church. What precisely have you got against your priests here?"

"Why are the priests all against us?"

"That's not it. Why are *you* against them?" As far as he could judge in the darkness the peasants were feeling, above all, perplexed; could they really trust those two officers? Their questions might have something to do with the protection of works of art.

"There isn't a single comrade here, that's done his bit for the common folk, who hasn't had the priests against him. That's how it is!"

The peasants blamed the Church for having persistently backed the upper class, condoned the punitive measures which had followed the revolt in the Asturias, approved of the spoliation of the Catalonians, and always taught the poor folk a meek submission to injustice, while now the Church was sponsoring a Holy War against them. One of them disliked the priests' voices "because they don't talk like proper human beings"; many resented the harshness or hypocrisy—according to their rank—of the men the priests employed to bolster up their influence in the villages. All were indignant that, in the conquered villages, the priests had denounced to the fascists those who were "irreligious," knowing full well that this consigned them to the firing squad. And all reproached the clergy for their wealth.

"Yes, that's so," one of the peasants muttered. "That's how they are. Just now you were asking about the church, why not turn it into a school? Well, my kids—they're my kids, and it isn't always too warm here in the winter. But sooner than have my children in that there building, I'd see 'em frozen stiff!"

Manuel handed the man a cigarette and clicked on his lighter. The speaker was a typical peasant, clean shaven, in the forties. The tiny flame lit up for a moment the face of the man beside him, a face shaped like a kidney-bean, the ill-defined nose and mouth slotted between a projecting chin and forehead. Asked for reasons, they had produced them; but what rang truest was the last speaker's voice.

Another voice came from the darkness, another peasant speaking. "And I say they're frauds, the whole lot of 'em."

"You mean it's money they're after?" Ximenes asked him.

"Every man's after the main chance. Those fellows say they're not, I know . . . but that's not it; I mean they're frauds deep down. It's something you can't explain. Yes, they're humbugs."

"Those priests! People who live in cities don't know the first thing about them!"

Dogs had begun barking in the distance. Another man spoke up, raising his voice a little.

"He was sentenced to death by the fascists, was Gustavito." His tone implied: And there's no more fooling him! And suggested, too, that all were hoping he would voice an opinion.

"Don't make no mistake." The new speaker was presumably Gustavo. "Collado and I, we're Christian folk. But we're against the priests, there's no denying it. Only, as it happens—I *believe*."

"That's the kind he is! He'd marry his daughter to Saint John of Compostella if he could!"

"I'd rather see her on the streets, by God I would!" Then went on in the slow voice of a peasant trying to explain himself.

"The fascists opened a door, you know. They shoved a poor

devil out, who cried 'What!' Then it started all over again. We
never heard the firing squad. The priest's bell, we heard that
all right. When that bastard started ringing, we knew what it
meant; one of us was in for it! Try to make us confess. To give
us absolution, says he. What for, I'd like to know? For defending ourselves against the generals? I heard that bell ringing
away for a fortnight. Then I says to myself: 'Those pardons
are a racket.' I know what I'm talking about. It isn't only a
matter of money. Now listen! What does a priest tell you when
he's confessing you? He tells you to repent. If so be there's a
single priest who got a single one of us to repent for having defended himself—well, nothing's too bad for him. Because re-
pentance—it's about the best thing a man has in him. That's
the way I see it."

Ximenes remembered Puig.

"Collado there, he's got something to say."

"Spit it out!" Gustavo commanded.

The peasant kept silent.

"Come along, man! Out with it!"

"One can't talk like that, to order," replied the man who
had not yet spoken.

"Tell us the same yarn you told us yesterday. Give us a
sermon."

"It ain't a yarn. . . ."

There was a clatter of rifles in the darkness. Some *milicianos*
were approaching. The darkness was now complete.

"All that fuss"—he sounded sarcastic—"because I told 'em
the King had once passed through the Hurdes' country. On a
hunting party. Those folks are nearly all goitrous, half-witted,
sick. And so poor, the King couldn't believe it possible to be so
poor. It's made dwarfs of them. So he says: 'Let's do something for these poor folk,' and his people said, 'Yes, sire,' as
usual. But not a thing was done, as usual. Then, as it was a
miserable sort of place, they found a use for it; they put the
penitentiary there. As usual. Then . . ."

The clear enunciation, the way he spoke, betrayed a man
accustomed to speaking in public, despite the sometimes rustic
turn of phrase. Though the man hardly raised his voice at all,
Ximenes caught every word.

"Then Jesus Christ thought, 'That isn't as it should be,' and
he says to himself, 'I'll go there.' The angel looks around for
the best of the women thereabouts, and one day he appears to
her. She says, 'Don't trouble, Lord. The child will come before

its term, seeing I'd not have enough to eat. There's only one man on our road has had a bite of meat this last four months; he killed his cat.' "

Already the tone of irony had given place to a fierce rancour. Ximenes knew that in some parts of Spain there were *improvisatori* who delivered homilies at the vigils for the dead, but he had never come across one till now.

"So Christ went to another woman. Round the cradle there was only—rats. Nothing much to keep the baby warm, and cold comfort for a friend. So Jesus thinks to himself: 'Things are as bad as ever in Spain.' "

From the centre of the village came the sound of lorries and grinding brakes, mingling with distant gunshots and the barking of dogs. A smell of smoke and stone drifted to them from the gutted church. For a while the rumble of lorries drowned the speaker's voice.

". . . and compelled the landlords to lease their farms to peasants. All the cattle-owners let off a howl saying they were being dispossessed by rat-owners. And called in the Roman soldiers.

"So Our Lord went to Madrid, and, to shut His mouth, the kings of the world began slaughtering the children in Madrid.

"So then Christ says to Himself: 'There's nothing to be done with mankind. They're that foul that even bleeding for them night and day throughout eternity wouldn't suffice to wash them clean.' "

The rumble of lorries persisted. They were waiting for Ximenes at the Commissariat. As the man went on speaking, Manuel was at once impressed and irritated.

"The descendants of the Wise Men didn't attend His birth, seeing as they'd all gone a-roaming—or settled down in government jobs. Then, for the first time on earth, from every land, men who lived near by and men who lived thousands of miles away, men from countries where it's hot and men from countries where it freezes—all who were brave and unhappy shouldered their guns and started marching, marching, marching . . ."

In the voice there was a note of loneliness so intense that Ximenes knew, despite the darkness, that the speaker had closed his eyes.

"And they understood in their hearts that Our Lord was living there, among the poor and oppressed ones of the earth. And so, from the ends of the world, they marched in, all who knew poverty well enough to die fighting against it; some had guns, and those who hadn't guns had their hands anyhow, and one after the other they came and lay down on the soil of Spain.

"They spoke all languages; why, there were even Chinese shoelace-sellers among them."

The voice sank lower still; the orator was speaking through his teeth, huddled up like a man with a belly-wound in the darkness. A ring of heads—Ximenes' among them, with its plaster cross—clustered round him.

"And when the slaughtering had gone too far and the last company of the poor had set out on the march . . ."

Each word was rapped out with the low-voiced intensity of a sorcerer's incantation.

". . . a new Star rose above them."

Manuel dared not kindle his lighter. The motor-horns on the lorries were baying in the darkness, with the frenzy of cars wedged in a traffic-jam.

"That's not the way you told it yesterday," a voice broke in.

Then Gustavo's voice, louder. "I haven't no use for such notions; once you start in with them, you don't know what you've got to do. Got to know what one wants, that's the only way."

"You're wasting your breath." A slow, resigned voice. "Those townsfolk don't know nothing about priests, and there's no help for it."

"They think it's got to do with religion."

"I tell you—those folk just can't understand."

"What was his job before the rebellion?" Ximenes asked.

"The man who was speaking?"

For a while there was an embarrassed silence. Then, "He was a monk," a voice replied.

Manuel led the Colonel off in the direction of the blaring horns of the cars.

"Did you see Gustavo's badge when you lit the cigarette?" Ximenes asked as they walked away. "The F.A.I., I suppose."

"That or another, it would be all the same. Personally, I'm no anarchist, Colonel. But, like all the rest of us, I was educated by the priests. And, do you know, there's something in me—though, as a communist, I'm against any form of destruction—that understands that man."

"Better than the other man?"

"Yes."

"You know Barcelona," Ximenes said. "On some churches there, instead of the usual notice, *Under the People's Management,* I saw *Owned by the People's Vengeance.* And yet . . . ! I remember how on that first day the dead were left lying about in the Plaza Cataluña. Two hours after the firing ceased the pigeons were back in the Square as usual, hopping about the pavements, over the corpses. And one day man's hatred burns itself out." He added in a slow, meditative tone as if he voiced the culmination of many thought-tormented years. "God, anyhow, has time to wait. . . ."

Their riding-boots crunched on the hard, dry soil, Ximenes' wounded leg still lagging a little behind Manuel's stride.

"But why," the Colonel murmured, "why must His time of waiting mean . . . all this?"

19

ANOTHER effort at mediation was impending. A priest was due to reach Toledo during the night and presumably he would enter the Alcazar next morning.

The gas-lamps in the little Square were out and the only light came from a hurricane-lantern hung rather low in front of the El Gato tavern. Attracted by the cat on the signboard of the inn, Slade took a seat at a table near the door and whiled away the time playing the shadow of his pipe at different angles on the wall of Toledo Cathedral.

Till two o'clock in the morning Slade was able to get wires through to his newspaper. Lopez should be back from Madrid well before that hour. It was he who had been deputed to bring the priest. A first-rate story in prospect, Slade thought. It was not ten yet. The utter solitude gave the Square, with its flights of steps and tiny palaces topped by the russet foliage of trees, the glamour of a stage-setting, to which somehow the last gun-shots up at the Alcazar added a touch of eerie unreality. A vision rose before his eyes of palaces forlorn in far-off India, with palm-trees sprouting in the rose-red halls, and in the emptiness huge radio sets bringing the din of distant war only to the ears of apes and peacocks. The stench of corpses in Toledo was like that of an Asiatic swamp. "Are there radios on the moon?" he wondered. "Wouldn't it be something if waves were carrying these vague sounds of battle to the dead stars . . . ?" The abandoned Cathedral, still undamaged and at this moment seething, most likely, with *milicianos,* gratified at once his dislike for the Catholic Church and his love of art.

Voices came to his ear; people talking inside the tavern.

"Our planes gave them a nasty jolt today. The fascists got their machine-guns into the bull-ring at Badajoz—that couldn't be helped—but only under the roof, not out in the open as they'd hoped."

"We'd better be careful about the barracks; they've put the prisoners inside them."

Another voice joined in, ironical, with a strong English accent.

"After the fight there was some excitement on the Plaza, I can tell you. I could see it—I was only five hundred yards away. Every woman was looking her youngest and prettiest, and guess what they were asking? 'Who's that pretty little Scotch boy up there?' "

Slade was still taking notes when at last Lopez appeared. Lopez with his regal mien, arms uplifted, and shock of hair all quivering like a cockscomb. He sat down heavily, lifted his hands again, and dropped them with a resounding smack upon his thighs. The brisk sound jogged the silence; some gunshots followed up the echo. His little hat pushed back on his head, Slade waited for his friend to speak.

"They're asking for priests. Well, they shall have their priests. But, good God . . . !"

"Do you mean they're asking you for priests, or is it you who're asking for your hostages?"

Lopez assumed the air of a man who has been through a trying day and had his fill of it.

"But don't you see it's exactly the same thing, you owl? They're asking us for priests. That's their affair. But, at the same time, these bastards don't want to evacuate the women and children. Neither ours nor theirs. That suits them fine, and they know it. . . . Well, as it happens, I know some priests, two of them. So I phoned to Madrid: 'Mobilize those two priests. I'll be along at two o'clock.'

"I suppose they think they're to be found at every street corner, priests who haven't cut and run. . . . Well, I went to Madrid. To begin with, no damned way of getting in touch with Guernico; he was out with his ambulance corps. At last I got the address of priest number one—a real good sort, by the way. He often used to visit the prison when we were there, in 'thirty-four. I rolled up to his place with four *milicianos*— we were all in our *monos*. The whole house was Catholic—the tenants were Catholic; the janitor was Catholic; the windows were Catholic; the walls were Catholic—every niche had its plaster saint. The motor hadn't died down before they started a racket, yelling on every floor. The fools thought we'd come to shoot them. I tried to explain to the janitor. No good. He had massacres on the brain, of course. When he saw our car roll up, the priest scampered across the garden. That disposed of number one."

The pale glamour of the moonlight seemed to have deserted the little square. As usually happened, wherever he might be, Lopez's presence made itself felt.

"As for priest number two, I knew he was in touch with the militia general staff. When I got to headquarters, the officers were eating. I called up a pal and told him what I was after. 'Right,' says he, 'I'll have your priest for you at four o'clock.' I had a hell of a lot to do, plaguing everyone for munitions all over the place, but I got back at four.

" 'You know,' my pal told me, 'the priest was there all the time, eating with us, but I wanted to give him fair warning. Looks as if you'd have some trouble getting him; he's backing out, the priest.' Backing out, was he? 'Those lousy swine, so they won't even do their jobs,' says I. Then they explained to me he was a canon at the Cathedral, one of the higher-ups, a big shot in the ecclesiastical hierarchy. If he'd been a country priest, he wouldn't have made such a fuss, it seems. As a matter of fact, I don't know much about country priests; sculpture isn't in their line, I guess. 'Right,' says I, 'I'll have a word with him. If there's any way of getting the kids out of this god-damned war, we've got to find it.' I was bone dry, so I hopped down to the beer cellar and no sooner had I turned the door-knob, than what do I see but a guy without a collar, in a filthy shirt and striped trousers, yanking at the beer-taps—and there at last was His Reverence, my priest."

"A young man? Old?"

"Badly shaved, and the stubble on his chin was white. Fattish. An ugly mug, but looked a good scout in his way. His hands—I'd have liked to draw them. I told him what was up —you know the way I put things. Well, his answer took ten minutes! Here, if a guy takes ten minutes to say what he could say in half-a-minute, we call him a faker—and he was a faker.

I said something to him, I don't remember what, and he says: 'That's the way soldiers talk, I know the style of it.' They must have told him I had a rank of sorts, though I was in a *mono*— without a badge of any kind. 'An officer like you!' That's what he said to me, to a poor devil of a sculptor! So I said: 'Officer or not, when I'm given orders to go to a spot and fight, well, I go. You, you're a priest; there's people over there who need you, and I want to save the kids. Are you coming or aren't you?' He hesitates a bit, then his voice gets serious. 'Do you guarantee me a safe conduct?' I'd had my bellyful of him by then. 'When I came here two hours ago,' I says, 'you were packing in the grub with the soldiers; what do you think, do you think they're going to eat you in Toledo for their dinner?' We both were sitting on the table. He stood up and struck a pose with his hand on his waistcoat. 'If you think I can save a single life I'll go.' 'Good,' says I. 'You look all right to me. Now, if you're going to save lives, you've got to do it mighty fast. The car's outside.' 'Don't you think maybe I'd better put on a coat and collar?' he asks. 'Well,' says I, 'personally I don't give a damn, but the others might like it better if you had your cassock on.' 'I haven't one with me.' I didn't know if it was true or if he was being prudent; most likely it was true. Anyhow he went off and a few minutes later I found him waiting by the car, in a collar, black tie, and alpaca coat. So off we go!"

A long gust of languid wind filled the air with a strong smell of burning; the smoke from the Alcazar was drifting down into the Plaza. And, now that the stench of rotting corpses was obliterated, Toledo seemed another city.

"They kept on stopping the car to check our papers. 'I should say it's a hard job getting out of Madrid, these days,' he said. Sounded to me as if he'd been thinking it over. All the time we were driving here, he couldn't seem to get away from trying to explain to me the Reds might quite as likely be in the right as the Whites, 'perhaps even more so,' and to find out just how the interview would be fixed up. 'It's a cinch!' I kept on telling him every few minutes. 'Just like we went about it with Captain Rojo. We tell them you're here; then we take you to the escort guard. They bandage your eyes and then they bring you to the office of the Commander of the Alcazar, Colonel Moscardo. Once you're there you can shift for yourself.' 'To Colonel Moscardo's office?' he repeats. 'Yes,' I says, 'Moscardo's office.' And so we were all set.

"Me, on my part, I tried to hammer into his head that he must refuse absolutions, baptisms and all the rest of it, if Moscardo declined to release the women and kids."

"He's promised to see it through?" Slade asked.

"To hell with his promises! If he feels like doing it, he'll do it. Otherwise his promise isn't worth a busted button! Anyway I did my best, but I expect I bitched it up. We reached Toledo. We went to the battery and I shouted to the Captain. *'Cojones!'* he bawls out, jumping on the running-board before I could get a word in. 'Where are the shells? They promised to send them today—tomorrow night we'll have run out of ammunition.' I wigwagged like a windmill for him to shut up. No matter how little a priest knows here, it's that much too much! No luck! At last the fool of a Captain understood. I introduced them. 'The priest—a comrade.' The Captain points at the Alcazar tower, all shot to pieces and standing on its last legs, and smacks his thighs. 'Looks pretty sick, old Moscardo's office, don't it?' There was a big triangular hole in it. 'Really, my dear Major,' says my priest—yes, we'd got that intimate— with the mulish look on his mug that kids have when they've plotted to play hooky, 'do you really expect me to have my interview with Colonel Moscardo in a place like that? For one thing, how on earth am I to get there?' 'That's for you to find out!' yammered the Captain. 'But I know God himself would have a tough time getting through that muck!'

"Well, it was getting better and better, but I finally made him understand we'd be able to fix it up somehow with Moscardo. The priest is catching a nap just now. I've got three sentries guarding him."

"Tell me," Slade asked. "Will he go, or will he back out?"

"Tomorrow at nine. There's a truce till noon."

"Any news about the kids?"

"Not a word. Well, it's up to the big shots and the would-be big shots to explain it all to my little priest. I hope they don't scare the pants off him! There's one tattooed guy among the anarchists—he's a nightmare!"

"Let's go and see what's happening up there."

Silently they trudged up to the Zocodover Square, pausing on the way to admire the *Terror of Pancho Villa* whose hat looked even handsomer by night. The higher they climbed, the more crowded the street. On the top stories of some houses rifles and machine-guns were keeping up an intermittent fire. Slade had been here three months earlier; here at

this same hour at night he had then heard the clatter of an
unseen donkey's clogs and a party on their way back from a
serenade merrily thrumming the *International* on their guitars.
Lit by the searchlights, the Alcazar loomed up between two
roofs.

"Let's go up to the square," he said. "I'll get my writing
done inside the tank." The newspaper men had got into the
habit of taking refuge in an old tank, which was rarely used,
bringing a candle with them and writing by its light.

At last they reached the barricade. On the left some *milicianos* were firing their rifles; others, on the right, lying on mattresses, were playing cards. Others were grouped round a
radio, taking it easy in wicker arm-chairs and listening to an
Andalusian folksong. Over their heads, from the second floor
of a neighbouring house, sounded the pit-a-pat of a machine-
gun. Slade walked up to the barricade and, peeping through
a chink, had a clear view of the square.

Completely empty, flooded by the rays of a powerful arc-
lamp, the city square, where in days of old Kings of Castille
on horseback fought with bulls, looked even eerier than the
Cathedral precinct. The reek of burning, mingled grotesquely
with the dewy fragrance of the night, brought to mind the
atmosphere of some dead planet rather than any spot on earth.
The fierce light of a film studio played on ruins like the wreckage of a temple of the East, on a gaunt archway, on derelict,
bullet-scored shop-fronts. On one side lay, singly or linked in
skeins of metal ribs, the chairs of an abandoned restaurant.
Above the houses flared an immense Vermouth poster, bristling with Z's; in corners of shadow glimmered the rooms where
look-out men kept vigil. Immediately in front, searchlights
bathed the narrow streets converging on the hill-top in a vivid,
theatrical effulgence, and at the end of each street, more
brightly floodlit than ever it had been for the tourists' benefit,
smouldered the Alcazar, extraordinarily squat against the dark
immensity of the sky.

Now and then a fascist fired a shot and Slade's eyes wandered from the card-players to those who fired back at the
enemy. Some of them, he supposed, had wives and children
up there in the Alcazar. At nightfall the peasants had brought
out their brown, country-made rugs; striped like the mattresses
on the barricades, they patterned the whole city in a curious,
piebald symmetry.

A mule came out into the main street. ("At midnight,"

Slade thought, "they'll exchange the mules for zebras, to carry on the pattern.") In front of the antiquated tank, the turrets of armoured cars, lit up within, fretted the shadows with little squares of light. The window of a milliner's shop near by was almost as bright as if its lamps were on and an old woman in a feathered bonnet was gazing in rapture at the display of hats, in the best provincial style, lit up by reflections of the search-lights raking the Alcazar.

Now and then an enemy bullet rapped the shield of a ma-chine-gun. Lopez started back to staff headquarters. When Slade entered the tank, the gunner made room for him. No sooner had he taken out his note-book than the gunner opened fire and, simultaneously with him, the armoured cars and marksmen. A machine-gun firing in a turret can make an in-fernal racket, and suddenly all the people in the street seemed to go frantic with excitement. What was happening? Slade jumped down from the tank. Was it a counter-attack from the Alcazar?

The fascists had just sent up a Verey light, and every marks-man in Toledo was blazing away at it.

20

THE priest had been in the Alcazar for half an hour. Journal-ists and various local officials were strolling slowly behind the barricade waiting for the appearance of the enemy represent-ative. In his shirt-sleeves, his hat well back on his head, Slade was walking with Pradas, a communist official, Golovkin, a Russian journalist, and a Japanese newspaper man. Every few steps he threw a rapid glance through the openings in the barricade. But nothing except the upended café chairs was to be seen in the square, as yet. The stench of death and that of burning came in alternate gusts as the wind veered about.

A fascist officer appeared at the corner of one of the little alleys issuing from the Alcazar. He went back, and once more the square lay empty. But now the emptiness was not oppres-sive as in the floodlit nights. The place seemed to have been deserted only for the moment; daylight had given it back to life, the life that had been only waiting like the fascists and *milicianos,* at each street corner, to re-enter it.

The truce had begun. But, having been so long an area no

combatant could cross without attracting enemy fire, the
square had a bad name. At last, however, three *milicianos*
decided to enter it. Some parts of the Alcazar had been captured, and in them had been found, so rumour said, mattresses
under archways and packs of cards, exactly like those used by
the militia manning the barricade. None the less the Alcazar,
if only because it was the enemy, had kept its mystery intact.
The militia knew they would not be able to enter it during the
truce, but they wanted to approach it anyhow. Still the little
group, walking across the square, was careful to keep in touch
with the barricade.

"Both sides are itching to be at each other's throats," Slade
thought as he peeped through a gap between the sandbags; the
sacking on which his forehead rested was already warming up,
his hat was farther back than ever. "Rather like cats, they
are!"

A group of fascist officers had just come out opposite him,
at the place where the first had disappeared. Confronted by
the empty square, they hesitated. *Milicianos* and fascists stared
at each other, unmoving. Some more *milicianos* crossed the
barricade. Slade adjusted his field-glasses.

He had expected to see anger on the faces of the fascists;
but all he could make out (he could not see their faces at all
clearly) was a look of embarrassment, accentuated by the
stiffness of their gait and, above all, the movements of their
arms, which the close-fitting uniforms made particularly
noticeable. The *milicianos* approached them.

Slade turned to a man who was peeping through the next
loophole. "What do you make of it?"

"Our fellows can't bring themselves to speak."

When men have been trying to slaughter each other for two
months, it is not easy for them to start talking to each other.
What made them keep their distance, what caused some to
slink beside the pillars and the others along the barricade was
less the mutual taboo of no-man's land than the idea that if
they approached each other they would have to speak.

More fascists came out of the Alcazar, more *milicianos* left
the cover of the barricade.

"Four-fifths of the garrison are Civil Guards, aren't they?"
Golovkin asked.

"Yes," Slade replied.

"Notice how they're dressed? They're only letting officers
come out."

As if to prove him wrong, just then some Guards appeared in yellow-braided uniforms, cocked hats—and incongruous white canvas shoes.

"The militia seem to have killed off boots," Slade observed.

Meanwhile conversations had sprung up in the square, though the groups took care to stand at least ten yards apart. Slade lit his pipe between two sandbags and walked towards them, followed by Golovkin and Pradas.

The two groups were slinging insults at each other.

The sight was all the quainter because each gesticulating group kept its distance, as if the intervening space were forbidden ground, and volleyed repartee without moving a step forward.

". . . because we, anyhow, are fighting for an ideal, you bastards!" they heard a fascist shouting as they came up.

"What about us? I suppose we're fighting for our moneybags, you son of a bitch? Your ideal, eh? Ours is a finer one than yours, seeing it's for everybody on earth."

"To hell with an ideal that's for everyone! It's only the *highest* ideal that counts, don't you know that much, you ignoramus?"

They had been sniping at each other for the last two months; now they kept up a war of words, for lack of an alternative. And yet . . .

"Say, call that an ideal, dropping gas on the Abyssinians? And throwing the German workers into concentration camps? And paying farm labourers a peseta a day? Do you call the massacre at Badajoz an ideal, you bloody butcher's boy?"

"Russia—call that an ideal?"

"What about it?"

"For those who haven't been there, perhaps. The worker's republic! A hell of a lot it cares for the workers!"

"Yes, I suppose that's why your bosses hate it! If you've a scrap of honesty, you can't deny that everything that's rotten in the world is on your side. And everything that's out for justice is on ours, even the women. Show us your militia-girls if you can. You're a policeman, not a god-damned prince. Say, why are the women on our side?"

"The women! They'd better keep their mouths shut, eh, you pimp! That's a good joke when people who burn churches start talking of ideals."

"If there weren't so many, we wouldn't have to burn them."

"Too many churches lined with gold, and too many villages with no food."

Slade, who was near the *milicianos*, felt vexed at being reminded of the futile altercations of Paris taximen and Italian cab-drivers.

A man beside him asked: "Who's that fellow?" pointing to Golovkin. Slade had been seen about with Lopez on the previous evening and so was looked on as a "comrade."

"Correspondent of a Soviet newspaper."

Golovkin had the prominent cheekbones and gnarled face of the peasants one sees on Gothic carvings. When Slade had visited Moscow on an assignment, he had been struck by the likeness between the Russians, so near their peasant origin, and the Western Europeans of the Middle Ages. "I look like an Indian," he thought; "that Russian like a field-labourer, and those Spaniards—like horses!"

The three *milicianos* who first had left the barricade had halted side by side without moving across the square. The others were still comparing "ideals."

"Anyhow," one of the fascist officers shouted, "it's all very well talking about an ideal when one sleeps at home every night as you do: what about us who have to live in a damned dungeon? You're living on the fat of the land. We haven't even got a cigarette to smoke."

"What's that?"

A *miliciano* crossed the forbidden area; a C.N.T. man, with one sleeve rolled up on an arm blue with tattooings. Almost vertical, the sun cast round his feet the shadow of his huge sombrero, and he seemed gliding forward on a black pedestal. A packet of cigarettes in his hand, he marched towards the fascists, as if he meant to strike them. Slade, who knew that Spanish etiquette forbids a man to proffer a packet of cigarettes, waited to see what he would do. He took the cigarettes one by one and handed them round, still looking black as thunder. The cigarettes seemed tokens of an attitude—as if he had said to the fascists: "You're right to kick about cigarettes. If you bastards haven't any, that's the fault of the war. You're a lot of filthy swine but we got nothing against them." He seemed to be calling the windows to bear witness as he doled out the cigarettes; when his packet was empty, the other *micilianos* who had joined him continued the distribution.

"What do you make of this damn-fool behaviour?" Pradas

asked. Pradas brought to mind a Mazarin who had pointed his beard in an attempt to look like Lenin.

"At one of the most heated sessions of the Belgian Parliament I saw all the parties join like one man to throw out a tax on carrier-pigeons. Eighty per cent of the members were pigeon-fanciers. Here there's a free-masonry of smokers."

"Ah, but it goes deeper than that, you know."

One of the fascists had shouted: "Well, anyhow, you get your morning shaves!" What made the remark still odder was that few of the militia were clean-shaven.

One of them, again an anarchist, started running back towards the town. The two journalists followed him with their eyes; he stopped to speak to a *miliciano* standing beside the barricade. The latter fired his revolver in the direction of the fascists, then started gesticulating with it as if he were indulging in a furious tirade. The anarchist went on his way, still running.

"Was it like this in Russia?" Slade asked Golovkin.

"We'll discuss that later . . . It's beyond me!"

The *miliciano* came back with a box of Gillette blades, opening it as he ran. There were at least a dozen fascist officers. Suddenly he halted, obviously perplexed; there weren't enough blades to go round. He made as if to throw them, as one throws sweets to a group of children, then hesitated; finally he handed the box, with an angry look, to the nearest officer. The other officers crowded round the man who held the box; but when the *milicianos* began laughing, one of them rapped out an order and they separated. Just then another fascist came from the Alcazar, and from the far side of the square, the man who had fired his revolver when the anarchist was passing came up and joined the group.

"That's all very fine, all this," he began, staring at each fascist in turn. Then he paused. The others waited for his silence to end. "But what about the hostages? My sister's up there, I'd have you know." There was a world of hatred in his voice; no question now of bandying "ideals."

"A Spanish officer has no right to question the decisions of his superior officers," one of the fascists answered. But the reply failed to take effect, for just then the last fascist to arrive spoke.

"I want to see the commanding officer, on behalf of Colonel Moscardo."

"Come along," said a *miliciano*.

The officer followed him. Slade and Pradas also followed, looking absurdly small beside the huge bulk of Golovkin. The crowd was growing denser, and by the way they moved might well have been the usual throng of idlers of a Sunday afternoon—had not all eyes been riveted on the Alcazar.

Hernandez was coming out of the bootshop, followed by the Negus, Mercery and two lieutenants as the fascist officer reached the door. The latter saluted and held out some letters.

"From Colonel Moscardo, for his wife."

Suddenly Slade had a feeling that all he had been seeing during the last twenty-four hours at Toledo and before that, at Madrid, had found its ultimate expression in those two men eyeing each other with languid hatred amid the reek of burning and the smoke pouring down from the Alcazar in trailing shreds like wisps of tattered flags. The cigarettes, the razor-blades had led up to those letters; so, too, had the hostages, the absurd barricades, the storming-parties and retreats and, when the reek of burning lifted for a moment, the stench of dead horses that seemed the normal odour of the soil.

Hernandez shrugged his right shoulder—a familiar gesture—and handed the letters to a lieutenant, conveying to him where to go with a jerk of his long chin.

"Of all the damned fools!" the Negus exclaimed, but his tone was cordial.

Hernandez shrugged both shoulders for a change but always with the same languid air, and signed again to the lieutenant to go.

Pradas steadied his glasses on his nose. "Is Moscardo's wife in Toledo?" he asked.

"No," Hernandez replied. "In Madrid."

"At liberty?" Slade's voice conveyed his amazement.

"In a nursing home."

This time the Negus shrugged, but in anger.

As Hernandez went back to his bootshop-headquarters, Slade could hear a busy typewriter within disturbing the silence of the truce. Startled by the sudden lull in the gunfire, dogs were beginning to venture forth into the steep streets. As in peace-time, a cheerful sound of steps and chattering voices filled the town. Pradas caught up the Captain and took a few paces by his side.

"What's the idea of sending on that letter?" he asked, tugging his little pointed beard. "Just courtesy?"

His brows were knitted and he sounded baffled rather than sarcastic. The Spanish officer seemed lost in contemplation of the shadows of the broad-brimmed hats stippling, like huge confetti, the cobbled roadway.

At last Hernandez answered him: "Generosity." And turned on his heel.

"Know that Captain well?" Pradas asked Slade. His eyebrows had not yet straightened out.

"Hernandez? No."

"What on earth prompted him to do that?"

"What should prompt him—to do otherwise?" Slade replied.

"That!" Golovkin pointed to a more-or-less armoured car that was passing by. On the roof lay the corpse of a *miliciano*. Judging by the way it was disposed, it was the body of a friend whom the men in the car were bringing home. The journalist tugged at the ends of his bow tie; a sign, with him, of uncertainty.

"Does that happen often?" Golovkin asked.

"Fairly often, I believe. The officer commanding here has sent on other letters of the kind."

"A regular officer, eh?"

"Yes. So's Hernandez."

"What's the woman like?" Pradas asked.

"That's your nasty mind!" Slade grinned. "I've never seen her, but I understand she's no chicken."

"Then why on earth . . . ? Or is it just Spanish solidarity?"

"Do you get any satisfaction out of big words like that? I suggest you go on to Santa Cruz, where he's lunching. You can wangle an invitation easy enough, and talk with him about it. You'll find some communists there, too."

Noticing the *Terror of Pancho Villa* strolling among the crowd, Slade realized that Toledo was a small town in wartime as well as in peace; that now he would come across the same odd characters at every moment whom in the past he used to see day after day; the selfsame guides and pensioners.

"On the fascist side," he said, "an attack is never made between two and four, because of the siesta. . . . Don't draw any hasty conclusions about what's happening here."

Almost intact on the side towards the city, the barricade of sandbags and striped mattresses was pocked like worm-holed timber on the side facing the Alcazar. Smoke-clouds were spreading everywhere a pall of shadow, and the houses burn-

ing their hearts out tranquilly as ever. And in the perfumed
lull another house began to smoulder close by the Alcazar.

21

Two tables at right angles occupied a corner of a room in
Santa Cruz Museum. Some jovial spirits were larking about in
the semi-darkness. Sunbeams squeezing through holes in the
brickwork flashed on the rifles slung across their backs, and
glinted on the sweating faces. Round them were heaps of
fruit and branches, and the air reeked with the characteristic
Spanish odour of crude olive-oil. Squatting, the *Terror of
Pancho Villa* was repairing rifles.

Hernandez' attitude was all the simpler as his bent back
hardly lent itself to soldierly postures, but the men of his escort, at the other table, were self-consciously martial. None of
the wounded men had changed his bandage. "Blood-proud,"
Pradas remarked. Golovkin and Pradas had planted themselves opposite Hernandez, who was talking to another officer.
With one fleck of light upon his forehead, and a second on his
undershot jaw—which gave him the look of one of Cortez'
compañeros—Hernandez seemed more of another epoch than
of another nationality. All the *milicianos* were dappled with
specks of light.

"Comrade Pradas here belongs to the technical committee
of the Party," Manuel said by way of introduction.

"I know."

"Look here, do tell us exactly why you sent on that letter,"
Manuel said continuing the previous conversation.

"Why did the men hand round those cigarettes?"

"That's just what interests me," Pradas grunted. A pinhead
of light glinted on his beard; he had just put a hand behind his
ear.

Did the curious gesture mean that he was hard of hearing?
But the hand was not steady; he began stroking the back of
his ear with it, like a cat washing itself. Hernandez answered
Manuel with an indifferent flick of his long fingers. Fitful
waves of sound from radios blaring outside under the blazing
sun seeped through the bullet-holes seeming to swirl around
Pancho Villa, who had fallen asleep among his rifles under the
fantastic hat.

"The Soviet comrade"—Pradas capped his head with his hand—"says this: 'In my country Moscardo's wife would have been arrested immediately. I want to know why you don't take the same line.' "

Golovkin knew French, and could understand Spanish a little.

"You been in prison?" the Negus asked.

Hernandez made no remark.

"In Czarist days I was too young."

"Fight in the civil war?"

"In the Service Corps."

"Got any kids?"

"No."

"Say, Negus," Slade broke in, "have you any kids yourself?"

"I . . . used to."

Slade dropped the subject. Pompous, Mercery oracled: "Generosity does honour to great revolutions."

"But," Pradas insisted, "our people's children are in the Alcazar."

A *miliciano* served up a superb ham garnished with tomatoes and cooked in olive-oil—Slade's pet aversion. The Negus, too, declined it.

"What!" Questions of cuisine always interested Slade. "You, a Spaniard, don't like *aceite?*"

"I never eat meat."

Slade picked up his fork; it was stamped with the arms of the archbishopric. Everyone was eating. In the ultra-modern showcases of the Museum—glass, chromium steel, and aluminum—all the exhibits were in perfect order, except certain small objects that bullets had reduced to dust; in front of each of these was a neat round hole starred out across the glass.

The Negus turned to Pradas. "Listen to me! When a man comes out of prison, nine times out of ten his gaze doesn't . . . doesn't *settle;* see what I mean? He's lost the way of looking at people like a man. In the proletariat, too, there's lots of folks can't look at people steadily. That's all got to be changed, to begin with—see?"

The words were meant for Golovkin as much as for Pradas, but he did not relish having Pradas translate them.

"Yes," Slade murmured with satisfaction. "I always knew that guy didn't have the 'big head.' "

One of the militia came up to him with a cardinal's hat in his hand. "We've just found this contraption. As it's no use to the community at large, we thought we'd make you a present of it."

"That's nice of you," Slade smiled. "I've noticed that good scouts—shaggy dogs and children and what they call extremists—usually like me . . . but not cats, woe's me! Thanks." He put the hat on his head, stroked the pompoms and went on eating his ham. "They remind me of the ball-fringe at my old grandmother's out in Iowa City. Around the bottom of the arm-chairs. Thanks."

The Negus pointed his stubby forefinger at a Crucifixion in the Bonnat manner, glimmering against a pitch-black background. It had been exposed to the enemy gunfire for several days. A cluster of bullet-holes almost severed the right arm; the left, protected by the stonework of the wall, had only a few punctures. A burst of machine-gun fire had stripped the body from shoulder to hip, forming a sort of bandolier, neatly picked out like a seam made by a sewing-machine.

"Even if we're beaten here and at Madrid," the Negus said, "at least the men will have given their hearts a few days' run. See what I mean? In spite of hatred. They're free today. They've never been that before. I'm not thinking of political freedom, but another kind. See what I mean?"

"Quite," Mercery put in. "That's what Madame Mercery always says: It's only the heart that counts."

"At Madrid things don't look so cheerful." Slade's voice was calm under the big red hat. "Still, you're right. During a revolution life takes a holiday. My today's article will be called, 'On Leave.' "

Pradas slid his hand up to the summit of his pear-shaped head. There had been a noise of chairs drawn aside, and he had missed Slade's last remark. They were making room for Garcia who had just come in smiling, a pipe stuck in the corner of his smile.

"It isn't so easy for men to hit it off together," the Negus went on. "That's sure. But there's not a great deal of courage in the world; and it's courage gets things done. Let's not fool ourselves! When men are ready to give up their lives for something, they sort of stand out from the rest. But we've no use for 'dialectics' or red tape; delegates are all right, but bureaucrats never! Or an army to defeat the army, or inequality to stamp out inequality, or playing the bourgeois' game. What we are out for is to live the way men ought to live, right now and here; or else to damn well die. If we fail, there's an end of it. No return ticket for me!"

Garcia's keen, squirrel-like eyes began to twinkle. "My dear old Negus," he said in a cordial tone, "when one wants to make the revolution a way of living, for the mere fun of it, it usually becomes a way of dying. And in that case, old fellow, one ends up by being as satisfied with martyrdom as with victory."

The Negus raised his right hand; the gesture of Christ addressing his disciples. "A man who's afraid of dying has an uneasy conscience," he said.

"And meanwhile," Manuel remarked, lifting his fork reprovingly, "the fascists are in Talavera. And, the way things are going, you'll lose Toledo."

"In the last analysis," Pradas announced pedantically, "you are Christians. And while . . ."

There, thought Garcia, he missed a good opportunity to keep his mouth shut.

"Down with the priests!" The Negus sounded exasperated. "But there's something in theosophy."

"No," Slade put in, toying with the pompoms on his hat. "But go on!"

"We're not Christians, not at all! But your lot are turning into a priesthood. I don't say communism's become a religion; but I do say that communists are turning priests. For you, being a revolutionary means just—being cleverer than the next fellow. It wasn't like that with Bakunin or Kropotkin— not by a long shot! You're soaked in the Party, in discipline, in plotting and scheming. If a man doesn't belong, you don't give him a square deal; you've not a scrap of decency towards him. You've lost even your loyalty. Look at us now! We've had seven strikes since 1934, just out of solidarity; not because we stood to gain a thing by them."

Anger had loosened the Negus's tongue, set him gesticulating and his hands fluttering round his fluffy crown. Golovkin had lost the thread of his harangue, but a phrase caught here and there alarmed him. Garcia said a few words to him in Russian.

"Concretely speaking, it's better to be disloyal than incompetent," said Pradas.

The Negus took out his revolver and laid it on the table.

Garcia laid down his pipe in the same position.

The room looked like a gigantic still-life, with the myriad pin-point rays piercing the shot-scarred wall caught by the plates and alembic-shaped carafes, making them sparkle like fireflies in the gloom. Fruit gleamed along the branches and a bluish sheen hovered on the squat, sleek barrels of revolvers.

"All arms are needed for the firing line," Manuel quoted.

"When soldiers were needed," Pradas said, "we were soldiers. Then, when organizers were needed, we were organizers. Yes, we've had to be all things in turn; engineers, factory managers and the rest of it. If, in the last analysis, we've got to be priests, well—damn it!—we'll be priests. But, mind you, we've built up a revolutionary state, and now we intend to build up an army. Concretely. With our qualities and our defects. And it's the army that will save the Republic and the proletariat."

"And me," Slade said suavely, both hands grasping the pompoms round his hat, "I don't give a damn! But what you do, all of you, is much more to the point than what you say. You guys are all too intellectual, that's how it is. And that's the trouble with your country, Golovkin; everybody's brainy, top-heavy with brains. That's why I'm not a communist. The old Negus, now, may be a little cockeyed, but I like him."

The tension in the air relaxed. Hernandez glanced at his watch again then smiled. His teeth, like his face and hands, were remarkably long.

"It's the same thing in every revolution," said Pradas fingering his beard. "In '19, Steinberg, a revolutionary socialist and commissar of the courts of justice, asked that the Peter-and-Paul Fortress should be permanently closed. Thereupon Lenin got his majority to vote that the White prisoners should be confined there; we had enough enemies of that sort behind the lines. In the last analysis, 'nobility' is a luxury no movement can indulge in—in its early phase."

"But the sooner it does, the better," Mercery said, emphatically.

The Negus spoke again. "Tomorrow there'll be free shaves all round, eh? . . . Nonsense! Parties are made for men, not men for parties. We don't want to build up a state or a church or an army. Just men."

"And I'd have them start behaving decently whenever the occasion arises," Hernandez said, clasping his long fingers in front of his chin. "We've enough ruffians and murderers who try to tag along with us."

"See here, comrades!" Mercery said. "You can't have it both ways. If we win, History will reckon up against the men we're fighting that business of the hostages, and honour us for Madame Moscardo's liberty. Whatever happens, Hernandez, you've given a fine, a noble example. In the name of the League of Peace and Justice to which I have the honour to belong, I take off my . . . *képi* to you."

Since the day of the flame-thrower attack when they first had met, Garcia had been puzzled by Mercery's personality. Must idealism, he wondered, always involve play-acting? Yet he discerned in Mercery an underlying sincerity; an authentic asset for the cause of anti-fascism.

The Negus was on the warpath again. "And don't go about pretending to take the 'anars' for a gang of lunatics. Spanish syndicalism has done some first-rate work during the last few years. Without compromising our principles, what's more. We haven't a hundred and seventy million men behind us, like you; but, if the worth of an idea is to be judged by the number of its supporters—well, there are more vegetarians in the world than communists, counting in the Russians. What about the general strike? It works, doesn't it? *You* were against it for years. Read your Engels again, that'll teach you. The general strike, that's Bakunin. I once saw a communist play with some 'anars' in it. Know what they looked like? Like the bourgeois idea of the communists."

From their shadowy background, the statues of the saints seemed to be egging him on with their ecstatic gesturings.

"It's wisest to go slow with generalizations," Manuel said. "The Negus may have had some—er—unfortunate experiences. Every communist isn't perfect. Except for our Russian comrade—I've forgotten his name. Sorry!—except him and Pradas, I believe I'm the only member of the Party sitting at this table. Look here, Hernandez, do you take *me* for a priest? Do you, Negus?"

"No. You're a decent sort! And you don't mind fighting. There are plenty of decent fellows among you. But there's the other sort as well."

"Another thing. You talk as if you'd a monopoly of honesty; and if anyone doesn't see eye to eye with you, you call him a bureaucrat. But you know as well as I do that Dimitroff's no bureaucrat. Dimitroff against Durruti; well, it's one set of principles against another—not a combination of the two against all morality. We're comrades; let's be honest with each other."

"Wasn't it that Durruti of yours who wrote: 'We're ready to relinquish everything but victory'?" Pradas asked the Negus.

"Yes," the Negus snapped at him with his prominent teeth. "Yes. But if Durruti came your way, he'd give you a good kick in the arse!"

"I'm afraid you'll very soon discover," Pradas observed, "that, concretely speaking, that moral code of yours has no utility for practical politics."

"No more has any other moral code," a voice put in.

"And yet the trouble about the revolution," Garcia said, "perhaps its tragedy, is that it can't get on without one."

Hernandez raised his head. On Manuel's knife a tiny spot of light was dancing; he was eating sunlight.

"There's one thing to the credit of the capitalists," the Negus went on. "A mighty good thing, too. In fact, what beats me is how they hit on it. I guess it's up to us to fix up something of the sort for each of the unions here, when the war's over. Yes, I take off my hat to them for that: the way they use the 'unknown.' The 'Unknown Soldier,' that was their stunt. We can go one better. On the Aragon front I've seen lots of graves with a plain F.A.I. or C.N.T. on a stone or a bit of wood. No name. I felt . . . well, I guess that was all right. At Barcelona when the columns going up to the front marched past Ascaso's grave, they all kept silent; that was right, too. Better than shootin' out one's neck."

A *miliciano* came to fetch Hernandez.

"Christians . . . !" Pradas mumbled in his beard.

Manuel stood up. "Has the priest come out?"

"Not yet. The commanding officer's sent for me."

Hernandez went out, followed by Mercery and the Negus. The latter picked up his cap—not the Mexican sombrero of the previous day but the red-and-black *képi* of the anarchists. There was a brief silence, broken only by the desultory noises that accompany the ending of a barrack-room meal.

"Can you tell me why he forwarded that letter?" Golovkin put the question to Garcia who, he felt, was the most respected by all, including even the Negus. Moreover, he spoke Russian.

"Let's take it point by point. Point one: he didn't care to refuse; parental authority sent him into the army; for many years he's been a Republican officer—out of liberalism—and he's more or less an intellectual. Point two: don't forget he's a regular army officer (there are others here) and that tells, whatever his political feelings are about the other side. Point

three: we're at Toledo. You know how every revolution is inclined to melodrama in its early stages; Spain just now is . . .
a Mexican colony."

"And what about the other side?"

"The telephone wire between our headquarters and the Alcazar hasn't been cut and both sides have been using it since
the siege began. During the recent parley, it was understood
that Major Rojo should be our spokesman. Rojo had been an
Alcazar cadet. He was led in blindfolded. When the bandage
was removed he found himself at the door of Moscardo's
office. You've seen what the left-hand wall looks like from
outside? Just one great hole. There was no ceiling to the office.
Moscardo in full uniform sat in his desk-chair; Rojo in the
chair he used to sit in. On the back wall, which was undamaged, just above Moscardo's head, hung—would you believe it?—Azaña's portrait; they'd forgotten to take it down."

"What about the morale of the troops?" Golovkin asked in
a lower voice.

"You better ask someone who's been in closer contact with
them than I have. Just now the Assault Guards are our best
troops. Manuel!" He translated Golovkin's question into Spanish. Manuel squeezed his underlip with his fingers.

"Mass courage in the field," he said, "can't stand up against
planes and machine-guns. The truth is that, well-trained and
armed, the militia is brave enough, otherwise they cut and run.
With enough *milicianos* and enough columns we can build up
an army. To give it courage is a question of organization. The
question is: Which men and how many will consent to being
'organized?' "

"Now that Captain," Pradas said, "don't you think, that as
a regular officer, he may feel some . . . attachment for the
cadets?"

"We had it out together. He tells me there aren't fifty cadets
all told in the Alcazar. That's true; it's garrisoned by Civil
Guards and officers. The 'young heroes defending their ideal
against an infuriated populace' are mainly—Spanish police-
men. So be it!"

"Tell me, Garcia, how do you explain what happened in the
Square?" Manuel asked.

"I think that the fellow who doled out the cigarettes and
the one who brought the razor-blades, and the others who
followed suit, and Hernandez when he took the letter—I think
all of them were yielding, without knowing it, to the same

impulse: the wish to prove to the men up there that they've no right to despise them. I dare say that sounds rather like a joke; but I'm in earnest. What separates the Right and Left in Spain is the taste for, or the horror of, humiliation. The Popular Front stands, among other things, for a combination of all the people with a horror of it. For instance, let's take the case of two impecunious *petits bourgeois* in a village before the rising. The one on our side was all for cordiality; the other for arrogance. The desire for fraternity on the one hand and, on the other, the cult of hierarchy are very definitely up against each other in this country—and in some others, too, perhaps."

Manuel distrusted the psychologist's views on such subjects, but he remembered the words of old Barca: "The opposite of humiliation, my lad, is not equality; it's fraternity."

"When I'm concretely informed," Pradas put in, "that under the Republic wages have been tripled and, as a result, the peasants have at last been able to buy themselves shirts; and when I hear that the fascist Government has restored the old wages and, as a result, thousands of newly opened shops where they sold shirts have had to close—then I understand why the lower middle class in Spain is with the proletariat heart and soul. 'Humiliation' wouldn't bring even two hundred enlistments."

Garcia was getting to recognize the pet expressions of the various parties; thus "concretely" was typical of the communists. He also knew the mistrust that Pradas, and even Manuel, felt towards psychology. His personal view was that the outlook of the anti-fascist struggle should be guided by economic consideration; but he also considered that, economically speaking, there was no difference between the anarchists (and their friends), the socialist masses and the communist groups.

"I quite agree, my friend. Still, it isn't from the Estremadura backwoods where people live on acorns that we get our best soldiers or the most recruits. But, for goodness' sake, don't ask me to work out a theory of humiliation as a stimulus of revolution. I am trying to understand what happened this morning, not the general situation in Spain. Concretely, as you'd put it, Hernandez isn't a shirt-merchant—even in a figurative sense.

"No, Captain Hernandez is a plain, straightforward man for whom the revolution means a way of realizing his moral aspirations. For him the dramatic times in which we live are a personal apocalypse. What's most dangerous about these semi-Christians is their desire for self-sacrifice; they'll indulge in the worst follies provided they pay for them with their lives."

To one section of his audience Garcia seemed all the more intelligent because they often had to guess what he was driving at.

"Obviously," he continued, "the Negus isn't a Hernandez. But between the liberal and the libertarian the difference is only one of terminology and temperament. The Negus told us his people were always ready to give up their lives. That's true of the best of them. Note that I say, 'of the *best* of them.' They're carried away by a fraternity which they know quite well is bound to take a different form one day. And they're quite willing to die after some crowded hours of ecstasy . . . or of revenge, in certain cases; dramatic hours in which their dreams come true. Don't forget what he said about their 'hearts' being in it. And, for them, a death like that justifies everything."

"I haven't much use for the sort of man who has himself photographed with a revolver pointing at the camera," Pradas remarked.

"Yet he's often the same man who on the eighteenth of July scared the rich folk into handing over their arms, by sticking his fist in his pocket to look like a revolver."

"The anarchists . . ." Pradas began.

"Anarchists," Manuel took him up, "that's only a label, and usually a damned misleading one. The Negus is a member of the F.A.I., I grant you. But, when all is said and done, what matters isn't what his comrades think; what matters is that millions of men—yes, millions—who aren't anarchists think as they do."

"Think as they think about the communists, you mean?" Pradas grinned.

"No, my friend," Garcia protested. "Not that. Think as they think about the struggle and about life. Ideas they have in common with, let's say, our French friend, the Captain. And, mark you, I found just the same spirit in Russia, in 1917; and, less than six months ago, in France. It's the adolescence of revolution. Yes, it's high time for everyone to realize that the masses are one thing, and parties are another—a fact that's been apparent ever since the eighteenth of July." He raised his pipe-stem to emphasize the words. "Nothing is harder than to make people think about what they're going to *do*."

"Yet that's the only thing that counts," Pradas said.

" 'Doomed to change . . . or to perish,' " Golovkin quoted in a sombre tone.

Garcia fell into a brown study. For him the term anarcho-syndicalism consisted of two opposed elements. The positive element was the syndicalist activity of the anarchists; the negative element, their ideology. Once the glamour was ruled out, anarchist theory fell absolutely into line with syndicalism; the more enlightened anarchists took their stand on Sorel's teachings, not on theosophy. Yet today's argument, from beginning to end, seemed to have been based on the assumption that anarchists were a race apart; that anarchism was to be defined in terms of *character*, that Garcia should have studied them in his capacity of ethnologist, and not as a political thinker.

"And to think that throughout Spain," he mused, "at this very hour exactly the same things are being said, most likely, at every luncheon table! How much better they'd employ their time hunting for some basis of co-operation, so as to implement the orders of the Government by joint action between the various groups, communist, C.N.T., F.A.I., and U.G.T.! It's odd the weakness people have for arguing about anything and everything rather than the practical line of action to be followed, even at a moment when their lives hang on the line they choose. Well, I suppose I'll have to tackle each of those fellows separately and see what can be done."

A *miliciano* who had just accosted Manuel came up to him. "Comrade Garcia, isn't it? You're wanted at the Jefatura. Madrid calling."

Garcia got in touch with Madrid.

A voice on the phone: "What about the negotiations?"

"The priest's not back yet. The time given him will be up in ten minutes."

"Call us as soon as you know anything. What are the prospects?"

"Bad."

"Very bad?"

"Just bad."

22

HERNANDEZ, who knew that Garcia had been called to the telephone, was waiting for his return at the Museum.

"One remark of yours particularly struck me. You said that, though a moral code is no concern of practical politics, it can't get on without one. Would *you* have had that letter forwarded?"

"No."

The click of rifles coming to the half-cock, the flash of canteens in the midday sun, and the smell of corpses, brought so vividly to mind the tumult of the previous day that an ending of hostilities seemed unbelievable. There were less than ten minutes to run before the truce expired, and already peace was getting to seem a romantic memory. Hernandez' long, loping steps glided beside Garcia's brisk, emphatic stride.

"Why?"

"For one thing, they haven't given back the hostages. For another, once you've accepted responsibility, it's up to you to see it through. That's all."

"But—I had no choice about accepting it. I was an officer and I'm doing my job."

"I tell you, you accepted it."

"How on earth could I have refused it? You know how short we are of officers."

For the first time the city took a siesta unbroken by gunfire, and lay plunged in an uneasy sleep.

"What's the point of the revolution if it isn't to make men better? I'm no proletarian, Major. As a slogan 'the proletariat for the proletariat' means as little to me as 'the bourgeois for the bourgeois.' But, all the same, I put up as good a show as I can—got to, you know!"

"Will the revolution be brought about by the proletariat or by the—the Stoics?"

"Why not by the most humane element of mankind?"

"For the simple reason, my dear fellow, that the most humane people don't stand for revolution. They stand for public libraries and . . . cemeteries. More's the pity!"

"A cemetery doesn't prevent an example from being worth the making. Quite the contrary."

"But meanwhile, we have—Franco!"

Hernandez caught Garcia's arm, with an almost feminine gesture. "Listen, Garcia. Let's drop the game of trying to put each other in the wrong. You're the only person I can talk to. Manuel's a decent fellow, but nowadays he sees things only from the Party angle. The enemy will be here in a week's time, you know it even better than I. That being so, whether I'm right, or you're right . . ."

"No!"

Hernandez looked towards the Alcazar; no move had been made as yet.

"And yet," he said, "if I'm to die here, I'd have liked . . . conditions to have been different. Listen! Last week one of my men—a comrade of sorts, who is or claims to be an anarchist —was accused of having rifled the company cash-box. He cited me as a witness. I gave evidence in his favour. But it seems that this man had been imposing the collective system on a village which was in his charge, and his comrades were beginning to extend that system to neighbouring villages. I quite agree that the whole idea was a bad one, that it's infuriating for a peasant who needs a sickle to have to sign a dozen forms before he gets one. I admit, too, that the communist method of dealing with such matters is the best.

"But ever since I gave that evidence, they've had it in for me. It can't be helped—damn it, I'm not going to have a man who cites me as his witness and who I know to be innocent labelled a thief."

"The communists—and all who want to get things going properly just now—consider that the fact your friend's an innocent man doesn't prevent him from playing into Franco's hands, if what he does leads to unrest among the peasants. The communists, you see, *want to get things done.* Whereas you and the anarchists, for different reasons, want to *be* something. That's the tragedy of a revolution like this one. Our respective ideals are so different; pacifism and the need to fight in self-defence; organization and Christian sentiment; efficiency and justice—nothing but contradictions. We've got to straighten them out, transform our apocalyptic vision into an army—or be exterminated. That's all."

"And, I suppose, people who have the same contradictions in their own hearts have got to be exterminated, too. That's all, as you say."

Garcia was thinking of Golovkin's view: "They've got to change—or die."

"Many men," he said, "hope to find in the apocalypse a solution of their own problems. But the revolution pays no heed to those innumerable drafts drawn on its future, and carries on."

"You think I'm under sentence of death, eh?" Hernandez grinned. There was no irony in his grin. "Anyhow suicide's a restful prospect." He pointed to the pre-war posters of films and vermouth above their heads and the grin broadened showing his long teeth, making him look like a dejected horse. "One's past . . ." he paused, then added: "But—to come back to Moscardo—I, too, used to have a wife."

"Yes?" Garcia said. "But we've not been hostages. Moscardo's letters, all you've told me—each of the problems that we're up against is a moral problem. And when one's life is linked up with a moral code, it's always a bit tragic. No less in a revolution than in other circumstances."

"And to think one believes just the opposite; till the revolution actually happens."

In the ravaged gardens roses and box-trees seemed to be sharing in the brief lull of truce.

"It's quite likely, Hernandez, that you're on the way to meet your . . . destiny. It's never easy to give up what one has loved, all the things one's lived for. I'd like to help you; but the cause you're staking on is doomed from the outset. Because you have to live politically, you have to act in terms of politics; and your duties as an officer bring you every moment into touch with politics. Whereas the cause you have in mind is not political. It is based on the contrast between the world in which you live and the world of your dreams. But action can only be envisaged in terms of action. The business of a political thinker is to compare one set of hard facts with another, one practical proposition with another; our side or Franco's; one system or another system. He is not fighting against a dream, a theory, or another apocalyptic vision."

"It is only for a dream's sake that men die."

"Hernandez, the habit of thinking about what ought to be instead of what can actually be done is a mental poison. For which, as Goya said, there is no antidote. The man who stakes his life on such a cause is bound to lose. It's a fool's game, my dear fellow. Moral uplift and magnanimity are matters for the individual, with which the revolution has no direct concern;

far from it! I am very much afraid the only link between them, as far as you're concerned, is the prospect you may lay down your life in the cause of both. You know Catullus: 'Neither with you, nor without you . . .'"

A dull boom of gunfire, the shrill scream of a shell, an explosion, a tinkle of falling tiles and rubble. A field-gun had opened fire on the Alcazar.

"The priest has failed," Garcia said.

23

YAGUE'S army was marching from Talavera on Toledo.

Citizen Leclerc, in a repulsively sloppy white flying-suit, with his grey cloak over his head and his thermos flask under his arm, was approaching the open door of the plane.

"Good God, what fool's been messing around with my 'Orion?'" he said in his hoarsest voice, as though it were himself that he was taking to task.

"That's all right, that's all right," Attignies said calmly as he slipped on a sweater. "I've fixed up a sight for you."

"Perfectly all right with me in that case," Leclerc answered condescendingly.

Leclerc disliked Attignies. He disliked his youthful earnestness, and he disliked his manners, which in spite of the latter's cordiality jarred on him as upper middle-class. He disliked his fund of knowledge (Attignies had been a military cadet), and his austere communism, though Attignies was far from making austerity a rule of life. And while the volunteers felt a debt of gratitude to the technicians, of the mercenaries, like Leclerc, they felt jealous. And Leclerc was obsessed by women.

He started up the engine.

Pelicans and wounded men were moving round the machine; Raplati came trotting after Scali. Jaime still came regularly to the aerodrome, blind though he was, his face straddled by a bandage. Some of the doctors said that he would get his sight back. But he had become unable to bear the presence of a dog near him. House likewise spent the whole of his time at the aerodrome, hobbling on two sticks, imperious, delivering himself of words of wisdom and instructions; he had become intolerable since his wounds had cloaked him with authority. Sibirsky had left Spain.

Ever since the Pelican Squadron had fallen back on night-flights as the only means of continuing their resistance, the atmosphere of the aerodrome had changed. The enemy pursuit planes were ruled out by these tactics; landing at night in the open country is not the easiest sort of joy-ride, but neither is landing on the wrong side of the lines in the daytime. Destiny, not combat, was now the decisive factor. If cavalry troopers feel the limitations of their horses in time of war, at least their horses are neither blind nor threatened daily with paralysis; but for these airmen the enemy was not so much the fascist army as the engines of the planes in which they flew, patched like old trousers. The war had resolved itself into an endless succession of night-flights in machines endlessly repaired.

The plane took off; rose through the clouds.

"Say, young man?"

"Well?"

"Take a look at me. I may spend all my time fooling around. But I'm a man!"

He did not like Attignies, but every airman on active service respected courage, and Attignies' courage was beyond question.

They went beneath the clouds again.

Listening to the reassuring yet constantly precarious throbbing of the engine, with his grey cloak over his head, Leclerc's feeling of godlike freedom took him back to the Great War, back to China; it was a freedom greater than sleep and war, greater than pain and passion.

A pause. Then, in the tone of a decision following ripe reflection, Leclerc said:

"You are a man, too."

Attignies did not want to hurt the pilot's feelings, but this kind of conversation got on his nerves. He grunted by way of answer, without lifting his eyes from the Milky Way etched in lights along the road beneath him; watching it streaming into the darkness in front of them, trembling in a wind they could not feel above, Attignies felt a desperate friendliness for that one sign of human life amid the dark, threatening, hostile solitude. There was no other light; to fall meant death. And as if some instinct more receptive than his conscious mind had forestalled his ears, Attignies suddenly perceived the reason for his feeling of distress: the engine was knocking.

"A valve!" he shouted to Leclerc.

"To hell with it!" the other shouted back. "We can take a chance."

Attignies tightened the strap of his crash-helmet; he was always ready to take a chance.

Talavera appeared on the horizon, magnified by its isolation amid the darkness. Level with the hills, its lights merged with the stars; they seemed to be coming forward to meet the plane. The stutter of the engine invested the town with an ominous reality. Amid the normal lights of a provincial town and the fretful, restless gleams which betokened military activity, the black patch indicating the darkened gas-works had something of the tense repose of a sleeping wild animal. Now the plane was flying over a tarred road, the wet surface of which reflected the light of the gas street-lamps after the recent rain. The mass of lights expanded steadily as the plane approached Talavera, and suddenly Attignies saw them from both windows at once as the old machine dived, like stars round a climbing plane.

He opened the improvised trap-door: the cold night air rushed into the cabin. On his knees up above the town, he waited, his field of vision limited by the bomb-sight like a horse in blinkers. Heading straight for the square black mass of the gas-works, his ears pricked up, Leclerc was bearing down upon the skeleton of light that was Talavera.

He swept over the black patch and turned round in a fury upon Attignies, of whom he could see nothing except his fair hair, gleaming faintly in the half-light inside the machine.

"What the hell are you doing!"

"Shut your choke!"

Leclerc tilted the plane sideways; still under the influence of the speed of the plane, the falling bombs were accompanying them, a little below them and a little behind, shining like fish in the moonlight. As pigeons veering in the air narrow into thin silhouettes, the bombs suddenly faded from their sight; their fall was becoming vertical. Close beside the gas-works a row of red explosions sprang into view.

"Missed."

Leclerc turned sharply and came back over the objective, going still lower. "Watch the height!" Attignies shouted; the change of height would alter the deflection. He looked at the altimeter, and then through the trap-door again. Seen from the opposite direction now, Talavera had changed in appearance like a man who turns round: the confused light thrown

upon the streets from the military staff offices had given place
to the lighted rectangles of the windows. The outline of the
gas-works was less clear. The machine-guns were firing down
below, but it was unlikely that the men handling them could
see the plane distinctly. Every light in the town went out,
leaving the illuminated dashboard and the shadow of Leclerc's
cloak upon the dial of the altimeter the sole things visible
against the starlit sky.

Its far-flung lights had given the town a vague semblance
of life, and the sharply defined lights revealed by the plane's
return journey had suggested something still more precise; but
now that it was in darkness the town really came into being.
Like sparks struck from a flint, the short flames of the machine-guns appeared and disappeared. The enemy town was
on the watch, seeming to move in response to each movement
of the returning plane, in which Leclerc was staring fixedly,
two wisps of hair protruding from the grey cloak covering his
head. Attignies was flat on his stomach, eyes glued to his sight,
through which the smallest bend in the river was coming into
view, mist-blue in the moonlight: the gas-works came into
view. He released the second rack of bombs.

They did not see them as they fell this time. The plane
nose-dived to the accompaniment of a stupendous crash, and
underneath there was a sudden burst of lightning-coloured
fire. To escape the blue flames surging up around them, Leclerc tugged frantically at the stick; the plane zoomed up
towards the impassive serenity of the stars; below, there was
nothing but a seething mass of red flames—the gas-works had
been blown up.

Bullets drove through the fuselage. Perhaps the explosion
had disclosed the position of the plane; a machine-gun was
following its outline as it entered the halo around the moon.
Leclerc began to zig-zag. Turning round, Attignies saw that
a network of red flames was spreading out below. The string
of bombs had also hit the barracks close beside the gas-works.

A cloudbank hid the ground from them.

Leclerc picked up the thermos flask beside him, then
stopped in amazement, holding the cup in the air, and signed
to Attignies; the whole plane was phosphorescent, glowing
with a bluish light. Attignies pointed to the sky. Till then they
had been looking at the ground, engrossed in their raid, and
had not noticed the plane itself; above and behind them the
moon, which they could not see, was lighting up the aluminum

on the wings. Leclerc put the thermos down; what human gesture would not have seemed trivial and inadequate? Taking them far away from their instrument-board—the only visible light in all the waste of air around them—that sense of well-being which follows on all physical conflict was merging into an almost geological tranquillity, incorporating them in the mystic union of moonlight and pale metal gleaming as precious stones have gleamed for countless ages on the extinct stars. The shadow of the plane moved steadily over the cloud beneath them. Leclerc raised his forefinger, grimaced in approbation, and shouted gravely: "Something to remember, eh!" Picking up the thermos again, he noticed that the engine was still knocking.

At last they were clear of the cloud. The roads, which now they could see again below them, seemed to be moving in places. Attignies knew the meaning of that vague nocturnal motion of the roads; the fascist lorries were advancing on Toledo.

24

TILL nightfall Manuel had been acting as interpreter. Heinrich, the General commanding one of the International brigades then being formed at Madrid, was inspecting the Tagus front —if front it could be called. From Talavera to Toledo, except in Ximenes' sector and a few others, there were no listening posts, no observers, no organized reserves, no proper defences. Machine-guns were badly placed and of poor quality.

In uniform, field-service cap in hand, with the sweat pouring off his bald skull (close-cropped to conceal his white hairs), his field-boots crunching on the brittle soil baked by the last fires of summer, Heinrich had been straightening things out indefatigably, with the dauntless optimism characteristic of the communists.

Manuel had learned from Ximenes how to lead men; now he was learning how an army is commanded. During the past two months he had believed he was acquiring the art of war; what he had actually learned was prudence, method, persistence and strictness. Above all he was learning to exercise these qualities instead of thinking about them. And as he walked through the darkness towards the Alcazar, a mass of leaping flame, shimmering like a huge luminous jelly-fish, he began to realize, after eleven hours' observation of the modifications made by Heinrich, what were the functions of an army division in the field. He felt them in his aching bones, and in his exhausted brain there echoed faintly through the rumble of the guns phrases of the great generals of the past: "Courage admits no hypocrisy"; "You listen to what you hear, you copy what you see"; the first remark, Napoleon's, the second, Quiroga's. Ximenes had introduced him to Clausewitz, and his memory harked back to the library at the Military School, not a bad library as it happened. The furnace of the Alcazar was reflected in the lowering clouds, like a ship on fire mirrored on the waves. Every two minutes a heavy shell crashed into the flames.

Heinrich's scheme was identical with that of the more enterprising elements of the Spanish High Command. He wished to reserve the Assault Guards for use as shock-troops and, pending the time when the Internationals could be moved up into the line, to expand the Fifth Regiment as much as possible. Once its units were sufficiently reinforced, he proposed to transfer them to the regular army, where they would constitute a nucleus capable of introducing revolutionary discipline into the whole army in the same way as, in the early days of the war, communist elements had disciplined the Fifth Regiment. Enrique's battalions were being made into an army corps. Manuel had begun with a motor transport unit, then he had commanded a battalion under Ximenes' orders, now he was transferred to Madrid to the command of a regiment. But it was not so much he who was "rising in the world," as it was the Spanish army.

A sprig of fennel in his hand, he walked against the blustering wind towards Santa Cruz, to see how the mine was getting on. The short angry flames burst from the Alcazar cast a red glow on his face. In the city Heinrich, his close-shaved German nape pleated like a fretful forehead, was waiting for a call from Madrid.

In each lull, when the sounds of rifle- and gun-fire died down with the wind, another sound made itself heard, faint but curiously dramatic: the sizzling of flames on the roof of the Alcazar. And somehow that faint sound was part of the smell that made the booming guns, the distant shouts and all the excited noises of combat seem strangely futile. The mingled reek of fire and corpses was so dense and pungent that it seemed the Alcazar alone could not account for it—it must surely be an elemental tang of wind and darkness.

It had become imperative to launch the Toledo militia into the battle of the Tagus. The Alcazar, with the exception of its subterranean vaults, was due to be blown up that night, and the town was being evacuated. An endless stream of peasants with their pigs and goats was passing, silently moving through the lurid darkness, lit not by the Alcazar but by the flaming clouds.

Manuel found one of the officers from Toledo in the mess-room at Santa Cruz; he was a man of forty, and wore his forage-cap well on the back of his head. His hands in his pockets, he had accosted Manuel with gruff, rather paternal good humour.

"Hello, my boy! What's up?"

"When will the mine be ready?" Manuel asked.

The officer stared at him. "When they're through with it. Tomorrow." His manner implied: "With fools like that, how can one tell?" There was a twinkle in his eye, as if the whole business rather amused him. If Manuel felt a certain sympathy with Hernandez' melancholy, this fellow's careless, patronizing humour got on his nerves. And, since his accident with Ramos, he had come to look on dynamite as a romantic and, as such, uncertain weapon of attack.

During a brief respite in the noise of battle he heard a rhythmic beat of dull, metallic thuds issuing, it seemed, from the floor and walls.

"Is that the mine?" Manuel asked.

The *milicianos* nodded. It struck Manuel that the fascists in the Alcazar must be hearing it, too, in much the same way.

The leader of the sappers came in.

"When do you expect to have it ready?"

"Between three and four."

"Sure?"

The sapper scratched his head. "For sure."

"What will it blow up exactly?"

"Ah, that's hard to tell."

"Well, what's your opinion?"

"All the front part will go up."

"No more than that?"

The sapper scratched his head again. "Well, the others say there'll be more. But I don't think so. The vaults ain't one

upon the other, they're spread-out like, following the formation of the rock."

"Thanks."

The man went off. Shifting the sprig of fennel to his left
hand, Manuel took the officer's arm. "If there's an engagement
tomorrow, comrade, you'd better see to your defences. Your
nest of machine-guns are too low down. And none of them is
camouflaged; why, they're visible even in the light of the fire."

He went out into the glowing darkness, into the reek of
corpses and white-hot stone. A gust of wind blew it momentarily away, then once more it settled thickly down upon
the garden.

After inspecting the various sectors one by one, he came
to the Alcazar outbuildings which had been captured by the
Republicans. There, things were very different; well-trained
milicianos, Assault Guards and Civil Guards. But he still felt
uneasy; the attack which was to be launched immediately after
the explosion had not been planned by a military expert.

Between crashes of the field-guns, he still could hear the
noises of the mine, welling up from the ground under his feet;
in their vaults the enemy must hear those sounds still better.

At the telephone Heinrich was waiting for a reply concerning the defence of Madrid. He wanted to defend Toledo, but,
whether Toledo held out or fell, he asked that the system of
small isolated units should be abandoned and large reserves
built up, with the Fifth Regiment as a nucleus. Franco was expecting great things of a fascist rising in Madrid and was actually beginning to commandeer white horses for a triumphal
entry; his troops were advancing with alarming rapidity.

The day's work finished, Hernandez was sitting at a table
with his friend, Moreno, at the Militia Headquarters, the only
place at Toledo where one could still get beer—tepid, at that.
On the day of the rising Moreno had been imprisoned by the
fascists and sentenced to death. He had made a lucky getaway
while being transferred from one prison to another, and had
come back to Madrid three days before. He had just been
called on to furnish some information; like Hernandez, he had
been a cadet at the Toledo Military School. Through the wide-
open window they could see a crowd of *milicianos,* pulsing
like the core of vivid blue from which the flames of the vast
furnace were racing skywards.

"A pack of lunatics!" said Moreno. His thick black hair, parted in the middle, straggled over his forehead and all but hid his face. Hernandez looked at him questioningly. They had known each other fairly intimately for fifteen years; but their friendship was half-hearted, made up of sentimental memories and secrets shared.

"I no longer believe in all I used to believe," Moreno said. "I believe in nothing now. Yet I'm going into the line tomorrow night."

He pushed back his hair. He had been famous at Toledo for his good looks; the conventional good looks of Latin countries —very large eyes and an aquiline nose. He had his hair trimmed but left unusually long, as though to keep in his appearance some reminder of the prison from which he had escaped. He was badly shaved and the stubble on his chin was grey. He had once been the lover of one of King Alfonso's mistresses.

A row of houses hid the Alcazar, but the clouds above were glowing with an ever-changing sheen of red, violet and purple, like ripe grapes, and the *milicianos* streaming by cast flickering shadows on the pavements. And always, punctually, the muffled thunder of the guns.

"Tell me, while you were in prison, what taxed your endurance most?"

"Learning to . . . to be indifferent."

For some time Hernandez had suspected Moreno of a perverse fondness for the tragic view of life. But now his distress, though his friend could not judge its motive, was obviously sincere.

For a moment they were silent, waiting for the next boom of the guns. The night was loud with creaking axles; the exodus from Toledo had begun.

"It wasn't being in prison that mattered so much, old man; it was the death sentence. Then something snapped in me. I used to think I took some interest in men. I used to be a Marxist, the first Marxist officer in the army, quite likely. It's not so much that I've changed my ideas; I haven't any ideas left."

Hernandez felt no desire to embark on a discussion of Marxism. With a clatter of rifles some *milicianos* ran by.

"Listen!" Moreno went on. "When I was sentenced to death, I was allowed to go down to the patio. All the men there had been sentenced for their political ideas. But nobody mentioned politics. Nobody. If anyone had done so, he'd have found himself completely isolated!"

A militia-girl, a hunchback, handed a letter to Hernandez. Moreno burst into rather hysterical laughter.

"From the point of view of the revolution," he asked, "what's your real opinion of all this play-acting?"

"It's more than play-acting."

Hernandez' eyes followed the humped, receding figure of the girl; but, unlike Moreno, all he saw in her was her fine zest, and he felt amiably disposed towards her. So, as far as he could discern across the livid darkness, did the *milicianos*. She, who till now most likely had been condemned to loneliness, was at last playing an active part in the world. The Captain's short-sighted eyes settled on Moreno; he was beginning to mistrust his friend.

"So you're off for the front, tomorrow?"

Moreno hesitated, knocked his glass over, but took no notice of it. He kept his eyes fixed on Hernandez.

"I'm leaving for France tonight."

Hernandez said nothing. A foreign *miliciano*, unaware that he did not have to pay, rapped his glass with a coin. Moreno took a copper from his pocket, and threw it up in the air as if he were playing pitch and toss. When it fell he covered it with his hand. without looking to see on which side it had fallen. There was a rather wistful smile on his lips; emotion gave the smooth, regular features a youthful, almost childish look.

"For a while, old chap, we weren't in a prison; they transferred us to an old convent. The change was made on purpose, obviously. In the prison we could see nothing, hear nothing—which was so much to the good. At the convent we were more favoured; we heard everything. Firing parties at work all night. . . ." The troubled eyes settled on his friend's face. In the childish features was a certain innocence, but grimness, too. "Can you believe the firing squads used searchlights?" he added.

Without awaiting the reply he burst out. "Imagine being shot with a spotlight on you! . . . Yes, we heard the volleys, and another sound as well. They'd taken all our silver, but left us the small change. And almost everyone was playing pitch and toss. Heads—we shall be sent for a walk in the patio tomorrow; tails—we're for the firing squad. They didn't chance it on one throw, but on ten or twenty. The noise of the volleys was muffled by the walls and the air cushion between. And all night on every side, I could hear the chink, chink of little copper coins. Yes, old man, I could judge the size of the prison by the differences between the sounds—if they were near or distant."

"What were your guards like?"

"One night a guard heard the noise. He flung open the door of my cell, yelled 'Tails! You lose!' and slammed it to again. Some of my guards were swine. Real swine. But not in that prison. . . . Listen! You hear those forks tinkling on the plates? Well, it was nearly as loud as that. Most likely we got to hear noises that didn't really exist; that sort of thing gets on one's nerves, you know. Sometimes I felt positively crushed by all those little jingling noises, as if I was buried in a snow-drift. The other fellows hadn't been arrested, as I was, on the first day; they'd been in the line. It was damn silly, and damn pathetic. Playing pitch and toss with death. Like heroes! But where did heroism come in, that's what I'd like to know?"

He picked up the coin again, tossed it.

"Heads!" He sounded surprised.

He put the coin back in his pocket. Hernandez had seen Moreno in the fighting-line during the war with Abd-el-Krim, and knew him to be brave. The guns were still battering the Alcazar; the strident creak of cart-axles mingled with the hiss of flames.

"Listen, old man! A hero can't make good without an audience; you get to know that once you're really alone. They say that blindness makes its own world; so does loneliness, take my word for it. Once you're in it, you discover that all the ideas you had about yourself belong to the other world, the world you've left. That fools' paradise. Of course, in your private world you can think about yourself, but it only makes you feel as if you were off your head. Remember Bakunin's confession? That explains it. The two worlds simply don't communicate. In one men die side by side, singing, or clench-ing their teeth, or any way they might wish; and beyond it there's that other world, that convent where . . ."

He took the copper from his pocket again, rang it on the table, shivered, and picked it up, without looking to see which side was uppermost. His eyes had never left the street.

"Look at 'em! Look at them, damn it! All those fellows simpering at each other: 'I'm a thinker, I'm making history.' Kisses. Slapping each other on the back. But put 'em in a cell . . . and then what? Pennies tossed in the air. . . . Oh, well, I suppose there'll still be lands without fascists on the earth, before I die. When I escaped I was crazy about getting back; I reported at once for duty. Now I know better. No one on earth can escape what's coming to him, *his truth*. And it isn't death, no, it isn't even suffering. . . . It's the spin of a coin, of a penny."

"I'd like to know why, for a sceptic like you, the moment of death should be more significant—more important, if you like—than any other."

"A man can put up with everything; can even go to sleep knowing it wastes some hours of life before he's shot at dawn; can tear up the photographs of those he loves because he's had enough of sapping his nerves by poring over them; can note with pleasure that he's still jumping in the air like a fox-terrier for another futile peep through the loop-hole up in the wall— and all the rest of it. With everything, I say. What he can't bear is to feel certain that, after being knocked about and trampled on, he's going to be killed. And that after that there's—nothing!"

The handsome face was tense with emotion. In the changing glow, red-brown and violet, reflected from the unseen flames, for all its screen-star symmetry, it had a real beauty.

"Just try to realize it! At Palma I spent a fortnight in the lock-up. Fourteen days. There was a mouse that came every day at the same time; I knew the hour by it. Man being *par excellence* the love-secreting animal, I got to love it. Well, on the fourteenth day they let me out into the patio and I had a talk with some other prisoners. When I went back to my cell, that mouse merely got on my nerves."

"A man can't go through what you've been through without feeling the effects. Look here! You'd better have a meal, a drink, and a sleep. And *think* as little as possible."

"Easier said than done. Get it into your head, old fellow, that a man isn't *used* to dying! It's outside all his experience. And, when he's up against it, he remembers that."

"Even without having been sentenced to death, one learns here quite a lot of things which go against the grain to learn. For instance, I've hit on a certain truth, oh, quite a simple one: one expects everything all at once from 'freedom,' but for man to progress a bare half inch a great many men must die. This street must have looked much like it does now in the days of Charles the Fifth. Yet the world has moved on since

then. Because men wanted it to move on, despite the pennies
—perhaps even with full awareness that those pennies were
waiting for them in the background. Nothing could be more
discouraging than fighting here. And still the only thing in the
world as . . . as important . . . as the experience you've
told me of is the help that we can give those fellows who are
streaming past us now without saying a word."

"That's the sort of thing I used to say to myself in my cell,
in the morning. But in the evenings the truth came back to me.
The evenings were awful. When one's been walking up and
down a room three yards by three all day, and the walls are
starting to close in—well, it sharpens one's wits, you know.
The graveyards of revolutions are just the same as other
graveyards."

"All seeds begin by rotting, but some of them germinate. A
world without hope is . . . suffocating. Or else, a purely
physical world. That's how a good many officers manage to
put up with it so well; almost all of them have always lived
on the purely physical plane. But that wasn't true of us. Look
here, you'd better apply for a fortnight's sick-leave. And if,
after that, you still can see only the comic-opera side of our
milicianos, if nothing in you responds to the hope that ani-
mates them, well then, go to France—there's nothing for you
to do here."

Behind the groups of silent wayfarers rolled farm-carts
bulging with sacks and baskets, in which sometimes there
showed the red glint of a wine-bottle. Peasant-women rode
past on donkeys; on their haunted faces was the immemorial
grief of a Flight into Egypt. In the reek of fire, to the strong
sonorous rhythm of the guns, the exodus streamed by.

From the quiet stars the hills fell steeply to the valley along
which the enemy tanks would presently advance. Groups of
men with dynamite were spaced along it, under cover of rocks
and clumps of trees and farmhouses.

The Republican front lines in the Toledo sector were a mile
and a half behind them. A dozen *dinamiteros* were lying under
a clump of olive-trees. One of them, his chin propped on his
hands, had his eyes fixed on the summit of the hill where the
observer had been posted. Most of the others had cigarettes,
still unlit, dangling from their lips.

The Sierra was holding out, so was the Aragon front, Cordova, Malaga, the Asturias. But Franco's motorized column

was advancing at full speed along the Tagus. And things were
looking bad for Toledo. As usual when things look bad, the
dinamiteros were beginning to talk of '34, the black year of
the Asturias. Pepe was describing Oviedo to the recruits who
had come from Catalonia. The Popular Front had followed
that setback.

"We took the arsenal," he was explaining. "And then we
thought, 'Now everything's all right. We're saved.' And then
we found we couldn't do a thing with the stuff inside it:
cartridge cases with no caps, shells without fuses. Duds. So
we used the shells as cannon-balls, there being nothing else to
do with them. Anyhow the noise made us feel good; so they
weren't wasted."

Pepe rolled onto his back. Moonlight was sifting down
through the olive-trees in a bright mist through the frail silvery sheen of the leaves.

"Yes, it gave us confidence—that much confidence it landed
us in prison."

A moonbeam was falling on his face, the face of a good-
tempered, friendly horse.

"Think they'll get Toledo?"

"The hell they will!"

"Don't be so darn sure, Pepe! Me, I guess things are in a
bad way in Toledo. I'm counting on Madrid."

"And weren't things in a hell of a bad way in the Asturias?"

"Without that dynamite," another voice put in, "we'd have
been wiped out in three days. We tried to get things straightened out at the arsenal, with the comrades who said they knew
all about priming. Nothing doing. The lads had to go off to
the front with five rounds each—just imagine that!—five
rounds per man! Say, Pepe, do you remember those women
with the baskets? I saw plenty of gleaners in my day but I
never saw 'em gathering empty cartridges before. They were
that keen on getting shells, we couldn't fire quick enough to
please them. . . . Mercy on us!"

No one had looked round to see who was speaking. It was
Gonzalez. Large men have a jovial quality of voice that is unmistakable. But, as they listened, all were straining their ears
for a distant rumble of tanks.

"Dynamite!" Pepe said. "That's the stuff! We did mighty
good work with it. Remember old Mercader's catapult?" But
it was to the Catalonians he turned, who certainly had never
heard of Mercader. "Mercader was a smart lad; he invented a

contraption for throwing big charges of the stuff. Sort of trench-mortar. Like in all the old wars, it worked with ropes and pulleys. And took three men to handle it. Well, it fairly knocked the stuffing out of the Moors the first time we used it on them. Real dynamite cartridges at two hundred yards— they hadn't looked for that. Another invention of his was shields; but they didn't pan out so well. Acted like targets."

In the distance a machine-gun started, stopped, started again; and like the sound of a sewing machine lost itself in the vastness of the night. But still no sign of tanks.

"The others, they made aeroplanes!" The voice sounded bitter.

In this valley, watching for the coming of the tanks, they exchanged tales of adventure, some heroical and others trivial. Without doubt *dinamiteros* are the last body of men who can face the machine on equal terms. The presence of the Catalonians here, was, so to speak, accidental; but the Asturians were continuing their tradition. They were the oldest revolutionary group in Spain and now at last an organized body; the only men for whom the golden legend of the revolution was being implemented by experience of actual warfare, instead of being disintegrated by it.

"They say the Moorish cavalry has been given machine-guns."

"To hell with them!"

"And Seville's overrun with Germans. And they're all trained men."

"Wardens of prisons, too."

"They say that two Italian divisions are on their way."

"Say, don't you think the boys will put up a good show against the tanks?"

"Well, they're used to them."

Once more they countered the menace of the new with reminiscences.

"The craziest thing of all in our show," Pepe said, "was the way it ended. The boys did pretty well at the peasants' central committee. But they had no help; they were outnumbered. The Moors came up; it took them three hours to close their circle round us. The boys were holding out and they had lots of dynamite, but nothing to put it in. So they fixed up a sort of hand-grenade with bolts and nuts and newspaper. Not a rifle to be had; they'd given out long ago. A comrade had gone round to the arsenal the day before, and all he brought back was a scrap of newspaper. The man that ran the arsenal had written on it in pencil, saying it was no good sending round for ammunition; not a cartridge left. The last ones had been shared among the comrades who had been loading them; five rounds each. And off they went to the front. So that was that. Everything was perfect, as you can imagine. They all sat round the table in the committee-room, scowling at each other. What else could they do? Some of the boys were standing around, but they didn't say a word. You could hear the machine-guns of the Moors getting nearer, just like now. And then there came a queer, rumbling noise, sort of muffled, so you couldn't hardly hear it, but all the mugs and knives on the table and the picture on the wall started trembling. What the hell was happening? Then they heard bells, and they understood. It was the cattle being driven in from the country. The Moors and their guns popping off in all directions had scared them, and there they were, herds and herds, stampeding up the street. Then one of the boys, a bright lad he was, had an idea. He jumps up and yells: 'Say, comrades, let's build a barricade! Hold up those cows and get the bells off them.' The bells they had on their necks weren't the thin sort, but fat, heavy ones such as the mountain cattle wear. Well, they yanked the bells off those cattle in no time and made 'em into bombs, and that's how they held out three whole hours, time enough to have everything evacuated that needed to be evacuated. . . . As for those tanks that're coming up, who gives a damn, now we've got the stuff and can hit back at 'em!"

Pepe hadn't forgotten the armoured train. We don't need guns, he thought; we can fight with our hands. And, now that they were trained, they could stop tanks, even without anti-tank guns.

A dog began barking in the distance.

"The donkey, the donkey, Gonzalez. Tell us that one!"

"When one thinks about this war, it's always the funny bits one remembers . . . !"

Most of the men were silent; they simply could not tell stories. Pepe, Gonzalez and one or two others were the professional entertainers and mirth-makers of the group. Presumably the tanks would not dare to attack till daylight. Not knowing the country well enough, the drivers would fear being ditched. But day would soon be breaking. Now or never for the donkey yarn.

"That was a grand notion, that one about the donkey. We'd

loaded him with dynamite, lit the fuse and shoo'd him off towards the Moors. Well, the old beast trots off, pricking up his ears; he had no idea what it's all about, poor fool. Only the others, you see, they start plugging away at him, good and hard. At the first shots he waggles his ears, like there was flies on them. After a bit he stops, puzzled-like. He sure can't make it out, and then he starts ambling back. But nothing doing. We too start firing at him. Only, you see, we were old acquaintances; so, after thinking it over, seeing how things are, he decides he'd rather come back to our lines . . ."

A terrific concussion, as if somewhere near by the earth had split in two, brought down on their heads a shower of dry twigs and leaves. A vast red flame was spouting up in the direction of Toledo, and as they stared blankly at each other, open-mouthed, their cheeks lit by the livid purplish sheen of flame and moonlight mingled, each saw the face that he would wear in death.

All the cigarettes had dropped.

They were used to explosions. But this was not a mine. Not dynamite. Not a powder magazine.

"An aerial torpedo?"

None of them had noticed anything of the sort. They listened. They fancied they could hear the drone of a plane high up. But it might be the rumble of the Moors' lorries.

"Is there a gas-works at Toledo?" Gonzalez asked.

No one knew. But all were thinking of the Alcazar.

One thing was clear: something had gone wrong for the fascists. Where the column of fire had just died down, the sky still glowed red. A fire? Or dawn?

Not the dawn. It was breaking on the opposite horizon. And, as the light grew, a coolness and a dewy scent of leaves seemed floating down from the olive trees.

Time for reminiscence was over. Now the *dinamiteros* were on the alert, at their posts. Daybreak, the enemy.

The cigarettes were back in their mouths, but still unlit. A vast silence brooded on the Spanish countryside, as on the day when the first Moors had come; the grey hush of how many peaceful and how many tragic dawns! On the horizon the silver streak of daybreak widened out, while overhead little by little the blackness waned. The air seemed charged with the unutterable sadness of the pale hour preceding the deep-toned call of day. Half-heartedly, forlornly, cocks began crowing in the farms.

Pepe shouted: "There's Ricardo."

The observer was racing back to them. And, advancing from the same grey limbo, tilted as if they threatened not the earth but the dim sky, the first enemy tanks came over the crest.

Gonzalez lit his cigarette; Pepe, then the others, followed suit. From all sides groups of men began creeping towards the tanks.

The crews of the tanks could not see them, though they may have known that they were there. The *dinamiteros* kept down in the valley bed, crouching or lying flat; the tanks reared up against the sky. On Gonzalez' right was a Catalonian boy who had not opened his mouth so far; on his left was Pepe. In the dim light he hardly saw them, but he was conscious of the swinging, manly strides of the two young men beside him. Somehow at such moments he always pictured his friends as molluscs who had been turned out of their shells; soft, lithe, defenceless creatures. He was acutely conscious of his own bulk and their fragility. The tanks—they, anyhow, had shells—were approaching, the rattle growing to a roar, while the wavering line of *dinamiteros* crept towards them in an uncanny silence.

The tanks were in two columns, but spaced so far apart that the *dinamiteros* took no account of this. Each group was allotted a single tank, as if they had been in single file. Some Catalonians had not hidden their cigarettes completely in their hands. "The idiots!" Gonzalez murmured. He was behind them. Let's hope, he thought, those tell-tale specks of red may be less noticeable from in front. Borne forward on the same tide of hard, fraternal exaltation, he advanced with them, and, as he kept his eyes fixed on the approaching tanks, he seemed to hear the deep-toned song of the Asturias echoing in his heart. Never again as at this moment was he to know all it can mean to be a man.

Soon he would be in the open. The sun was rising. Pepe had taken cover. Gonzalez dropped back on the ground. The tank must be some four hundred yards away, but the tall grass level with his eyes concealed it. It was the sort of grass he used to play with as a boy, an oat-grass with long palms, the heads of which he used to slip inside his playmates' sleeves, up which they wormed their irritating way. Already, he noticed, some ants and a tiny spider were crawling on it. On the ground, in their grassy forest, other creatures were going their small, warless ways. Then, just behind a pair of busy ants, loomed up the lurching, roaring bulk of a swiftly moving tank. The ground where Gonzalez lay was uneven. When throwing his dynamite, he might have toppled over. He shifted his position to one side.

The tank would pass on his right. The embankment would screen him from the turret till the tank had actually come level with him. It was a question—a question of life and death —who would deliver the first blow. Anyhow the gunner would have the sun in his eyes. Gonzalez made sure that there was nothing to hamper his right arm.

Where the hell was that Catalonian? The tank on the right had opened fire. Gonzalez' tank was approaching at full speed, tilted up, just above the ants that looked like monsters at six inches from his eyes. Steadying himself with his left hand, Gonzalez brought all his weight onto his bent knee. Here it comes! He jerked himself erect, launched his dynamite into the clatter of gun-fire and machinery, and in the same movement flung himself flat on the ground, as if he were diving into the explosion.

There was a patter of falling gravel. He looked up. The tank was standing on its turret, upside down. The only entrance into it was through the top of the turret. One of the caterpillar bands was still turning, glinting in the dawn. Like a roulette wheel, gradually it slowed down.

Gonzalez had one bomb left and he was holding his cigarette ready beside it. The machine-gun on the tank was silent. The two men inside were dead or wounded; in any case they were trapped inside the turret with no hope of escaping. The full weight of the machine rested on the turret. If the gasoline tank had upset, they'd go up in flames within five minutes. That is civil war!

The band had stopped revolving. Everything was still. Gonzalez looked round. Not a shot had been fired by the Republican artillery—if Republican artillery there was. He rose to his knees. The valley was scored by the trails of caterpillar bands, like the wakes of passing ships; the tank in front of him and four others had been put out of commission. Ditched or bottom upmost, they had a quaintly prehistoric look. (When he saw the first one upside down, he had taken it for some new type of tank.) Two were on fire. Far away, in the bright light that now was flooding all the countryside, the rearguard of the column of tanks was gradually disappearing over a patch of rising ground, on its way to the Republican lines, the last lines before Toledo.

The tanks had got through.

"Where's that Catalonian boy?" Gonzalez asked.

"Killed," Pepe answered.

The sun was well up by now, but the dead bodies in the grass could not be seen. Bullets were beginning to whiz round the two men; Pepe gave an imitation of their foolish whistling, then dropped under cover again.

A line of white dots, the Moors' turbans, was advancing over the crest of the hill.

Mingling with the dewy freshness of the dawn, the smoke from the explosion, which still enveloped the Alcazar, had clotted into a dank mist heavy with the stench of corpses. A gust of wind had forced the smoke against the still unfallen walls like reefs beneath the surface of a lagoon. When a more violent gust dented the smooth expanse, jagged blocks of stone emerged. Lower down, on the right, it was spreading out towards the town, not in billowy masses, but like a quiet tide, seeping into every hole and crevice. Manuel thought: The Alcazar is leaking like a cistern.

Foot by foot advancing down each shattered street and by-way as if it, too, were an invading foe, the smoke was penetrating the Republican positions. The mine had blown up the advance posts of the fascists, though not the underground chambers, and the opposing troops were now at a greater distance from each other.

For a moment the sound of firing died away and Manuel heard someone stamping his foot on the rock behind him. It was Heinrich; a ray of sunlight fell on his flabby, furrowed neck.

Manuel spoke first, his sprig of fennel in his hand. "Madrid?" he asked.

"The answer's: No." The General spoke without looking at him. His eyes were fixed on the high rocks slowly emerging from the smoke as from an ebbing tide.

"Why?" Manuel asked.

"The answer's: No. We had men in front of the building, eh?"

"They were moved away before the mine went up."

"It seems there's no way of getting at the part that's being blown up except through the main building, eh?"

He was still watching through his field-glasses the battered headland from which the smoke was clearing. His face, for all his years, had the chubbiness of a Polish peasant-woman's. He handed the glasses to Manuel.

"Have we machine-guns on the flanks?"

"No."

"It wouldn't stop them, but it would hold them up a while."

Tiny specks were moving on the crest-line of the rock, clinging to it like flowers. The smoke had spread far beyond the old front line which the Assault Guards had evacuated before the explosion. Behind the smoke the fascists were approaching. Like a gas barrage it covered their advance.

All the positions occupied during the last ten days had been lost.

"We must see about defending the town," Heinrich said.

The Jefatura telephone was still silent. Santa Cruz reported that the Moors were only six miles away.

They went to Hernandez' headquarters in the little boot-shop.

In one of the streets where the crowd was thick, as in the approaches to a station during the summer holiday rush, a *miliciano* handed Manuel his gun, a Mauser.

"Want a rifle, Major?"

"You'll be needing it soon," Heinrich said to the man, in German.

"I'm through with it. So you may as well . . ."

Heinrich's white brows usually gave his blue eyes a look of childish wonder. But when, as now, they settled to a stare, the shaved skull and almost invisible eyebrows gave him an expression of utter ruthlessness. . . . But by now there were twenty or more people between him and the *miliciano*.

The rifles dropped in doorways were being picked up by sharp-shooters, who were firing on the *milicianos* from the shuttered windows. For the first time Manuel felt the same oppression in a street that overtook him in closed-in places; he dared not set a foot down without first prodding the ground with his big toe. No previous crowd in Toledo, not even that of the Corpus processions before the war, nor the crowds that gathered in Madrid on great occasions, had ever been so dense as this one. The *milicianos* were carrying their Mexican hats like circus hoops, at arms length. Twenty thousand men seethed in a frenzied mass. On every doorstep lay abandoned rifles.

Hernandez' office was wide open. A man in a red-and-black *képi* was asking, "Who's in charge here?"

"I am. I'm Captain Hernandez."

"See here, Captain! We were in Number 25, Commercial Street. They were bombarded. We moved on to Number 45; they bombarded us there, too. I'd like to know if it's you who puts them wise each time we shift, so they can wipe us out more easily, the Captain who is on the other side."

Hernandez eyed the man with disgust. "Continue," he said.

"I'd have you know we've had our bellyful of it. Where are our planes?"

"In the air. Where else should they be?"

The Government had no more than ten up-to-date machines fit to take the air against the Italian and German planes.

"I'd have you know, if our planes don't show up within a half hour, we down rifles, see? Think we're out to act as gunfodder for the bourgeois, or for communists? Not us. We're going to down 'em. Understand?"

He was staring at Manuel's large red star. The hardness had come back to Heinrich's eyes.

Hernandez took the man by the lapels of his tunic and said in a calm peremptory voice, "You, down them right away," and pushed him out of the room. The man had not said another word. Then, turning, Hernandez saluted Heinrich and shook hands with Manuel.

"That man's either a fool or a knave—both, I dare say. Those men have treachery on the brain. Perhaps they're not so far wrong . . . And so long as things are that way, there's nothing to be done."

"There's always something to be done," Manuel said, correcting him.

His hands were shaky; his sprig of fennel had been lost in the crowd.

Hernandez shrugged his shoulders. "Very good, sir."

"If that man has quitted his post, he should be shot."

"By whom?"

"By you, if necessary. Is there anyone else we can count on?"

"No one. There's nothing to be done here. And yet . . . Look here! Don't let any of the good troops enter the city; they'll become infected in an hour. It's a hotbed of deserters. Let's put up a fight, if we can, outside it, and with other troops. What troops have you available?"

"There are thousands of men here," Heinrich said, "and thousands of rifles. Surely we can put some of them to use. We've got to make the most of the situation."

"Not a soldier is here. Only three hundred *milicianos* who'll fight to death; and a handful of Asturians. The rest are a pack of cowards who try to justify their cowardice by finding fault with everything! They've dumped their rifles in the doorways, and the fascists are beginning to use them against us. Even the women aren't afraid of shouting abuse at us from the windows."

"Well, try to gain five or six hours, anyhow."

"The Visagra Gate could be defended, but they won't lift a finger."

"It's up to us to defend it," Heinrich said. "Let's go there."

After a long detour through side-streets they reached the Gate. It looked like a rifle dump.

The sight of all those abandoned rifles made Manuel furious. Something had to be done to calm his nerves. He found a fairly straight branch to replace his lost sprig of fennel. A dozen *milicianos* were squatting over a game of cards. As he passed them, Heinrich stooped, swept up the cards under the players' noses, and put them in his pocket.

"It's sheer insanity," he said. "With all those roofs and terraces we could perfectly well hold out here, anyhow till they brought up their field-guns."

They went back into the town. The General kept on glancing up at the roofs. "*Ach,* what a nuisance it is not knowing Spanish!"

"I know Spanish," Manuel said.

With Hernandez' help he began assigning posts to the men available, one by one, sending others to fetch ammunition and despatching such of the abandoned rifles as were in good condition to the sharp-shooters already posted. Three Lewis guns were unearthed. In an hour's time the Gate was being defended.

"Comrade, you'll think I'm a bit cracked," said Heinrich to Manuel, "but now I'd like you to get them to sing the *International*. As they're all under cover, they can't see each other; so they've got to *feel* their comrades are near by." The General's remark lost none of its authoritativeness by his use of the word "comrade."

"Comrades!" Manuel bellowed.

From every window, at each house-corner, heads popped

out. Manuel began singing the *International*, but was worried by the leafy sprig in his hand, which kept on wanting to beat time. He had a powerful voice and, as the firing against the Alcazar had practically ceased, everyone could hear him. But the *milicianos* did not know the words of the *International*.

Heinrich was amazed. Manuel confined himself to the refrain.

"Well, it's better than nothing." Heinrich sounded bitter. "We'll be at Madrid in about four hours. They'll hold out till then."

Hernandez smiled sadly.

Manuel appointed section leaders; then the three officers walked to the Puerta del Sol. In three-quarters of an hour defenders had been posted at that gate as well.

"Let's go back to Visagra," Heinrich said.

Through half-opened windows the fascists were firing more and more frequently. Down the whole length of the street, the officers were greeted with abuse. But the crowd had thinned out. In one hour, more than ten thousand men had left. The city was being drained of its population as a dying man is drained of blood.

Their car was locked up in a shed.

"Better get it out right away," Hernandez suggested. "If we wait . . ."

A small-moustached officer was standing by the door.

"I hear you're going to Madrid," he said. "Can you give me a lift?" He showed them a written order to proceed to Madrid.

They drove to Visagra first, Manuel at the wheel. Abandoned rifles lay on every doorstep. While the car was slowing down for a corner, a door was pushed ajar and a hand reached out from within towards a gun. Heinrich fired; the hand went back.

Toledo was putrefying like a corpse.

"The Spanish people have failed to rise to the occasion," Heinrich said, and for the third time his eyes had that look of brutal fixity which Manuel had already noticed. "In such cases," Heinrich continued, "it's always the General Staff that's to blame."

Manuel remembered Ximenes and the *milicianos* who were to be seen in every Madrid street, learning to march in step as children learn to read.

When they reached Visagra, Manuel shouted to his men. No answer. He called again. Still no answer. He climbed to the

top storey of the first house from which he could see the neighbouring roofs. At each point where he had posted a sharp-
shooter lay an abandoned rifle. Even the three Lewis guns had
been discarded. Visagra was being defended—by guns that
had no men behind them!

And, on the Malaga, the Aragon and the Cordova fronts
they were short of guns. Also at Madrid.

On a threshing-floor near by someone was threshing corn.

At last Manuel flung away his branch and staggered down
the stairs; his legs were giving way beneath him. Every door
stood open. And on every roof, from behind each chimney-top,
a rifle was peeping out, with a little pile of ammunition near it.

Manuel told Heinrich what had happened. Hernandez had
guessed it already.

"We've got to rush some of the young troops to Toledo,"
Heinrich said. "Let's dash off to Madrid. As things are it will
be an easy task evacuating Toledo."

"Too late!" Hernandez replied.

"Let's try anyhow."

Manuel turned to Hernandez. "What do you intend to do?"

"What do you expect me to do?" A bitter smile parted his
lips, baring his long yellow teeth. "There are twenty of us here
who can make good use of a machine-gun." He pointed to the
cemetery with indifference. "There or here."

"No, we'll be back in time."

Hernandez shrugged his shoulders.

"I tell you," Manuel repeated almost angrily; "we shall be
back in time."

Hernandez gazed at him with an almost startled air, and
Manuel realized that he had never used such a tone before
when speaking to Hernandez. It is impossible to convey orders
in an unemphatic voice; for some hours he had been trans-
lating for Heinrich, and he had acquired the General's way
of speaking. He had picked up the language of command, as
one picks up a foreign language by repetition.

"Well, if you can scrape up twenty men," he added, "try
anyhow to defend this gate."

"Have new men posted here at once," Heinrich said, "before you leave."

"Very good, sir," Hernandez replied with the same forlorn
indifference. When the men had been assigned their posts, the
officers went back to the bootshop. The firing from the win-

dows and the hostile cries were steadily increasing in volume as they walked down the street.

"Those people," Manuel remarked, "would like to see Philip II back on the throne. Look here, Hernandez, will you have all the rifles lying about collected, except the ones on the doorsteps? I'll send you some lorries with Assault Guards to fetch them."

"It's easier to get them collected than to get them used."

The death-throes of Toledo were hastening to their climax.

"Let them hold out during the day," said Heinrich. The *dinamiteros* will take care of the night. Once the young troops and the Fifth Regiment have come we can hold the town for a week. And in a week lots of things can happen. . . ."

25

HERNANDEZ had discarded his *mono* and was in mufti, like most of the last men holding out at Toledo. Now he pondered for a moment. Judging by the sounds, the Republicans were on his right. What did he really want? Was it to be saved? Two hours earlier, leaving Toledo would have been as easy as catching a peacetime train. Or was it to fight to the end? Most of all he wanted not to be alone again. Nothing could be worse than that. He had been separated from his men when the Tercio launched their first attack. The great thing now was to rejoin them.

He ran beside the wall of a little by-street. On his left the Tercio machine-guns were steadily approaching. At last he reached a larger street where shots from the Republicans were flaking the high, pale house-fronts, throwing up small white puffs of plaster. Louder and nearer sounded the enemy's machine-guns. The Tercio must have reached the corner Hernandez had just left. He was under fire now from in front and from behind.

Ten yards ahead a street-lamp was lit up. When Hernandez came below it he waved his revolver in the air to make known who he was; a sledge-hammer crashed down on the barrel, knocking it to the ground. He dived into a doorway. Here he was sheltered from the fire of the Tercio by the corners of the street, and from that of the Republicans by the walls on each side of the threshold. Machine-guns were firing spasmodically on his right and left; obviously the men behind him could see little to aim at. Presently a gust of bullets brought the street-lamp down in a melodious tinkle of broken glass. After that the machine-gunners could see nothing at all; could only aim at the sudden bursts of bluish flame flickering at each end of the street.

Hernandez went down on all fours, thrust his head forward below the criss-cross stream of bullets, retrieved his revolver and crept back to the doorway. He had stayed thus for ten minutes when he gave a sudden start. He had felt the muzzle of a revolver prodding his ribs.

"Hernandez! That you, Hernandez?"

"Er . . . yes."

"Move back to the wall."

The *miliciano*—he, too, was in mufti—fired three shots at intervals of a second, and both men dashed out. The Republican machine-gun ceased fire.

As they came up to it, another *miliciano* ran up behind them.

"The Moors are coming!"

"Run to the bull-ring!" The man who spoke was a machine-gunner; he seemed to be in command of the group.

All made a dash for it along the side-streets, the machine-gunner bristling on all sides with the mountings of the Hotchkiss in his arms.

Hernandez did not wish to die alone.

The gunner halted, turned, set down his Hotchkiss, reeled off a drum of fifty bullets, and started off again. He was a poor shot. After pausing for a moment, the Moors, too, pressed forward again.

A few isolated shots zipped by. Then, from the opposite direction, there came to the ears of the Republicans a sound of music, wafted on the breeze—big drums and trumpets, the brassy din of circuses, and country fairs, and armies. Hernandez was puzzled. Could there be a merry-go-round somewhere near? At last he recognized the fascist anthem; the Tercio band was playing in the Zodocover Square.

The machine-gunner halted and began to shoot again. Ten, fifteen seconds, passed. Then the man beside him started bawling, "Get a move on, idiot!" and kicked the gunner's backside with all his might. "For God's sake, get going!" The kicks took more effect than the bullets of the advancing Moors. The gunner picked up his Hotchkiss and started running again.

At last they reached the bull-ring. Some thirty *milicianos* were there already. Seen from below, the huge, tiered walls looked stately as a fortress.

"A cardboard castle." Hernandez smiled grimly to himself. He went up to a window and looked outside. The Moors were beginning to post sentries round the entrances. "We're in for it at the first shot of their cannon," an artillery-man remarked. He, too, was in civilian clothes.

"The civilian fascists have started wearing white armlets," a *miliciano* said.

"They're having a *Te Deum* at the Cathedral. The priest is there. Seems he was in hiding here all the time." So much for our mass executions! Hernandez thought. He was still watching the scene outside; on the left the city was not yet invested.

"There's the Moorish cavalry!" someone shouted.

"You're crazy!" a voice replied.

So he was—or nearly so.

"It's a fool's game staying here," Hernandez said. "They'll be pouring in all the time, and you'll be caught like rats in a trap. The coast's still clear on the left. Don't trouble about the entrances. I'll just mop up a street with the machine-gun; you can jump down from the first storey—see you don't break your necks, though! Lay out the Moors who haven't been hit and try to stop you. There won't be many. Then cut round to the left. You've better things to do than just be slaughtered here. If they bring up reinforcements I'll look after them till you've made your getaway."

He put the machine-gun in position, rattled off two long belts, there-and-back—flaying the street from end to end. The Moors fell, or bolted. The men in the arena jumped down and drove back the few remaining Moors easily enough. Some fascists came up on the right. The machine-gun enfiladed them, forcing them back under cover of the doorways. The last Republicans vanished up the street in a confused mass, treading on each other's heels. His mind void of thoughts, Hernandez pressed his shoulder to the butt of his gun; he was utterly happy, happy without reserve.

No one was left in the bull-ring. At last he, too, jumped down. A glancing blow, like a whiplash, seared his forehead; he felt his eyes growing blurred with blood. Another blow crashed down on his back with a lumbering thud; a rifle-butt most likely. His arms beating the air, he collapsed on to his back.

26

IN THE courtyard of the Toledo jail a man began shouting at the top of his voice. That was very unusual. The real revolutionaries kept their mouths shut—because they were revolutionaries; the others, men who thought they were revolutionaries because those about them were, and had discovered, faced with death, that all they really clung to was life—life on any terms—kept silent, too. Silence is the prisoner's safeguard; thus insects try to be indistinguishable from the leaves in which they live.

And there were those who had lost even the desire to make their voices heard.

"You sons of bitches, you god-damned fools!" The voice was yelling. "I'm a bus conductor!" And, nearly bursting his lungs: "A bus conductor! That's my job, you fools!"

Through the bars of his cell Hernandez watched for the man, unseen as yet, to come into view. When he appeared, he was slapping an alpaca coat which he held in his left hand, as if to beat the dust out of it. In several towns the fascists had condemned to death workers whose coats were shiny on the shoulders—showing that a rifle had rested there. And the men who had carried cartridge-pouches had similar marks, due to the leather straps.

"I don't care a damn for your politics, you bastards." After taking breath, he burst out again. "Blast it! Just look at my shoulder! A rifle leaves a bruise there, don't it? Well, have I a bruise? I tell you I'm only a bus conductor."

Two guards led him off. To a cell more likely than to freedom, Hernandez thought. Order must be maintained.

The prisoners walked round and round the yard, each terrified by his own destiny. The cries of newspaper-boys drifted in from the city.

There were the newcomers, too. Daily, a batch of them. As usual Hernandez looked at them, and, as usual, they looked away, shrinking from his gaze. Hernandez was beginning to realize that men condemned to death are considered contagious.

A sound at the cell door, a bolt drawn back; the crucial sound just now.

He had had enough of it; he was looking forward to being shot. The men with whom he would have wished to live were all marked for death; with the others he had no wish to live. There was nothing particularly repellent in the prison system here, as prison systems go. His jailers, professionals imported from Seville, knew their job. Prison life was another matter. Sometimes a batch of twenty or thirty prisoners was led out; there was a sound of a volley and, after it, a desultory shot or two, finishing off the wounded. Sometimes, at night, there came the click of a bolt and a voice—almost invariably the same word: "What?" Then the chime of a priest's bell. Nothing more. But boredom set him thinking, and a condemned man's thoughts all turn on death.

A guard led Hernandez to the office of the Secret Service police, and stayed there with him. The officer had not come yet. Here, too, a window opened on the yard; the same prisoners going the same round.

The men who had not yet been "tried" were in the patio, the condemned men in the death-cells. Hernandez attempted to catch a glimpse of the men behind the bars on the far side of the yard, facing the window. They were too faraway. All he could make out was the portion of each hand clutching the bars on which the light fell. Behind the bars, nothing; only darkness.

In any case, he did not greatly wish to see them. It was with life, and not with death, that he wanted to exchange a friendly glance.

The Chief of the Secret Service entered. He was an officer, a man of about fifty with an elongated neck, small skull and moustache—the image of Queipo de Llano. He had Hernandez' wallet in his hand.

"Is this your wallet?"

"Yes."

The officer took out a wad of notes.

"These your notes?"

"I couldn't say for sure. But I remember having had some notes in my wallet."

"How many?"

"I really can't tell you."

The officer rolled his eyes towards the ceiling, as if invoking heaven to witness the carelessness of the Reds.

"Seven or eight hundred pesetas," Hernandez added, after a short pause.

"Do you recognize this note?"

The officer with the pin-head skull watched Hernandez' face, expecting, presumably, some tell-tale change of expression. Hernandez, utterly bored by the proceedings, glanced at the note; a bitter smile pursed his lips.

What was puzzling the Secret Service officer was a currency-note on which, among a jumble of obviously pointless scrawls, a dotted line had been traced in pencil, up and then down, forming an inverted V, and looking like some kind of symbol.

Moreno had drawn it. (He had not gone north to France, but to the Tagus front.) What was it Moreno had said? "In the prison, old boy, they talked about everything on earth—except politics. Never a word of politics. If anyone had started saying, 'I've fought for what I thought was right, and now I've lost, I'm willing to pay,' he'd have found everyone edging away from him. When a man dies, Hernandez, he dies alone; remember that!"

Were they thinking about politics, he wondered, those men there in the yard; or about rifles pointed at them—or about nothing?

Hernandez had said then, "I don't attach so much importance to death. To torture, yes." To which Moreno had replied, "I asked the fellows in prison, who had been tortured, what they were thinking about while it was going on. Almost all told me they were thinking: 'What next?' Even torture doesn't amount to much, compared with the certainty of death. The principal thing about death is that it makes all that has preceded it irremediable, eternally beyond redress. Torture and brutality *followed by death*—those are the really terrible things. Like this . . ." Then Moreno had begun drawing the pattern on the note. "Every sensation, however terrible it may be, is like that. But when it's over . . ."

"Do you recognize this note?" The Secret Service officer repeated.

"Oh, yes, I recognize it." Hernandez' smile disconcerted his interlocutor. No charge was made for drinks at the Militia Headquarters; Hernandez had laid the note on the table in an absent-minded moment.

"What do those signs mean?"

Hernandez did not answer.

"I'm asking you to tell me what that means."

Such men, it seemed, took themselves seriously. Hernandez

stared at the little head, the long neck which would look still longer when the man was dead. And he'd die the usual sort of death; a nastier one, perhaps, than the quick work of a firing squad. Poor fool!

Prisoners were walking past the window, their eyes averted.

"A fellow on our side," Hernandez said at last, with the same harsh smile, "made those 'signs.' He'd escaped from one of your prisons, where he'd been in cells for over a month, under sentence of death. He was explaining to me how in life everything is always offset by something else; and as he talked he drew those two lines, one of which stands for, let's say, misfortune, the other for its compensation. But, as he said, the tragedy of death is that it halts the process once for all, irrevocably. After death nothing can be compensated for. That, he said, is what makes the moment of death so terribly important even for an atheist.

"But," Hernandez added in a lower voice, "he was mistaken." He felt as if he were delivering a lecture to a slow-witted audience.

Now it was the Secret Service officer's turn to hesitate before replying. Had he understood? If so, it was a wonder! Still even the stupidest always understand a little. How living people waste time over futilities! Supposing now the fellow demanded further explanations—the devil of a nuisance!

For, despite his courage, there was one word Hernandez would not utter: "Torture."

At last the Secret Service officer came out of his brown study. "That depends on how you look at it," he said.

Again the prisoners walked past the window.

The officer spoke again. "Those were queer opinions for an officer. He'd have done better to go and see a priest."

"He wasn't on duty then," Hernandez said, unsmiling.

"Well, now! What about those dotted lines?"

"They're meaningless. The subject of our discussion had got his nerves on edge. That's all." There was no provocation in his tone, only complete indifference.

A bell rang and a guard entered.

"Break off!" the officer said.

Hernandez was still thinking about Moreno. One spring morning—how far away it seemed now, far as the romantic epoch of the "Cid,"—at the self-same table, in Toledo, he had heard Ramon Gomez de la Serna say, "Of course man has descended from the monkey; you need only watch him shelling nuts!" The age of Spanish humour—where was it now? Hernandez saluted and began to move towards the door.

"Halt!" the officer roared in an angry tone. Then added: "I've been given special orders about you, recommending that you should be treated with leniency, but . . ."

Lost in a maze of memories, Hernandez had been thrown off his guard by the order "Break off!" rapped out in a military tone. And automatically he had saluted, as he had been saluting for the last two months at Toledo, with his fist clenched. Were they to engage in another argument—about that gesture?

" 'Leniency,' " he said, "when a man's kept in the death-cell! And, anyhow, why those 'special orders?' "

The officer stared at him, puzzled—or exasperated. "Why do you think? Because they like your looks?" Then, struck by a sudden idea, he wagged his forefinger, as if to dispel an illusion, as if to say: "No, there's no need to be on your guard—with me anyhow," and added with a smile: "I know all about it."

"About what?" Hernandez calmly enquired.

"A little touched," was obviously the fascist's judgment of him. A Red, of course . . .

"Why, obviously because of your conduct towards the officers at the Alcazar."

A man does not go mad out of disgust. But suddenly Hernandez was conscious of his unkempt four days' growth of beard—keeping him warm. He ceased smiling. His fingers, resting on the table, clenched.

"Let's hope," he said, looking the officer in the eyes and steadying his clenched fist on the table, "let's hope such an opportunity doesn't present itself again." His shoulders were quivering.

"I do not think that such an opportunity will present itself again—for you."

"So much the better."

"That depends how you look at it. . . . Why did you keep this note?"

"One usually keeps a note, till one spends it."

Another officer entered. The Secret Service officer handed the note to him. And the guard led Hernandez back to his cell.

27

ONCE again Hernandez was walking in the Toledo streets. The prisoners were linked two by two. A car passed. Then two little girls walking side by side. An old woman with a pitcher. Another car, carrying fascist officers. Ah, yes, Hernandez thought, I'm sentenced to death—for "mutiny." Another woman passed with a parcel of groceries, another with a pail. A man, with nothing.

Living people.

Death comes to all. He had seen a friend of his, a woman, die of malignant cancer; her body had turned the colour of her chestnut hair. And she had been a doctor. A *miliciano* at Toledo had been crushed to death by a tank. And there were lingering deaths—from uraemia, for instance. To all death comes. To all except those Moors escorting the prisoners; killers are beyond life and death.

Just as they set foot on the bridge, the man beside Hernandez whispered: "Gillette blade. Come close."

Hernandez squeezed up to him. A family passed. (Yes, there still were families!) A small boy eyed them. "Why, they're quite old," he said. Old! Hernandez smiled and thought: He exaggerates. Is death giving me a sense of humour? A woman passed, in black, riding on a donkey. She'd do better not to give herself away, he thought, looking us over with such concern. All that Hernandez could feel of his long body was the pressure of the ropes upon his wrists. The blade was sawing through the rope.

"Done it!"

Hernandez gave a gentle tug. Yes, the rope was cut. For the first time he looked round; the man beside him had a small, very bristly beard.

"There's still some of our comrades behind the hill," the man said. "At the first cross-roads."

They had crossed the bridge. Just as they reached the buttress, the man jumped.

Hernandez did not jump.

He was too tired, and tired of life as well. It would mean an effort, another effort. What was beyond the embankment—bushes? Impossible to see. He remembered Moscardo's letters.

Some Moors were jumping down after the man, firing. There were not enough of them; they daren't leave the column. Well, he would never know if that bearded man had carried it off. Perhaps he had; the Moors had a surly look as they climbed back on to the road.

The dark procession set off again. There was a slight rise in the ground ahead of them, and in it a longish hollow to the bottom of which he could not see. In front of it stood ten falangists with arms at rest, and an officer. On the right Hernandez saw some more prisoners; with the newcomers there would be fifty, all told. Their civilian clothes made the only dark patch in the brilliant sunlight; the khaki uniforms of the Moors were the exact colour of Toledo.

It had come, the moment which had always haunted him, that moment when a man knows he will die without the least chance of resistance.

Seemingly the prisoners were as indifferent to dying as falangists and Moors to having to shoot them. The bus conductor was with the rest, precisely like them now. All looked a little dazed, like men who are over-tired; no more than that. The firing-squad, however, showed signs of restlessness, though all they had to do was to await the order to fire already-loaded rifles.

"Atten-tion!"

The command was rapped out more peremptorily than usual, and the ten members of the squad stiffened up, to act their parts in the comedy of "honour." Already far beyond all histrionics, Hernandez and his fifty companions stared into vacancy.

Three fascists had just led off three prisoners and, after posting them on the edge of the ditch, had withdrawn.

"Ready!"

The condemned man on the left had a mop of round-cropped hair. The three men were posted on a ridge above the level of the watching group, and stood out, taller than life, against the historic mountain-range beyond the Tagus. But how small a thing is history beside living—still living—flesh and blood!

The three men somersaulted backwards. They were already in the ditch when the squad fired. Absurd! How can they possibly escape? Hernandez thought. The other prisoners giggled nervously.

They would not have to escape. The prisoners had seen the somersault first, but the squad had fired before it. A trick of the nerves.

Three more men were lined up. It was unthinkable, knocking all those fifty men over in threes, like ninepins, into the pit behind. Something was bound to happen, had to happen. . . .

One of the prisoners on the ridge glanced down over his shoulder into the ditch and instinctively began to move away from it. Then, as he brought his eyes round, without raising them, and looked ahead he saw the feet of the firing squad quite near, pointing in his direction. He stopped. The prisoner on the right began to shout something. Then all three crumpled up, their hands clasping their bellies, and toppled over. This time the squad had aimed lower.

The rest of the prisoners stood by, silent and impassive. From the city came the forlorn braying of a donkey, and the cry of an alcarraza-seller; far-off sounds, dying upon the golden air.

One of the men who had been leading the prisoners to the place of execution on the ridge, bent over the ditch, with his revolver pointing forward. A fisherman's attitude. The sky was quivering with light. Coffins at least, Hernandez thought, are *clean*. Europe may have no love left for most things, but she still has for her dead. The soldier crouching above the ditch was following with his revolver something that moved in it. He fired. It is as painful to picture the *coup de grâce* administered to an unconscious man as to picture it given a dying one. And, at this hour in half the land of Spain young men were playing their grim part in the same tragic comedy, firing across the same bright morning air; peasants like these were falling sheer or leaping back into a pit . . . It struck Hernandez that he had never seen men turn back-somersaults before except at circuses.

Three men were standing where the others had stood, waiting for the plunge.

If, Hernandez mused, I hadn't had Moscardo's letter sent on, if I hadn't tried to "behave decently," would those three men be there? Two were standing awkwardly, too far forward and looking to the side; the third seemed wondering whether to turn his back on the rifles or to face them. Like seeing a train off, Hernandez thought, with a touch of hysteria; one never knows how to stand! And, damn it, even if I'd acted otherwise, it would have made no difference! There were plenty of fellows who acted otherwise.

The organizers of the death parade went back to the three blunderers and, taking them by the shoulders (not in the least brutally), set them straight. The prisoners, too, seemed trying to help them out—to grasp what was expected of them and behave accordingly. Like mourners being lined up at a funeral . . . But these men were attending their own.

"Seventeen, eighteen, nineteen, twenty." The prisoners were in three ranks. The man who was numbering them was counting up the men who would be shot before him. "No. Seventeen, eighteen, nineteen . . ."

He could not get the count right; Hernandez was on the point of telling him the correct number. There were only seventeen men all told; not nineteen, not twenty. Somebody made a remark, about dying, most likely. "All right! All right!" a voice replied. "Oh, shut up! There's worse than that."

Let's hope, Hernandez thought, this isn't all a dream. Just think of waking and having to go through it all again!

Would they never manage to get the prisoners facing the rifles like a wedding group facing the camera into the correct pose?

Bright air shimmered on the Tagus hills and bathed Toledo in a crystal sheen. Hernandez was beginning to learn how history is made. Once more in this land of black-clothed women, as so often in the past, a generation of widows was in the making. When such things are being done, what is the meaning of "nobility?" Or "generosity?"

Hernandez felt his eyes yearning towards the fresh-turned earth. Earth inert, reposeful . . . Only living men are torn by anguish and disgust.

The most appalling thing about the prisoners was their courage. Obedient they were, but not passive victims. How inept was the symbol of the slaughter-house! Men are not felled like cattle; killing them is an intricate process. Hernandez remembered Pradas, their conversation about generosity. At last the three had taken the right pose; yes, all was ready for the camera. Generosity is the virtue of the conqueror.

A volley. Two fell back into the ditch, one onto his face. A minion of death stepped forward. Was he going to push the body over with his foot? No. Stooping, he dragged it by an arm and leg—a heavy corpse, and the ground sloped up.

Tiresome unto death; and after! Into the hole with him! . . .
But would this business *never* end?

They were getting into the routine; those on the right—of
killing, those on the left—of being killed. Three more lined
up on the ridge where the others had stood. The drab expanse
of ruined mansions and closed factories was taking on an aspect of eternity, the agelessness of graveyards: as if up to the
crack of doom in never-ending sequence, groups of three men
would take their stand there, waiting to be killed.

"You wanted the earth," a fascist exclaimed. "Now you
have it!"

One of the three men was the bus conductor; the smooth
patch on the shoulder of the overcoat which had led to his
death-sentence glinted in the sun. He had ceased protesting.
He stood there waiting; like the others he had let himself be
lined up calmly, without a murmur. "I don't give a damn for
your god-damned politics, you bastards!" He was a puny little
man with a complexion the colour of black olives. Simultaneously with the movement of the rifles brought up to the
shoulder, he raised his fist in the Popular Front salute.

Hernandez watched the uplifted fist; a moment hence those
fingers would be clenched on earth.

The firing-squad hesitated, not because they were impressed,
but waiting for the prisoner to be called to order—the conqueror's order, pending that of death. The three men in charge
of operations walked up to him. The little man gazed at them,
stolid in his innocence as a stake rooted in the soil, and gave
them a look of undying, elemental hatred that had already
something of the other world in its intensity.

Ah, Hernandez thought, if that man could get away now
. . . ! He was not to get away. The officer had just given
the order to fire.

Another batch of prisoners took their places in front of the
trench. Their fists were raised.

"Hands down!" The officer shouted.

Under the clenched fists the prisoners' shoulders lifted in a
brief gesture of disdain. The officer stooped to tie a shoe-lace.
Then, straightening up, he too, shrugged his shoulders and
gave the order.

Three more prisoners, including Hernandez, walked up to
the ridge. Fumes of hot steel and fresh-turned soil hung on
the air.

Part Two

THE MANZANARES

I. Action and Reaction

1

THE panic-stricken mob that had fled from Toledo, the un-armed *milicianos* from the Tagus and the remnants of peasant battalions from Estremadura were flocking into Aranjuez Station. Like leaves whirled together and then dispersed by the wind, groups that had arrived in such a hurry vanished among the red-flowered chestnut-trees of the park, or, like lunatics in their asylum garden, tramped up and down the avenues of majestic plane-trees.

The draggled remnants of so many dramatically named formations—the Unconquerables, the Red Eagles, the Eagles of Liberty—were moving to and fro excitedly on a carpet of fallen flowers, thick as the dead leaves on a forest path. Their arms hung down, dragging their rifles after them like dogs on a leash; now and then they stopped to listen to the sound of the approaching guns on the far side of the river. Between the shots, rising up from the ground and deadened by the heavy curtain of decaying chestnut-flowers, they could hear the faint sound of an ancient bell.

"A church bell at a time like this!" Manuel exclaimed.

"It sounds more like a gardener's bell to me," Lopez replied.

"It comes from the direction of the station."

Other bells, large and small, bicycle bells, motor-horns and even a clatter of cooking-pots, were mingling now with the deep notes of the bell they first had heard. And, across the violet-leaves as large as a man's hand, there poured out of the recesses of the park the wreckage of the revolutionary dream, like wild tribes rallying to their tom-toms, with their para-phernalia of swords, striped blankets, garments made of cur-tains, sporting guns and even the latest Mexican hats.

"And to think that at least half of them are brave . . . !" Manuel said.

"The strangest thing of all, you owl," Lopez observed, "is that they haven't broken a single statue."

From end to end of the park, the famous plaster busts, rose-pink now in the reflection of the weathered bricks, remained unharmed under the romantic plane-trees. Manuel did not look at them. Eddying like some aviary brought from the Americas by Spanish princes for their Aranjuez garden, the fantastic rout straggled down towards the station, under the brick arcades bathed in the rosy light of the royal vistas.

As Manuel and Lopez began following the crowd towards the station, one word grew clear, and the word was "Locomotive." On no account must they go to Madrid! Manuel thought. Only too easy it was to picture the effects of ten thousand demoralized men arriving there, full of the most hair-raising yarns, immediately after the fall of Toledo, just when Madrid was desperately organizing her defences.

They were now quite near the station. "Drid-drid-drid-Madrid-drid-drid" sounded on all sides like the chirring of a swarm of frenzied crickets.

"Having cut and run, they'll try to make out the Moors are invincible," Lopez said; "the Moors must be better armed, and all the rest of it—just to account for their running away!"

"They bolted because they weren't properly led. Before that, they fought as well as we did."

Manuel remembered Barca and Ramos, his comrades in the armoured train, and the others on the Tagus. And, last of all, an old trade-unionist who had been standard-bearer at a popular demonstration some years before. Held up by a large body of police, the demonstrators had been told they might go ahead provided their flags were furled. "Furl the flags!" the leaders had shouted. Manuel had a very powerful voice. When he impatiently repeated the order, the old man had stared at him without a word, but his eyes seemed to say: "As we have to do it, we'll do it—but the slower the better. You've still a lot to learn, my lad." Manuel had never forgotten the incident. It wasn't, he reflected, always the same people who behaved badly. The link between Manuel and the proletariat was made up of too many memories, too many loyalties, to be snapped by any passing madness—even a lapse as grave as this.

"It's easy enough," he said, "being loyal to one's friends when they're in the right; the hard thing is when they're behaving badly."

"Well, one can always have a shot at it."

A man with a beard, who looked like the Negus elongated by a distorting mirror, had climbed onto the roof of a limousine in front of the station entrance. Inside, the waiting-rooms and passages were packed with people; on the platform there was no more room for a single child. Above them loomed majestically the tall trees of the square.

"Who knows how to drive an engine?" yelled the bearded man. "There's a train, there's an engine, there's everything we need!"

Suddenly, silence. Everybody was waiting for someone to come to the rescue.

"Set her going . . . set her going."

"What?"

"Set her going. . . ."

The speaker, at first invisible, was pushed and pulled amid a clamorous outburst of enthusiasm until he reached the roof of the car.

"I can set her going." He was a meek, furtive creature, spectacled and slightly bald. "I tell you, eh, if we go carefully about it, I can drive her."

The temperature dropped. Step by step Manuel and Lopez were nearing the car.

"Can you slow up?" a voice cried.

"Er—aye—I think so."

"Eh, boys, we can hop on her when she's moving."

Manuel clambered on to the roof of the car.

"And the wounded?" he called out. "Are *they* going to hop on too?"

A number of the crowd began trying to climb on to their comrades' shoulders. What was his game? To march on Madrid or what? Another officer!

"Comrades, listen to me! I am an . . ."

He could no longer be heard. The shouting on all sides drowned his words. He lifted up both arms, got three seconds' silence and shouted: "I'm an engineer, and I tell you you can't control that engine."

"It's the man who commanded the motorized column," someone in the crowd muttered.

"Drive her, you!"

"I don't know how to drive her, but I do know what an engine is that's out of control. The men who risk it will be responsible for the death of two thousand of their comrades. And what about the wounded?"

Fortunately the volunteer driver did not inspire confidence.

"Then what about it?" someone yelled from the crowd.

"Make a suggestion."

"Spit it out!"

"Do you want us to walk?"

"Supposing we're cut off?"

"Is it true that Navalcarnero's fallen?"

"What about it?"

"Stay here!" Manuel roared at them.

The crowd surged round him in baffled, sullen fury. A hundred hands rose up and fluttered like leaves tossed by the wind, then sank down again into the swirling mass.

"It's two days since we . . ."

"The Moors are on their way!"

Manuel knew that there were no supplies.

"Who's going to feed us?"

"I am," he answered.

"And find shelter?"

"I shall."

A breathing-space, he thought; a breakwater—but there was no knowing whether the waves wouldn't prove the stronger.

"It's easier to fight the Moors than make Madrid in a runaway train."

Again hands shot up above the crowd—clenched fists, now. But not in comradely salute.

"In a quarter of an hour we'll be shot to bits," Lopez murmured. He had joined his friend on the roof of the car.

"I don't care. So long as they don't go barging into Madrid." He remembered a remark of Heinrich's. "Every situation has at least one positive element; the thing's to find it, and to build on it." He began shouting again.

"The orders of the Communist Party are strict discipline and obedience to the military authority. Communists, hold up your hands."

The communists were in no hurry to declare themselves. Manuel noticed that the bald little mechanic beside him wore the Party star.

"Where's your gun?" he asked him. "A communist never gives up his gun."

The mechanic looked at him and said, without the least humorous intention: "But he does! You can see it for yourself."

"Then he dismisses himself from the Party. Give me your badge."

"Certainly, old boy. You don't need to yell like that. Here it is. What the hell are you going to do with it?"

Seven or eight badges fell on the roof of the car with flimsy, feeble thuds.

"In five minutes they'll be pumping lead into us," Lopez said.

"No fear! They haven't the guts for it."

He began again, as loud as ever but more slowly so that the crowd could understand each word.

"We've all taken up arms against fascism. We all knew we might be killed. If any of you had been killed at Somosierra that would have been all in the day's work, wouldn't it? What has made the difference? Because there has been an awful muddle. The Party and the Government, they've said it straight: military discipline first. We're two Commissioned Officers here, and we take the responsibility. We're going to clean things up. This evening you'll get your rations, and you won't sleep out. You've got arms and ammunition. We won at Somosierra. We'll win here. Let's fight the same way, that's all that's needed. The river's easy to defend, and the tanks can't cross it."

"What about planes?" cried a dozen voices.

"We'll be in trenches tomorrow morning. Bomb-proof dug-outs in 'em. And the shelter of the hill-sides. There's no question of fighting at Madrid or Barcelona or the North Pole. Or of giving in to Franco, and shaking in your shoes for the next twenty years for fear you've been given away by your tart, or the busybody next door, or the priest. Think of the Asturias! In a day or two our new planes will be ready. The whole country's with us. We've got to hang on—here and not elsewhere. Not drag an army of tramps into Madrid. We've got to stay here with the wounded."

"Right! Good for you!"

"No! They're kidding you again!" The voice seemed issuing from the rotten leaves underfoot.

"Who is? Let's have a look at you, my lad." The man who had spoken made no sign. Manuel knew that to Spaniards it was the personal guarantee that counted. He went on.

"Who d'you mean, by 'they?' Listen! We two, and the comrade beside me, have been fighting from the very start, and it's we who're taking the responsibility. I tell you, you'll get food and shelter. You know it's one of yourselves who's talking. We stood together on the eighteenth of July. Today you're panicky, you're hungry, you're badly armed. But don't forget there's men among you who knocked out the field-guns with light cars, who forced the Montaña Barracks with a battering-ram, who licked the Triana fascists with knives, and the Cordova fascists with slings. Tell me, boys, did you do all that only to scuttle now? As man to man, I tell you—for all your bellyaching! I *know* that I can trust you.

"If by tomorrow you haven't had all I promised you, you can shoot me. Until then, do as I tell you."

"Where d'you live?"

"Aranjuez isn't a big place. And I've no escort."

"Why doesn't he tell us . . . ?"

"That's enough. I promised to get you organized, you promise to defend the Republic. Who's with me?"

In a flurry of dead leaves swirling up to the tree-tops the crowd surged this side and that, as if groping to find the way. Bent heads wagged to and fro, shoulders swayed as in a barbaric dance, hands fluttered in the air. Lopez realized that, in the last analysis, a speaker's influence depends on what lies behind it. When Manuel had said "I trust you," all of them knew he meant what he said and the better part of all their personalities came to the fore. For they could not doubt that he was bent on helping them; many knew, too, that he was a good organizer.

"Communists, fall in by the lorry. You've no more rights than the others, but you've more duties. Got it? Volunteers, on the left."

"Let's begin digging trenches now," a voice cried out of the confusion.

"You'll go into trenches when those in command tell you."

They were all wanting to be doing something now; they were shoving each other into line as they had shoved each other out of the way in their stampede towards the train.

"Militia and Party Section-leaders, empty the waiting-room and occupy it. Other comrades, stay where you are. Each man will be served with a mattress or bedding."

He jumped down from the car, and Lopez after him.

"It'll start all over again in five minutes, won't it?" Lopez said.

"No. They've got to have something to do until they go to bed. It'll be all right now. You stay here."

"What the hell can I do?" Lopez had no illusions about his incapacity to command.

"Make 'em number off. That's essential, as I shall have to get them bedding. Have each group leader get together his militia unit, or whatever the formation is, and report to you their number. That'll give me an hour. There must be quite fifteen hundred men there."

"Sure! Go ahead!"

Lopez was not very efficient, but he was plucky and keen.

Quite worn out, Manuel was huddled up on what had been a bishop's chair, in the cell of the Superior of a convent. With almost vacant eyes, he was staring out at the plaster busts in the park, glimmering like moonlit statues in a Persian garden.

Lopez' idea was to take the busts to Madrid and after the victory replace them by "significant" animals. But Manuel paid no attention to his friend's remarks. As soon as he had left Lopez, he rushed off to see the Popular Front Committee. Among them he found an enterprising few who knew the town well. They had spotted this convent for him, and collected six hundred straw pallets, beds and mattresses. The little orphanage girls had given up half their bedding and were sleeping two in a bed. Everything available in convents, barracks, and guard-rooms had been commandeered. But there was not enough to go round. Some men would have to do with a shake-down on straw, or rugs.

When he was half way through the job a delegation arrived; it had been elected by the soldiers for liaison between them and their commanding officers. It was ten o'clock and everybody was in bed. Manuel, after being glued to the telephone for an hour and a quarter in communication with the Communist Party, the Fifth Regiment and the War Ministry, had extracted a promise of three days' rations. He would use that time to organize his supply system. But the lorries would not arrive before daybreak, though a few were on their way, with enough food for two hundred men. Manuel had announced that they would eat at eleven. Moreover, the Fifth Regiment was to send him some trained soldiers who could start instructing the men here, and form the nucleus of a new regiment.

There was a knock at the door. The delegation had come back.

"Hello!" said Manuel, his head ringed by a halo of Virgins and Sacred Hearts. "What's the trouble now?"

"There's no trouble. It's the other way round. You see, you and your pal, you're not soldiers, though you're in command. There's no getting round that. In one way, that suits us better. What you said to us was sense; we haven't done all we have done just to end up like this. And you've kept your promises. At any rate, up to now. And we know it's not so easy. So we —the delegation, and the other boys—we've been putting our heads together. See? We've decided—about the train, for instance, you were quite right."

The spokesman was a cabinet-maker with a drooping grey moustache. Out in the park the famous nightingales were in full-throated song.

"So we thought if we put a guard at the station, what happened today probably wouldn't happen again. We've got the men, all right. So we came to suggest this guard."

Behind the speaker his comrades in *monos* stood against the white background of the cell, one in front, three behind; that was the formation the workers' delegations always used to adopt. That these men realized they were representing their own men, their lives, their faults, their responsibilities, before one of their own side, was so evident that it was as if the revolution itself, in its simplest, most significant form, stood there personified by them. For the speaker the revolution meant just the right to talk like that. Manuel embraced him in the Spanish way, and said nothing. For the first time he was in the presence of a fraternity that expressed itself in action.

"Now we eat!" he said to them.

They went down together. As Manuel had hoped, all the men were plunged in the heavy sleep of soldiers on active service—in the dormitories and vaulted halls, at the feet of the blue and gold statues of the saints—warrior saints with red flags on their lances.

"Who wants food?" Manuel asked—but not too loud. The only reply was a series of sleepy snorts and grunts. There wouldn't be a hundred men to feed, and the supplies from Madrid would suffice. He went on his way, his boot-heels clattering on the flagstones like the sound of footfalls in a church. He wanted to laugh, and at the same time felt ashamed.

When the meal was over, he went back to the Popular Front headquarters. That night he would have to organize his equipment, find soap, and be ready at dawn to designate the new formations. "Who'd have thought," he smiled to himself, "that soap was needed to make war!" The trees were invisible in the gloom, but he was vaguely aware of the dense profusion of their leaves above him stirring in the night breeze. A faint perfume came from the rose-gardens, smothered by the bitter

tang of boxwood and plane-trees, as if it were being wafted
across the river by the muffled clangour of the guns. There
was no sign of the lorries as yet. The members of the Committee were on watch, too.

When he got back, Manuel was challenged at the convent
gate.

"What the hell are you playing at?" he asked, after making
himself known.

"We're the guard," was the answer.

How many fascist surprise attacks had succeeded through
the lack of guards! In the dim glow that came from the convent, Manuel saw the glint of three rifle barrels against three
dark great-coats; the first self-appointed guard of the Spanish
war.

2

The night of November 6th

THREE of the bombers had been repaired. Magnin's plane,
known as the "Jaurès," was flying over the sleeping Balearics.
For the last hour it had been alone above the sea. Attignies
was piloting. All around the badly extinguished lights of Palma,
the anti-aircraft guns were spitting up shells against the invisible plane; the town below was defending itself like a blind
man screaming. Magnin was looking for a Nationalist cruiser
and the ships loaded with arms in the harbour. Searchlights
were stabbing through the darkness behind and in front of
him, intersecting each other. He thought tensely that it was
like using thin wands to catch a fly. Except for the pilot's
cabin, the bomber was in complete darkness.

Were they fighting against an enemy or against cold? It was
more than eighteen degrees below freezing point. The gunners
detested having to fire with their gloves on, but in the intense
cold to touch the metal of the guns meant burns. The bombs
threw up spouts of water into the night, lighting them with
an orange glow. They would have to find out from the War
Ministry whether the ships had been hit.

Each one of them was watching the anti-aircraft shells
burst around him. With ice-cold faces and bodies enclosed in
the warmth of their fur-lined flying-suits, they were alone in
the vast darkness stretching over the sea.

The plane suddenly lit up.

"For Christ's sake, put that out!" Magnin shouted. But the very next moment he saw the shadows of the plane's wings, and realised that the light had come from outside.

The searchlight returned, catching the plane again. Magnin saw Pol's good-humoured face and Gardet's back with the little rifle slung across it. They had carried out the bombing of the ships in complete darkness, broken by the blue lightnings of the anti-aircraft shells they had so far avoided. It was their comradeship in arms which had brought them into that cabin filled with menacing light; for the first time since they began their flight, those men could *see each other*.

One and all were peering down at the searchlight to which that blinding beam linked them—aiming at them. They all knew that focussing itself along the same line there was a gun.

Down below lights were going out, pursuit planes were no doubt taking off and the darkness stretched away to the horizon. And in the midst of darkness, with the plane shaking them about like shot in a box as it spun earthwards in an unsuccessful attempt to free itself from the searchlight, were those seven men bathed in blue effulgence.

Magnin sprang to the side of Attignies, who was tugging at the stick, his eyes closed to escape from that blinding dazzle. Three seconds more, and the anti-aircraft guns would have opened fire.

The left hand of every occupant of the cabin went to the buckle of his parachute.

Attignies banked, teeth clenched and feet tensed against the controls, wishing with every fibre of his body, from his toes upwards, that he were in a pursuit plane: the bomber was turned with the unwieldiness of a lorry. And the light was still after them.

The first shell—thirty yards away. The plane jolted violently. The anti-aircraft guns would correct the error. Magnin tore aside the ear-flap of Attignies' flying-helmet.

"Falling leaf," the pilot shouted, indicating the manoeuvre with his hand.

It was the device by which a plane frees itself from a hurricane when the controls no longer function: a dive with all the weight of the machine behind it.

Magnin's moustache registered a frantic protest, visible but inaudible in the white glare and the noise of the engines. The searchlight would follow their dive down. He made another movement indicating a sideslip, followed by a turn.

Attignies went into a skid that seemed like a fall, with a noise of clanking metal and cartridge-clips rolling about the cabin. He fell headlong into an abyss of darkness, turned and made off in a corkscrew curve. Above and below, the search-light went stabbing through the sky, like a blind man feeling his way with a rapier.

The plane was well clear of the searchlight zone now—lost once more in the protecting night. As if sinking into the repose of sleep, the crew of the plane had regained their posts and were luxuriating in the relief which was the invariable sequel to an engagement; driving through the freezing darkness above a lightless sea. But each of them had vividly before him the picture of the features of his comrades as they had been thrown into relief for that brief moment.

After a short halt at Valencia among the orange-groves, Magnin had left the "Jaurès" at Albacete, from where it was going on to Alcalá-de-Henares. Albacete was the last aero-drome in the possession of the Republicans on that side of Madrid. A section of the squadron had remained at Albacete to test the repaired planes; the remainder was fighting at Alcalá.

At Albacete the International Brigade was in process of formation. In the bright morning air keen with a touch of winter, thousands of men thronged the little pink and yellow town. The market-place, with its promiscuous display of knives, quarter-litre drinking mugs, pants, suspenders, shoes, combs and badges, was humming like a country fair. The shoe and hosiery shops could be picked out by the queues of soldiers in front of them. A Chinese pedlar was offering his shoddy wares to a sentry who had his back to him. The sentry turned round and the pedlar made off: they were both Chinese.

When Magnin arrived at Brigade Headquarters, the dele-gate for whom he was looking was at the instruction camp and would not return for another hour. Magnin had had no lunch. He went into the nearest bar.

Amid the throng inside, a drunk was shouting at the top of his voice. In spite of every precaution, an extraordinarily mot-ley collection of recruits was arriving for the various inter-national contingents. Rejected and packed off by the noon train, they made themselves a general nuisance all the morning

beforehand. On one occasion all the hobos of Lyons had set
out to join the Brigade, only to be stopped at the frontier and
returned to the station they started from. The Brigade was
made up of men who could fight, not "extras" from a film
studio.

"I'm fed up with it!" the drunk was bawling. "Fed up!
Haven't I flown the Prince of Monaco across the Atlantic, and
served with the Legion? You call yourselves revolutionaries!
Know what you are? A gang of lousy, yellow bastards!"

He had flung a glass on to the ground and was trampling
on the broken pieces.

A socialist rose to his feet, but an equally wild friend of
the drunk put out a restraining hand.

"Let him alone. He's a friend of mine. He's easy game when
he's like that. I'll fix him."

The friend went up behind the glass-breaker and rapped
out:

"Fall in! 'Shun! Eyes front!"

The drunk immediately went through the correct motions.

"Right—turn! Quick march!"

The drunk made for the door and disappeared through it.

"Good as gold, eh?" the friend said, and went back to his
cognac.

Magnin was looking round for faces he knew, but failed to
find any. He went up to the first floor. Three of the paid air
force volunteers were playing knuckle-bones on the floor beneath a portrait with a waxed moustache.

A considerable number of the mercenaries had returned to
France. This lot had their backs to Magnin, their attention
concentrated on their game. The window was open, letting in
the cold morning air. Accompanying the click of the big
Spanish bones came a sharper noise like hammering, as distinct as the beat of horses' hoofs, but with the regular rhythm
of flails and forges. It was the dull tread of marching troops.
The man who had just thrown the bones still had his hand in
the air: his bones went on quivering. The hammer-beat of
the boots, right beneath the window, was setting the cobwork
houses trembling; the shock of the rhythm of war had invaded even the local pastime.

Magnin went to the window. Still in civilian clothes, but
shod with military boots, with their dogged communist faces
or the pale cast of the intellectual, the Brigade was tramping
down the narrow street, resonant as a passage-way. There were

old Poles with walrus moustaches and young ones whose faces recalled Soviet films, Germans with shaved heads, Algerians, Italians looking like Spaniards who had strayed by mistake into the International fold, Englishmen with more colour about them than any of the others, Frenchmen on the lines of Maurice Thorez, of Maurice Chevalier; and all alike inspired, not with the young Madrid recruits' earnest desire to learn, but by memories of military service or of actual fighting against each other. They were nearing the barracks, and they started to sing. For the first time in history, the strains of the *International* were rising from men of every nation united to do battle together.

Magnin turned round. The mercenaries were going on with their game. They were not going to let anyone pull that sort of stuff with them.

He had some hopes now of being able to build up an efficient foreign air force. It had taken him more than a fortnight in Barcelona to organize a repair service, and his absence had increased to no small extent the disorder of the Pelicans. But six reconditioned planes would be able to take the air again within a week.

The delegate whom he had to see was with the men passing beneath the window. Magnin started back towards Brigade Headquarters, his eyebrows puckered pensively, pondering his half-formed project.

3

"No, BUT I mean to say is this going on for long?"

Wearing overalls and a crash-helmet that endowed him with Roman dignity, Leclerc was ranting and gesticulating in front of his plane crew at the Alcalá aerodrome. Thirty yards away, out of hearing, a squadron-leader friend of Sembrano, by the name of Carnero, was studying the Madrid sky through field-glasses. Filthy weather.

"Why can't we get a move on? They'd still be Fritzolinis to me, even if they were to rig themselves out like archangels!"

Leclerc classed Germans and Italians indiscriminately as "Fritzolinis."

Carnero climbed into his plane, which drew into line ready to take off. The carburetor of the machine he normally com-

manded was out of order, and he was in charge of the
"Jaurès," with a Spanish crew. Leclerc and a Spanish bomber
followed him. The Republican fighters were already circling
over Alcalá—a miserable collection. A few planes had arrived
from America, but still without up-to-date machine-guns. The
Government air force was still fighting with the 1913 Spanish-
made Lewis.

Since the breaking up of his "Orion" and his installation as
pilot of the "Pelican I," pieced together from two other machines, Leclerc had abandoned his grey hat in favour of a
leather crash-helmet which he contrived to wear with a stu-
pendously official air.

"What about the thermos?" asked the forward gunner in
the "Pelican I." It was just beside Leclerc's seat, out of his
sight.

"Thermos be damned! I'm due today for a Caesarian! Got
to do it myself. It's no joking matter, me lad!"

A few minutes later, escorted by their fighters, the three
planes were over Madrid. With the exception of Barajas, all
the aerodromes which the Pelicans had used were now in
enemy hands. Every road was packed with jostling traffic: in
front of Getafe, a field had been transformed into a parking
place for lorries. Yet the lack of protection everywhere was
such that it seemed impossible that it could be enemy territory.
From his position on the right, Leclerc was carefully watching
the other two planes as they came out of the very low clouds.
Above them was their escort of fighters. For one moment the
clouds lay so near the ground that they had to go above them.
Between two layers of grey, the silhouettes of the planes in
battle formation filled the pale void with the black wings of
war. As the planes came out of the clouds, the lorry parking
field lay beneath. The roads on both sides were solid with
Franco vehicles. The mechanized column from the Tagus had
reached the gates of Madrid.

The fascist pursuit planes swooped down from the upper
clouds. Seven Fiats coming head-on, unmistakable with their
W-shaped stays between the wings. The uppermost Republican
fighters opened their throttles to the maximum and rushed
forward to meet them.

The enemy barrage began.

German anti-aircraft guns had reached Madrid in large
quantities. The shells from the quick-firers were bursting at
intervals of fifty yards. Leclerc thought of his plane's wing-

spread of twenty-six yards. Even in 1918 he had not seen such a barrage. The German gunners were not aiming at the bombers but some hundreds of yards ahead of them, exactly at their height, so that the latter seemed to be throwing themselves deliberately into the danger-zone. Far beyond, the pursuit planes were engaging each other. Leclerc dived: the shell bursts followed suit.

"They've got electric fire-directors," the bomber said.

Leclerc could scarcely follow the battle between the fighters, whose intertwined parabolas gave the impression of crashes and of acrobatics at one and the same time.

The machine-gunners were watching the fight, and the bomber the ground below. Leclerc had his eyes glued to Carnero's plane, which was climbing, diving, side-slipping, still confronted by the bursting shells, which suddenly came closer. Following his leader through the wild confusion like a blind man linked to his guide, with no thought for anything but that he must not diverge from the same course, Leclerc was rushing into the barrage with the stoicism of a man driving a tank.

The barrage was only a hundred yards away now.

Shells and planes both drew together at the same time. Leclerc's machine bounded ten yards higher; the "Jaurès," broken right through the middle, hurled its eight occupants into the leaden sky like a handful of seeds broadcast on the air. Leclerc felt suddenly as though the arm on which he was leaning had just been severed. In front of the falling men, black specks grouped round a single parachute, he saw the terrified faces of his bomber and forward gunner. He banked still more sharply and made for Alcalá at top speed.

"Never seen that, even in the War," Leclerc had kept repeating ever since he had shut off his engine before landing.

Grouped round him on the landing-ground, the crew did not answer. With tragic mouth and haunted eyes, Leclerc slouched off towards the aerodrome headquarters.

Vargas was waiting for him, sitting in an armchair with his long legs stretched out, his narrow face turned towards the low clouds drifting past the window. He was in uniform now.

Leclerc began a heroic account of his flight. When he got as far as the fall of Carnero's plane, Vargas cut him short.

"What were your orders?"

"To bomb the Getafe column."

"Were there already some lorries *in front of* the parking place, coming up in line?"

"Yes. But getting through was out of the question with that barrage. Carnero proved that!"

On the occasions when Leclerc did not dare to use his slang, his speech became stilted rather than natural.

"Was the barrage over the lorry-park?" Vargas repeated.

"Yes."

"But there were lorries *in front,* nearer you?"

"Well, yes."

"Tell me why you brought your bombs back."

It had just dawned on Leclerc that he had run away.

"There were the enemy fighters . . ."

They both knew that the battle between the pursuit planes had taken place more than a mile from there. And even if he had been attacked, Leclerc should have dropped his bombs, parallel to the barrage: it was for the pursuit planes to do the fighting. Magnin had carried out several such bombings in the middle of an engagement.

"You did bring your bombs back, didn't you?"

"Well, there was no point in dropping them just anywhere, on our own men. . . . And besides the engine was knocking."

Vargas' feeling that Leclerc was far from being a coward as a general rule merely increased the bitterness of hearing him answer now like a schoolboy who had broken bounds.

He sent for the bomber, the leader of the machine-gunners, and the mechanic, who all came in and stood waiting.

"How was the engine?" he asked.

The gunner and Leclerc fixed their eyes on the mechanic.

"Well . . . not too good," he answered.

"What was wrong?"

"Just not running well."

Vargas got up.

"That's all I wanted, thank you."

"Bombing was out of the question," said Leclerc.

"That's all, thank you."

4

WEARING a uniform for the first time, on the instructions of the Ministry of War, Scali found himself in command of the aerodrome as the result of Magnin's absence at Albacete. Of those who had a better claim, one was in hospital and the other, Karlitch, had been summoned urgently to Madrid to organize machine-gun units. The lack of all means of compulsion was as complete in the International Air Force as in half of the whole Spanish army, and had the same effect of limiting the efficacy of orders to the range of the personal authority of whoever issued them. Two men were obeyed at the aerodrome: Magnin and the chief pilot, who was little more than a boy, but whom everybody liked, and who had brought down four fascist planes. But for the last twenty-four hours his personal authority had been expended upon fever and an amputated arm.

Scali was chuckling over the discovery that one of the Pelicans had imprinted the rubber-stamp of the squadron upon Raplati's pink belly so that he should not get lost, when he was called to the phone.

"I am sending you back one of your pilots."

It was Sembrano speaking.

The said pilot was evidently well on his way. For a few minutes later Leclerc arrived in a lorry—trussed like a turkey and escorted by four *milicianos* with fixed bayonets. He was accompanied by the chief gunner and the mechanic from the "Pelican I," who were less drunk. The *milicianos* went off alone.

Leclerc had decided to go and get royally drunk after he left Vargas. Taking his two particular pals along with him, he had commandeered one of the aerodrome cars without so much as a word of explanation and driven off to Barajas, where he knew drinks would be waiting for him. Still keeping silence he had drunk six Pernods.

Then his tongue had begun to wag.

Hence the lorry.

He was slowly sobering up. Holding his dog under his arm, Scali was wondering what he was going to do if Leclerc ran amok. That great ape with the clownlike mop of hair and the overlong arms was certain to be extremely strong. Scali was determined not to call the *milicianos* back unless there was absolutely no alternative. The other Pelicans were regarding Leclerc somewhat aloofly, with mingled hostility and mirth. Attignies had silently reappeared, after having left them. Scali had no doubt that he had come back in order to lend help if the need arose. At last he put the dog down.

Leclerc had begun a harangue as he was being unbound:

"So I'm stingy and tough, eh? Let me tell you that's a sure sign of class, the sort of class that really makes revolutions! And if you don't mind my saying so, I've got no use for little sailor boys like you, nor for retired tin-gods from the town hall, either! To hell with them! They're a lot of fools. I'm an old communist, I am, not a stripe-hunter or a red-tape merchant. Are you going to tell me what it's all about? Or are your yellow guts getting you down?

"I've known the type that lines up with Franco ever since the Wrangel army and all the ex-gentlemen came and tried to drive our taxis for us. Knew it long before Franco's time! I'm one of the pre-war communists, I am."

"Dating from before the big split," Darras said gently. "That's all right, old chap, we all know you've nothing to do with the Party. That doesn't stop you from being a fine fellow, but you've nothing to do with the Party."

His wounded foot had mended, and on the previous day he had carried out a raid with Scali similar to the one over which Leclerc had just come to grief.

Leclerc looked at them both: Scali with the round spectacles, overlong trousers with balloon-like legs, and the appearance of an American comedian taking part in a film about aviation; Darras with his flat red face, white hair, calm smile and wrestler's chest-muscles. The gunner and mechanic remained silent.

"So now it's the 'Party,' eh? Did I have to show you my Party card before sending the Talavera gas-works sky-high? A lone wolf, that's me! A communist all on his own. But I want to be left in peace. And that's a warning to all the ruddy crocodiles who'd like to come nuzzling under my ribs where they don't belong, get me? Talavera, are you there? Is that you, Talavera darling?"

"We all know it's you," Scali said, taking his arm. "Don't worry; come along to bed."

Like Magnin, he took the view that Leclerc's turning tail was more in the nature of an accident than actual cowardice. And he was touched by the way in which he clung to the memory of Talavera at such a moment as this. But there is always something repellent about anger; especially in the variety which accompanies drunkenness. In Leclerc's case distended nostrils and swollen lips had reduced his comic face to an expression of sheer bestiality.

"Come to bed," Scali said again.

Leclerc squinted sideways at him, beneath wrinkled eyelids. From below the drunken mask, the cunning of some peasant ancestor rose to the surface.

"Think I'm tight, eh?"

He was still looking at him from the corner of an eye.

"You're right. Let's go to bed."

Scali gave him his arm. Halfway up the stairs Leclerc turned round.

"You lousy bastards! You can all go and . . . !"

On the first floor he threw his arms round Scali.

"I'm not a coward, not really. I'm not a coward!"

He was crying.

"And I'm not goin' to let it go at that. Just you wait!"

Nadal had been sent, under the protection of the Spanish embassy in Paris, to do some reporting on the Pelicans, some of whom showed themselves disposed to play up to him, with outward superiority and inward glee. The crew of the "Marat" —Darras, Attignies, Gardet and the others—were drawing up a manifesto. Jaime Alvear, sitting at the far end of the hotel dining-room with Scali, wearing black spectacles instead of his bandage, dismissed any suggestion of an interview as useless. He was seated near a window shutting out the Alcalá night, listening to the radio. House had dictated three columns.

Nadal was a little, thick-set, frizzy-haired youth, with eyes that were almost mauve, who might have made a successful gigolo if everything about him had not been too rotund; his face and nose, even the over-elaborate sweep of his gestures, were almost childisly in keeping with his too wavy hair. Leclerc had been announced to him as the most colourful of the Pelicans. But Leclerc's view of journalists was that they were a bad enough joke to make the archangels weep; and if one of them took it upon himself to approach him he would, so he declared, "push his face in." Moreover, he was in bed.

Attignies came back with the manifesto prepared by the crew of the "Marat."

"We came here without any thought of adventure. Revolutionaries unattached to any party, socialists or communists resolved to defend Spain, we shall carry on the fight wherever and however we may give the most effective service. Long live the liberty of the Spanish people!"

None of this was of any use to Nadal, who was not really

out to investigate the volunteers. His paper's readers included more than a million members of the proletariat. What was expected of him was to provide his editor with good liberalism, tributes to those nice airmen (the French especially), "atmosphere" on the mercenaries, sob-stuff on the others; shedding a heartfelt tear over the dead and the badly wounded (a pity that man Jaime . . . ! Still, after all, he was only a Spaniard). No communism, and the absolute minimum of political ideology.

He also wanted to pick up one or two anecdotes, preferably of a sexual character, to retail in private. The most picturesque features of a dramatic assignment come out when the reporter is back among his friends.

His immediate preoccupation was with the liars. Not that he was taken in by them. But they made good copy. There is something of the novelist in every half-wit, he thought; it is merely a question of choosing one. His first choice talked of "my men" (not too loudly, though).

Next came the turn of those who had deserted from the French or English armies, in order to go to Spain. Several of them had since got married, and he got them to give him photographs of their wives. "My paper has a lot of women readers." Next there were the "aces" among the paid pilots, those who were officially credited with having brought down more than three fascist planes. They referred to the volunteers as "the politicals," and to themselves as "the fighters"; but there was no bluffing about them. They let him see their logbooks, but discreetly.

Next there were a certain number of would-be "bad lots," and a few shirkers who had been allowed to remain. He had given up the volunteers as a distinctly unprofitable field.

He was engaged in taking notes from a log-book, and half the contents of a box of jujubes which he had been unwise enough to disclose had already found its way into Pol's pocket, when a lull in the talk and a feeling of tension in the air made him lift his head.

His face twisted in a leer and his back hunched, Leclerc was coming down the stairs. The grey hood had made its appearance again, with the wisps of black hair protruding from it. His smile was far from reassuring and his arms seemed longer than ever. Pointing to Nadal, a gunner from the "Pelican I" called to him. "Here's a writer come to see us.

Come and have a drink with your colleague." Leclerc sat down.

"So you're a writer, too! What do you write?"

"Short stories. And you?"

"Pot-boiler novels. I've been a poet, too. There's never been another airman poet who sold all his stuff like me. If the tough boys got hold of a fool of a tourist or one who was tight, they'd pick every sou off him. But did I? Not me. But I used to palm off my stuff on them, as there was work had gone into that. Only fifteen francs. Sold out every copy. *Icarus at the Wheel,* it was called. Because of the poetry and the flying, see?"

"Are you writing just now?"

"Given it up. But now I write with a machine-gun."

"What sort of guns do you use?"

Having signed their statement, Attignies and Darras had joined Scali and were listening to Jaime's radio. Since he had lost his sight, Jaime spent half his life listening-in. Darras moved away from the radio; Nadal's last question was not at all to his liking.

Still he decided not to interfere. Their conversation was just a comedy of errors. Leclerc knew nothing about pursuit planes; he had never handled a machine-gun since joining up. And Nadal, as he went on talking, chewing at his pipe with the wise look of an expert of long-standing, was under the impression that submachine-guns with ammunition belts were being used, not knowing that the Spanish Government planes were fitted with drum-loading Lewis guns—and failed to understand a word of what Leclerc was talking about.

"You like it here?" he asked casually.

"Yes. This is the life! What the hell should I be doing if I'd stayed in Paris? Piloting a passenger-bus, as like as not. Might as well push a baby-carriage! If you're a Leftist, you don't stand a chance; you got to take what comes along. No, thank you! Over here, a man's a man. Look at me now! I was at Talavera, I was. Ask anyone about it. The gas-works blazed like Christmas puddings. One in the eye for Franco. Me, Leclerc, I stopped Franco. Get me? And look at these fellows! Do they look the sort that'd go round job-hunting just to get the order of the boot? Not they!"

Round the huge kitchen-stove they had fitted up at one end of the room, under the revolutionary posters, the cook and his family were busy as usual, and some Pelicans were engaged in wheedling "extras" out of them.

Attignies, too, was listening to the conversation, keeping an ear on the radio at the same time. For the last few minutes he had been watching with interest the way the two men reacted to one another. Leclerc was rolling bread-balls between his fingers and flicking them almost into Nadal's face. His voice was by no means as friendly as his words.

"And my bus at Talavera was an 'Orion'—you know what that means! This may be the land of fighting bulls; but all we got to shoo round's a bunch of half-grown heifers. But we kept our end up with 'em, with our little heifers. Get me?"

A bread-ball landed smack on Nadal's nose. Attignies, more and more interested, watched the game. Nadal was pretending to laugh; well, he could afford to. He'd get even in his interview.

"What sort of equipment did you have at Talavera?" he asked.

"Awful! A machine-gun through a window, and the privy-hole made bigger to drop our bombs through."

"And an aviation Hotchkiss on a tripod," Gardet put in, in his best expert manner.

"Just what we had at Villacoublay," Nadal said, with an air of aggrieved indignation. It was an outrage, he clearly implied, to ask any man to fight with arms like that. The Pelicans tittered. That Hotchkiss existed only in Gardet's imagination.

"Stop talking!" Attignies shouted.

The speaker from the rebel station to whom he was listening—perhaps a hook-up from the Seville radio station—had just announced "Aviation," and Jaime had turned the radio on louder.

"Our planes have successfully bombed the front lines of the Reds, forcing them back from Carabanchel into Madrid.

"The city was bombarded from three o'clock to five, without any Red plane putting in an appearance.

"Five Government machines have been brought down behind our lines.

"I have already announced from this station that the plane of the communist Magnin, the notorious renegade and Stalinist agent, would soon be disposed of. Today it was brought down within our lines. All the crew perished in the crash.

Magnin's body has been identified at Getafe. One scoundrel less. Let the others take warning! Good night, all."

The Pelicans exchanged glances.

"Don't you worry," Scali called to them, "they've made a mistake!"

Nadal began to put questions, but he soon saw that he should not press the matter. On this subject, the Pelicans, even the toughest, were superstitious, and their manner became unfriendly. Most of them believed that the airplane referred to was the "Jaurès," manned by Carnero and his crew. Still, Magnin had come down at Albacete; there was nothing to prevent his having fought that afternoon on the Madrid front.

"What do you know about it, you fathead!" Leclerc grumbled.

Scali knew a great deal. Since noon, he had felt things were turning out badly, and he had telephoned to ask Magnin to come to Alcalá that night.

But Magnin had already received fuller information than Scali was able to give him. Sembrano had telephoned directly to him—and in greater detail. Leclerc, dead-drunk, had started denouncing the Spanish pilots, though he knew quite well that, whatever shirkers might be hiding in Valencia, the Spanish pilots, with their decrepit planes, were daily equalling the Talavera "stunt" of which he was so proud. He had gone on to prove to the Spanish mechanics flocking round him that the war was as good as lost, that their patched-up machines were bound to crash—and so forth. Smarting with a sense of shame, he had given free rein to his malevolence. Scali, too, was well aware that Leclerc, after his return, had gone out and talked on the same lines to the Pelicans, button-holing each in turn. And the worst of it was that he had some influence among them; they were attracted by the man's picturesque personality, and by his open-handedness, genuine enough, though due primarily to his craving for being liked. Scali knew, moreover, that the Pelicans of Leclerc's own crew had "played up" to their loquacious comrade.

At first Scali had been surprised at this attitude of Leclerc's men. Of unfailing insight when dealing with men whose character he understood—with intellectuals—he was all at sea with personalities like Leclerc's. Gardet had drawn his attention to the fact that the crews, the personnel of which was modified each time a man was sent to hospital, tended to crystallize around a certain type of mind. When Leclerc had turned back, his companions had not clearly understood what he was about. There were thick clouds; the visibility was poor. And now they were involved in a tragedy far too intricate for their comprehension. Leclerc could not forgive himself for running away; he now was set on involving all his associates in his own disgrace. To get them all to feel as disgusted as he felt with himself gave him the same sort of gloomy satisfaction as he got out of absinthe.

"Magnin phoned us at seven o'clock," Scali announced.

But everyone wondered if he was speaking the truth or merely trying to reassure them. The latter was quite possible, considering the prevailing mood.

A longish silence greeted his announcement. Nadal was the first to speak.

"What prompted you to come here?" he asked Leclerc, pencil in hand. "Was it the revolution?"

Leclerc shot him a vicious glance from the corner of an eye.

"What the hell's that to do with you? . . . Anyhow everyone knows what I am; I'm a left-wing mercenary. And if I'm here, it's because I've got guts. And I'm air-minded, as they say. That's a man's job, flying; it's no job for lily-livered skunks, or weaklings, or—journalists! Every man to his own taste. Get me?"

Looking more emaciated than ever, his nostrils dilated, his hair all ruffled, chest thrown out, and forehead puckered, Leclerc sat at the table gripping a bottle of *tinto* with long simian fingers. A thrill of uneasy suspense seemed rippling in the air.

Gardet, who had drawn his chair up to Jaime's, ran his fingers nervously through his close-cropped hair, vaguely smiling.

"Whatever it is," Attignies said to him, "weakness or cowardice, if Magnin doesn't squelch them soon, these fellows will infect the whole squadron, like dry rot. What's happening? The wine going to their heads?"

"Whatever it is," Gardet replied, "I've had enough of it. Leclerc's beginning to get on my nerves. I don't like fighting beside fellows who're all nerves. Watch him now, though, playing the hero, puffing out his chest. It's enough to split your sides laughing."

"You can see he's sick with Nadal for making him play the part. Look at his face. He could kill Nadal, this minute."

"But grateful, too, for the chance he's giving him of showing off."

"Grateful? I'm not so sure. See the look on his ugly mug."

Nadal realized that things had an ugly look, and after ordering drinks all round, slipped out with his notes; a small, foxy figure, with a long pipe aggressively belying the crafty smile upon his lips.

"I'm not tight," Leclerc was bellowing. "But as for the revolution . . ."

Obviously he meant to say "to hell with it!" but dared not. Not because of his comrades, whom he might well have liked to challenge. But beyond the two shutterless windows there was Madrid.

The radio was near one of the windows. Looking round, Attignies saw the sleepy plaza of Alcalá-de-Henares, with its monuments and, half hidden behind the columns of the porticos, rows of diminutive taverns where snails were sold, and where just now, most likely, some Pelicans were sipping real Pernods. And all the little town, with its pillared streets and quiet gardens, churches with pointed towers, and ornate palaces, romantic walls and balconies that seemed to invite guitars and serenades—all that old Castille, which looked like the stage-setting of a Spanish comedy, was chipped and frayed by air-bombs, and slept with one eye open, and ears alert for the sounds of war.

"When Magnin comes," Gardet said to Scali, "please tell him that with the men from the 'Marat,' yourself, and some of the others, we can always fix up crews for a raid."

"You're going to Madrid tonight?" Jaime asked.

"Yes. Garcia's sent me a special order to see him."

"I wish you'd look up my father. And bring him here."

Scali knew that Jaime's father was very old. It was probably a sense of dignity that prevented Jaime from trying to justify his request. He had never made his wound an excuse for special consideration.

"Right. I'll do so."

"Say, Mr. Scali," Leclerc snarled, "when's the grub going to be a bit better?"

"Ah. So it gives one an appetite, does it, being shown up?" Gardet retorted, from the far end of the table.

Leclerc stared at Gardet, whose unfriendly smile disclosed small cat-like teeth, but said nothing.

"And what about our contracts?" the bomber of "Pelican I" enquired.

"They're not back yet from the Jefatura," Scali replied.

"Me, I'm not one to make complaints. But all the same, if I'd been killed today—might have happened, you know—what would have become of my contract?"

The tone was at once aggressive and apologetic. The bomber who spoke had little staring eyes and ineffectual-looking hands, and the lieutenant's stars had been sewn on his pale-blue leather jacket the day following his wedding in Barcelona. "By artificial light he looks more than ever like a teapot in an animated cartoon," Gardet murmured to himself.

Scali's view was that these fellows should not be taken too seriously, and his plan usually worked. But today things seemed different.

"Your pay would have been handed over to your wife, of course. Now, leave us in peace."

"And supposing Franco got to Madrid before it was all fixed up?"

"In that case, I damned well hope Franco'd have you shot," Gardet said, smoothing his hair. "And then we'd hear no more of you and your pesetas."

Usually the dangers shared in common by volunteers and mercenaries brought them together far more effectively than the business of the contracts estranged them. But tonight the patience of the volunteers was sorely tried.

"And why don't they send us enough pursuit planes?" asked the mechanic of "Pelican I."

"I must say, they don't look after the wounded as well as they might do," put in House.

House would have found he was not sufficiently well treated had the King of England himself come to Madrid to visit him.

"It's no cinch, this job," said Leclerc's chief machine-gunner. "Not enough pursuit planes, not enough bombers, God-awful equipment, lousy machine-guns!"

The Spaniards, however, cheerfully fought the anti-aircraft guns with obsolete Breguets. And without complaining.

Moving back towards Leclerc's table, Attignies overheard a conversation among some Pelicans.

"That's all very well, but he hasn't been seen since this morning; there's no getting over that."

"You should have seen those poor devils. Slithering down through the air in bunches."

"Never saw anything like it, even during the War."

"Yes, but the worst was the 'Jaurès.' It broke right in two."

"Seems the bastards got Carnero with their machine-guns."

"Was that Carnero with the parachute?"

"Yes, it was Magnin's parachute, with Carnero hanging on to it."

"At the start one could stick it out, but against a telemeter barrage, what the hell can you do? I don't call that fighting."

"What's worst is when the plane splits in two."

"We're short on organization, that's our trouble. No planning. Everyone starts a hullabaloo in the evening about what's to be done next day!"

"By bucketfuls, the poor devils, the plane just vomited them out by bucketfuls."

"Of course, Magnin's got a swelled head. But if the fool wants to commit suicide, that's no reason for us to do the same."

How shame corrupts men, thought Attignies. Reacting as he did, automatically, to ideas, the whole business seemed to him both trivial and profoundly sad. Here were men fussing and fuming about a few dozen mercenaries hired by the Republic; while he was thinking of the thousands and thousands of Italians and Germans and the interminable lines of Moors sanctified "for the duration" by their Sacred Hearts. Forty thousand Moors, at so much a day—with a court-martial behind them. How long can one keep confidence in men? But to have confidence in men who would be faithful unto death, is it necessary to rely on so-called experts, who are rotting away, as good as dead already? . . . Meanwhile, at Albacete and Madrid, the first International Brigades were being formed.

Gardet's voice rose above the muffled hum of conversation.

"Listen to me!" he called out, sitting on the table, his under-jaw thrust forward. "You've all been disgusted by the smart boys who come to give us the look-over, putting on airs and sucking at their pipes—men who never once go into the lines and who trot back to Paris and pick holes in all that Magnin's doing—not to mention what we are doing—without the first idea of what we're up against. Well, tonight, it strikes me that you're backing up those bastards. Everything's wrong here, is it? Let me tell you, my lads, if you were with Franco, your mouths would damn well have been shut up long ago. Perhaps for ever."

"And that's why I'm here and not with Franco," the mechanic said.

Pol jumped up, enormous, fuzzy-haired, purple in the face, furiously wagging his forefinger.

"No you don't! I'm not fooled that easy! I see your little game: you'd like to do us out of our bonuses. And you, Bertrand, you're not a bad fellow, but when I hear you crabbing Magnin's work it makes me vomit."

"Then we haven't the right to express an opinion nowadays? We're just so much dirt, and got to keep our traps shut?"

"Call that expressing an opinion? You're drivelling because you've lost your nerve. And, mind you, I don't hold that against you. Accidents will happen, as they say, and I'm not the one to blame a comrade for a thing like that. It might happen to anyone. Yes, by and large, we all know you did your bit. But what I saw now is that you want the whole world to rot because you're fed up with yourself. Well, I'm not fooled by you, and that's straight! Nothing doing! You're grousing, are you? Well, who'd you put in instead of Magnin? Name someone. Just name one! And if what the bastard on the radio says is true, well what? That he—that he'll not come back. What then?"

"Bonus for me: ten per cent."

"Moral for you: you boys are acting like a lot of goddamned fools."

Leclerc came up to Scali and grasped the back of a chair beside him, his eyes aflame with hate. There was a silence as he spoke.

"About the revolution. I told you just now and I say it again: let everyone carry on with it. But as to the way this show is run, I don't care what you say, it stinks. They mobilize us for a fight and then they keep us on ice for two days. Forty-eight hours without a razor! It's lasted long enough. Get me?"

Scali, his eyes black with disgust behind his glasses, made no reply.

"Without a razor? You don't mean to say so!" All were startled to their feet by the voice which rang out from the far end of the room.

Since Jaime had come back from his plane for the last time, he had never spoken to any except isolated comrades round his table, in a corner. Now it was as though he had recovered his singing voice of the old days, that voice which recently had fallen on silence as if something in it had gone blind, too. Not a man present but knew that each time he went up he was threatened with a like fate. Jaime was their comrade, and he was also the living, ominous image of what might befall each of them. With his large nose jutting out between the black glasses, his hand scrabbling at the tables, on the under side, so that his groping fingers should not be seen, he advanced, moving from empty plate to empty plate, and all the Pelicans shrank back as though horrified by the thought of touching him.

"And the men in the trenches," Jaime asked, in a lower voice, "do they shave?"

"Ah, it's you!" Leclerc muttered between his teeth. "We all know you're a hero of the revolution. But get the hell out of this!"

Scali was standing four or five yards away to the left, near the wall, hitching up his service trousers (which were far too long for him), but his eyes had never left Leclerc. Suddenly Leclerc went towards him, leaving Jaime to his slow, groping progress along the table-edge.

"I'm fed to the teeth with machine-guns that are only fit for the shooting-gallery at a fair," Leclerc shouted. "Fed to the teeth. I got hair on my chest, I have, and I'm going to act like a bull, not a god-damned stool-pigeon. Get me?"

Scali, too disheartened for words, made a gesture of disdain.

Leclerc mimicked his gesture. He was wild with anger, his teeth clenched with rage.

"You! I say shit to you! Get me? Shit to you!"

His face was convulsed with bestial fury.

"The same to you," Scali stammered lamely. He had no knack of repartee in vulgar brawls, any more than for giving orders. Like a good intellectual, he not only wanted to explain, but to convince. And as for physical violence, he had an aversion to it amounting to disgust. Leclerc, who felt instinctively this disgust, mistook it for fear.

"No, *I* said it first. Not you. Get me?"

Pol thought of the day when they had all waited together for the coming of the first plane filled with wounded.

"*Salud!*" Magnin cried out, waving his fist like a handkerchief in the air. Statue-like he stood on the threshold, his moustache flattened by the wind.

He strode forward among looks of hostility, relief, or feigned indifference, and stopped before Leclerc.

"So you had your thermos with you?"

"It's not true! I hadn't a thing to drink!"

Leclerc screamed the words in a tone of righteous indignation; it delighted him to be unjustly charged with drunkenness now that he wished so urgently the charge of cowardice should likewise seem unjust.

"Not a thing? That was unwise," Magnin said.

He preferred a drunken pilot to a demoralized one.

Leclerc hesitated, puzzled, groping for a way out.

"The Pelican's crew will return to Albacete at once," Magnin announced. "The lorry's at the door."

"A lorry! What, a lorry! Why not a wheelbarrow? . . . I want a real car!" Once more Leclerc's face was working with insensate rage.

"Can't we even have time to pack our kit?" the bomber grumbled.

A pointless remark. Everyone knew the crew had arrived by plane, without so much as a toothbrush. Magnin shrugged his shoulders.

He looked at Leclerc, then at Leclerc's men, who were now scattered about the room. Had they died this morning, he mused, we'd remember only what is best in them. And even were they to be killed tomorrow . . . The memory of Marcelino was stronger than Leclerc's presence. He looked at them, volunteers and mercenaries, as if all they were saying, doing, thinking about themselves were a mere passing madness, a dream from which they must awaken sooner or later, stiff under their flying uniforms, real with the reality of death.

Leclerc marched up to Magnin as he had done to Scali. On his face was an expression of undiluted hatred, terrifying in its intensity, though the features had changed little; only his furrowed brows seemed to have sunk lower.

"Magnin, I say shit to you!"

The hairy fingers at the end of the long ape-like arms were quivering convulsively. Magnin's eyebrows and moustache seemed to bristle, his eyes grew curiously still.

"You'll leave tomorrow for France, all arrears paid. You will never again set foot in Spain. That's all."

"I'll come back whenever I damn well choose to, contract or no contract. You lousy son-of-a-bitch, think you can stop me? I was in the Legion once, don't you try taking me for a doormat."

Scali, Attignies and Gardet had taken their stand beside Magnin. Against the table stood Jaime, with his black glasses.

"I want a real car," Leclerc repeated, his hands twitching more and more convulsively. "Get me?"

Magnin walked to the door, swift, indifferent, with his slight stoop. At the far end of the room the only sound now audible was that of forks plied in the kitchen. All eyes followed Magnin. He opened the door and said some words, as if addressing the high wind sweeping across the great plaza of Alcalá.

Six guards entered. They were armed.

"Forward, everybody!" Magnin shouted.

Determined to maintain his sense of importance, Leclerc went out first.

Silence hovered over the room. Then it echoed with the roar of the starting lorry, of grinding gears and racing pistons; gradually the noise died away, merged into the roar of the wind. Magnin had been standing in the doorway, looking out. The moment he turned round, there was a sudden din of clinking glasses, clattering dishes, sneezes, exclamations—as at a theatre the audience relaxes when the curtain falls. Magnin sat down at the table and cut short the suspense, rapping a glass with his knife to call for silence.

"Comrades," he began, in a conversational tone, "two or three miles from that door at which you have been looking are the Moors. Only a mile from Madrid. One mile.

"With the fascists at Carabanchel, men who act as the men who have just left acted are behaving like counter-revolutionaries.

"They will all be in France tomorrow.

"From today on, we are incorporated with the Spanish regular air force. Each one of you must procure a uniform for Monday. All contracts are cancelled as from today. Darras is appointed chief mechanic, Gardet chief machine-gunner, Attignies civil commissar. Those who do not accept this arrangement leave tomorrow.

"The business about the Pelican crew is definitely settled. And we must try to forget all but their previous good service. Let us drink to the Pelican crew."

The tone in which he spoke made the toast seem a farewell, a peremptory dismissal of the subject.

"Officers and N.C.O.'s will kindly join me in my room," he added, when the glasses had been put down.

Magnin explained his views on the reorganization of the squadron.

"But how are we going to find our crews and ground staff?" Darras asked.

"The International Brigade. I went to Albacete about that. Everything is fixed up with them. They have some fellows who served in the air force, and quite a few hands from aviation factories. All the men who have had anything at all to do with aviation will be transferred to us tomorrow. It's up to you to sort them out, and detail each man to the job that suits him. We shall have more than we need, I understand. As for discipline—at least thirty percent of the men being sent are communists. There are two communists among you. It's for you to see to that among yourselves."

Magnin remembered Enrique.

"How about pursuit planes?" Attignies asked.

"I hear we shall be given some."

"Enough?"

"Quite."

Obviously he was expecting to receive some Russian machines.

"Are you contemplating joining the Party?" Darras asked.

"No. I am not in complete agreement with the Party."

"Can't you stop proselytising for five minutes, Darras?" Gardet smiled.

There had been some trouble in persuading Gardet to take a commission. "When the machine-gunners get balled up," he had once remarked, "I give them a hand. I like that, and they have confidence in me. But as for commanding them—that's not up my alley." "And if the officers aren't just those men the comrades have confidence in, who the devil should they be?" Darras had said. And finally Gardet had given in.

"Did you come by way of Madrid?" Attignies asked.

"No. But I had a telephone call from there just now. Fighting is going on at the gates of the city."

5

THE Government had moved from Madrid to Valencia, and the Ministry of War was empty. On a gilded chair, in solitary state, sat a French officer who had come to volunteer his serv-

ices and been told to wait. He was still waiting; it was eleven
P.M. The white marble staircases and the florid carpets lining
them were lit up only by the glimmer of candles planted on
the steps and upheld by their filaments of tallow. Once the last
wick had drowned itself in a little grease-pool, darkness un-
qualified would reign on the majestic staircase.

The only lamps lit were those in the attics, occupied by
Miaja's staff and the Military Intelligence Department.

Scali sat down, while Garcia opened an untitled file of
papers. The fascist advance, it seemed, was being held up at
Carabanchel.

"You know Madrid well, Scali, don't you?"

"Pretty well."

"You know the Plaza del Progreso?"

"Yes."

"And of course you know the Calle de la Luña, the Plaza
de la Puerta de Toledo, the Calle Fuencarral, and the Plaza
del Callao?"

"I used to live on the Plaza del Callao."

"And the Calle del Nuncio, the Calle de los Bordadores, and
the Calle de Segovia?"

"Not the second street you named."

"All right. I'm going to ask you a question; think it over
before answering. Is it possible for an exceptionally skilful
pilot to hit just those five places"—he repeated the names—
"which I've mentioned?"

"To hit them? What do you mean? To hit the houses along
those streets?"

"No, to drop bombs on the streets and open places beside
the houses, but without touching any of the roofs. Only the
streets themselves. And always at crowded spots. A tram on
the Plaza del Callao, for instance."

"A tram? That would obviously be a matter of luck."

"Quite so. And the other places?"

Scali ran his hand through his hair; behind the glasses his
eyes looked thoughtful.

"How many bombs?"

"A dozen."

"That would be extraordinary luck. What about the other
bombs?"

"There aren't any others. Twelve bombs—and a direct hit
with each. On women in front of the grocers' shops, children
at the Puerta de Toledo."

"I'm trying to find an answer. But my first reaction, let me tell you, is to say all that's beyond the bounds of possibility. Even if the plane flew very low."

"Well, this particular plane was flying high—so high nobody heard it."

The more fantastic Garcia's questions were, the more uncomfortable Scali grew; for he knew Garcia's scrupulous regard for accuracy.

"Look here—the whole idea's too grotesque for words."

"You must allow for the possibility of the bomber being highly proficient; a regular air force officer, for instance, who has won bombing contests."

"He can be anybody you like. But it simply couldn't be done. Did anyone see the machine?"

"Now, they're claiming to have seen it. But on the first day not a word was said about it. And no one heard it."

"It can't have been a plane. The fascists must have a gun with a longer range than those we've reckoned for. It's the 'big Bertha' stunt all over again."

"But if it *was* a plane, how do you account for the accuracy of the bombing?"

"I don't account for it. Look here, why not issue orders and let's go up together tomorrow? I'll fly you over the Calle de la Luna at whatever height you wish. You'll find your theory hasn't a leg to stand on, or else that everyone below will see the machine as clearly as one sees a car bearing down on one. There's a high wind; the pilot won't even be able to keep his course above the street."

"Even if the pilot's Ramon Franco?"

"Even if it's Lindbergh!"

"Right. There's something else. Here's a plan of Madrid. You see those red rings; they show where the bombs landed. Don't take any note of those pencil-marks. Does this map suggest anything to you?"

"It bears out what I've just said. All those streets don't follow the same direction. So our hypothetical bomber must have had the wind at right-angles to his course now and then. And to expect to hit a given street from some height up under such conditions is . . ." Scali tapped his forehead, to convey: "sheer lunacy."

Meanwhile Garcia was thinking to himself: How, my dear Scali, could shells fired from a long-range gun and necessarily falling at a pretty steep angle land on streets running in different directions without touching a single wall?

"A final point," he said aloud. "Could a really first-class pilot fly over Madrid for some considerable time at a height of, say, sixty feet? In bad weather, let me add."

"No."

"The Spanish pilots, I may say, entirely share your view."

The mention of Ramon Franco's name had made Scali suspect that Garcia was referring to the bombardment on October 30. . . .

After Scali had gone, Garcia studied once more the photographs he had had taken of the various points where bombs had fallen. Artillery officers had told him these bombardments could not possibly have been the work of heavy guns; the angle of descent definitely ruled that out. Moreover, fragments of the missiles had been discovered; they were not shells but bombs. On the photographs were comments by different branches of the Staff; Garcia, without explaining why he required the information, had asked the experts to give answers to his questions. One of the answers ran: "This projectile was launched from a height not exceeding sixty feet." It was noteworthy that the pavements had been little more than chipped.

Sad at heart, Garcia put the photographs back in his drawer. For him the problem was solved. No aeroplane, no field-gun was responsible; the so-called Fifth Column had been at work. Twelve men operating at the same moment. He had contended, not without success, against the "phantom cars"—the fascist cars, that armed with machine-guns, had roamed Madrid by night; against the shopkeepers who at dawn fired down at the *milicianos* through their shutters; against all a civil war may stand for. But such things had only been what one expects of war; a blind man firing impersonally on his enemy. In these cases, however, each man before launching his bomb had looked down on the line of women queued up outside a grocery, had seen the old men and children in the square. The women had been slaughtered without a qualm—perhaps it was a woman who had thrown those bombs; pity for women is a man's emotion. But what about the children? Garcia had seen photographs taken immediately after the explosion.

One of his colleagues, who had just come back from Russia, had talked to him of sabotage. "Hatred of the machine is a new thing in emotions; but when all the enthusiasm and the hope of a people centres in *work*, that very fact is enough to inspire the enemies of the régime with bitter hatred for the work that is being done." Nowadays, at Madrid, the fascists hated the people—whose very existence a year earlier they may well have questioned—and hated them so bitterly as to see in a group of children playing in a city square no more than an embodiment of the people.

Very likely, he thought, at this moment the twelve killers were gloating over their impending victory; that afternoon the prisoners in the model jail had sung the fascist anthem.

And it was his duty to keep silence; no incitement must be given the brute that slumbers in the heart of man. And he knew that if torture is so prevalent in war, a reason—*another* reason—is that it seems the only apt rejoinder to treachery and cruelty. Did he speak out, that tense, excited crowd whose distant rumour came to him on fitful gusts of the night-wind, would take the first step towards sheer bestiality. Masses, like individuals, are apt to run amok in their desire for vengeance on atrocities. And so, in the fine frenzy of its barricades, Madrid would go on believing in the exploits of Ramon Franco.

The Intelligence Service and Secret Police would deal with it themselves, as usual. A picture rose in Garcia's mind of the Gran Via as it used to be, in the gay light of an April morning; shop-windows, restaurants, women who were not to be slaughtered, and on the café terraces sugar-sticks dissolving like hoar-frost in glasses of water, beside cups of cinnamon-flavoured chocolate. And now he sat alone in a deserted palace, confronting a polluted world, the very air of which was stifling. Whichever way this war ends, he mused, what sort of peace can possibly prevail after such bitter hatred? And what will the war make of me?

Moral problems! Yes, a man can never get away from them. He shook his head, picked up his pipe and, rising with an effort, started out for the Secret Police Bureau.

6

A THIN, bent figure, alone in the midst of the vast staircase, Guernico had come to the War Ministry to enlist official support for the ambulance corps he was trying to reorganize. As the tide of war drew nearer to Madrid, the ambulance corps he had built up in the Toledo days was losing its efficiency. On the ground floor of the Ministry was a display of armour, and in the gathering dusk the Catholic writer with the tall, spare form and the fair complexion we find in so many of Velasquez' portraits, looked as if he might have stepped out of one of those historic coats of mail, pledged to return to it before the break of day. Garcia, who had not met him for the last three weeks, was wont to describe Guernico as the only one of his friends in whom intelligence took the form of charity. And, for all the gulf that yawned between them, Guernico was perhaps the only man for whom Garcia had a real affection.

The two set out together for the Plaza Mayor.

Shadows glided along drawn shutters and bare walls, shadows parallel and bending forward, like haulers towing a boat upstream. Tawny smoke-clouds from the suburbs were rolling over the city. "The exodus," Garcia thought—but then he saw that none of the passers-by carried bundles. All were walking very fast in the same direction.

"It has pluck," he said, "our city of Madrid."

A blind man, his begging-bowl before him, was playing the *International*. In their lightless houses, the fascists, a hundred thousand strong, were waiting for the next day's battle.

"There's not a sound," Guernico said.

Only a sound of footsteps. The street was throbbing like a vein. The Moors were at the south and western gates, but the wind was blowing away from the city. Not a rifle-shot could be heard, not even the boom of cannon. Only the constant rustle of the moving crowd, like an army of moles digging their tunnels underground. And the accordion.

They walked towards the Puerta del Sol, in the same direction as the reddish smoke that drifted overhead and the unseen river bearing the crowd on its futile way towards the plaza—as though the Carabanchel barricades had been erected there.

"Supposing we stop them here . . ."

A woman plucked Guernico's sleeve and addressed him in French. "Do you think I ought to leave?"

"She's a German comrade," Guernico explained to Garcia, but did not answer her.

"He says I ought to go," the woman went on. "He says he can't fight properly when I'm around."

"And I'm quite sure he's right," Garcia said.

"But I just can't *live* if I know he's fighting here and I don't even hear what's happening."

Another accordion playing the *International* droned an accompaniment to the words; a second blind man, begging-bowl on lap, was carrying on the tune from the point where the first had dropped it.

The women are all alike, Garcia mused. If that one goes, she'll take it hard at first, but she'll see it through; whereas, if she stays, he'll be killed. He could not see her face; she was much shorter than he and her face was screened by shadows of the passers-by.

"Why do you want to stay?" Guernico's voice was gentle.

"I don't mind dying, but food's the trouble; I've got to eat my fill, and now that won't be possible. . . . I'm pregnant."

Garcia did not hear Guernico's reply. The woman drifted away on another stream of shadows.

"What can one do . . . ?" Guernico murmured.

Some *milicianos* in overalls caught them up and passed them. Paving-stones had been pulled up and phantom figures were building a barricade across the street.

"When are you leaving?" Garcia asked.

"I'm not leaving."

Guernico would be among the first for the firing-squad when the fascists entered the city. Though Garcia did not turn towards his friend, he visualized him now, as he walked beside him, with his little fair moustache, his tousled hair and long, lean arms. The defencelessness of that body touched him in the way that children always stirred his pity, for it ruled out all ideas of fighting. No, Guernico would not fight; he would be killed.

Neither mentioned the Madrid ambulance section, for neither really believed it would materialize.

"So long as one can serve the revolution, it's up to us to do so. But getting oneself killed doesn't help in the least, my dear fellow. The Republic's not a matter of geography and its fate isn't sealed just because one town more or less gets captured."

"I was at the Puerta del Sol on the day of the Montaña affair, when the crowd was being fired on from every window. The people in the street lay flat; the whole square was a mass of prostrate bodies, on which the enemy were firing. On the next day but one, when I went to the Ministry I found a long queue of women outside it; they had come to offer their blood for transfusion. Twice I've *seen* the Spanish people. This war is the people's war, whatever the outcome; and I'll stand by it wherever it is. There are two hundred thousand workers here and *they* haven't any cars to take them to Valencia."

Obviously nothing Garcia might say could have weighed with Guernico as the lives of his wife and children must have weighed with him. And Garcia could not bear the thought that if they were never to meet again their last conversation should have ended on a sort of wrangle.

Guernico made a spacious gesture with his long, slender hand. "After all," he said, "perhaps I'll leave at the last moment." But Garcia felt sure that he was lying.

A thud of heavy footsteps echoed down the street, seeming to precede the body of men who now emerged into the light. "It's the diggers," Garcia said. They were off to the front just behind Carabanchel for trench-digging and laying mines. In front, another company of shadows, dim in the mist, were building another barricade.

"They're staying right enough, you see," Guernico said.

"At a pinch they've a retreat open by the Guadalajara road. But your rooms and the Association premises are positive death-traps."

Guernico made the same gesture of uncertain fatalism. Another blind beggar; still the *International*. The only tune blind men played just now. And more shadowy forms, building more barricades.

"Perhaps," Guernico said, "more duties are imposed on us, as Christian writers, than on other people." They were passing the Alcalá Church. Guernico pointed vaguely towards it. By his tone Garcia guessed that his lips were twisted in a bitter smile, as he continued. "After a sermon by a fascist preacher in French Catalonia—the text was: 'Be ye not unequally yoked together with unbelievers'—I saw Father Sarazola go up to the preacher. After the preacher had gone away Sarazola said to me: 'Once to have known Christ leaves its mark. Of all the fascists I've seen here, he's the first to be ashamed of it.'"

A lorry passed, laden with a serried mass of *milicianos* squatting on the floor, the muzzles of their obsolete machine-guns swaying above them. When Guernico spoke again, his voice was lower.

"Only, you know, when I see the way they're behaving now, it's I who feel ashamed."

Garcia was about to reply when a little weasel-faced *miliciano* suddenly gripped his arm.

"They'll be right here tomorrow!" he said.

"Who's that fellow?" Guernico asked in an undertone.

"He used to work in Magnin's squadron, as a clerk."

"This Government—there's not a bloody thing to be done with it," said the weasel-faced man. "Why, ten days ago I brought them a plan, worked out in detail, mind you, for the large-scale culture of typhoid germs. Fifteen years' research, and I didn't ask a sou for it, just to down the fascists. They wouldn't do a thing about it. Turned it down, like they turned down my bomb. Well, the fascists will be here tomorrow."

"Oh, shut your mouth, you!" Garcia exclaimed.

But already the little man had bobbed back like a jack-in-the-box into the stream of passing shadows; the *International* had accompanied his appearance and eclipse.

"Come across many of his type?" Guernico inquired.

"At first, yes. . . . The sort of volunteer we got at first was usually a bit of a lunatic or a bit of a hero. Sometimes, both at once."

On the Alcalá, as on all the narrow streets, brooded the feverish expectancy of nights when history is in the making. And here, too, there was no sound of guns, only the throbbing of accordions. Suddenly at the far end of the street a machine-gun loosed off a strip—a gunner opening fire on ghosts.

More barricades were being hastily thrown together. Garcia had no great faith in the utility of barricades; these, however, looked business-like enough. Everywhere in the dim light spectral forms were flitting to and fro, with here and there a stationary wraith that, after a brief gesture, resumed its immobility—a man directing operations. The mist was steadily thickening. Men and women carrying building materials sped through the gloom, and workers from the various building unions were carrying out the tasks of supervision assigned them by their foremen. Experts from the Fifth Regiment had trained these foremen in two strenuous days. And in this silent phantasmagoria the Old Madrid was passing away; for the first time, behind the drama of private lives, of personal dreams and aspirations, beyond the lesser hopes and fears that urged these people on their diverse ways, a will commensurate with the collective soul of New Madrid was developing in the fogbound dusk of the beleaguered city.

The lamps along the avenue were dwindling to dismal, ineffectual blurs of light under the prehistorically monstrous forms of the intricate skyscrapers. And Garcia recalled what his friend had said: "More duties are imposed on us, as Christian writers, than on other people."

"What the devil can you expect from them—things being as they are?" he asked, jerking his pipe in the direction of another church.

They were under a street-lamp. On Guernico's face was the pensive smile that so often gave him the look of an ailing child.

"Don't forget I'm one of those people who believe in an eternity." He took Garcia's arm. "I suspect that what's happening here just now—even the burning of churches in Catalonia—may do far more for my Church than the last hundred years of Spanish Catholicism have done for it. For twenty years I've watched the priests officiating here and in Andalusia. Well, in all those twenty years, I've never had a glimpse of a truly Catholic Spain. Only rites and ceremonies, and in the people's hearts as on the face of nature—a wasteland!"

At the Puerta del Sol all the doors of the State Building were open. Just before the rebellion an exhibition of sculpture was being held in the vestibule, and statues of all kinds— nudes, groups and animals—were awaiting the coming of the Moors in the vast empty hall. Only the click of a distant typewriter fretted the silence; evidently the building was not completely abandoned.

And in all the streets radiating from the square, ubiquitous as the mist, similar wraiths were building similar barricades.

"Is it a fact that Caballero asked your advice about reopening the churches?"

"Yes."

"What did you say?"

" 'No,' of course."

"You told him not to open them?"

"Obviously. That may surprise you, but it doesn't surprise Catholics at all. If I'm shot tomorrow, I'll have the usual fears for myself, like any other man; but not one on that score. I'm neither a heretic nor a Protestant; I'm a Spanish Catholic. If theology were in your line, I'd tell you I'm appealing to the soul of the Church against its body; but that's another story. Faith doesn't imply a lack of love. And hope doesn't imply a world that would justify itself by making people worship once again, like a fetish, that crucifix at Seville which they call 'The Rich Man's Christ'. (Simony, not heresy's the trouble with our Church.) Nor is it looking forward to a Spanish empire as the be-all and the end-all of the world; a régime in which no sound is heard because those who suffer must hide themselves to weep. 'Order'—you find that in a convict prison, too. Even the best of the fascists hasn't a single hope that isn't founded on pride. But what has Christ to do with such a world?"

Garcia tripped over a large dog and nearly fell. There were numbers of magnificent dogs—abandoned by owners who had fled—straying in Madrid. With the blind men they had taken possession of the city, pending the issue between Republicans and Moors.

"Those priests of Navarre," Guernico continued, "who permit men to be shot for the glory of the Holy Virgin, what have they to do with 'charity'? No, it's the Basque priests who stand for charity; those priests who till the fascists killed them went on administering the benediction, in the cellars of Irun, to the anarchists who'd burned their churches. I'm not anxious, Garcia. I recognize the Church of Spain, but—all the faith I've in me bears me out—I'm against it in the name of the three major virtues of our creed: Faith, Hope and Charity."

"Where will you find the church that answers to your faith?"

Guernico stroked back his hair, which was falling on his forehead. Almost soundlessly the crowd was flowing to and fro between the arcades and hoardings which all but blocked the Plaza Mayor. The earthwork going on in the square had been held up, and it was littered with heaps of stone and paving-blocks; over these the moving stream of shadows skipped or glided in a tragic nocturnal ballet, against a background of haggard pinnacles resembling those of the Escorial. Madrid tonight seemed so thickly covered with barricades that in the whole city not one open space remained.

"Look!" Guernico exclaimed. "In those squalid houses, and in the hospitals, there are priests at this very moment, dressed up in waistcoats like Parisian waiters, and collarless —and they're hearing confessions, giving extreme unction, perhaps baptising children. I said to you that for twenty years I've not heard Christ's word in Spain. But those priests are being heard now. Yes, they're being listened to, and nobody, will listen to the men who turn out tomorrow in the cassocks they've fetched out of hiding, to bless Franco. How many priests are carrying on their ministry just now? Fifty, perhaps a hundred. Napoleon once walked under these arcades;

in those days the Church of Spain shielded its flock; but since then I doubt that there's been a single night, till these last few nights, when Christ's words were *living* in our midst. Yes, tonight His Gospel is a living presence."

His foot caught on a displaced paving-block and his hair sagged forward again.

"A living presence," he repeated. "There aren't many places in the world of which one can say: 'His Word was present here.' But soon it will be known that here, in Madrid, during these recent nights, His Word was among us all. In this land something is dawning for my Church, something which may well be its renaissance. I saw the last sacrament administered to a Belgian *miliciano* yesterday at San Carlos Hospital, do you know it?"

"Yes, when we were running that armoured train, I had some casualties treated there."

The enormous, musty rooms came back to Garcia's mind, the foliage sprouting through the narrow windows. How far away all that seemed!

"It was a ward for arm cases. When the priest said, *Requiem aeternam dona ei Domine,* several voices made the response: *Et lux perpetua luceat.* . . . Four or five voices, just behind me."

"Do you remember Manuel's *Tantum Ergo?*"

Five months earlier several of Garcia's friends, including Manuel and Guernico, had spent with him the last night before he started out on a journey; at daybreak they had all gone together to the hills overlooking Madrid. As the pale, mauve forms of the buildings loomed slowly forth against the shadows and the dark mass of the Escorial woods, Manuel had sung some Asturian folksongs and the others joined in the refrains. Then he had said, "Now for Guernico's benefit, I'm going to sing the *Tantum Ergo.*" All had been educated by priests and all had joined in the last verse, singing the parts in Latin. As those half-forgotten Latin phrases had come back to his friend that morning, charged with a certain amiable irony, so to the wounded revolutionaries in the San Carlos Hospital had recurred the Latin of the death-bed.

"The priest said to me," Guernico went on: "'When I came in, they all took off their hats; they knew that I was bringing them consolation in the hour of death.' He was wrong. They took off their hats because the priest who'd entered might have been their enemy, but was not."

He stumbled against another loose stone; uprooted paving-stones lay everywhere is if the square had been through a bombardment. His voice was different when he spoke again.

"Oh, I know our 'realists' are out to make us see all that from a new angle. The Son of God came down on earth merely to talk a lot of idle nonsense; His sufferings must have turned His head a little—considering the time he was hanging on the Cross, of course. . . .

"God alone knows the trials He is about to impose on the priesthood; but I think that the priest's vocation *should* become a hard task once again." He paused for a moment, then added: "As indeed every Christian life is hard."

Garcia watched their twisted shadows gliding in front of them along the iron-shuttered shopfronts and remembered the twelve bombs of the thirtieth of October.

"What's hardest," Guernico continued in a low tone, "is the problem of the women and children. Anyhow, I've that much luck, my family's not here."

Garcia turned to see his friend's face, but could make out little of his features. There was still no sign of battle; yet somehow, like a presence in a darkened room, the crescent of the fascist army made itself felt closing in upon the city. Garcia recalled his last meeting with Caballero, and how the words "eldest son" had cropped up in their conversation. He was aware that Caballero's eldest boy was held prisoner by the fascists at Segovia and would be shot. That had been in September; they had sat at the table facing each other; Caballero in dungarees, Garcia in a *mono*. Through a window open on the autumn sun a grasshopper had blundered in and fallen upside down on the table between them. Half-stunned, the insect tried to keep from moving, but its brittle legs were quivering and, as Garcia watched him, both men had kept silent.

7

IN THE FOG shadowy forms were drifting ceaselessly past the shop-fronts and the street was loud with unseen footfalls. In the huge dining-room at the Gran Via, the waiters were serving three forlorn customers (whom they took to be the last guests of the Republic) with surly stupefaction. In the lobby of the hotel, men of the Fifth Regiment were withdrawing their fists, bristling with bullets, from large sacks of ammunition and, filing out one by one, were falling in by companies along the pavement. At Tetuan and Cuatro Caminos, women were carrying all the gasoline they had been able to collect to the top floors of the houses. In the worker's districts the possibility of surrender or escape was not so much as mentioned. In lorries or on foot the Fifth Regiment was proceeding to Carabanchel, the Western Park and University City. . . .

There was not much room in the car, and a suit-case was the most that Jaime's father would be able to take with him.

The door opened and Scali saw a very tall, robust old man, with a sharply pointed beard that seemed wedged between his stooping shoulders. Once they were under the electric lamp in the hall, Scali noticed how curiously the hair modified the old face, much as a baroque copyist might modify an El Greco portrait; above the large keen eyes whose intensity seemed a little dulled by the heavy, puckered lids, the restless eyebrows tapered off, like the beard, into little comma-like wisps, and the long hair at the back of the bald head fluttered in all directions.

"You're Giovanni Scali, aren't you?" he asked with a friendly smile.

Scali was surprised to hear his first name used. "Did your son talk to you about me?"

"Yes," the old man answered. "But I've read you, too; I know your work."

Scali remembered Jaime telling him his father had been a professor of the history of art.

They entered a room entirely lined with books, except for two high alcoves on each side of a divan. In one of the alcoves were some baroque, primitive statuettes, the work of Spanish-Mexican artists; in the other was a very fine Morales.

Holding his glasses to his eyes, Alvear looked down on Scali—he was a head taller than his guest—with the meticulous attention one gives to objects out of the common run.

"You seem surprised," Scali remarked.

"Yes. To see a man with brains in that get-up always surprises me."

Scali was in uniform. On a low table, flanked by large leather chairs, were some open books, a bottle of liqueur brandy and a filled wine-glass. Alvear stamped heavily out of the room—his shoulders seemed too bulky for his legs—and came back with another glass.

"No, thanks," Scali said.

The shutters were closed, but he could hear a sound of hurrying footsteps, and an accordion in the distance.

"You're wrong. Our Jerez liqueur brandy is extremely good, quite equal to the French. How about something else instead?"

"My car's waiting below," Scali said. "It's at your disposal. You can leave Madrid at once."

Alvear sank into the nearest arm-chair. Huddled up in it, he looked like a sturdy old eagle in its eyrie, an old eagle shorn of its plumage, with a large but not unattractive beak, like Jaime's.

Raising his eyes, he stared at Scali. "What for?"

"Jaime asked me to call for you on my way back from the Ministry. I'm going to Alcalá de Henares."

Alvear's smile seemed even older than his body. "When a man of my age travels, he takes his library with him."

"I suppose you know it's quite possible the Moors will be here tomorrow."

"Quite so. But what on earth can I do about it? Well, well, we've met, you and I, under most remarkable circumstances. I'm grateful to you for your offer of help; please thank Jaime for having asked you to make it. But what reason can there be for me to leave Madrid?"

"The fascists know your son is in the army. Do you realize that you stand a good chance of being shot?"

"Certainly." A smile rippled down his thick eyelids and sagging cheeks. Then he pointed with his spectacles to the bottle. "I've bought that brandy."

The old man had the knobby face, the lean, hook-nose of Jaime, and the selfsame eyes, now that a shadow was casting two black disks, like smoked glasses, on his forehead.

"Do you mean," Alvear went on, "that the risk's enough to separate me from . . ." He pointed to the book-lined walls. "Why? But why? It's curious. I've lived for art, immersed in art, for forty years and how can you, an artist, wonder if I prefer to go on doing so? Listen to me, Monsieur Scali; I ran a picture-gallery for many, many years. I was the first to show people here the Mexican baroque art, Lopez' sculpture, Georges de Latour, our primitives. A woman would come to my gallery, look at a Greco, a Picasso or an Aragonese primitive. 'How much?' Usually she was an aristocrat, who came in her Hispano, with all her diamonds . . . with all her miserliness. 'Excuse me, Madame; why do you want to buy that picture?' Almost always she replied, 'I don't know.' 'Then Madame, go home and think it over. When you know why, you can come back.' "

Among all those with whom Scali came in contact and with whom he had been living since the war began, Garcia was the only man with any sense of mental discipline. And Scali felt all the more affected by the intellectual fellowship which was growing up between him and the old picture-dealer, because he had had a particularly trying day—and because, painfully conscious of his weakness as a leader, he was drawn to a world in which he felt at ease.

"They came back, those women?" he asked.

"They did their best to 'know why' on the spot. 'I want that picture because I like it . . . because I think it's fine . . . because Mrs. So-and-So has one.' Everyone knew that the finest Grecos in Spain were to be had at my place. Well, I wouldn't sell to her."

"When did you consent to sell?"

Alvear raised a gnarled finger, matted with curly hair. "When she said: 'Because I *need* it.' Then, if the woman was rich, I sold it to her—at a fabulous figure. But if it was somebody poor who 'needed it', I sometimes gave it away."

Two gunshots rang out close to the house, followed by a clatter of footsteps scattering out fanwise.

"With these inside shutters," Alvear remarked in a casual tone, "it's impossible for people outside to see the light in here. . . . Yes," he continued, "I sold according to the faith that's in me, Monsieur Scali. Sold my wares. I doubt if anyone would carry his faith further! Tonight it keeps me company. The Moors are coming? Well, why should I care?"

"So you'd let yourself be killed—out of sheer indifference?"

"Not indifference." Alvear half rose, and, his hands still resting on the chair-arms, gazed intently at Scali, as if to emphasize what he was saying. "Not indifference. Disdain. Still —d'you see this book? It's *Don Quixote*. I was trying to read it just now. Couldn't manage it."

"In the churches of the South where there'd been fighting, I sometimes saw great pools of blood in front of the pictures. And the pictures . . . had lost their efficacy."

"We've got to have new pictures, that's all," Alvear said, slowly winding the tip of his beard round his forefinger; the

tone of voice was that of a picture-dealer who suggests changing the pictures in a client's flat.

"I see," Scali said. "But surely it's rating works of art very
high?"

"Not 'works of art', but *art*. It isn't always the same works
that give access to what is purest in ourselves; but it's always
this work of art or that."

At last Scali realized what had been worrying him ever since
the beginning of the conversation. All the expression of that
old face was concentrated in the eyes. And, with its usual
fatuous malevolence, instinct was leading him, every time old
Alvear took off his glasses, to expect to see a blind man's eyes.

"Tonight," Alvear continued, "neither philosopher nor novelist has any message. People who deal in life are unavailing
in the face of death. Wisdom is more vulnerable than beauty;
because wisdom's an impure art. But poetry and music hold
good for life and for death. You should read *Numantia* again.
Remember it? War is striding through the beleaguered city—
with just that distant rumour of running feet. . . ." He got
up, looked for his collection of Cervantes' works, but failed
to find it. "Everything's topsy-turvy, what with this war . . ."

Alvear had taken another book from one of the shelves and
was reading aloud the last two lines of Quevedo's famous
sonnet.

> *¿Qué pretende el temor desacordado*
> *De la que a rescatar piadosa viene*
> *Espíritu en miserias anudado?*

The gnarled forefinger following the lines betrayed the
pedagogue of old. His shoulders hunched against the chair-
back, like a weary old eagle who had taken shelter in this
shuttered room, in the arm-chair, in poetry, he read the lines
slowly and with a feeling for their rhythm all the more impressive that his voice was toneless, senile as his smile. Muffled
footsteps scattered into the distance, far-off explosions, and all
the sounds heard from dawn to dusk that still were haunting
Scali's memory seemed circling now like startled animals
round that voice already committed to death.

"Quite possibly the Arabs may kill me. For all I know,
your people may do so, in the end. Really it doesn't matter.
. . . Is it so hard, Monsieur Scali, to await death—that may
or may not come, quietly sipping one's drink and reading

excellent poetry? By the way, there's a very deep-seated feeling towards death which no one seems to have mentioned since the Renaissance. . . . And yet in my young days I was afraid of death," he added parenthetically in a lower tone.

"What feeling?"

"Curiosity."

He replaced the Quevedo on a shelf. Scali had no desire to leave now.

"You don't feel any curiosity about death?" the old man asked. "Any fixed opinion on the subject is, of course, ridiculous."

"I used to think about it often." Scali ran his fingers through his curly hair. "But since I've been on active service, I've ceased to do so. Death for me has lost all—what shall I call it?—metaphysical validity. I cracked up once. Well, between the moment when the nose of my plane struck earth and the moment I got wounded—very slightly, as it happened—I didn't think at all; I was just an animal at bay, watching desperately where and when to jump. I suppose it's always like that. A fight to the death with death. All the rest is just association of ideas. There's no need to take death seriously; but pain's another matter. And where there's suffering, art is pretty futile. No picture can stand up against a pool of blood—more's the pity!"

"Don't be so sure of it, my boy. When the French were besieging Saragossa, the grenadiers took canvases of the great masters from the convents and made tents of them. After a sortie, the camp was crowded with wounded men, among whom Polish hussars were to be seen kneeling, saying their prayers in front of Virgins painted by Murillo and serving now as tent-flaps. Yes, art, and not religion only, entered into it, for they never prayed thus before the 'popular' effigies of the Virgin. You are deeply versed in art, Monsieur Scali, but you've much to learn about suffering. You're too young now, but you'll discover later that suffering becomes less poignant once one realizes there's no changing it."

A machine-gun began to stutter in short sharp bursts; a lonely, rancorous voice cutting across the little creaking sounds that filled the silence.

"You hear?" Alvear said in a listless voice. "But the portion of himself which that man who's firing just now is bringing into play isn't, to my mind, the part of him that really matters. What's to prove that the benefits, the 'economic liberation'

they talk about may bring, will be greater than the losses en-
tailed by the new order—threatened as it's sure to be on every
side, and scared into acts of violence, repression, perhaps
treachery. I grant you economic servitude's a dreary state of
affairs; but if, to do away with it, they're obliged to enforce a
political, military or religious servitude, why should I take
sides?"

Alvear was bringing home to Scali a form of experience
hitherto outside his range, and one which had a tragic aspect
for the little curly-headed Italian. For Scali, what threatened
the revolution was not the future but the present. From the
day when Karlitch had so surprised him, he had been watching the physiological element of war getting a stronger and
stronger hold on many of his comrades, and he had been
deeply shocked by it. Moreover, the meeting he had just left
had not been calculated to allay his fears. He was feeling
baffled, perplexed.

"I like to be able," the old man went on, "to clarify my
ideas."

"That's all very well. But it cramps one's life."

"Perhaps." Alvear's tone was pensive. "But don't forget the
least cramped life is that of lunatics. I like to consort with
people for what they are, not for their ideas. I want true
loyalty among friends, not the sort of loyalty that hangs on a
political opinion. I want a man to feel responsible to himself
—and that, you know, Monsieur Scali, whatever people may
say, is the hardest thing of all—not to any cause, even the
cause of the oppressed." Alvear lit a cigar. "In South America"
—a puff—"every morning"—another puff—"the monkeys always set up a terrific outcry in the forest. Once upon a time,
the folk-tale tells us, God promised to change them into men at
dawn. Morning after morning they hope for the best, are once
again disappointed, and scream their grievances from tree to
tree.

"Hope 'springs eternal' as they say, and it's a terrifying
thing! A man who has been unjustly sentenced, or has run up
against more than his share of ingratitude or baseness or
stupidity—well, he's bound to stake his hope on some new
order. Among other functions, the revolution plays a part
that an 'eternal life' used formerly to play; that explains many
of its characteristics. If only each man would direct upon himself one-third of the efforts he devotes nowadays to politics,
Spain would become quite a habitable country."

"But he'd have to do that *by himself;* that's the point."

"A man devotes to any line of action only a limited part of himself; and the more that line of action sets up to be 'totalitarian,' the smaller is the part of him involved. You know very well Monsieur Scali, how hard it is to be a *man,* far harder than the politicians think." Alvear had risen from his chair. "But good heavens!" he exclaimed. "How can a man like you, the interpreter of Masaccio and Piero della Francesca—how can you endure the present state of things?"

Scali wondered whether the words conveyed Alvear's real thoughts, or his grief.

"So be it!" he replied after a short pause. "Tell me, have you ever lived among uneducated men?"

It was Alvear's turn to muse before replying. "I don't think so, but I've a good imagination."

"Do you know some of the famous sermons of the Middle Ages?"

Alvear nodded.

"Well," Scali continued, "those sermons were listened to by men still more ignorant than those who are fighting at my side. Do you think those sermons were understood?"

Alvear rolled the tip of his beard around his fingers; his look implied: I can see what you're leading up to.

"Certainly," was all he said.

"You spoke of hope just now. Well, men who are joined together in a common hope, a common quest, have, like men whom love unites, access to regions they could never reach left to themselves. And there's more nobility in the *ensemble* of my squadron than in almost any of the individuals composing it."

Scali had taken off his glasses and Alvear's eyes were intent on the face that seemed lit up with beauty, now that he was expressing what he was meant to express: ideas. And there was a mysterious symmetry between the thick lips and the rather narrow eyes.

"I am sick and tired," Scali continued, "of many things in my present life, and yet I find it's just such circumstances bring out what is—how shall I put it?—most fundamental in men. 'In the sweat of thy face shalt thou eat bread.' And that's true for us, you know; truest of all when the sweat is icy cold."

"Yes, of course, you're all of you hypnotized by what is 'fundamental' in man!" Suddenly Alvear's voice grew earnest.

"The age of fundamentals is returning. And reason has to be rebuilt on a new basis."

"Do you think Jaime was wrong to join up?"

Alvear's hunched shoulders quivered, his loose cheeks sagged a little lower. "Let the world go fascist," he said, "but let my son get back his eyes." Shrill with speed, a car sped past, receded. "Do you think he'll get back his sight?"

"The doctors say it's possible."

"So they say that to you! To you, as well! Of course they know you're his friend. And you're in uniform. Yes, they'd lie to any officer in these days; they're afraid of being taken for fascists, if they tell the truth, the wretched fools!"

"Why must what they tell me be necessarily untrue?"

"Do you think it's easy to believe even the truth, when it hangs on just one man's word, and when all one's happiness is staked on it?" He was silent for a moment, then continued listlessly, though in a firmer voice: "The only hope that the New Spain has of keeping that for which you and Jaime and so many others are fighting, is that somehow the thing which we've been trying our best to inculcate year after year may be preserved. . . ."

He listened to something in the street, got up and walked to the window.

"Meaning—what?" Scali asked.

The old man turned. His voice was like a sigh of regret. "The human element; the quality of man."

He stood listening a little longer, then switched off the lights, and set the window ajar. Across a counterpoint of footsteps the *International* drifted in. In the darkness his voice was more remote than ever, like a voice coming from a smaller body, a sadder and still older voice.

"Well, if the Moors are here presently, the last song I'll have heard will be that hymn of hope played on a blind man's concertina."

He spoke quite unemotionally, smiling perhaps a little to himself. Scali heard the shutters closing, and for a moment the room was plunged in darkness. Alvear found the switch, and turned on the light again.

"For if they need our world," he said, "in the hour of defeat, they'll need it too when the time comes for rejoicing." He glanced at Scali who had just sat down on the sofa. "Yes, Monsieur Scali, it wasn't the gods who created music, it was music created the gods."

"Or perhaps what's happening outside there is what created music."

"The age of fundamentals is returning," Alvear said again. He poured out a glass of brandy and drank it off. His face was expressionless. Scali was sitting just within the range of the lamplight, which glinted on his forehead and crisp hair.

"That's where Jaime always sits when he comes to visit me. You, too, are wearing glasses. When he takes his off I can't bear to look at his face."

For the first time a note of grief throbbed in the old, toneless voice as Alvear murmured slowly to himself in French:

Que te sert, ô Priam, d'avoir vécu si vieux!

He raised his head, his brows puckered under the wisps of straggling hair, and looked Scali up and down; there was something at once childlike and haunted in his gaze.

"Nothing's more horrible than the mutilation of a *body* that one loves."

"I'm his friend," Scali said, in a low voice. "And I'm used to wounded men."

"It so happens," Alvear said, "that exactly in front of his eyes, on those shelves over there, are all my books on painting, with thousands and thousands of the photographs over which he used to pore. . . . Still, do you know, when I turn on the gramophone—when there's music in the room—I can look at him, even if he isn't wearing his spectacles."

8

MANUEL, too, had found the Ministry of War given over to dying candles. Those vast, lugubrious halls where the last Spanish Kings had staged their tawdry imitations of the spacious days of Charles the Fifth—Manuel had known them packed with *milicianos* sleeping on the sofas, each with a revolver on his chest, while the Premier listened in at a radio set in a far corner; then, after that, he had seen them neat and orderly under the strict, rather pettifogging discipline of Caballero. Orderly they still were, but now the windows gaped upon a nerve-racked city, and when he switched on a lamp the arm-chairs had a positively startled air. The one exception was the War Minister's room, where all the lights were on, and the French captain still was waiting, by himself. On the staircases the candles had ceased to shed the theatrical illumination

Garcia and Guernico had seen; now, on the point of guttering out, they shed no more than a dim religious glow. Here and there, along an arcaded inner corridor, hung little lanterns such as are lit by night on hand-carts, or to mark blocked roads. Their rays seemed lost on the majestic staircase climbing into the darkness.

The room which General Miaja occupied and Manuel was approaching was high up under the roof. Here, too, the corridors were unlit, but lamplight showed under each door. The General himself was out, but half the staff-officers of the "Junta of Defence" were sitting in the room, which looked like the lounge of a second-class hotel. The leader of the *dinamiteros,* the chief sapper, Miaja's personal staff and officers of the Fifth Corps were there. None of the latter had been a soldier six months earlier; among them were a fashion designer, a contractor, a pilot, a factory manager, two members of joint committees of the various parties, steel-factory hands, a composer, an engineer and a garage-keeper. Enrique and Ramos, too, were present.

Manuel remembered the blind *miliciano,* with his legs paralysed by wounds, who had accosted Azaña.

"What do you want of me?" the President had asked.

"Nothing. Only to say to you: 'Good luck and keep your courage!'"

Then the blind man had hobbled away on his crutches.

It was not a council of war—but that night every gathering was a council of war. The destiny of all these men, formed in active service, followed the same lines as that of Manuel and of Spain.

"There's one rifle for—how many men just now?" Enrique asked.

"One rifle among four men," an officer replied. The officer was the ex-fashion artist and a friend of Manuel's. He was directing the mobilization of the civilians; on the previous day the Communist Party had asked for orders for a general mobilization of the Syndicates.

"We've got to make arrangements to collect the rifles," Enrique said. "When the first men fall, their rifles must be picked up and taken to the rear. The same procedure as the stretcher-bearers'. Fix that up tonight, will you?"

The artist went away.

"Is it absolutely impossible to unearth any more weapons at Madrid?"

Another voice replied: "There's not a rifle left except at Police Headquarters. Even the sentries, escorts and patrolmen have only kept their revolvers. No one's armed in Madrid tonight."

"If we lose Madrid, we stand to lose the Government offices —and, of course, all the leaders and ministers, if there are any left."

"How are the fortifications coming along?" Miaja's second-in-command enquired.

"Twenty thousand men," Ramos said, "are working on them, hammer and tongs. All the members of the building syndicates are there, and with them plenty of volunteers. A man from the Fifth Corps is directing operations at every barricade. As things are now the Moors will have a good half mile and more of solid fortifications to fight their way through. And the day after tomorrow Madrid will be completely surrounded by barricades—not to mention the other defences."

"The women's barricades are rotten," an officer remarked. "Much too small."

"We've done away with them," Ramos replied. "The only ones we're keeping are those which are built on the lines I've just described, and the ones the Fifth Corps boys have checked up on and passed as trustworthy. But you're wrong about the women's barricades. They're not too small; quite the contrary. There was no holding the women once they'd started!"

"What the women are doing—about the stocks of gasoline in each house, I mean—is pretty futile," another voice put in.

"Futile perhaps. But excellent for the morale."

"Look here! Why couldn't all that have been done before?"

"Half our people here—more than that, nine-tenths of them—can't conceive of defending Madrid except *inside* Madrid. A fellow said to me only this morning 'If ever they reach Madrid, we'll teach them what's what!' 'Look here,' I told him, 'you know where Carabanchel is—or don't you?' He only said: 'Madrid's Madrid, and Carabanchel isn't Madrid.'"

"Are they advancing on Carabanchel now?" Manuel asked.

"Yes, they're being held up there by the Fifth. But they're advancing from the South, and they'll be attacking on your side as well."

Manuel had to leave that night for Guadarrama. He was now a Lieutenant-Colonel. His hair was cut short and, on the face that had grown darker, the greenish eyes shone paler than ever.

"I hear that Durruti's men have turned up. Is that so?"

"The railway's cut. We've sent lorries to Tarancon. They're on their way there now."

"Are they still expecting the planes we've bought in Soviet Russia for the day after tomorrow?"

No one answered. All knew the planes were being assembled. But how long would that take?

"Who'll they come up against in the South?"

"That depends on the time; just now the International Brigade is being brought up from Vallecas."

More officers were entering the room.

The last candles on the huge staircase had burnt out. The French captain had left. Only a few decorative lanterns which formerly had hung beside the entrance-gates shed a funereal light, like the lamps in a death-chamber, at the far end of the long, lugubrious vistas. Empty as the last restaurants of Madrid, deserted as its streets, the old palace, like the city, was maturing its defense in silence and in gloom.

9

West Park

A BLACKBIRD'S song rose through the air in seeming interrogation—and drew an answer. It came again with a note of growing uneasiness; a furious protest followed, then a burst of laughter through the fog. "You're right," a voice said; "they shall not pass."

The blackbirds were Siry and Kogan, of the first International Brigade. Kogan was a Bulgarian and knew no French. They were whistling to each other; question and response.

"Quiet."

A dozen shells answered.

Germans, Poles, Belgians, and a few Frenchmen stood waiting, listening to the explosions getting nearer. Suddenly they turned round; there was firing behind them.

"Explosive bullets," the officers shouted. "Nothing to worry about."

The sound of bullets cut through the mist so clearly that the ear could follow their actual flight. The battalion had been named after Edgar André when they first started training. On the previous night the Germans had heard that Edgar André's imprisonment under Hitler had been ended by the headsman's axe.

For months past, almost all the Germans had lived the wretched, maladjusted life of newcomers in a strange country. They were waiting. They had been waiting for three years. Now at last they were on the point of showing that they were no longer uninvited guests of the revolution.

The Poles were tensely awaiting orders.

The Frenchmen were talking.

The shells were getting nearer. Half-unconsciously, many of the men were touching each other—a leg or a shoulder—as if the physical nearness of their companions were their sole defence against death.

Siry and Kogan were clinging to each other. They were too young to have been through the Great War, but old enough to have done their military service; fit for the front, therefore, after a fortnight's training. Siry was short and sturdy, with the gestures of a comedian and a broad, triangular face of pronounced swarthiness. Kogan looked like a tousled feather-duster, with his shock of hair always bolt upright.

They had shared the same blanket that night; all the troops had slept in pairs, for the November night had been cold. Kogan thought that he had never developed such a feeling of friendship for any man in so short a time. Whenever a shell fell near them, Siry gave vent to his birdlike whistles indicating approval, protest or indifference. A "155" failed to explode, disappearing through the mud, towards the bowels of the earth. Siry flapped imaginary wings, protesting frantically.

"The Moors!"

No—overstrained nerves. The mist was beginning to thin, but there was nobody in sight. Nothing but explosions, and a deserted wood.

"Down!"

They flung themselves with one accord upon the scented moss, evocative of childhood. A batch of men hit in the face were falling back down the slope, with fingers already red with blood pressed to their wounds. Their comrades rose to salute with clenched fists, despite the bullets. But only one of the wounded saw them, disclosing, as he raised an answering fist, a face that might have been the incarnation of war. Branches were falling all round them, like so many men. "If only there was a way down into this blasted ground!" Siry said.

"Forward!"

Bent double, they began to advance through the wood. They could hear the Moors advancing too, but could see nothing except a tree or two which, through the mist, resembled spouts of earth thrown up by the bursting shells. There was no whistling now. Since they had started to move forward, since their legs had begun to carry them into action, they were thinking of nothing but the moment when the Moors would appear. And yet even the most ignorant of them felt also that events of incalculable significance depended upon their conduct on that misty morning.

The Belgian on Siry's right (Kogan was on his left) was hit in the leg. He bent down to feel his calf, received two more bullets in his chest, and fell. The Moors had established a cross-fire. Siry was amazed not only that so many bullets should be directed at him personally, but that there could be so many bullets in the whole world. But he was delighted to find that he had such control over himself. Fear was there, but not to the point of utter mental or physical inhibition. He was all right. "We'll teach them a thing or two about Frenchmen!" Each member of the Brigade felt that in such a moment he was the custodian of the military prowess of his particular nation. An officer began to shout an order, and fell with a bullet in his mouth after the first two syllables. Siry felt a surge of anger; this assassination of his comrades was becoming something personal. A wounded captain was carried past by two soldiers. "Stick it out," he said. "And above all don't throw your lives away needlessly." Between the crashing shells, Siry noticed the silence of the men. Only one phrase could still be heard, from several throats:

"They've got me!"

The Brigade was advancing through the haze. Were they ever going to get a sight of the Moors?

Heinrich was feverishly directing operations amid the telephones and hubbub of field-headquarters. A civilian arrived. He had stiff grey hair and a moustache.

"What do you want?" Albert asked him. Albert was the general's adjutant; a sturdy, crisp-haired Hungarian Jew, ex-student, ex-dishwasher.

"I hold the rank of Captain in the French Army. I have been a member of the World Anti-Fascist Committee since its formation. I've spent the whole day sitting on a chair at the War Ministry. Surely I can do something better than that. Finally they sent me here. I am at your service."

He handed Albert papers showing his army record

and membership of the Committee.

"That's all right, sir," Albert said to Heinrich.

"A Polish company have just lost their second captain," said the general.

"Very well."

The captain turned to Albert.

"Where are the uniforms?"

"No time," Heinrich grunted.

"Very well. Where are the men?"

"You'll be shown the way. I should warn you that the position is not . . . a sinecure."

"I served through the War, sir."

"Good. Splendid."

"I was born lucky. Bullets don't worry me."

"Splendid."

In between the trees in West Park, so unsuggestive of war, beyond the motionless bodies of those who were taking no further interest in the fighting because they were dead, Siry at length had his first glimpse of turbans moving behind the trunks like fat, furtive pigeons.

"Stick your bayonets in the ground!"

He had never seen the Moors. But a few nights before, detailed for liaison work, he had spent an hour within a hundred yards of their trenches. The November night was thick and foggy. Though he could see nothing, during the whole of that time he distinctly heard the beat of their drums rising and falling beside their fires; and he awaited them now as he would have awaited the onslaught of a savage tribe. The Moors were supposed to be drunk when they attacked. Standing up, lying prone or dead, aiming, firing, aiming and firing, all around him were his comrades from Ivry, and with them workers from Grenelle, Courneuve and Billancourt, Polish emigrés, Belgians, exiles from Germany, men from the Budapest Commune, dockers from Antwerp, representatives of proletarian blood from half Europe. The turbans were dodging about behind the tree-trunks, as if taking part in some fantastic variation of "puss-in-the-corner."

Nearer and nearer they had been coming ever since Melilla.

Long blades of bayonets and sabres were moving through the mist; steel, sharp and without sheen.

Where cold steel decides the issue, the Moors are among the finest troops in the world.

"Fix bayonets!"

The International Brigade were going into action for the first time.

They drew their bayonets. It was Siry's first battle. He was not thinking that he would be killed or that he would get through the day. He was thinking: "Niggers just don't realize!" Would it be like the bayonet practice on the training ground? Or just a quick rip through the guts?

Between two shells, a distant voice could be heard behind the trees:

"For the Republic! Forward, Comp . . . !"

The end of the order was inaudible.

Every eye was fixed on the approaching Moors. Then another voice, much nearer, shouted across the mist words which each of them might have guessed in advance—words less important in themselves than in the vibrant fervour of their utterance—words which made each one of the crouching men stand needlessly erect.

"For the Revolution and for Liberty, Number Three Company—Forward!"

His shaven neck as furrowed as an anxious forehead, Heinrich was sitting with a telephone receiver to each ear. Company by company, the Brigade was launching bayonet attacks.

Albert put his receiver down.

"I can't make things out at all, sir. Captain Mercery reports: 'large quantities of booty. Objective in our hands; at least two tons of soap captured!' "

Mercery was in command of a Spanish company on the right of the International units.

"Soap! What on earth does the damned fool mean?"

Albert picked up the receiver again.

"What? What factory? What factory, Christ Almighty?"

"He's explaining how useful the soap will be," he said to Heinrich. The General was studying a map.

"What is the map-reading?"

Heinrich changed receivers.

"That's it," he said. "He got the wrong co-ordinate and he's captured a soap-factory which was already ours! Ask the general in command of the Spanish troops to have that idiot relieved right away."

The bayonets they were about to use were longer than they

had thought. All that Siry could remember of the last quarter of an hour was a nightmarish chaos of bushes and large trees hurtling through the air, crashes of bursting shells drowning the noise of the explosive bullets, and the advance of the Moors, with their gaping mouths emitting unheard yells.

A detachment of Germans had just relieved Siry's company, which was retiring to form again behind the line. The wood was strewn with Moors lying as thick as litter after a picnic. But while the battalion was charging, he had not noticed them. A Polish company was rumoured to have crossed the Manzanares.

"What about the captain with the Poles?"

"When he saw how things were, he said: 'This position is untenable; you must abandon it. Those who reach our lines are to say that it was evacuated by my orders. You'd better leave by the back windows. You'll run into just as many shells that way, but not quite as many bullets. Carry on! And say that I did what had to be done.' He put on the dead captain's tunic, went downstairs, and shot himself through the head. He fell right across the doorway."

"How many got clear?"

"Three."

Siry had lost touch with Kogan; neither of his new neighbours understood French (other than words of command), and they could not whistle. Siry knew that behind his battalion there were nothing but barbers carrying rifles; their reserve was known as "The Figaro Battalion." When the diabolical din slackened, he heard the firing of the Durruti column, which was steadily advancing, and the "Ironsides" were advancing; the socialists were advancing.

Behind the bloody confusion which reigned in West Park, a line of attack was developing over a front extending the full length of the city. The Spaniards who, posted between the houses, had beaten off three attacks that morning, had just received the order to launch an attack. The houses captured by the Moors were being retaken with hand-grenades; dynamite was holding up the tanks, and the Moors, driven back by the bayonets of the International Brigade, were meeting the anarchists pushing the Republican field-guns through the streets towards the front line.

Behind them the mobilized syndicates were waiting to take over the rifles of the first casualties.

The fascists had been gaining ground ever since they left Morocco, but now that they had reached West Park they were yielding it.

Now that the line of the Moors had been broken, the decimated detachments of the International Brigade were retiring, and, after forming in new companies, returning to the attack. The Moors were in full retreat. The Durruti anarchists, the units representing the various Catalan parties, the socialists, the bourgeois "Ironsides"—all were pressing their advantage.

"Hallo!"

It was Albert who held the receiver now.

"The enemy are counter-attacking again, sir." The General was beside him.

"More tanks?"

Albert repeated the question over the line.

"No, no new tanks."

"Any planes?"

Again Albert put the question.

"Usual number."

He did not hang up the receiver, but sat staring at his foot, which was shaking. On the table the receiver quivered.

"That's the stuff, sir! They're falling right back to the Manzanares. And they're going to recross the Manzanares, sir!"

Company after company was streaming past Siry's detachment with fixed bayonets, and the ground which he and his comrades now were occupying yard by yard was strewn with men with haggard, war-worn faces. Company after company charged past them, nation after nation, stooping, rifle in hand, advancing at the double through a mist that was clotted with the smoke of battle. It was like a battle-scene in a film—and yet how different! Each of these men Siry knew for one of his kind, a brother. And some were coming back with fists pressed against their faces or clutching their bellies with both hands— if they came back at all. They had accepted that; and so had he. And he still accepted it. Behind them lay Madrid, loud with the incessant roar of distant rifles.

Another forward surge brought them to a narrow river.

Men were shouting: "The Manzanares!"

A blackbird broke into ecstatic song. Somewhere in the mist, his life-blood gushing out on to the fallen leaves from a bayonet wound in the thigh, Kogan answered for the wounded, for the dead.

II. Comrades' Blood

IN THE profound silence crept an even deeper note, till presently it seemed to Guernico that the whole sky was full of it. It was not the crisp hum of a racing car—which reveals the presence of a single plane—but a very massive throbbing that grew deeper and deeper, sustained like a ground bass. Whenever he had heard planes before, the sound had been irregular, rising and falling. But this time the engines were so numerous that everything was merged into a single, implacable, robot progress.

The city was practically without searchlight. How could the Government pursuit planes, such as were left, hope to find the fascists in that blind darkness? The deep, full drone which permeated sky and town and night alike set the nerves tingling at the roots of Guernico's hair in the long moment of intolerable suspense before the bombs fell.

At last a muffled explosion rumbled through the ground like a distant mine, then one by one, he heard three very violent detonations. Another dull explosion; then nothing more. Another; somewhere above Guernico the windows of a big apartment house opened all together.

He refrained from using his electric torch; the *milicianos* were all too ready to imagine that a light was a signal. The drone of the engines went on, but the bombs had ceased. In the pitch darkness, the fascists were quite invisible from below and the city was almost invisible from above.

Guernico tried to run, but stumbled at every step over heaped-up paving-stones. And the utter darkness made it impossible to follow the sidewalk. A car dashed past, with its headlights tinted blue. Five more explosions, some rifle-shots, a desultory burst of machine-gun fire.

The concussions still seemed to be taking place somewhere below the ground, and the bursts about ten yards up in air. Not a glimmer of light; more windows were flying open, impelled by some mysterious agency. Following an explosion nearer at hand, shattered panes of glass fell from a great height on to the roadway. By the sound Guernico realized that he could only see up as far as the first storey. Like an echo from the broken glass, his ears caught the clatter of a bell. It came nearer, passed in front of him, and was lost in the darkness—the first of his ambulances. Finally he arrived at the headquarters of the first-aid service. The street was filling up in the darkness.

Doctors, nurses, surgeons and those with organising jobs were all, like him, reporting for duty. At last he had his ambulances. The responsibility for the purely medical side lay with a doctor. Guernico looked after the organisation of the relief units.

"We're all right at present," the doctor said, "but we soon won't be, if they go on like this. We are having to send out the ambulances in relays, with the swine bombing San Geron-imo Hospice, San Carlos Hospital, and so on. . . ." An institution for old men, and a hospital. Suddenly Guernico pictured the wounded stumbling through the wards at San Carlos—in the dark.

"Have the ambulances all got the right number of torches?" he asked calmly.

"Look at that blaze! The fascists must be using incendiary bombs."

The doctor opened the inside shutters.

"Look!"

On all sides, gleams of rosy light were flickering behind the dark houses. Guernico thought that the burning of Madrid had begun. He repeated his question with patient insistence.

"The torches are in the ambulances all right, aren't they?"

"I don't expect so. But I'm telling you, we won't have any need for them."

Guernico organised things with a calmness that astonished the surgeons; he was impervious to life's comedies and trag-edies. He gave orders for the torches to be placed in each ambulance; in that impenetrable darkness, light was the first essential for the work of rescue.

Another explosion; the windows shuddered. While one of the nurses was closing the shutters again they heard the bells of two ambulances go clanging through the night.

Another detonation. It seemed as though the bombs, light ones no doubt, were being thrown with the savage accuracy of grenades rather than dropped from planes. Guernico had sat down and begun examining the telephone messages which were being handed to him on slips of paper.

"They're all round the Palace," he said.

"One thousand wounded," said the doctor. "And so it goes."

The hospital and the Soviet Embassy were in close proximity.

"Calle San Augustin," said Guernico. "Calle de Leon. Plaza de las Cortes."

"Anyhow they're hitting able-bodied men and women now, not wounded," a doctor remarked.

An assistant half-opened the windows from which the doctor had drawn back the shutters; dominating all other sounds—words of command, buzzing telephones, the tramp of marching feet (almost indecently unflurried), and the continual clanging of ambulance-bells—the even drone of the fascist air-fleet came flooding into the room.

A sudden draught sent some papers whirling into the air; one of the nurses who had accompanied the ambulance sent to the old men's hospice was coming in.

"Well, this is a nice business! Guernico, my dear, they'll need at least two more ambulances at the Institution!"

"Shut the door, Mercedes," the doctor shouted, while chasing his papers like so many butterflies.

"What brutes they are!" she said, as if she had been speaking of the engines upon whose drone the window had been closed once more. "Things are in a shocking mess over there. Those poor old men are trampling each other down on the stairs. They're in a panic, naturally."

"How many casualties?" Guernico asked.

"Oh, the first ambulance will take all the casualties. The problem is, how to evacuate the others."

"The ambulances are intended for casualties; and we shall have quite enough of them. Are the old men in the cellars at least?"

"I should say so!"

"And the cellars—are they pretty solid?"

"Rather! They're like catacombs."

"Good."

He ordered one of the assistants to warn the Junta.

"You know, Guernico," Mercedes said in a low voice—she had suddenly grown calm—"some of them are going crazy."

"What sort of bombs are they? Incendiary?" the doctor asked.

"The people who seem to know about that sort of thing call them calcium bombs. Green they are, like absinthe. Horrible things, you know; it's impossible to put them out. And those poor chaps running down the corridors, groping in the darkness like blind men! And others hobbling on crutches! It's ghastly!"

"Where did the bomb fall?"

"In a passage between the wards."

Was one of the windows badly shut? The persistent drone of the planes was echoing inside the room now, punctuated by bursts of fire from a Republican machine-gun—an attempt to raise morale, no doubt. But from below, as though it were coming up from the foundations of the building, a long, incessant rumble like the roll of muffled drums was rising and falling on the air; along the Manzanares, the International Brigade was launching a new attack against the Moors.

"Where's the fighting taking place?" Guernico asked.

Mercedes answered him. "Everywhere."

"At the Casa del Campo and University City," the doctor said.

An explosion in their immediate neighbourhood made the pens jump on the table. There was a noise of tiles falling on distant roofs, the scurrying footsteps of a crowd running for shelter. Then, after a moment's silence, a scream, sudden and intolerably shrill, jarred the darkness. Then silence fell again.

"An incendiary bomb on the French Embassy," Guernico said; he had taken up the telephone-receiver again: "Another present from non-intervention." He turned to an assistant. "The motorcyclists are at their posts, aren't they? . . . Two bombs have fallen near the Plaza de las Cortes. . . . Send six dispatch-riders to Cuatro Caminos at once."

Another assistant whispered something into his ear.

"Send another ambulance to San Carlos," he continued. "There are a number of casualties there. And tell Ramos to go and have a general look round, please."

Since the beginning of the siege, Ramos had been given the task of directing the help of the Communist Party to the points where it would be most efficacious. Though he had rendered useful service to the medical staff, which was short of anaesthetics and X-ray plates, he had not so far played an active part in ambulance work. But henceforth first-aid was to be one of the principal functions of the Junta at Madrid. . . .

11

RAMOS was travelling as fast as his blue-screened headlights would permit.

He stopped the car at the first big fire. The darkness was loud with muffled cries, echoes of racing feet, explosions, calls for help and the long-drawn crashes of falling buildings, sounding above the never-ending din of battle. A convent was collapsing in a cataract of toppling masonry, over which sleek scarlet flames were scurrying, like hungry beasts of prey, through the red rolling smoke. The building had been evacuated and *milicianos*. Assault Guards and first-aid parties were watching the scene, fascinated by the exultant havoc of the flames, their irrepressible vitality. A grey cat sitting on the kerb raised his eyes to watch.

Was the air-raid over, all were wondering.

A faint glow kindled on the left. In a sudden lull a tramp of heavy boots and a sound of shouting in the distance jarred the silence.

The faint glow grew to an incandescence shaped like the head of a tremendous artichoke, then sank again, and presently a vast glare began to light up the sky and houses. Though the bombers had flown back—their landing-grounds were near, and November nights are long—under the roofs innumerable fires were surreptitiously alive, creeping from floor to floor; to the left four more houses were ablaze, not with the blue-green flare of calcium, but vomiting great bursts of tawny flame. When Ramos passed, the big conflagrations had dwindled to a horde of little restless wisps of fire, battening on the houses like a plague of insects. There was a general exodus in progress; hand-carts, piled with mattresses and chairs, lumbered past him, followed by old women, the last to leave. Ambulance sections were speeding up. Doing their work well, too. Ramos counted ten of them.

At San Carlos, where the houses acted as a screen, it was pitch dark in nearly all the streets around the Plaza. Ramos ran into a stretcher; the bearers cursed him roundly. Like a cloud of fiery confetti, a flurry of sparks swept across the bodies of the wounded, laid out in rows; and for a second their limbs glimmered faintly in the darkness. Three yards farther on Ramos collided with another stretcher; this time it was the wounded man who cursed him. On an islet of roof, at a street corner, the black forms of a group of firemen swayed above the huge flames they were fighting with their preposterous little hoses. At last Ramos reached the Plaza.

The gusts of smoke were coming faster and the glow was increasing. Everything was becoming visible; the cats in the street, the lint bandages round the heads of the wounded. And, like an accompaniment to the roaring of the flames, once more the dim sky throbbed with a deep drone of motors.

So desperately anxious was Ramos that these wounded men should have some peace—they were being gradually evacuated in ambulances—that he almost persuaded himself the sound was only that of heavy cars coming towards him. But then a slithering avalanche of rafters stifled for a moment the fury of the flames and a great cloud of sparks whirled up across the sudden silence—and in the lull there was no mistaking the drone of aeroplanes deploying overhead. Two batches of four bombs each, eight crashes, were followed by a confused, startled din of voices, as if the whole city had wakened in alarm.

A peasant *miliciano,* whose dressing had come undone, was standing beside Ramos, watching the blood trickle down his bare arm and splash drop by drop upon the mud. In the sombre flamelight his skin looked red and the blood, pale brown as it ran down his arm, turned in falling to a bright, diaphanous yellow, like the tip of Ramos' cigarette. He had the man evacuated at once. Other wounded men with arms that seemed to be in splints were drifting past in measured cadence, like the mimes in a dance of death, showing at first as flat black silhouettes, till as they crossed the square and came into the dark glow of the fires, their light-coloured pyjamas grew a bright and brighter red. All the casualties were soldiers; they showed no signs of panic, but observed a self-imposed discipline, the discipline of weariness and helplessness, of rage and resolution. Two more bombs fell and the long line of wounded men rippled like a wave. . . .

There was a telephone-box a hundred yards off, up a dark side-street. As Ramos switched on his torch, he stumbled over a body; the man uttered a cry, his mouth wide open. One of the stretcher-bearers, felt his hand.

"He's dead."

"No," Ramos said, "he cried out."

They could hardly hear each other speak across the roar of aeroplanes, the shrilling of far-off sirens, boom of guns, crashes of bombs. But the man was really dead, his mouth wide open, as if in the act of crying out; perhaps he had cried out. Ramos walked on. More stretchers, more shouting, and then a sudden glare shattered the darkness into a multitude of crouching forms. . . .

Manuel rang up, asking for ambulances and lorries; a good many of the wounded could be evacuated in lorries. Evacuated where? he wondered, as he said it. One after the other, the hospitals were going up in flames. Guernico told him to go to Cuatro Caminos. It was one of the poorest quarters and had been a favourite target since the siege began. (Franco, rumour said, had announced that he would spare the fashionable quarter, Salamanca.) Ramos got into his car again.

In the glare from the conflagrations, through the spectral sheen of misted street-lamps, and along streets of total darkness, one of the great migrations of the century was silently afoot. Many peasants from the Tagus had taken shelter with relatives here, each family with its donkey. With their quilts, alarm-clocks, canary cages and pet cats in their arms, all were streaming out—why they knew not—towards the richer quarters, unflurried, stolid as the poor are stolid. Bombs were falling, falling to teach the under-dog to "keep his place."

Driving past some gutter houses, Ramos saw in the weak glow of his blue headlights some twenty bodies laid out parallel on the road; of all shapes and sizes, they looked alike beside the havoc of their homes. He stopped his car and whistled for an ambulance, thinking how effectively the interminable thunder of those planes far overhead had ranged all sorts together—anarchists, communists, socialists and republicans—in that ultimate fraternity of death.

In the darkness sirens wailed, nearing, meeting, crossing each other, with long hootings that died out on the clammy air like the hooting of liners putting out to sea. One car halted and its call, motionless amid the moving patterns of shrill sound, rose forlorn as the baying of a lost dog. In a reek of burning wood and scorched masonry, under flurries of bright sparks that raced along the streets like mad patrols, the vicious detonations of the bombs seemed to be hunting down the jangle of the ambulances, spraying them with showers of flying steel, whence they emerged, as from a tunnel, clanging their way between the frenzied sirens. The slums of Cuatro Caminos were as full of poultry as any country village, and with the crashes of the first bombs cocks had started crowing by the thousand; now the ferocious racket of the aerial torpedos had sent them crazy. And, furiously, frantically, all crowing together, they blared a shrill chorus, brazen with rage, the battle hymn of poverty, towards the menace of the sky.

Restless as an insect's feeler, the slender beam of Ramos' torch probed the darkness; it lit on another body lying at a lower level than the bodies aligned along the wall. The man was wounded in the side and was groaning. An ambulance-bell was clanging somewhere near by. Ramos whistled. "It's coming for you," he said. The man made no reply, but went on groaning. Directed from above, the beam of the torch cast on his face a tracery of shadows from the tall grass growing between the paving-blocks. With the frenzied crowing of the cocks still ringing in his ears, Ramos looked down compassionately at the man's quivering cheeks fretted with a delicate pattern of waving grasses, dainty as the line-work of a Japanese print.

On the corner of his mouth fell the first drop of rain.

12

THE first big fires that Madrid had known were glowing behind the trenches of the German section of the International Brigade. The volunteers could not see the planes. But in that silent night—no longer the friendly silence of the country-side —the mysterious silence of war hung quivering like a train changing tracks. The Germans were all together; some had been exiled for being Marxists, some for being romantic and thinking themselves to be revolutionaries, some for being Jews; and there were some, too, who were not by nature revolutionaries but who had become so and accordingly found themselves there. Since the assault on West Park, they were beating off two attacks a day; the fascists were trying in vain to break through at University City. The volunteers watched the ruddy glow spread over the background of clouds; as with electric signs, an aura of prodigious size is given off by big conflagrations on a hazy night, so the whole city seemed to be ablaze. None of the volunteers had yet seen Madrid.

For over an hour a wounded Republican had been crying out.

The Moors were only about half a mile away. They must surely know where the wounded man lay; no doubt they were waiting for some of his comrades to come and fetch him; already one volunteer who had left the trench had been killed.

The volunteers were quite ready to play this stool-pigeon game; what they were afraid of, on this pitch dark night with only the sky lit up by the fires, was that they would not be able to find their way back to their own trench.

At last three Germans got permission to go and look for the man whose cries came to them through the black mist. One after the other they crossed the parapet and were engulfed in the murk; in the trench the silence could be felt in spite of explosions.

The cries were coming from at least four hundred yards away. It would be a long job; they all knew by now that a man does not crawl very fast. And then there was the load to bring back. Provided they did not stand up and provided the dawn did not break too soon.

Silence and battle. The Republicans trying to affect a junction behind the fascist lines; the Moors trying to break through at University City. Somewhere in the night, enemy machine-guns were firing from the Clinic; Madrid was in flames. The three Germans were creeping along on their bellies.

The cries from the wounded man came every two or three minutes. If a flare were to go up, the volunteers would never come back. They must be fifty yards away from the trench by now; the others could smell the stale odour of the mud outside, not quite the same as that inside the trench, as if they had gone with them. It was a long time since the wounded man last called. If they could only keep their sense of direction, if they could at least keep heading straight towards him. . . .

Flat on their stomachs, the three men waited, waiting for the cry to guide them through the flame-punctuated haze. The voice was silent. The wounded man would not call again.

White-faced they raised themselves up on one elbow. Madrid was still burning, the German trench still held out; and to the dull boom of artillery, the Moors were still trying to force University City in the night-fog.

13

SLADE stopped before the first gutted house. The rain was no longer falling, but he felt that it was still in the air. Black-shawled women had formed a chain behind *milicianos* from the salvage corps who were dragging from the ruins a gramophone horn, a bundle, a little chest. . . .

From the third storey, cut in cross-section like a stage set, a bed hung down, one foot still caught in a wrecked door; the contents of this room had tumbled out into the stream, almost at Slade's feet: pictures, toys, cooking utensils. The ground floor, though ripped open, was still intact—as peaceful as in normal life, its inmates having been taken away *in extremis* by an ambulance. On the first floor, above a blood-spattered bed, an alarm-clock was ringing; a small, shrill sound forlorn in the grey desolation of the morning.

The rescue corps were passing their finds from hand to hand. The last *miliciano* passed a bundle to the first woman. She did not take it by the middle with her hands, as it was offered to her, but held it in her arms; a head fell backwards, for the child was dead. The woman looked along the line, found what she was looking for and began to weep; perhaps she had seen the mother. Slade moved on. Mingling with the damp morning haze, a smell of burning was filling the city with the peaceful, pleasing smell of wood burning in autumn forests.

At the next house there were no victims; the occupants, minor employees of some kind, were silently watching their shattered house burn. It was Slade's business to be on the constant look-out for picturesque and tragic details, but his job revolted him; the picturesque was grotesquely out of place in the circumstances, but tragedy in plenty was to be found in this banal scene, in these thousands of human lives one like another, in these grief-stricken, sleep-starved faces.

"You are a foreigner, sir?" The speaker stood watching beside him.

The face was refined and old, with vertical lines—the face of an intellectual. He pointed towards the house, without speaking.

"War horrifies me," Slade said, pulling at his little tie.

"You're getting plenty of it." And then, more quietly, "If you can call this war.

"The electric lamp factory is on fire over by the Alcalá road, my friend. San Carlos and San Geronimo are alight. All the houses round the French Embassy; many of the houses round the Plaza de las Cortes and the Palace. The Library . . ." He did not look at Slade as he spoke; his eyes were fixed on the sky. "I, too, find war horrible. But less horrible than assassination."

"Nothing is as bad as war," Slade said stubbornly.

"Even the giving of power to those who use it as these are using it?" He was still watching the sky. "No, I cannot accept war, either. And how is one to accept this? What is one to do?"

"I wonder if I can help," Slade asked.

The speaker smiled as he pointed to the burning house, from which pale flames were rising through the grey morning, beneath a dismal pall of smoke.

"Every paper I possessed, my friend. I am a biologist."

A hundred yards in front of them a heavy shell burst in a square. The last remaining windows clattered down; and in the middle of the broken glass a donkey, without making any attempt to run away, brayed despairingly as the rain began to fall again.

By the time Slade reached the institution which housed the old men many of them had emerged from the cellars. The fire was no longer burning, but among those inoffensive and defenceless old people, with their infirmities and their shrunken movements, the signs of the bombing struck a note of supreme incongruity.

"How did you manage?" he asked one of the old men.

"Oh, sir. We're no age to go running about. Running like that . . . Especially for the ones on crutches. . . ."

He took hold of Slade by the sleeve.

"What is going to happen to us, sir? I used to be a barber, with my own special class of customer. All my gentlemen counted on me for their death-bed shave, haircut, everything . . ."

Slade had to listen hard to hear him, for a stream of lorries was passing, shaking intact and fallen walls alike.

"The Popular Front put us here, sir. Very nice and comfortable, it was. But what good has it been? It's just going to begin all over again. I suppose it will have an end sometime. But so shall I . . ."

On the first floor the more robust of the old men were working away at something or other which Slade did not quite
understand. There were a dozen of them, all with the traditional gravity of aged Spaniards. They worked as if they had
been condemned to silence, straining to catch every sound,
watching the sky. On the floor above, surrounded by the gongs
of the ambulances which were traversing the city in all directions and the ceaseless noise of the lorries, were some *milicianos* who had been specially detailed to try to drag some of
the old men forcibly from under their beds where they had
taken refuge in their frenzy during the bombing, and whose
iron legs they were now unwilling to release. Suddenly, like a
sinister echo of the ambulances, the warning sirens shrilled
through the city. Abandoning the beds, the old men ran
towards the doorway of the stairs leading to the cellar, carrying their bedding on their backs; one of them took his whole
bed with him, tortoise-like.

Within ten seconds, the first explosion pulverized the fragments of glass that lay on the tables and under the windows
shattered by last night's bombs. And as if all Madrid were
replying with a leisurely tocsin, above the roll of the guns in
University City, one after another, the clocks began to strike
nine.

"There they are!" one of the *milicianos* cried.

Slade went down to look from beneath the hospital gateway. First his long pipe, then his nose peered round the
corner. Broad-bellied like the German commercial planes he
had so often used since he came to Europe, the Junkers came
into view from behind a gable, black, prows bulging in front
of them, flying very low beneath the rain clouds. They crossed
slowly over the street and disappeared behind the roof opposite, followed by their pursuit planes. Chance alone directed
the incendiary bombs. They burst right and left, in rows. Some
pigeons took to the air; above their flapping circles the rigid
flight of the bombers swept on, inexorable as fate. The utter
haphazardness of this death flung from the sky filled Slade
with horror. Hadn't the Government enough pursuit planes
left to bring a single machine back from the front? The lorries
were still churning past the door, their covers streaming wet;
it was raining near by.

"There's a cellar," a voice said behind him.

He stayed beneath the gateway, though he knew it was poor
protection. Shadows were passing along the walls, stopping

for a few moments in front of every door, then moving on. He had often visited the front, but he had never had this feeling before. War was war, but this was something other than war. What he wanted to see the end of was not so much the aerial torpedoes themselves as the particular slaughterhouse shambles which they caused here. The bombs continued to fall; no one knew where they would fall next. Slade thought of his interviews and his notes, of the tables laid for dinner in houses that had been sliced open, of the shattered glass of a picture with a little jet of blood beneath it, of a travelling coat hanging above a suit-case—in preparation for another world; of a donkey of which the hoofs alone had been left; of the long trails of blood left on pavements and walls by those wounded at the Palace, like the tracks of hunted beasts; of the empty stretchers with a blood-stain where each wound had touched. How much blood there was for this rain to wash away! There were shells intersecting the falling bombs now. After each explosion Slade waited for the sound of falling tiles. In spite of the rain, the smell of fire began to pervade the streets. And still the lorries went by.

"Where are they going?" Slade asked, tugging at the ends of his little bow-tie.

"Reinforcements for Guadarrama. 'They' are trying to break through up there."

14

MANUEL's brigade was advancing from the Sierra de Guadarrama through blinding sheets of driven rain, across a land of shattered church-towers—a 1917 landscape. Slowly they crept down the slopes—clumsy dark forms ploughing their way across the mud. Long lines of ancient furrows streamed down to a deep valley that climbed again towards a draggled horizon, grey in the wan morning light that looked like nightfall. That skyline seemed to end the world, but behind it lay the vast Segovia plain, like sea beyond a cliff-wall, stretching out to infinity. And throughout that unseen world, drenched in lethargic rain, the guns were thundering. Behind it lay Madrid.

The men moved steadily on, floundering deeper and deeper in the deepening mud. Now and then among the shell-bursts came another sound, the long-drawn swoo-oosh of a dud diving into the slush.

Manuel's headquarters were quite near the lines. Some other regiments had been attached to his and he was now commanding a brigade. His right wing and centre were doing well; but the left was wavering. In the last engagement sixty percent of the officers and political commissars had been wounded. "Be so good as to stay at your posts," he had told the latter an hour before, "and don't go into battle in front of your men, singing the *International*." The counter-attack was working out well—except for the left wing.

The men on that wing were not those who had fought at Aranjuez, not the Fifth Corps which had reinforced them, nor the new troops attached to them; the latter were fighting in the right wing and centre. The left wing consisted of companies from the Valencia area, so-called anarchist companies, though actually the men had never belonged to any syndicate before the war. And since the last day but one not one of the veteran sergeants was left among them; all were dead or in hospital.

Manuel's tanks were advancing in front of the left wing. With the mechanical stolidity, that air of merely taking part in field manoeuvres peculiar to tanks, they were driving through an artillery barrage of the same volume as that directed on the infantry behind them. But it was not so much the shells that seemed to trouble them as the condition of the ground, which looked as if it had been blown to pieces by land-mines. One tank vanished, as though dissolved into the rain; it had fallen into an anti-tank ditch. A column of mud and pebbles shot into the air, and alongside it another tank started to topple over slowly, very slowly. The rest went placidly ahead, through showers of heavy clods that, soaring briskly up, floundered to earth between the downward-flashing shells in limp parabolas, forlorn as the interminable cadence of the rain.

For months Manuel had been watching tanks advancing just like this; only, for months, they had been enemy tanks. One day the Aranjuez brigade had built a wooden tank—by way of sympathetic magic, to conjure up real ones. But today those were his own tanks forging ahead, as far as eye could reach; far ahead on the right, and on the left more slowly, followed by the infantry. The Republican heavy guns were pounding the enemy lines; the enemy were retaliating, but failing to hold up the counter-attack. In the grey immensity little specks of a darker grey were advancing behind the tanks: the *dinamiteros*. And the machine-gun sections were occupying small, cramped islets of semi-solid ground won foot by arduous foot from the all-encroaching mud.

Were more tanks being sent in support of the troops on the extreme left wing, Manuel wondered. And was it because the advance was not progressing at that point? Viewed from end to end, the line of tanks was gradually taking the form of a crescent. It seemed to Manuel that the tanks on the left had actually turned back; those he could see were moving towards him, not against the fascists. Then he understood; those were not reinforcements, they were enemy tanks.

If now the left wing faltered, the whole brigade was as good as wiped out, and through the gap the enemy might sweep down on Madrid. But if the left held, none of the enemy tanks would get back to the fascist lines.

His reserves were in readiness beside the lorries. He could throw them bodily into the battle, as another contingent of reserves was on its way up from Madrid.

The left-wing liaison car pulled up in front of him; the yellow upholstery made it recognisable at once. The commanding officer was sitting in the back of the car, an arm crooked over the folded hood and his head resting on it. He seemed to be snoring.

"What's up?" Manuel asked, flicking his boot with the pine-branch he had in his hand.

The major had ordered him, the chauffeur said, to drive to headquarters. And what Manuel heard was not snoring, but the death-rattle.

"Where's he hit?" Manuel asked the chauffeur. There was no sign of a wound.

"Back of the neck."

For an officer in action to be wounded in the back is rare; presumably this one had turned.

"Put him down here," Manuel said, "then drive back and bring Gartner."

Manuel had already telephoned orders to get in touch with the political commissar and send him over.

The car lumbered off, vanished into the deluge. Manuel took up his field-glasses. On the extreme left of his sector he could see men running towards the fascist tanks, which were, apparently, not firing, for no one fell. Manuel turned the screw of his field-glasses, blurring the landscape, then focussed it anew behind the rain. The men were holding up their hands. Going over to the enemy.

They could not be seen by the company behind, as there was some rising ground between.

Behind the small dark specks running with their waving arms above their heads, like insects waving their antennae, the ground sloped. Sloped all the way down to Madrid. It crossed Manuel's mind that, since the arrival of the new recruits, falangist inscriptions had been found in the billets.

The other companies in the rear were firing now. Thinking that the first line was advancing, they were moving ahead, towards certain death. Manuel was puzzled. Couldn't their captain recognize Italian tanks?

Just then he saw the captain being carried up, on a blanket —the dressing-station was just behind Manuel's headquarters. Dead, too. A bullet in the back.

He had been one of the best officers of the brigade, and had formerly led the Aranjuez delegation. Now he lay curled up on his blanket, his grey moustache clotted with raindrops.

There were falangists among the recruits; and the officers were being shot from behind.

The right wing was still advancing.

"The commissar has just bumped off a fellow," the chauffeur said.

Manuel told another officer to carry on, and, with all his reserves, made haste to the left.

Gartner, the political commissar with the brigade, scrupulously obeying Manuel's orders "not to go singing the *International* at the head of the troops," had taken up his position in a pine-wood at the beginning of the nearest valley—on which the enemy tanks were now advancing.

A soldier had come running up to him. It was Ramon, one of the old-timers, one of the fifty men from Aranjuez with whom Manuel had "salted" the recruits.

"Look here, old man, there's half a dozen swine among the rookies, who want to bump off the Colonel. Six of 'em. Want to go over to the other side. I pretended to be in with them. They said: 'Let's wait for the others.' Then they said: 'We got the Captain laid out, we got the Major, now we'll have a shot at the chap in the white tunic.' About the Captain—that was O.K., you know. The dirty bastards!"

"Yes, I know. . . ."

"They want to go over to the enemy. Maybe it's not they who are going to finish off the Colonel, but some of the others. Anyhow, when they said that, I said, 'Just a minute, some of my pals want to go over, too.' 'All right,' they said. So I've come to you."

"How can you get in touch with them again? Now that the whole line's moving up."

"That doesn't matter. They won't budge, not they. They're waiting for the enemy tanks to show up. Some dirty trick they've planned. Oh, and then, there's another gang of the boys that's raising hell; they say we ought to beat it, we can't hold out against the tanks. The way they yell—there's something up. It doesn't sound natural to me. So my pals sent me to let you know."

"What about your regimental commissar?"

"Killed."

Gartner had ten Aranjuez men with him.

"Boys," he said, "there are traitors in the line. They've shot the Captain. They're out to kill the Colonel and go over to the fascists."

Gartner exchanged clothes with one of the soldiers, who stayed behind. His angular, clean-shaven face which always looked rather vacant in repose, looked even more so when he took care not to betray emotion. Most vacant of all just now when, taking off his service cap, he set a faded képi on his mop of hair, which in a few minutes was sopping with rain. Handing over the post to a regimental commissar, he went off with his men.

All the paths in the rolling landscape seemed to converge, either on Manuel's headquarters and the casualty-clearing station, or else on the road to which Ramon now was taking Gartner.

As they passed a little clump of pine-trees, dripping with rain, two infantrymen came running down a slope towards them, shouting: "Come on, boys, they're beating it!"

"They're the ones," said Ramon to the commissar.

"Of the six, you mean?"

"No, not them, but the chaps who've got cold feet, the bellyachers. They've all got to pass this way."

"Where are you going?" Gartner shouted. "Are you crazy?"

It was unlikely the six recruits had ever set eyes on him; their regimental commissar was the only one they knew. Prob-

ably they had often met Gartner before, but just now their
thoughts were far from him; and they had no suspicion.

"They're hopping it, I tell you! Not a dog's chance up
there. The tanks are coming up! In a half hour we'll be cut
off. They'll mow us down!"

"Madrid's there, at the rear."

"What the hell do I care?" said the other, a good-looking
youth, who now seemed dazed with fright. "If the officers
knew their bloody jobs, we wouldn't have to beat it. Come on,
boys! Let's save our skins while we can!"

"Know what they're doing, the men who're bolting now?
They're letting the enemy turn our flank. They're letting down
their comrades who're holding on, in the centre! You'll hear
about it, tonight. Now, up you go, lads! Up the hill again!"

He barked out the harangue, rather than spoke it, across
the downpour. Gartner was facing one of the soldiers, his
mouth looking grotesquely small in his enormous face. The
soldier brought his rifle to the ready.

"Say, you big cod-face, are you trying to win a stripe? If
you're that keen on getting yourself smashed up by the tanks,
go to it! I'm not stopping you. But if you think you're going
to get the rest of us killed, you have another think coming!"

Ramon's fist crashed on the man's ribs, sent him sprawling
in the mud. The fugitives were disarmed, and, escorted by
four of Gartner's men, led off to the rear. Gartner pushed
forward, at a run. The khaki great-coats of his men showed
grey through the rain.

The six men Ramon had described to Gartner were waiting,
crouching in a twenty-foot shell crater, thickly smeared with
mud. But they were not standing by for an attack.

"Here they are," Ramon said to them, as if to introduce
Gartner and the others.

"Everything set to go?" Gartner asked.

"Hold on!" said the man who seemed to be in command.
"The others are up there."

"Who?" Gartner asked, with his best dazed air.

"You want to know too much, pal!"

"I don't give a damn. What I want to know is whether
they're to be trusted or not. You see, I've got some guns. But
not to hand out to the first idiot I meet. How many can you
do with?"

"Us? Six."

"Me and my pals, we can have ten machine-guns right now."

"No. Six will do us. No more."

"Mind, these are the goods. Big ones—with the large pans."

The man merely patted his rifle, shrugging his shoulders.

"Not that we need them," said another one of the six. "But all the same, they might come in handy. We could do with the lot."

The man who had spoken first nodded acquiescence, as if taking an order. The last speaker had delicate hands. That's a falangist, the commissar thought.

"Can't you see, men," Gartner went on, addressing the first speaker, "it's in a different class from that popgun of yours? This is no pocket-pistol. See here. You shove in the pan like this. Got it? Now it's loaded. Fifty rounds. There's six of you . . . That makes eight rounds—and two to spare—for each of your dirty mugs. Hands up!"

The one who had talked first had barely time to stretch his hand an inch towards his rifle, when he collapsed into a puddle, a bullet through his head. The blood oozed out through the water, black in the grey light. The enemy tanks were still coming on.

Gartner's men had covered the others with their guns, and were escorting them towards the rear. On their way to the farm, they met Manuel and his lorries. Gartner jumped into Manuel's car and told him what had happened. Manuel had already despatched the anti-tank section of his reserves to the left wing.

The fascist tanks would reach the sector in a few minutes. If the centre held, the reserves could take over the left wing, and if the right kept on advancing, all would go well. This was a critical moment.

The centre was made up of the men from Aranjuez, together with all those who had joined the same unit, experienced troops who had fought at Madrid, Toledo, the Tagus, even in the Sierra; workmen from the villages, *junteros,* farm labourers, small shop-keepers, metal-workers, barbers, textile-workers, bakers. They were fighting over ground criss-crossed with low dry-stone walls, running parallel like the curving lines on military maps. From where they were now they could not help seeing that if the enemy tanks advanced another mile—a matter of five or ten minutes—not one of them would come out of it alive. Manuel had given them the order to hold on; and they held on, hugging their bits of wall, lying flat in folds of the ground, or taking what cover they could behind tree-trunks slenderer than themselves. The enemy trench-mortars were in front and behind, machine-guns were cross-firing, heavy shells coming over through the curtain of rain, searching the whole position. Manuel had first made a tour of inspection of the centre, and there he had seen his men falling one after another, engulfed at once in the mud thrown up by the next volley of shells.

Across the paroxysms of the riven earth roaring up to the streaming clouds, vomiting across the downpour great cascades of clods and stones and blood, Manuel could see a wave of enemy troops advancing, with fixed bayonets. They had no sheen, for the rain melted to liquid slime all that was hurtling up into it from the sodden plain, yet Manuel could feel those bayonets as if they were jabbing at his own flesh. Something was happening among those preposterous low walls, in the dim chaos of the deluge. And the enemy—they were not Moors this time—were surging back, as though repulsed not by the old *milicianos*, but by the never-ending rain, which was already beating their dead into the earth, sweeping away towards their unseen trenches the attacking waves, in a seething spate of dissolution, across the welter of a cloud-burst shuddering with explosions countless as the rain-drops.

Four times the fascists launched a bayonet charge, four times it melted away into the blinding rain.

The line held. But, pressing Manuel's left, the tanks of the fascist right wing were now engaging his anti-tank section.

Pepe was in command of the section. All the old *dinamiteros* who had survived the August fighting and shown the least gift for leadership now held commissions. Pepe was grousing. It was damned bad luck, he said, that his mate Gonzalez was not there with him, to see the stunt he was going to try out. But Gonzalez was fighting at University City. All the same, Pepe was jubilant. "I'll teach 'em a thing or two, this time!" Followed at some distance by the infantry, the fascist tanks were advancing at full speed towards the first valley, where they would be under shelter from the Republican gunfire. There is a track or road of some kind through every valley of the Sierras; the lorries had brought up Pepe and his men in good time.

On each side of the road the country was fairly open, with occasional clumps of pines that showed black against the rain. Pepe's men took up their positions, lying flat on the sodden pine-needles, amid an earthy odour of mushrooms.

The first tank started to traverse the valley, on the right of the road. It was a German tank, very swift and mobile. The *dinamiteros* all had the feeling that the works must be going rusty in that never-ending rain. Fleeing before it was one of the packs of dogs that had gone wild and taken to the Sierras.

The other tanks were coming into view. From his hiding-place, Pepe could not see across the undergrowth the ground between him and the tanks which, from where he was, seemed to be advancing along the road, dipping their turrets and jerking them up like restive horses' heads. They had already opened fire, and it seemed as if their caterpillar bands were emitting, not a light mechanical patter of turning links fretting the hiss of the rain, but the hoarse roar of the machine-guns. Pepe was used to machine-guns, and he was used to tanks.

He waited.

Then, his teeth bared in an unamiable grin, he opened fire.

Even a machine can seem startled on occasion. The moment they heard the machine-guns, the tanks charged. Four of them —three in the first line, one in the second—tilted up simultaneously, with an air of puzzlement—"What on earth is happening to us now?"—and stayed there rageful, rearing forms, looming across the nightmare rain. Two swung round, one toppled over, the fourth came to a halt, standing on end, against a lofty pine.

It was their first brush with anti-tank machine-guns.

The second wave of tanks had seen nothing of all this—a tank is practically blind. They came on at full speed. The second line of machine-gunners, also lying flat, began firing over the heads of the front line. The tanks were all knocked out—all but four, which got past Pepe and bore down on the second line.

But Manuel had reckoned with this possibility, and given the necessary orders to his men. The second line of machine-gunners slewed round two of their guns, while the others and the men in the front rank continued firing on the main body of tanks which was scattering through the black pine-woods, in drunken zigzags. Pepe, too, swung round. Those four tanks might prove more dangerous than all the rest, if driven by determined men. The brigade, on which they would presently bear down, would think that other tanks were coming after them.

Three had already crashed against three separate pines. Runaways; their drivers had been killed.

The last tank was still advancing under the fire of the two guns. Suddenly it swung on to the empty road and roared away along it, the clatter of its caterpillar bands jangling across the din of the machine-guns. Its own guns silent, it was making a good forty miles an hour along the road, absurdly small and futile between the steepening slopes, a lonely fugitive on the rain-drenched asphalt that gleamed with broken lights reflected from the livid sky. At last it came to a bend, crashed against a cliff, and stayed propped up against it, like a child's toy.

The unhit tanks had taken the same direction as the Republican tanks, and were charging down on their own lines, which were beginning to break up in panic. In front, among the pine-trees, grouped round the tank which, standing up on end, looked like some prehistoric effigy of war, other tanks sprawled in every attitude of havoc. They were gradually being coated with broken twigs, pine-needles and cones that had been ripped off by flying bullets, and seemed already succumbing to rain and rust, as though they had been lying derelict for many months. Manuel, who had just come up, could see, beyond the lurching turrets of the last enemy tanks, the fascist right wing breaking up. The Republican heavy artillery was beginning to shell the line of their retreat.

Manuel went at once towards the centre of his front.

The retreat of the enemy right wing before its own tanks was turning into a rout. The men of Pepe's section who were not manning machine-guns, together with the *dinamiteros* and Manuel's reserves, were now following on the tracks of the fleeing tanks as though they had been their own. The enemy right centre was also beginning to give way. Manuel's troops, reinforced by detachments from the contingent which had been rushed up in lorries from Madrid (the remainder staying in reserve) emerged from the stone walls behind which they had been hiding, and dashed impetuously forward.

These were the men who, on the day of the fight for the Montaña Barracks, had lain flat in the surrounding squares while snipers were shooting at them from every window. And these were the men who had fought in units which had only one machine-gun to the half-mile and had had to lend them round wherever they might be needed; and these the men who, armed with shot-guns, had attacked the Alcazar. There were some, too, who had done nothing yet, some who had run away at the sight of a plane, and whimpered at the hospital that their comrades had "let them down." And there were men who had fled before the tanks; and others who had faced the tanks with dynamite. All were men who knew that *señoritos* judge the poor man's worth by his servility; they were the innumerable, predestined victims of the firing-squad, impersonal as the drumfire thundering against them along the line.

Guadarrama would not be taken by the fascists today.

His pine branch to his nose, Manuel stood watching the brilliant advance of the men of Aranjuez and Pepe's company, watching his first victory in progress, marching on through the viscous mud, through the steady, slanting curtain of the rain.

By two o'clock all the fascist positions had been captured; but there a halt had to be called. There was no question of driving on to Segovia. All the reserves of the centre were already in the front line and the fascists were strongly entrenched ahead.

15

AT THE "Granja" the tables along the boulevard were empty, but the back of the restaurant was crowded. The rain storms from the Sierra, which had been deluging Madrid, had passed. There was a new sound in the explosions; less loud than bombs, they seemed to be taking place some fifty feet above the ground.

"Have our anti-aircraft guns arrived?" Moreno asked, handsomer than ever. Everyone at the Granja knew now what had been the common talk at Toledo: that Moreno had been the lover of one of King Alfonso's mistresses.

No one answered. All the men drinking in the café were more or less acquainted with each other. Glasses shivered in rhythm with the incessant gunfire from University City. It was the early afternoon and the lamps had not been lit; the only light in the café came from outside, a cavernous half-light filling the long room from end to end.

An officer entered by the swing-doors, flashing the silver facets of a lark-mirror on the grey November air.

"Fires are breaking out again everywhere," he said. "And coming our way."

"We'll put 'em out," a voice replied.

"Easier said than done. They've started on the Calle San Margos and the Calle Martino de Los Hijos."

"On the Avenida Urquijo, too."

"The San Geronimo Hospice, San Carlos Hospital and the buildings round the Palace are on fire."

More officers entered. The swing-doors whirled into the café a smell of red-hot stone.

"The Red Cross Hospital."

"San Miguel Market."

"Some of those fires have been extinguished. At San Carlos and San Geronimo they're out."

"What's that noise? Is it our anti-aircraft?"

"Waiter, an absinthe." The speaker was a man with ragged, unkempt hair, sitting beside Moreno.

"I can't say. But I doubt it."

"That's shrapnel," said the officer who had just entered. "It's coming down in bucketfuls on the Plaza d'España. But they're not getting through at Guadarrama."

He took a chair beside Moreno, who also was in uniform. Moreno looked quite young now that he had shaved and had his hair cut.

"How's the man in the street taking it?" Moreno asked.

"They're only just starting to crowd into the shelters. Somehow they all seem rooted to the spot, especially the women. Others drop on the ground, others just start screaming. Of course, there's some who want to see the show. And others who go tearing all over the town. The women with children keep on the move."

"All the morning," Moreno said, "I've felt as if an earthquake were taking place." He meant that it was not so much fear of the fascists that gripped the crowd as the sort of terror a cataclysm inspires; the idea of "giving in" never entered their heads—one doesn't talk of giving in to an earthquake.

To a jangle of bells an ambulance sped past.

A black crash and the glasses on the tables sprang up like toy rabbits into the air and landed tinkling back among saucers, split liquor and V-shaped splinters from the windows. The panes had caved in like drum-heads as the bomb exploded on the boulevard outside. A waiter's tray toppled over, bounded on the floor with a thin clash of cymbals, muted by the silence. Half the people in the room rushed for the stairs leading down to the cellars, in a clatter of falling teaspoons; others stood their ground in blank suspense . . . waiting for the second bomb. None came and, as usual, cigarettes were extracted from dozens of pockets, and dozens of matches flared across the smoke-clouds swirling round the room. Once the smoke had ebbed away through the two large saw-edged gaps of what had once been mirrors, a dead man was seen leaning on the bar of the swing-door between the splintered panels.

"They're aiming at us," said Moreno's companion.

"Oh, cut it out!"

"You're all a pack of fools—can't you realize how things are? You'll all be killed like rats in a trap. I tell you, they've got us . . ."

"The hell they have!" Moreno growled.

"Sorry, old fellow. I've done my share of fighting, that you can't deny. A straight fight—I've nothing against it. But, as for getting wiped out by an air-raid, nothing doing. I've been working all my life till now, and all the things I've dreamt of lie ahead of me."

"Then what the hell are you doing here? Why aren't you down in the cellar?"

"Yes, like a damned fool, I'm staying upstairs. I wonder why."

" 'Watch how I act, don't listen to what I tell you,' as the philosopher said."

Shells were bursting on all sides and wan gleams of wintry sunlight, caught on the scraps of broken glass that littered floor and tables, kept flickering imperceptibly amid little quaking pools of vermouth, absinthe and manzanilla. The waiters began coming up again from the cellar.

"They say Unamuno's died at Salamanca."

A civilian came from the telephone booth.

"A bomb has just fallen," he announced, "on the Puerta del Sol Metro station. There's a thirty-foot hole."

"Let's go and see." Two voices.

"Were there people seeking shelter in the Metro?"

"Can't say."

"Over two hundred killed and five hundred wounded; that's what the ambulance corps reported at noon."

"And that's only a beginning."

"They say there's been a battle at Guadarrama."

The man who had just been at the telephone seated himself before the wreckage of a vermouth.

"I've had my bellyful of it," grumbled the long-haired man at Moreno's side. "I tell you once again, they're aiming at us. What the hell are we after here—staying in the heart of the city? It's ridiculous."

"Hop it, then."

"Yes, to China or the South Seas, any old place that isn't here!"

"Look! The Del Carmen market's ablaze," someone began shouting in the street. The clangour of another ambulance cut across the voice.

"To the South Sea Islands? And what will you do there, I'd like to know! Make necklaces of sea-shells? Organize the savage tribes?"

"What will I do? I'd get a boat and go out fishing goldfish! I'd do anything, any darned thing, to get away from all this."

"Why, man, you hate the thought of breaking with the rest of us so much that you can't even bring yourself to go down to the cellar. But I'm used to that sort of thing. I used to talk like that myself, in the old days. To Hernandez, poor chap."

Suddenly he cast an apprehensive glance at the man beside him. Then it had been Hernandez. "Hernandez is dead," Moreno thought, "very likely it's my turn next!" But then the superstitious dread passed from his mind, like the smoke clouds ebbing from the room.

"I'd meant to cross the frontier to France; then I hesitated, then I was caught up by all the old associations, by life. When I'm under fire I don't believe in 'thinking things out' or the 'eternal verities,' or anything at all. I believe only in fear. Real fear, not the sort that makes one talk, but the fear that sets one running. If you've decided to bolt, I've nothing more to say. But, since you're staying here with us, that settles it and you'd do better to keep silent. See?

"When I was in jail I saw all sorts of things—men playing pitch and toss with their lives, and I looked forward to each Sunday, as no one was shot on a Sunday. I saw men playing games of *pelota* against a wall spattered with human brains and tufts of hair. There were over fifty men under sentence of death whom I used to hear playing pitch and toss in their cells. Oh, I'm not making it up; I was there. Right on the spot. Only, old chap, there's something else to it, and don't you forget it.

I fought through the Moroccan War; there too it was a sort of magnified duel—with an even chance of survival. But here in the front line it's a very different story. After the first ten days you're an automaton, a sleep-walker. You see too many men die. There's too much of the machine in what's against you: tanks, artillery, planes. Fate takes charge, and you're only sure of one thing—that you haven't a dog's chance. You're like a man who's drunk a poison that kills after a certain number of hours, or like a chap who's taken the monastic vow. Your life is over.

"Then the whole world's changed. You get a new line on the truth, and it's all the others who are off their heads."

" 'A new line on truth.' That's you all over!"

"Yes, that's how it is, one pushes ahead into the barrage; nothing, not even one's own life, makes the least difference. Hundreds of shells are falling, hundreds of men going forward. You're just another case of suicide, yet at that moment you're sharing in all that's best in all of them. You're sharing in . . . in something that's rather like the ecstasy of the crowd at Carnival. I wonder if you see what I mean . . . I've a pal who calls that the moment when the dead start singing. Yes, for a month now, I've known dead men can sing."

"Like hell they do!"

"And there's something else which even I, the first Marxist officer in the army, never dreamt of. There's a fraternity which is only to be found—beyond the grave."

"There are fellows who guessed they'd had enough of it when they had to fight planes with rifles. And there are others who've had enough of it when they had to fight tanks with rifles. Me, I've had enough of it, right now!"

"My nerves used to go all on edge, like yours, but I've got over that!"

"Well, they'll be quieter when you're dead."

"Yes. But now I don't give a damn about it." Moreno's smile disclosed his white, beautifully formed teeth.

All the ornamental bottles above the bar dived off the shelf together, with a clatter of empty glass. The table seemed to stiffen at the impact of the explosion; a vermouth poster fell on Moreno's back, ending his smile as if a hand had sealed his lips. The noses peeping from the cellar stairs hastily retreated.

A wounded man, bearded, in civilian clothes, flung himself on the café entrance, trying to get in. The door swung round violently, hit the dead man's chest, and jammed half way round. A dull thud jarred the silence following the explosion. The wounded man pressed on the frayed glass panels, battered and banged them with his fists, then suddenly collapsed.

All around, the din of explosions broke out again.

16

HEAVY shells were dropping between the Central Telephone Building and the Calle de Alcalá. One was a dud, and two *milicianos* carted it off, one in front, the other behind. The late afternoon sky lay colourless and clear over Madrid. The city was full of driven sparks and tiny tongues of flame. The smell of dust and explosives was mingled with the more sinister odour which Lopez remembered having already smelt at Toledo; it was, he, supposed, the smell of burnt flesh.

Two Grecos and three small Goyas from a palace abandoned by its owner had been expected that morning by the Commission for the Protection of Works of Art, to which Lopez had been appointed; but they had not yet turned up. He wanted to be present when they were being sent away. Little good at fighting, Lopez had turned out quite brilliant at the job of rescuing works of art. Thanks to him, not a single Greco had been destroyed in the Toledo débâcle. Eminent old masters had been dug up by the dozen out of the dust where they had lain mouldering in convent attics.

At some distance ahead, in front of a church, a small shell exploded. No sooner had the pigeons flown away than they came back, interested, to examine the latest cracks in the stonework of their cornice. Through the windows of a gutted house, now gaping to the winds of heaven, one could see the high tower of the telephone building, with its baroque escutcheon, gaunt in the thickening November dusk.

That the little skyscraper which towers above Madrid as does the Church of the Sacré-Coeur over Paris had not yet been blown to smithereens was nothing short of a miracle. Only one corner was chipped off. But all the window-panes were smashed. Behind the tower rose the smoke of a shellburst. "Good heavens," Lopez thought, "sooner or later they'll be plonking one on my Grecos!"

A panic-stricken crowd, in flight from perils known to the

unknown, seethed in the streets. Others, indifferent, curious or excited, moved along, peering skywards. A second shell fell near by. Some children, accompanied by women or old men, fled in panic. Other children, unaccompanied by any parents or relatives, discussed the shot like experts.

"What fools those fascists are! Can't even shoot, not they! Popping off at the soldiers in the Casa del Campo—and just see where they land their stuff!"

One morning, in the nursery-school of the Plaza del Progreso, three kids were playing at soldiers, looking skywards like the people Lopez now saw before him. "A bomb!" cried one. "Get down!" And all three fell flat, like well-disciplined soldiers. It was a real bomb. The other children, who were not playing soldiers, remained standing, and were killed, or wounded. . . .

A shell dropped somewhere to the left. Some dogs trotted past across the road in single file. Another small pack issued from a neighbouring street, running in the opposite direction. Those dogs, turning in the mazes of a hopeless quest, seemed to portend the coming plight of human beings. Lopez watched them, as he would have done formerly, with the eye of a sculptor and lover of animals. But other animals were awaiting his attention . . .

The house to which Lopez was going was, like most of the requisitioned palaces, such as the Casa d'Alba, lavishly adorned with stuffed animals. Many of the Spanish aristocrats preferred their blood sports to paintings. And, if they preserved their Goyas, they were very apt to mingle them with their hunting trophies. The inventories of the houses of the great who had fled—and only the houses of proprietors who had fled were requisitioned—often included a dozen masterpieces (when these had not been sent abroad the week before the uprising) and a surprising number of elephant-tusks, rhinoceros horns, stuffed bears, and divers other animals.

When Lopez, heralded by a shellburst a hundred yards away, entered the gardens of the house, a *miliciano* ran out to meet him.

"Well, you owl," Lopez bellowed, slapping him on the back, "what about my Grecos, damn it?"

"What? The pictures? There wasn't any transport for them. They make good fat packages, you know, now that your fellows have packed them in cotton-wool like eggs. Anyhow your lorry's gone by."

"When?"

"About a half-hour ago. But it wouldn't take these here cattle of ours."

Planted among the trees, and around a neat pile of elephant-tusks under the portico, the bears, stuffed in realistically life-like poses, seemed indeed to be alive. The ground was slightly shaken by the shellbursts, and the derelict bears, their paws flapping in the twilight, seemed to proffer threats or benedictions.

"They, anyhow, aren't fragile," Lopez said complacently. He refused to regard these natural-history specimens as the concern of his department. It was the business of another section of the Works of Art Commission to collect and store them.

"Yes, but see here, comrade," said the *miliciano*, "if the shells are bad for the pictures, then they're not too good for the elephant-tusks. What the hell am I supposed to do with all this stuff? And it's going to rain again!"

A shell exploded, quite near. The whole menagerie leapt into the air and tottered, while a canary in a cage which had been left behind in the gilded halls of the West Indies Company burst into frantic song.

"Right. I'll phone for someone to shift your bears."

Lopez lit a cigarette, and went away, carrying the canary cage. At each explosion the canary sang more shrilly, then quieted down again. A building was burning, from top to bottom, a moving-picture conflagration. Behind an elaborately ornamental façade, as yet intact, the gaping, shattered windows on every floor were lurid with the flames within, as if the house were inhabited by elemental Fire. Farther along, at a street corner, a bus stood waiting. Suddenly Lopez stopped, breathless for the first time since he had come out. He started frantically gesticulating—the bird-cage flew out of his hands—he shouted. "Get down!" The people in the bus stared at him as though he had been any one of the hundreds of crazy people exhibiting their antics in a hundred other streets. Lopez dropped flat on the ground. There was an explosion. The bus went up in flame.

When Lopez got to his feet again, blood was streaming down the walls. Among the dead stripped by the explosion, a whiskered gentleman, naked but unhurt, picked himself up, screaming. The shelling, still pounding the vicinity of the telephone building, grew more intense.

17

SLADE was at the Central Exchange. It was the hour for sending off his article. Shells were falling on the whole quarter; but here, in the telephone building, each was convinced they had him personally spotted.

There had been a direct hit on the building at five-thirty. Shells were dropping now, one after another, all round it. After the direct hit the enemy had lost the range. Now they were feeling out for it again. Operators, journalists, messengers, *milicianos,* all felt as if they were in the front line. Shells followed each other in quick succession, like the interminable echoes of a clap of thunder. Perhaps the bombing planes were at it again. Darkness was falling, the clouds hung low. But amid all the noises of the Exchange, no drone of aeroplane engines could be heard.

A *miliciano* came for Slade. Major Garcia requested the presence of all the newspaper-men in an office of the Central Exchange. All correspondents of any importance were there, waiting. "Why just now?" Slade wondered. But Garcia was in the habit, when he had any dealings with the Press, to meet the journalists where they imagined they were most exposed to danger.

In one of the old board rooms of the Central—all leather, wood, and nickel—Garcia had the duplicate copies of all articles sent out from Madrid brought to him. They were brought in two files, labelled respectively "Political" and "Descriptive." While waiting for the correspondents to arrive, he glanced through the second file. It made one feel weary of belonging to the human race. Every article was overflowing with atrocities. Garcia read:

"For *Paris-Soir*. On my way to the Telephone Exchange, I was the witness of a moving scene of horror. Last night a three-year-old child was picked up near the Puerta del Sol, where it had been wandering in the darkness, crying. There happened to be a woman in one of the bomb-proof shelters of the Gran Via who had lost her child, a little boy of the same age as the child found at the Puerta del Sol, and fair like him. Upon being informed of the finding of this child, she ran to the house in the Calle Montera where it was being cared for. There, in the gloom of a shuttered little shop, the child was munching a piece of chocolate. I happened to be there when the mother arrived. Holding out her arms, she approached him. Then her eyes widened and settled into a look of horrible, insane fixity. It was not her child.

"For several long minutes she stood there, motionless. Then the lost child smiled at her, and the woman sprang towards him, gathered him up into her arms, and carried him away . . . thinking, most likely, of her own child who had not been found . . ."

"They won't pass that," Garcia reflected. He read on:

"For *Reuter:* A woman was carrying a child, a little girl scarcely two years old, whose lower jaw was missing. But she was still alive, and the wide-open wonder-struck eyes seemed to ask who had done this to her. Another woman crossed the street; the child in her arms was headless."

Garcia had seen, time and again, that terrifying gesture of a mother shielding in her arms what remained of her child. How many similar gestures could be seen in the streets today?

Three shells burst at a distance with a muffled sound like the three hammer-strokes in a French theatre before the curtain rises.

The door opened, and the correspondent entered. On a low table, some artificial flowers in glass, as yet unbroken, shivered with each explosion. Through the broken panes of the two windows came the smell and smoke of the burning city.

"Whenever a line happens to be free," said Garcia, "the person who has asked for it will be advised here immediately. As you know, I only summon you here to convey to you the contents of documents. Before communicating to you the document which is the reason for our present meeting, I'd like to draw your attention to this fact: According to the fascist despatches we have destroyed enemy planes on nine flying-fields since the beginning of the war. It is, of course, easier to bomb Seville than it is to bomb the Seville aerodrome. Now, if it has happened that some of our bombs have missed their military objectives and wounded civilians, at least we can assert that never has a Spanish town been systematically bombed by us.

"Here, then, is the document. I am going to read it to you. Each of you is requested to examine the original. Which we shall take steps, in any case, to make known in London and Paris, I assure you. It is simply a little circular addressed to senior officers in the rebel army. This copy was found on July 28 in the possession of an officer, Manuel Carrache, taken prisoner on the Guadalajara front." Garcia spread out the document and read:

One of the conditions essential to victory is that the morale of the enemy troops shall be shaken. The opponent has at his disposal neither sufficient troops nor sufficient arms to resist us; nevertheless, it is indispensable that you adhere strictly to the following instructions:

To secure our occupation of the hinterland, it is essential to inspire a certain salutary dread in the population.

It must therefore be made a rule that all measures adopted shall be impressive and spectacular.

All points situated in the line of the enemy's retreat and, in a general way, all points to the rear of the enemy front, must be considered as zones of attack.

Whether or not these localities harbour enemy troops makes no difference. Panic prevailing among the civilian population along the line of the enemy's retreat has a lowering effect on the morale of his troops.

Experiences during the World War showed that damage unintentionally inflicted on enemy ambulances and hospital trains greatly contributes to the demoralization of the troops.

Following our entry into Madrid, heads of all units must immediately install, on the roofs of buildings commanding the more dangerous areas—on public edifices and in belfries as well—nests of machine-guns capable of commanding all adjacent streets.

In the event of any attempt on the part of the population to resist, it will immediately be fired upon. Considering the large number of women fighting on the opposite side, the sex of the combatant need not be taken into account. The more uncompromising our attitude and the more ruthless our elimination of all resistance on the part of the population, the sooner will our triumph bring about the renovation of Spain.

"May I add," Garcia continued, "that *from the fascist point of view* I find these instructions logical? It is my personal opinion that terrorization is one of the means expertly and systematically employed by the rebels since the first day of the war, and that you are here and now witnessing a drama of which Badajoz was only the rehearsal. But enough of personal opinions!"

As the journalists went out, he added:

"You will also receive the Franco interview of the 16th of August, the one beginning 'I shall never bombard Madrid . . . Innocent people are there . . .' "

Shells were still dropping, but a good distance away. At the Central no one any longer paid any attention to them.

A secretary entered.

"Has Colonel Magnin telephoned?" Garcia asked.

"No, sir. The Internationals are fighting in Getafe."

"Lieutenant Scali hasn't come?"

"They telephoned from Alcalá. He will be here at about six o'clock. I came to tell you Dr. Neubourg is here, sir."

Neubourg, head of one of the Red Cross units, had come over from Salamanca. He and Garcia had previously met at two Geneva conferences. Garcia was aware that Neubourg could have seen but little in Salamanca; he knew, however, that the doctor had spent some time with Miguel de Unamuno.

Unamuno, the greatest contemporary Spanish writer, had just been deprived, by Franco, of his rectorship at the University. And Garcia realized how dangerously the menace of fascism was weighing on this man who had been its eminent defender.

18

"For the last six weeks," said the doctor, "he has been staying in his small bedroom, lying in bed, reading. After he had been removed from the University staff, he said, 'I shall leave here only as a condemned man, or a corpse.' He went to bed, and is staying there. Two days after his dismissal, the University was handed over to the Order of the Sacred Heart."

Neubourg glanced, as he passed, at his own face reflected in the only mirror in the room; his thin clean-shaven face which aspired to look alert and shrewd but succeeded only in being the ruined reminder of his youth.

At the beginning of the conversation, Garcia had taken a letter out of his pocket-case. "When I heard that you were coming," he said, "I went through our correspondence of the old days, and I found this letter which he wrote ten years ago, in exile. There's a passage I'd like to read to you."

Truth alone is justice; there is no other justice. And truth, as Sophocles said, is mightier than intellect. As life is mightier than pleasure or pain. Truth and Life, then, shall be my motto; not Intellect and Pleasure. To live in Truth, even though it means to suffer, rather than to exercise intelligence in pleasure or take pleasure in intelligence.

Garcia placed the letter before him on the polished desk which reflected the red sky.

"That," said the doctor, "is the gist of the speech which caused his dismissal. He said, 'Politics may lay certain demands on us, into which it is needless to enter here . . . As for the University, it must serve Truth.' Miguel de Unamuno could not remain where lies ruled. There's something else he said. 'As to the Red atrocities of which we constantly hear, there can be no doubt that the least of the women combatants, even were she, as we are told, no better than a prostitute, is less contemptible to the reasoning mind, when she fights, rifle in hand, and risks her life for her beliefs, than are the women who have never been able to dispense with flowers and fine linen, those bare-armed women whom I saw leaving our banquet the other night to go and see the Marxists being executed.'"

Neubourg had a well-known gift for mimicry.

"And as a physician I may say," he went on in his natural voice, "that there is something pathological in Unamuno's horror of the death penalty. Also, he was doubtless rather flustered at having to reply to the General who was the founder of the 'Tercio.' When he defended the cultural unity of Spain, the heckling began."

"What sort of heckling?"

"'Death to Unamuno!' 'Death to the Intellectuals!'"

"Who were the interrupters?"

"Silly young undergraduates. So then, General Millan Astray stood up and shouted: 'Death to intelligence, long live death!'"

"What do you think he meant?"

"Of course he meant, quite simply: 'Go to the devil!' As to

'Long live death!'—perhaps he was alluding to Unamuno's protests against the executions by the firing squads?"

"In Spain that cry comes from pretty deep down. The anarchists went in for it once."

A shell dropped in the Gran Via. Proud of his courage, Neubourg continued to pace Garcia's office, his bald head shining in the light that poured down from the lurid sky. On each side of his skull there stood out tufts of black curly hair. During twenty years Dr. Neubourg, though distinguished enough in his own domain, had rather prided himself on looking like an eighteenth-century ecclesiastic, and he still retained some vestige of that resemblance.

"It was at that point," the doctor went on, "that Unamuno made his famous reply: 'A Spain without Biscaya and Catalonia would be a country lacking both an arm and an eye—as you do, General Astray.' Which, coming as it did after his well-known remark to Mola, 'To conquer and to convince are two different matters,' could not be dismissed as a mere witticism.

"That evening he went to the Casino, where he was openly insulted. Whereupon he returned to his room and announced that he would never leave it. . . ."

Garcia, while listening attentively, had his eyes fixed on Unamuno's old letter which lay on his desk. He picked it up again:

> Will the crusaders of revenge abandon the idea of imposing upon the Rif tribesmen the *guardia civil,* that is, of decivilising them? When shall we give up that hangman's notion of "honour?"
>
> I don't wish to hear anything of what is going on over there, or in Spain. I am even less interested in what is called 'Greater Spain' by the people who shout so that they may not hear. For my part, I take refuge in that other Spain, my little Spain. I wish I had the strength of will never to read a Spanish paper. Our papers are appalling. Not even the snapping of a broken heartstring can be heard, as one reads them. Only the creaking of the strings and pulleys by which puppets are moved. Our giants are only windmills . . .

A vague murmur was coming up from the Gran Via. The glow from the conflagrations flickered on the walls of the room, as the reflection of a sunlit river trembles on a bedroom ceiling.

" 'Not even the snapping of a broken heartstring,' " Garcia repeated, tapping the bowl of his pipe against his thumb-nail.

"What I would like to know is what he is *thinking*. I can picture him, with his lordly airs, his goggle eyes and wise old owl-like stare, telling off Millan Astray. But that's only a picturesque incident. There's more to it than that."

"We talked a lot, in private, afterwards. He did the talking, I only put in a word or two. He can't bear Azaña. To him the Republic, and only the Republic, is still the one means of achieving Spanish federal unity. He is against an absolute federalism, but he is also against forcible centralisation. And he now sees, in fascism, that very centralisation he dislikes."

An incongruous scent of eau de Cologne was mingling with the reek of smoke and fire that poured into the office through the broken windows. A perfumer's shop was on fire.

"He wanted to shake hands with fascism, you see, doctor, but he forgot that fascism has feet as well. That he still has his desire for federal unity explains more or less his inconsistencies."

"He is sure Franco will win, and when interviewed by the journalists, says to them, 'Write that, whatever happens, I'll never be on the side of the conqueror.' "

"Which they are careful not to write. What did he say to you about his sons?"

"Nothing. Why?"

Garcia looked at the red sky, musingly. "All his sons are here, two as combatants . . . I can't believe he doesn't think of them. And he hasn't so many chances of seeing someone who knows about both sides."

"After the speech he went out once. They say that, in reprisal for his remarks about the women, he was summoned to a room from which he had a view of men being executed by firing-squads . . ."

"I have already heard that—and don't much believe it. Have you exact information on the subject?"

"He said nothing to me about it—which is quite natural. And I certainly did not mention the matter to him. But, by the way, his uneasiness has much increased of late, what with the country's eternal recourse to violence and irrationality."

Garcia dismissed the phrase with a vague gesture of his pipe.

"But really, my dear Garcia, it strikes me that what we are saying is, after all, a little beside the point. Unamuno's opposition is purely ethical. Our conversations bore on that aspect only indirectly, but pretty constantly."

"Evidently, the question of firing-squads has nothing to do with centralisation."

"When I left him there in that bed, a sad and embittered man surrounded with his books, I felt as if I were leaving behind me the nineteenth century."

Rising to show Neubourg out of the room, Garcia pointed with the end of his pipe to the last lines of the letter which he held in his hand.

When I turn my mind's eye towards my last twelve troubled years, ever since I tore myself away from that little study in Salamanca, where I had dreamed my sheltered dreams—ah, how I used to dream there!—it all seems to me like the shadow of a dream . . . You ask if I read. Not much, except about the sea, with which each day I grow a closer friend.

"Written ten years ago," Garcia said.

19

AT THE moment, when, having got Paris, Slade was called into the telephone room, a shell dropped quite near. Then two others, nearer still. Almost all the occupants of the room rushed to the wall farthest from the window. Despite the electric lights, all in the room were conscious of the fierce red glare in the street; it seemed as if it were the fires outside that were bombarding the Central, with its thirteen stories of windows, at none of which was the least shadow of a human form. Finally an old journalist with a big moustache ventured away from the wall. One by one the others followed suit. But they kept glancing back at the wall, as though looking to see if they had left their traces here.

More shells were falling. Scarcely farther away than the first ones. Yet now they had regained their places no one moved again. They say that wherever people gather, every twenty minutes an angel of silence passes. Here an angel of indifference passed.

Soon Slade was able to begin dictating. As he went on describing his experiences of the morning, the shells came nearer. At each explosion, all the pencil-points leapt up at the same instant from the writing-pads. When there was a pause in the firing the tension increased. Were the guns, over there, correcting their range? Everyone was waiting, waiting, waiting. Slade went on dictating. Paris relayed to New York.

"This morning, comma, I saw bombs falling all round a hospital where lay a thousand wounded, full stop. On the sidewalk, comma, on the walls, comma, were spoors of blood, comma, such as are left by wounded animals . . ."

The shell dropped less than twenty yards away. This time there was a general rush to the basement. In the almost empty room there remained only the operators and the correspondents on the wire. The operators listened to the messages, but their eyes seemed watching for the coming of the shells. The journalists who were dictating went on doing so; once cut, the communciation would not have been made again in time for the morning edition. Slade dictated what he had seen at the Palace.

"This afternoon I arrived a few minutes after a shell had exploded in front of a butcher shop; there, where women had been standing in line, waiting their turn, were stains: the blood of the slain butcher ran down the counter between the sides of beef and carcasses of mutton hanging from iron hooks, and dripped on to the floor where it was washed away by the water from a burst pipe.

"And, mind you, all this serves no purpose. None whatever. The inhabitants of Madrid are far more shaken with horror than with fear. For instance, while bombs were falling all round us, an old man said to me: 'I have never meddled in politics. I have always regarded them as beneath contempt. But we can't let power fall into the hands of people who use power this way—power which even is not yet theirs by right—can we?' I stood a whole hour in a queue in front of a bakery. In the queue were only a few men, but about a hundred women. And everyone, remember, feels it is more dangerous to stay for an hour in the same spot than it is to walk about. Five yards away from the bakery, on the other side of the street, the dead collected from a demolished building were being put into their coffins. (The same thing is being done at this very moment in all the shattered houses of Madrid.) There was no noise of guns or of airplanes, and the hammering sounded in the silence. At my side a man said to a woman, 'Juanita's arm has been torn off; do you think her young man will marry her in that state?' They were all talking about their own personal affairs. Suddenly a woman shouted out, 'It's horrible to be obliged to eat as we do!' Another woman answered gravely, with something of the manner they have all picked up more or less from La Passionaria: 'You haven't got much to eat, none of us has got much to eat; but in the old days we hadn't much to eat either. Well, anyhow, our children are better fed nowadays than they have ever been for at least two hundred years.' To the general approbation of the others in the queue.

"All these people who are being disembowled, maimed, beheaded, are being martyred in vain. Every shell that falls only confirms the people of Madrid more deeply in their faith. In the bomb-proof shelters 50,000 people can take refuge. And there are a million people in Madrid. In the sections of the city that are being most constantly bombarded, there is not one objective of military value. But the bombardment will go on.

"As I write this, shells are bursting every minute in the poorer quarters of the city. In the uncertain light, at this moment, the glare of the conflagrations is such that the night into which the daylight is fading is wine-red. The curtain, a smoke curtain, is rising on Fate's dress rehearsal for the coming war. Fellow Americans, I say to you: Down with Europe!

"Let us find out what it is we want. When a communist addresses an international conference, he puts his fist down on the table. When a fascist addresses an international conference, he puts his feet on the table. A Democrat—be he American, English, or French—when he addresses an international conference, scratches his head, and asks questions.

"The fascists have come to the aid of fascists, communists have come to the aid of communists and have even assisted the Spanish democracy. But democracies do not come to the aid of democracies.

"We, the democratic people of the world, believe in everything except ourselves. If a fascist state or a communist state disposed of the combined strength of the United States, the British Empire, and France, we should be struck with terror. But since it is *our* strength, we don't believe in it.

"Let us find out what it is we want. Either let us say to the fascists—or to the communists, if need be—'Get out of here! If not, you will have to deal with us!'

"Or let us say, once and for all: 'Down with Europe!'

"The Europe I see from this window no longer has anything to teach us, neither strength, which it has lost, nor faith, which it now manifests by decorating Moorish mercenaries with Sacred Hearts. Fellow Americans, all you who desire peace, who hate those who blot out ballots with the blood of butchers murdered on their counters, turn your eyes away from this continent; We're through with this old Uncle Europe who has gone out of his mind, yet, with his passions of a savage, his shellshocked face, presumes still to come and read lessons to us!"

When he had done dictating, Slade went up to the top storey, the best observation-post in Madrid. Four other correspondents were already there. They seemed relatively calm, for in the open air nerves are never so taut as in a confined space; and also because the little *mirador* of the Central, being smaller than the tower itself, seemed less vulnerable. That evening had no sunset, and nothing seemed alive except the dancing flames; it was as though the city of Madrid were stranded on the face of some dead planet, and the nightfall had made it over to elemental chaos. All trace of human life seemed buried in the dank November mist, blotched with angry red.

A huge burst of flames shot through a roof so small that Slade wondered how a house so tiny could have contained it. Instead of spreading upwards, the flames slithered along the house-front downwards to the street. There they fixed on another house and went soaring up it, to the roof. Then, as at the close of some spectacular display of fireworks, the conflagration ended in a whirl of brilliant sparks across the mist. A shower of red-hot cinders compelled the journalists to duck for a moment. As the fire approached the buildings which were already gutted, it lit them up from behind. They showed as gaunt, phantasmagoric skeletons, against the flames that prowled behind the ruins, like beasts of prey loath to leave their kill. The ghastly twilight seemed ushering in another

Age of Fire. The three largest hospitals were burning. The
Savoy Hotel was burning. Churches and museums were burning, the Biblioteca Nacional was burning, the Ministry of the
Interior was burning, a market was burning, all its little
wooden stalls were blazing, houses were crumbling, collapsing
in volleys of sparks, two entire quarters were glowing fiery
red, scored with long black walls like gridirons placed upon
a coal fire. With impressive slowness, but with grim persistence, the fire advanced, by way of Atocha and the Calle León,
in the direction of the centre, towards the Puerta del Sol,
which was also burning.

"The birth-pangs of a world," Slade murmured.

The bunches of shells were now dropping farther over to
the left. And from the depths of the Gran Via, immediately
beneath Slade and almost invisible to him, there rose a sound,
audible at times even above the clanging of the ambulance
bells, a sound as of barbaric litanies. Slade strained his ears
to catch the sound which seemed to come from some far-off
prehistoric age, congruous with this world of fire. After a
phrase rhythmically recurring, it seemed that everyone in the
street was uttering a response which imitated the clang of
funeral gongs: *"Dong-ding-a-dong."*

At last Slade guessed what is was, though he could not
catch the words. He had heard the same rhythmic chant a
month previously. In response to words he could not hear,
that human gong was beating out: *"No pasarán."* Slade had
seen La Passionaria, dark, austere, widow of all the slain
Asturians, had seen her leading a fierce and solemn procession
marching beneath red banners inscribed with her famous
phrase, *Better be a hero's widow than a coward's wife;* had
heard twenty thousand women chanting, in answer to another
long, incomprehensible phrase, this refrain: *"No pasarán."*
He had been less moved by them than by this smaller, but
unseen crowd, whose desperate courage rose towards him
through the smoke-clouds of the burning city.

20

STILL holding his pine-branch, Manuel left the town-hall
where the court-martial (its members were elected by the
soldiers) had been held. The death penalty had been pro-

nounced on both murderers and fugitives. It was the genuine
anarchists who had shown themselves most obdurate regarding those who had run away. "The whole proletariat is responsible," they had said. "Even if these men were fooled by
the falangist spies, that's no excuse."

A motor-car went by, the bright flails of its headlights pitted
by the rain.

"They can bomb Madrid at their ease, now," Manuel
thought. One couldn't see a thing.

As he passed the little side-door of the town-hall, marked
only by the light that issued from the corridor, he felt someone
seize him by the leg. Gartner and the others who were close
behind him turned on their electric torches and, in the rain-
drenched light, they saw two soldiers of their own brigade.
They were kneeling in the deep mud, clinging to Manuel's legs.
He could not see their faces.

"They've no right to shoot us!" one of the men was shouting. "We're volunteers! You got to tell them!"

The gunfire had ceased. The face of the man who was
shouting was not raised, but bent towards the mud, and his
cries were deadened by the hiss of the downpour. Manuel
said nothing.

"They can't do it! They can't do it!" the other began to
shout. "They can't, sir!"

His voice sounded very young. Still, Manuel could not see
their faces. Around their forage caps, pressed against his hips,
in the blurred radiance of the electric torches, droplets which
seemed rising from the ground danced across the lines of
driven rain. Suddenly, as Manuel still did not reply, one of
the condemned men raised his head and gazed up at him. He
was kneeling, his arms dangling, his shoulders thrown back
the better to see Manuel's face above him, and against the
timeless background of the rain-swept night the man looked
the very symbol of defeat—the eternal scapegoat, he who
pays. He had been rubbing his cheeks frantically against
Manuel's muddy top-boots. His forehead and cheekbones
were thickly smeared with mud, and on the darkness of the
face only the eye-sockets showed, blobs of cadaverous white.

Manuel felt inclined to say: "The court-martial's nothing to
do with me." But he was ashamed of such a disavowal. He
could think of nothing to say, and he knew he could only
shake off the second condemned man by pushing him away
with his foot. And the idea of that revolted him. He could

only stand there motionless, looking down at the frantic eyes of the suppliant, whose breast was heaving and down whose cheeks the rain was streaming as though all his face were dissolved in tears.

A picture rose in Manuel's mind of his men at Aranjuez and those of the Fifth Corps crouching in rain like this behind their little parapets. He had not lightly come to his decision that a court-martial must be held; but now he did not know what to do, caught between two alternatives, one odious and the other hypocritical. To shoot men down was bad enough, he thought, without adding moral sermons.

"You got to tell them!" the man who was looking at Manuel wailed. "You got to tell them!"

Manuel wondered what he could say to them. The argument for their defence was something inexpressible in words; it was in that streaming face, that open mouth which had made Manuel aware that here was the everlasting visage of the man who pays. Never had he realized so keenly the necessity of choosing between victory and compassion. Stooping, he tried to push aside the man who was still clinging to his leg. The man clung desperately, his head still bowed, as if in the whole world nothing but that leg could save his life. Manuel all but fell, then thrust more heavily against the man's shoulders; it struck him that several men would be required to dislodge his grasp. Suddenly the man let his arms fall, and he, too, looked up at Manuel, slowly raising his eyes till they met Manuel's. He was young, though not so young as Manuel had imagined. He had passed beyond resignation or despair, as though at last it all were clear to him—not for now only, but for ever and ever. And with the forlorn detachment of men who are speaking almost from beyond the grave, he said:

"So that's it? You've no voice now, as far as we're concerned?"

Manuel realized that he had not spoken a word.

He took a few steps; the men were left behind him.

The elemental fragrance of the rain on leaves and branches was drowning the odour of the wool and leather of wet uniforms. Manuel did not look back, but he still felt the presence of the men behind him, kneeling unmoving in the mud, felt their eyes haunting his receding steps.

21

SUDDENLY there was a blinding flash that left the lighted room in twilight for a moment. For Garcia and Scali to have noticed it in spite of the electric light, it must have been caused by a terrific burst of flame. They both crossed over to a window. The air was cold now, and a light mist was rising from the ground and mingling with the smoke from hundreds of houses smouldering in the darkness. No warning sirens could be heard, but there were fire-engines and ambulances everywhere.

"This is the hour when the Valkyries come down to glean the dead," Scali remarked.

"I seem to hear Madrid speaking to Miguel de Unamuno tonight, saying with its tongues of fire: 'What good to me are all those thoughts of yours, if you can't give my tragedy a thought?' Let's make a move. We'll go to the other office."

Garcia had been describing to Scali his conversation with Dr. Neubourg. Of all the men he was to see during that day and night, Scali was the only one who would feel as he had felt about it.

"When an intellectual who was a revolutionary once," Scali said, "attacks the revolution, it always comes to this: he is judging the political methods of that revolution by his own moral standards. But seriously, Garcia, would you rather such criticisms were left unsaid?"

"How could I wish such a thing? Intellectuals are always rather inclined to think that a party means a collection of people rallied round an idea. A party is really much more like a living, acting personality than an abstraction. Take the purely psychological side; a party is surely more than anything else a means of organizing for common action an aggregate of feelings that are often incompatible. In this case they include poverty—humiliation—apocalyptic vision—and hope. For the communists: love of action, organization, intensive production and the like. Yes, my dear fellow, to draw conclusions about a man's own character from the programme of the party he belongs to would be much the same as if I'd set out to deduce the psychology of my Peruvians from their religious myths."

He picked up his cap and revolver and switched off the light. The glow of flames outside, invisible so long as the lamps

were on, now suffused the room, which was filling with smoke
clouds that rasped their throats with the acrid fumes of burning wood, as the fires advanced slowly, resistlessly, towards
the Puerta del Sol. The fiery sky seemed lowering in the
darkened room. Clouds were piling up in dark-red masses
that seemed almost solid to the touch, above the Telephone
Exchange and the Gran Via. Coughing and sneezing, though
the smoke was no thicker, only more visible, than before,
Scali went back to the window. Had the paving-blocks caught
fire? No, they were only reflections, those little wisps of flame
gleaming red on the smooth surface of the asphalt. A pack of
stray dogs began howling, grotesquely, senselessly, aggressively, as though the world of men had passed away and they
were rulers of its desolation.

The automatic elevator was still working.

They walked as far as the Prado through the black streets
beneath the angry sky. Here in the utter darkness they were
still surrounded by the sounds they had heard from the window of the telephone building; Madrid was licking its wounds.
As they advanced another sound came to their ears, a sound
of countless tiny footfalls drumming on the asphalt.

"Unamuno will have made a fine mess of his death," Scali
said. "Here, in Madrid, fate had prepared for him the funeral
of his dreams."

Garcia thought of the room at Salamanca.

"Here he'd have found another tragedy," he said, "and I'm
not so sure he would have understood it. The great intellectual
is a man of subtleties, of fine shades, of evaluations; he's interested in absolute truth and in the complexity of things. He is
—how shall I put it?—'antimanichean' by definition, by nature.
But all forms of action are manichean, because all action pays
a tribute to the devil; that manichean element is most intense
when the masses are involved. Every true revolutionary is a
born manichean. The same is true of politics, all politics."

Just then he felt a pressure on his legs, a moving mass
hemming them in. He groped round with his hands. Was it a
pack of dogs? But where could that dusty smell of country
fields have come from?

The pressure increased; there was no getting through. The
patter of feet on the pavement was too sharp, too rapid for a
pack of dogs.

"What on earth's happening?" Scali shouted; the moving

mass had carried him a good five yards away. "Can it be sheep?"

He was answered by a bleat close by. Half-suffocated, Garcia managed to get out his torch and the thin ray rippled along the surface of a fleecy mass scarcely denser than the smoke-clouds overhead. Up to the limit of the light a flock of sheep was surging around. There seemed no end to it; they could hear bleat after bleat far into the distance. And not a trace of a shepherd.

"Bear to the right," Garcia shouted.

Fleeing from the battlefields, the flocks were passing through Madrid on their way down to Valencia. Somewhere behind, or coming down the side-streets parallel to the boulevard, there was doubtless a band of shepherds armed as they all were nowadays. But in the meantime, the nightbound flocks, masters of the Prado as they might be hereafter when men had passed away, were pressing forward between the smouldering houses in a warm, compact mass, their stolid silence broken now and again by a plaintive bleat.

"Let's go and fish out our car," Garcia said. "That's about the best thing we can do."

They made their way back towards the middle of the town.

"Go on with what you were saying, Garcia."

"Remember this, Scali. In all countries, in all parties, the intellectuals are always at loggerheads. Adler against Freud, Sorel against Marx. But in politics a dissenter is an outlaw. The intelligentsia always has a tremendous sympathy for the outlaw; out of generosity, or because they apreciate his cleverness. But they forget that what a party wants is to make good, not to find good reasons for its programme."

"I grant you that those who, on humane or intellectual grounds, may feel inclined to pick holes in revolutionary politics know nothing of the stuff of which a revolution's made. And the men with practical experience of revolutions never have the talent of Unamuno; often they are incapable of expressing themselves at all."

"If, for instance, as we are always being told, there are too many pictures of Stalin in Russia, it's not because that ogre Stalin, squatting in a corner of the Kremlin, has decreed it should be so. Why, look at the craze for signs and badges right here in Madrid, and, heaven knows, the Government doesn't care a damn one way or the other! It would be interesting to analyze the reasons for all those portraits. The trouble is, to talk about love to a lover, you've got to have been in love yourself; it's not enough just to have dissected love in the laboratory. It isn't by approving something or resenting it that a thinker proves his worth, but by his power of exposition. Let the intellectual first explain why and how things are as they are; then he can lodge his protests if he thinks fit—only, by then, it'll be a waste of breath. Analysis is a great force, Scali. I don't believe in ethical systems which exclude psychology."

Not a sound from the fires. Streaked with clouds of dense smoke hanging in tattered shreds, the glowing sky was mottled with great blotches of angry red, like red-hot iron cooling on the anvil; one would have thought the whole of Madrid was ablaze. Now and again a rustle of small sounds—absurdly out of keeping with the tragic sky—fretted the silence; the patter of thousands of small hoofs trotting up from the Prado.

"All the same," Scali said, after a moment, "soon men will have to be taught again the art of living." A memory of Alvear crossed his mind. "To be a man, in my view, one needn't necessarily be a good communist. For Christians, to be a man used to mean being a good Christian. Well, I mistrust that sort of thing."

"The question is far from being a trivial one, my friend; it raises the whole problem of civilization. For quite a while, the philosopher—let's call him that—was more or less explicitly regarded as the highest type of European man. The intellectuals were the 'clergy' of a world in which the politicians represented the nobility, for better or for worse. Their claim to act as spiritual advisers was uncontested. It was they, the intellectuals—Miguel de Unamuno and not Alfonso XIII indeed, for that matter Miguel and not the bishops—who were responsible for teaching men how to live. But nowadays the new political leaders claim to rule our minds as well; Miguel against Franco (against *us*, till the other day), Thomas Mann versus Hitler, Gide versus Stalin, Ferrero versus Mussolini; it's a conflict of prerogatives."

The street began to turn and above them now a lurid glow was filling the sky, reflected from the flaming masses of the Savoy, invisible behind the houses.

"Or Borgese rather than Ferrero." Scali raised a pointing finger in the darkness. "The whole business, to my thinking, turns on the famous and preposterous notion of 'totality' as they call it. It's a sort of mania with our intellectuals; in the twentieth century such a phrase as 'totalitarian civilization' is meaningless. It's as absurd as if one said the army constitutes a totalitarian civilization. And, as for the truth about things in general, the only man who aims at a 'totalitarian reality' is, precisely, the intellectual."

"Perhaps, my dear fellow, he's the only one who needs it. The close of the nineteenth century was an entirely passive epoch, whereas activity seems to be the keynote of the new era. Which indicates a pretty drastic contrast between the two periods."

"From that point of view, the political leader cannot but be regarded by the intellectual as an impostor, since he preaches a solution of life's problems, without telling us what those problems really are."

They were in the shadow of the house. The pink glow of Garcia's pipe described a semicircle as if implying: That would lead us too far afield. From the moment they had left that day, Scali had been conscious that Garcia was feeling worried —an unusual state of mind for the robust officer with the pointed ears.

"Tell me, Major, how can one make the best of one's life, in your opinion?"

An ambulance bell, shrilling like a danger-signal, sped past them and receded. Garcia was pondering.

"By converting as wide a range of experience as possible into conscious thought, my friend."

They were passing a movie theatre that spanned an angle of two streets. An aerial torpedo had ripped it open, peeling off the entire wall giving on the narrower street. A rescue party with electric torches were burrowing about among the ruins, searching for victims, most likely. And, as if summoning men to watch this search for the dead or dying, as it had once called them in to dream, the cinema bell was buzzing away behind an almost intact façade in the winter night.

Garcia was thinking of Hernandez. And, as he watched the flames rising above Madrid, he realized with a rush of agony how similar are all the tragedies of man's estate, each turning in his sad small orbit of despair like a madman turning in his cell.

"The business of the revolution is to solve its own problems, not ours. Ours depend on ourselves alone. If fewer Russian writers had cut and run along with the flood of émigrés, very

likely the relations between writers and the Soviet Government
wouldn't be what they are today. Miguel made the most of his
life—I mean, he lived as nobly as possible—in monarchical
Spain, which he loathed. And he'd have also made the most
of it in a less rotten social order. It might still have been
difficult, perhaps. No state, no social structure can create
nobility of character, nor intellectual qualities; the most we
can expect of it is favourable conditions. And that's a good
deal."

"You know, of course, that some claim to do so."

"What a party claims in such respects only goes to demon-
strate either the intelligence or the stupidity of its propagan-
dists. What interests me is what a party *does*. What are *you*
doing here?"

Scali stopped, amazed to find that he could give no definite
answer, and pushed back the tip of his nose as he always did
when thinking hard.

"Personally," Garcia continued, without waiting for his
reply, "I'm not in this uniform because I expect the Popular
Front to put the noblest into power, but because I wish to see
a change for the better in the lot of our Spanish peasantry."

A remark of Alvear's crossed Scali's mind.

"And if to give them economic freedom," he suggested,
"you've got to have a system which will enslave them politically?"

"In that case, as no one can be perfectly sure of the purity
of his ideals in the future, there's nothing for it but to let the
fascists have their way. But once we're agreed on the vital
point—that we've *got* to put up a resistance, we've taken up a
line of action which commits us once for all to a programme,
with all its inevitable consequences. In certain cases, the choice
is a tragic one. For the intellectual, it's almost always so, above
all for the artist. Yet, even so, wasn't it up to him to resist?

"For a thinker, the revolution's a tragedy. But for such a
man, life, too, is tragic. And if he is counting on the revolution
to abolish his private tragedy, he's making a mistake—that's
all. I've heard almost all your problems stated already by a
man you may have known, Captain Hernandez. As a matter
of fact, they led him to his death. There aren't fifty ways to
fight, there's only one and that's to fight to win. One doesn't
engage in a war or a revolution just to please oneself.

"Some writer—I don't remember who—once said: 'I am as
thronged with corpses as an old graveyard!' For four months

all of us have been 'thronged with corpses,' Scali. The path that leads from moral standards to political activity is strewn with our dead selves. Always there is a conflict between the man who acts and the conditions of his action—the line of action he must follow to win, not that which he must take to lose all that we want to save. The whole thing's not a matter for debate but a matter of hard facts and, in a way, of personal talent. Yes, it's a conflict, almost a rough-and-tumble!"

A rough-and-tumble! Scali remembered the struggle between Marcelino's plane and its own flames.

"There are just wars," Garcia went on, "such as the one we're waging now—but there's no such thing as a just army. And that an intellectual, a man who's business it is to think, should go and say like Miguel: 'I'm leaving you because you are not just'—well, it strikes me, my friend, as downright immoral. Yes, one can have a policy that's just, but there's no such thing as a just party."

"That point of view opens the door to every kind of racket."

"Every door's open to those who are set on forcing it. The quality of one's life is like the quality of one's mind. The only guarantee that an enlightened policy will be followed by a popular government isn't our theories but our presence, now and here. The moral standard of our government depends on our efforts and on our steadfastness. Enlightenment in Spain will not be the mysterious outcome of some vague aspiration; it'll be exactly what we make it."

A fresh fire broke out close by.

"Anyhow, my good friend," said Garcia with a touch of irony, "it's the workers themselves who'll bring about their own emancipation."

22

MOTIONLESS as marksmen taking aim, the firemen stood on their ladders, between the flames of the Savoy and the cascades of their fire-hoses. Suddenly they gave a start, and the long nozzles shook like anglers' lines when a fish bites. For a moment even the flames seemed to stand still, quelled by a terrific crash like the noise of an exploding mine. An aerial torpedo had just landed somewhere in the rear.

Mercery was watching the scene with professional interest.

"They're quicker at lighting fires than we are at putting them out."

Once he had fancied he might serve the Spanish Republic best as an adviser, maybe as a strategist. But after that regrettable incident of the soap factory, he had gone back to his old post of Captain in the Fire-Brigade. And never before had he been so useful nor so popular. Never, at the front, had he faced the enemy as he had been doing here during the last twenty hours.

"Fire's a tricky beast to handle," he would say, giving a dexterous twist to his moustache; "you've got to know the ropes, of course . . ." And so forth.

He stood on the pavement in his fire-fighting uniform, watching each nest of flames as if it were an enemy advance-guard he were fighting. The smouldering furnace was constantly flaring up again. The calcium flares were inextinguishable. On the left, where the fire seemed to have died out, bursts of dense white smoke were rising, frayed into long level streamers by the wind from the Sierra, and reddened by the flames below.

There were only four hoses to fight three separate fires, but these were now only a few yards away from the nearest building. The fire on the left blazed up again. The conflagration might be prevented from spreading if it were mastered where it was fiercest, on its extreme right, before the fire on the left got out of hand.

Again the nozzles gave a sudden jerk, and the flames seemed to stand still. A second torpedo had dropped, just in front, this time.

Mercery tried to distinguish the various sounds he heard. Despite the darkness, numerous fascist planes were about. The blazing fires in Madrid made perfect landmarks for them. Ten minutes previously four incendiary bombs had been dropped. Heavy shells were still coming over in the workers' districts and in the centre of the town. And, further away, the firing of the field-guns could be heard, mingled with the sounds of battle. Now and then they were drowned by the long shrieks of sirens and the clang of ambulance bells, the crash of buildings toppling over amid geysers of sparks. But Mercery listened in vain for the sound of fire-engine horns announcing the arrival of the sorely needed extra hoses.

A third bomb dropped, in line with the others. When

Mercery was fighting fire a dozen bombing planes could not have made him budge an inch.

The central patch of flames spread out suddenly, but as quickly writhed and flattened down. "After the war," Mercery thought, "I'll turn gambler!" The fires on the extreme left remained stationary. If only those reinforcements would hurry up! Mercery felt quite Napoleonic. He tugged his moustache cheerfully.

The fireman on the extreme right suddenly dropped his hose, hung for a moment on the ladder by one foot, then fell into the fire. The others hurried down their ladders rung by rung in parallel lines.

Mercery ran up to the first man who reached the ground.

"They're firing at us!" the man said.

Mercery looked round. None of the neighbouring houses was high enough for anyone to be firing from the windows. But someone might be shooting at them from a distance; there were plenty of fascists in Madrid.

"If ever I lay hands on the bastard!" a fireman exclaimed.

"If you ask me, it's a machine-gun," another man put in.

"Say, are you off your head?"

"We'll soon see," Mercery said. "Come on, lads. Up the ladders again! The fire is picking up. Come on, lads! For the People, and for Liberty!

"Immortal Liberty!" he murmured, as he turned to grasp the ladder. He took the place of the fireman who had fallen into the blazing furnace.

From the top of the ladder he looked round. No one was shooting at them; there was no place from which anyone could shoot. A machine-gun can be camouflaged easily enough, but the sound would have given the alarm to the patrols. He aimed the nozzle of the hose. The seething mass of flames on which he played it was the fiercest of all. It was an enemy with more life in it than any man, more life than anything else in the world. Facing this enemy of a myriad writhing tentacles, like a fantastic octopus, Mercery felt he was terribly slow, as though made of lead. But, for all its tentacles, he would best the monster. Behind him avalanches of smoke were pouring, black and garnet-red. Through all the noises of the conflagration he could hear people coughing in the street, scores and scores of them. He seemed floundering in a dry, dazzling sea of incandescence. The patch of fire died down.

The last smoke-wisp lifted, and Mercery could see Madrid below him in a lightless pit. All lights had been extinguished and the town was outlined only by the distant fires, flapping, like bull-fighters, their scarlet capes across the darkness. He had given up all, even Madame Mercery, to help to make a better world. He pictured himself stopping with a gesture those little children's hearses, white and quaintly decorated like wedding-cakes. For him each explosion he heard, each fire he saw, meant those poor, heartbreaking little hearses. Carefully he aimed the jet of water from his hose on the next patch of fire. Suddenly he felt as though a racing car had gone by at full speed. As if he had been blown from his foothold by a gust of wind, another fireman dropped off his ladder. This time, Mercery understood. They were being machine-gunned by a plane.

There were two of them.

Mercery saw them coming back, flying very low—not more than ten yards above the fire. They were not shooting. The pilots, who could see the firemen only when their forms showed up against the glow of the flames, had to wait till they flew behind them. Mercery had his revolver under his fireman's suit. He knew it was useless; and anyhow he could not get at it. But he felt a mad desire to shoot. The planes came back, and two firemen dropped, one in the flames, the other on the pavement. Mercery was filled with such passionate disgust that, for the first time, he felt completely calm as he saw the planes swooping towards him across the glowing sky. They struck him with the rushing tempest of their wings as they passed, before the return journey that would enable them to "spot" him. Mercery climbed down three rungs and faced them, erect on his upright ladder. As the first plane bore down upon him like a hissing shell, he turned his fire-hose on the cockpit of the machine, drenching it from end to end. Then he fell back against the ladder, with four bullets in his body. Living or dead, he still clung to the nozzle of his hose which was notched between two rungs.

Below, the spectators had taken shelter in doorways from the machine-guns that now were flaying the streets.

At last, slowly, Mercery's hands began to open. His body rebounded twice against the ladder, crashed upon the empty street.

23

IN THE main room of an old suburban house, the walls of which were completely covered with maps, the officers were waiting for Manuel, who had been called to the telephone.

"One of the falangists has killed himself," a captain observed.

"But another has given away the entire organization," Gartner replied.

"Isn't it amazing? Of course, to take on a job like that, a man has to be a scoundrel—but he must have courage as well."

"We've still a lot to learn about human nature, old man. You saw the state they were in. When the morale is at a low ebb, as the Colonel puts it, there's always someone ready to turn traitor."

"Have you seen the German tanks?" another voice put in. So far they had seen only the dim outlines in the rain.

"I went into one, it was open. One of the fellows had got away, the other was dead. Dead at his post, in the turret, and his pockets turned inside out. And the rain coming down outside. I shan't forget it in a hurry!"

The rain was still streaming down the window-panes, interminably.

"Had his comrades rifled his pockets, do you think?"

"Yes—so that no papers might fall into our hands. But they hadn't time to tuck back the lining of his pockets."

"That's natural enough, damn it! Taking things out is one thing—they might come in handy. But tucking back the lining, after—that's another matter."

"Have those chaps been executed?"

"Not yet, I believe."

"What are they saying at the base?"

"The comrades are very firm. Especially the ones from Toledo. The men who ran away when they had neither officers nor ammunition can't forgive these men who bolted when they had everything."

"Yes, I got the same impression; they're much more down on them than the others."

"Well, you see, these particular fellows remind them of the one thing in the world they're most anxious to forget."

"Yes, it's like they'd been building up something with a

hell of a lot of trouble and then these fellows barge along and lay it flat!"

"They've had a tough deal—like a lot of us, for that matter. But don't forget that the story of the bastards who killed their Captain won't do the others any good."

Manuel came in. His lips were drooping. In his hand was a fresh pine-branch.

On the wall, among the maps, hung a case of mounted butterflies. A shell burst near the villa; the bombardment had begun again. Another shell. A butterfly came loose and fell, pin upwards, to the bottom of the case.

"Comrades," said Manuel, "Madrid is burning——"

He was so hoarse that his voice was almost inaudible. He had been shouting all day; but that alone could not account for his voicelessness. He went on speaking in the same low tone to Gartner, who repeated his words more loudly.

"The fascists are attacking all along the south-east sector. The International Brigade is holding out. The bombardment is now being carried on by artillery and planes co-operating."

"And they're holding out?" A voice enquired.

Manuel raised his pine-branch. Holding out? That went without saying.

"The executions will take place," he went on. "Some Civil Guards are being sent to us."

Gartner repeated. By now, Manuel had lost his voice altogether.

More shells exploded. No one paid any heed to them. But at each explosion, one or two more butterflies broke loose and fell.

Manuel scribbled a phrase on the margin of one of the staff maps lying on the table.

Gartner glanced at it, then looked at each of his comrades. His small mouth pursed in his flat face, he swallowed hard, then said at last, in the tone of one announcing a definitive event: victory or defeat or peace—"Comrades, the Russian aeroplanes have arrived."

24

THE enemy was retreating on Segovia. The Republicans had too few adequately armed troops to harry their retreat, nor did they wish to deplete the Madrid defences. Manuel's regiment, and the troops attached to it, were resting. Now they were marching off by companies for drill.

The rain had stopped, but in the drab morning sky the tattered clouds were drifting low, skimming the flat roofs of the Castilian houses and turning their stones and tiles a dirty grey. Standing on the steps of the town-hall, Manuel watched the arrival of these men, for whom he was responsible.

In front, a huge half-ruined castle, of the kind to be seen in every village of the region, seemed dissolving into the soft, crumbling rock on which it stood. To the right was a steep street, up which the troops were marching to parade on the plaza between the town-hall and the ruined castle. Manuel had not seen his men since the executions of the previous night.

The first company, in formation as correct as that of regulars, the heavy boots of the men keeping punctual step on the sharp cobbles, came up to the saluting point. And as they passed the town-hall steps, the Captain rapped out an order.

"Eyes—Left!"

All heads turned smartly towards Manuel. It was the first time the command had been given in the regiment; it was perhaps the first time it had been given on the entire Madrid front. The order for the salute which bound the volunteers more closely to their commander had been given by the revolutionary officers; and Manuel felt it was not unconnected with the events of the night.

When the second company marched past, the same order was given, and so on for each successive company. Manuel watched these troops pass in fighting order, as efficient now as their opponents. They were the defenders of the people of Spain; he would be their defender. He would protect them from everyone, even from themselves. And yet he could not forget the mud-smeared faces he had seen gazing up at him; he could not forget the words: "So you've no voice, now, as far as we're concerned?" Still, the eyes which now met his, as the men marched past, were not indifferent or expressionless; they were full of the events of the night, full of a tragic fraternity.

The castle looked much like the one on the Tagus front, near which Ximenes had advised him never to court his men's affection. Well, there was now no longer any question of courting the affection of his troops. It had been necessary to kill—not enemies, but men of his own, and volunteers. And he had done it because he was responsible to each of the men who now were passing before him. Responsible for their lives. Each man pays in the coin of his responsibilities, and, from now on, Manuel would have to pay in lives. . . .

With ever-growing sadness, with ever stronger resolve, Manuel's eyes encountered his men's eyes, rank by rank, and their gaze told him that today they were pledging themselves to him in a blood-bond.

After the regiment had passed, Manuel was left alone on the empty plaza, with only some stray dogs and the sound of distant gunfire to keep him company. Gartner was away with the Brigade. Never had Manuel felt so much alone.

He had three hours to while away. The castle made him think once more of Ximenes, who was also in a rest camp six or seven miles away. Manuel got him on the telephone. Yes, "Old Quack-Quack" was there. Manuel gave some instructions and got into his car.

The village in which the Ximenes brigade was quartered lay behind the village Manuel had left. Peasants were still fleeing along the road, and Manuel reached the Colonel's headquarters through lines of donkeys and carts, herds of cattle of every sort.

They walked out together. The damp air made Ximenes' slight deafness worse. Enemy batteries were in action at some distance to the right and the gunfire at Madrid was audible. The Segovia plain showed through gaps in the Sierra.

"I believe that yesterday I lived through the most important day of my life," said Manuel.

"How's that, my boy?"

Manuel told him what had happened. They walked in silence for a while.

The change in Manuel's appearance, his cropped head, his air of authority, had immediately struck Ximenes. All that remained of the young man he had known was the rain-drenched pine-branch in his hand.

According to report, there were big fires in the direction of the Escurial; and dark clouds were hanging on the slopes of the Sierra. Farther off, towards Segovia, a village was burning. Through his field-glasses, Manuel could see peasants and donkeys hastening away.

"I knew what had to be done, and I did it. I'm determined to serve my Party, and I'm not going to let myself be deterred by any personal psychological reactions. I don't believe in regrets. But there's something else. You said to me once: 'It takes more nobility to be a leader of men than just to be oneself. Because it's harder.' Well, I'm becoming less and less 'myself.' Music, for instance . . . All that's over, so far as I'm concerned. Look here. Last week I slept with a woman whom I'd loved in vain . . . for years. Well, after two wretched shots at it, I found myself wanting to get away. No, I haven't any regrets on that score. But if I give up all that, it must be for some good reason. To command is to serve, nothing more and nothing less. I take upon myself the responsibility for those executions. They were necessary to save others' lives . . . our men's. But there's something else; every step I've taken towards greater efficiency, towards becoming a better officer, has estranged me more and more from my fellow-men. Every day I'm getting a little less human. But I expect you've been up against the same thing?"

"All I could tell you, my boy, would be things you wouldn't understand. You'd like to lead men and yet remain their comrade; well, in my opinion, no man's big enough for that."

He was thinking that fraternity of that kind was only to be found in fellowship in Christ.

"Still, I imagine, our humanity takes care of itself better than we think. All that estranges you from your fellow-men is bound to link you up more closely with your Party. . . ."

Manuel had thought so too, and sometimes with dismay.

"To be linked more closely with the Party is worthless, if one's to be estranged from the very men for whom the Party's working. Whatever the Party is aiming at, that aim exists only as the aim of each and every one of us. One of those condemned men said to me: 'Ah, so you've no voice now, so far as we're concerned!' "

He did not mention that as it so happened he had, at that moment, lost his voice. Ximenes linked his arm with Manuel's, but did not reply. From the height where they were standing, the activities of the men below seemed dwarfed to insignificance by the stately pageant of the rolling clouds and the slow sheets of fire streaming across them. As though, in the gods' eyes, mankind were nothing but so much combustible material.

"And what did you expect, my boy? That you could sentence men to death without a qualm?"

Ximenes looked at Manuel affectionately. His eyes seemed dark with perplexing, perhaps bitter memories.

"But you'll get used even to that!"

As a sick man seeks the company of a fellow-invalid to discuss death, so Manuel was drawn to speak of a moral conflict with a man to whom such conflicts were familiar. But it was much more for the warm humanity of his remarks than for their meaning. As a communist, Manuel did not question the rightness of his decision; he had done what he had done, so be it! Any problem of that kind should, he held, be settled either by modifying his actions (and there could be no question of doing that) or else by simply refusing to consider it. And words, as he knew, tend merely to wear down the edge of insoluble problems.

"The real struggle," Ximenes said, "begins when you have to contend against a part of your own self. Up to that point, it's all plain sailing. But it's only from such inner conflicts that a real man emerges. Yes, we've always got to fear the world within ourselves; there's no escaping it."

"I remember something you once said to me. Something like this: 'The first duty of a leader is to make himself be loved without courting love. To be loved without "playing up" to any one—even to himself.' "

Through a great rent in the rocks of the Sierra the farther slopes had just come into view. From Madrid, scarcely visible across the grey expanse, pillars of dense black smoke were slowly, mournfully spreading across the sky. Manuel knew only too well what that smoke meant. The city was veiled in the shroud of its conflagration as warships are veiled in swirling banks of battle-smoke. The smoke was rising from buildings whence no glow of fire was visible, towering in columns that frayed out across the murky sky. And all the clouds seemed to have welled up from the unseen furnace, progressing like an army on the march in the direction of their drift. Above the thin white line of the beleaguered city, nestling in its woods, brooded an infinite distress, a holocaust of agony, filling the whole immensity of heaven. And to Manuel it seemed that even the memory of the night was being borne away by the slow, stagnant breeze, that brought to him the reek of the smouldering fires of Cuatro Caminos and the Gran Via.

One of Ximenes' officers came up in a car.

"Lieutenant-Colonel Manuel is being asked for on the telephone. By General Headquarters."

They hurried back, Manuel feeling vaguely uneasy. He rang up G. H. Q.

"Hullo? You asked for me, I believe?"

"The general staff wishes to congratulate you on the way you handled your men yesterday."

"At your service."

"You may have heard that some of the militiamen who ran away the other day have asked to re-enlist."

"Yes?"

"The general staff has decided to form a brigade composed of these units. They will be quite the most difficult troops to handle of any we have now."

"Yes?"

"The Chief of Staff believes you have the qualities required for the command of such a brigade."

"Ah, yes."

"Your Party is also of that opinion."

"Yes."

"General Miaja thinks likewise. You will be immediately put in command of this brigade . . ."

"But what about my regiment? My own regiment!"

"I believe it will be incorporated with another division."

"But I know each man in it! Who could . . ."

"General Miaja thinks that you are qualified for this command."

Coming back from the telephone, he found Heinrich waiting for him. The Internationals were planning a counter-attack on Segovia, and Heinrich was going in the direction of Guadarrama. They went away together.

The car was coming down the slopes of the Sierra. Manuel thought he understood Heinrich, because he knew his qualities as a commander. But as he recapitulated to him the events of the day and of the previous night, and repeated his conversation with Ximenes, it became obvious that the only human contact he had with the General was the strange affinity which always springs up between an interpreter and the person he interprets.

Heinrich's head was bent forward; his shaven neck was smooth, and his lips, reflectively pursed up, gave a childish look to his grizzled old face.

"We are, both of us, engaged in changing the conditions of this war," Heinrich said. "Surely you don't believe you can change things without being changed yourself? From the day you take a commission in the army of the proletariat, your soul is no longer your own."

"What about that brandy?"

Manuel had seen Heinrich handing out bottles of brandy to all the drunkards of his brigade; the labels on the bottles had been replaced by others reading: *Presented by General Heinrich. To be drunk when off duty; not a drop on duty.*

"You can keep your heart: that's another matter. But you must lose your soul. You've already lost your long hair—and the sound of your voice has changed."

Heinrich's vocabulary was almost the same as Ximenes's. But the tone was Heinrich's hard tone, and his lashless eyes were set as they had been at Toledo.

"What do you, as a Marxist, mean by 'lose your soul?'" Manuel asked, a little stiffly.

Heinrich watched the pine-trees scudding by in the melancholy light.

"All victories involve losses," he said; "and not only on the battlefield."

He gripped Manuel's arm, and added in a voice which might have been bitter, or merely practical and firm—Manuel could not guess which: "And now, you must never again waste pity on a lost man."

25

Madrid, December 2nd

Two corpses were lying in front of the window. A wounded man had been dragged back to cover by the feet. Five of the Internationals were holding the staircase, with their dumps of hand-grenades beside them. There were some thirty members of the International Brigade occupying the fourth floor of the house painted pink.

An enormous loud-speaker, one of those which the Republicans drove round in propaganda lorries more than half-filled by the huge funnels, was bellowing through the failing light of the winter afternoon:

Comrades! Comrades! Hold on to your positions. The fas-

cists will be out of munitions by this evening. The Uribarri column blew up thirty-two of their lorries this morning. Comrades! Comrades! Hold on . . .

The loud-speaker, knowing there was no answering it, re-iterated. . . .

The fascists would be out of munitions by the evening, but for the time being they had plenty; they had counter-attacked, and were holding the first two storeys of the building. The third floor was a no-man's-land. The Internationals occupied the fourth.

"Dirty swine!" a voice yelled up the chimney, in French. "You'll soon see whether or not we have enough munitions to lay you out!"

That was one of the Tercios, down below. Chimneys made good speaking-tubes.

"Dirty ten-francs-a-day hirelings!" Maringaud yelled back, getting down on all fours. Heads were in the line of fire, even at the back of the room. Formerly Maringaud had believed all the usual romantic stuff about the Foreign Legion. Rebels, tough fellows, those boys! Well, there they were, just below, the Spanish Foreign Legionnaires, come here to defend they knew not what, full of vanity, and crazy to fight. Maringaud had been in a bayonet charge against them a month before, in West Park. What price the Tercios then? That pack of trained bloodhounds, servile to their unknown masters, now utterly disgusted him. The International Brigade, likewise a foreign legion, hates above all that other Foreign Legion.

The Republican six-inch guns continued to fire on the Hospital at regular intervals.

The apartment in which Maringaud and his men were look-ing for good sniping posts had formerly been a dentist's. One of the rooms was locked. Maringaud decided to break open the door. Maringaud, squat to the point of tubbiness, had black eyebrows and a short nose set in a round, genial face, bringing to mind the smiling baby of an advertisement. Under his weight the door burst open, and the dentist's operating-room appeared. There, sprawling in the dentist's chair, was a dead Moor. The Republicans had occupied the two lower floors of the building only the day before. The window in this room was wider and lower than the others. The enemy's bullets had broken the dentist's glassware only above a height of three feet from the floor. It would be possible to look out of the window and shoot from there.

Maringaud was not a commissioned officer as yet—he had not done his military service—but he was not without authority in his company. Everyone knew that he had been secretary of the Workers' Union in one of the largest munitions factories, and what he had done there. The Italians had given the firm an order for two thousand machine-guns, to be delivered for Franco. The factory-manager was a fire-arms enthusiast, and would not let the packers box the arms for shipping until they were absolutely perfect. So each night, when the day's work was over, lights burned until late in a portion of the factory where the old boss was working by himself indefatigably in a quiet work-room, tinkering with a bolt on a minute piece of mechanism, putting the last touch to an all-important gadget which would make those machine-guns "top-notch, I'm telling you!" And at four in the morning, the militant workers, following Maringaud's instructions, would come, one after another, to the factory and, with a few strokes of a file, put out of gear the piece to which such patient industry had gone. So it went on for six weeks. For almost forty nights the dogged struggle persisted in the munitions factory between the workers' solidarity and the technical zeal of Maringaud's employer. (He was not a fascist, but his sons were.)

All the men knew—they now had reason to know!—that this work had not been in vain.

In the pink house, Maringaud's men had at last installed themselves below the line of fire.

That house, in which fighting had been going on now for six days, with attacks and counter-attacks, was impregnable, except by the staircase, where five Internationals with hand-grenades kept constant guard. The space round the house provided no possibility of training a gun. Rifle-bullets took no effect on it. The place might be mined. But so long as the Tercio held the lower floors, it was certain that the mine would not be set off.

The six-inch guns of the Republicans went on firing.

The street was empty. In a dozen houses insults were being hurled up and down the chimneys.

Now and then an attacking party from one side or the other made an effort to rush the street, failed, and fell back. Behind the windows the look-out men, bored even by death, waited idly. Had a misguided journalist come along to survey the situation, he would at once have had a load of lead in his body.

There was a machine-gun or a rifle behind every window.

The loud-speaker drowned with its hoarse blare the insults bawled up the chimneys, and the street was empty, seemingly forever.

But to the right stood the Hospital, the best fascist position on the Madrid front. A thick-set skyscraper, standing apart in wooded ground, it overlooked the whole suburban quarter. From their fourth floor, Maringaud's men could see the Republicans in every street near by, crouching in the mud; had the Hospital not been visible, its proximity might have been inferred from the way the men kept below the line of fire from its windows.

The Hospital looked deserted, as did the neighbouring houses. But from all its windows machine-guns spat unceasingly. There it stood, stolid and ox-like, a gloomy, murderous skyscraper, a ruined Babylonian tower, amid the bursting shells that scoured it with flying débris.

One of the Internationals, after searching all the cupboards, had found a pair of opera-glasses.

Some grenades exploded suddenly in the stairs. Maringaud went out on the landing.

"It's nothing," one of the International guards informed him, above the roar of bursting shells.

Nothing; only the Tercios trying again to come up the stairs.

Maringaud took the opera-glasses. Seen in close-up, the Hospital changed colour, grew red. Its clean-cut outline was seen to be due merely to its bulk. That it was undamaged was an illusion. The glasses showed that under the pounding of the six-inch guns it was being hollowed out, dented, flattened, like red-hot iron under hammer-blows. A close-up view of the windows gave it the look of an abandoned beehive. Yet even at a considerable distance from that ruined fortress, men crept warily along the rain-drenched pavements and rusting tramlines.

Suddenly Maringaud began waving his fat arms frantically. "Oh, boys, look! Look! It's begun! Our fellows are attacking!"

The men crowded up between the window and the dead Moor in the dentist's chair. *Dinamiteros* and bombers could be seen, dark specks rising from the ground round the Hospital. They raised their arms, sank into the mud again, then reappeared where, five minutes before, their dynamite cartridges and hand-grenades had made a ring of red beads.

Maringaud rushed to the chimney, and bellowed to the Tercios:

"Just have a look what's happening to your Hospital, you
bloody fools!"

Then he ran back to his place at the window. The *dinamiteros* were closing in. From the smashed beehive a swarm
of insects was pouring out towards the fascist lines, swept by
their own machine-guns.

No reply had come from the chimney. One of the fellows,
a Czech, suddenly crouched lower than his comrades and,
bringing up his rifle, started banging away. From the houses on
the opposite side of the street, some other besieged Internationals were also firing. Hugging the wall, the Tercios were
filing out of the pink house. It was mined, and now that the
Tercios had left, the mine would be set off.

Cautiously the Negus crept along the counter-mine. For a
whole month he had ceased believing in the revolution. The
apocalypse was over. There remained the struggle against
fascism; and the Negus' respect for the defenders of Madrid.
There were anarchist members of the Government; other anarchists, in Barcelona, were fiercely defending their doctrine
and their status. Durruti was dead. But the fight against the
bourgeoisie had been, for such a long time, the breath of life
to the Negus that he found it easy to go on living for the
fight against fascism. He had always fought for negative emotions. Yet things were not going well with him. He listened
to his own men making their radio appeals for discipline, and
he envied the young communists who spoke after them. *Their*
lives had not been transformed in the last six months! With
the Negus now was Gonzales, the fat man with whom Pepe
had attacked the Italian tanks advancing on Toledo. Gonzales
belonged to the C.N.T. But that made no difference to the
Negus. The fascists must be mopped up first, he guessed;
plenty of time to argue afterwards. "You know," the Negus
once remarked, "the communists are good workers. I can
work with them. But as to liking—no! I've done my damned-
est, but I can't get to like 'em!" Gonzales had been an Asturian
miner; the Negus had been a dockhand in Barcelona.

Since his exploit with the flame-thrower at the Alcazar, the
Negus had taken to mine-laying. He liked that underground
warfare in which nearly all the fighters are foredoomed and
know it; in which, for the most part, each plays a lone hand.
When up against insoluble problems, the Negus always fell
back on violence or self-sacrifice; best of all, on both together.

Now he was creeping forward, a thin figure, followed by fat Gonzales, along the gallery which was believed to extend a little beyond the pink house. The ground sounded more and more hollow. That meant either that the enemy mine was very near (but he could hear no thud of spades) or . . .

He set the detonator of a hand-grenade.

The last blow of the pick landed on emptiness, and his momentum carried the miner through the hole into a sort of chasm in front.

The Negus groped round with his electric torch like a blind man with his hands. Earthenware jars were everywhere, jars the height of a man. Obviously, a cellar. He switched off his light and jumped. In front of him shone another electric torch, groping about. The man who held it could not have seen the Negus' lamp, put out a moment before. A fascist. The Negus hesitated. Should he fire? No, he could not see the man. The pink house must be almost directly above them. Gonzales was still in the communicating trench. The Negus threw his grenade.

When the smoke-clouds, swirling across the ray of Gonzales' torch, had lifted, two fascists came into view sprawling in a slimy pool of oil or wine, from which their heads emerged. Fragments of the enormous jars stood up like cliffs from the pool which, slowly deepening, rose to the dead men's shoulders, then to their mouths, then above their eyes.

The Republican counter-attack was over. Maringaud and his men were rescued, Gonzales and his men returned to brigade headquarters. They had to cross a section of Madrid to get there.

The city had acquired the routine of bombardment. As soon as pedestrians heard an explosion, they ran for shelter to the nearest doorway; then, when the danger was past, they went on their way. Here and there, smoke-streamers trailed in a languid breeze, recalling in the midst of tragedy the peaceful smoke of cottage chimneys as supper-time approaches. A dead man had fallen in the street. He was still holding a lawyer's brief-case which no one had dared to touch. The cafés were open. A draggled crowd, like the denizens of some sinister dive, was streaming from each Metro exit. Others were swarming down the entrances, with mattresses, towels, baby-carriages, handcarts heaped with kitchen pots and pans, tables, family portraits, and children clasping cardboard bulls. A peasant was trying to push a stubborn donkey into one of the entrances. Since the twenty-first, the fascists had been shelling the city every day. Round the Salamanca quarter, queer negotiations were in progress to claim the tenancy of doorways. Sometimes a mass of wreckage in the street would begin moving, and a hand, with its fingers fantastically splayed, emerged. But in the bombarded areas, among the horror-stricken faces of the fugitives, children could be seen playing at "pursuit planes." Stories, worthy of the Arabian Nights, were going round of women who had come back to their homes in Madrid packed up in baskets or tucked inside mattresses. . . . A tram-driver joined the soldiers who were returning to headquarters, and began talking to Gonzales.

"I don't mean to grumble, but it's a rotten life nowadays, this job of mine. I start off, I do my run, I reach the terminus —with half my passengers alive. The others have been knocked out on the way. What I say is, what kind of a job is that now?"

Suddenly the tram-driver stopped. Gonzales and Maringaud stopped. All the people in the street stopped, or ran for doorways. Five Junkers, escorted by fourteen Heinkels, were approaching overhead.

"Keep your chin up!" a voice said. "You'll get used to it!"

And then, before Gonzales or Maringaud had noticed anything in the grey evening sky, a huge crowd of people came pouring out of shelters, cellars, doorways, houses, underground railway-stations—with cigarettes in their mouths, kitchen-ware or newspapers in their hands—variously clad in overalls, jackets, blankets, and pyjamas.

"They're our planes!" a civilian was shouting.

"How the hell do *you* know?" Gonzales asked.

"Can't you hear? The sound of the motors. It's louder, clearer."

From the other side of Madrid, for the first time, thirty-six Republican pursuit planes were approaching. The planes sold by the U.S.S.R. after the Soviet Union's denouncement of nonintervention, had at last been assembled. Some had already fought over Getafe, and the patched-up machines of the International Flight had flown over Madrid, dropping pamphlets announcing the reorganization of the Republican Air Force. But these four squadrons of nine planes each, in V formation, with Sembrano in command, were being used that day for the first time for the protection of Madrid.

The leading Junker swerved to the right, swerved to the left, hesitated. The Republican squadron swooped out upon the bombing planes. Men's hands gripped excitedly the shoulders of their women. In every street, on all the house-tops, at each cellar opening, at all the underground entrances, the people who for eighteen days had gone their ways in terror of the bombs, raised their eyes, looked up in wonder and delight.

And then—they saw the enemy squadron turn tail towards Getafe; the roar of half a million voices, a wild, inhuman, exultant paean, rose to the dim sky, loud with the thunder of the people's planes.

In the gathering darkness, Heinrich watched from his window a crowd of soldiers in the street below. They had been cut off from their units and had come there to join up again. Before him lay a map on which he noted the movement reports which Albert, tethered as usual to the telephone, was transmitting to him. On all sides it was being confirmed that, cut off from their supply train by the Uribarri column, the fascists had run out of ammunition.

"The attack on Pozzuelo-Aravaca has been repulsed, sir," Albert said.

Heinrich marked the new positions on the map. The creases at the back of his fat white neck puckered like a smile.

"The attack on Las Rosas has been repulsed," another staff-officer reported.

Again, the telephone.

"Good. Good. Thank you," Albert murmured. Then he turned to Heinrich. "The attack at La Moncloa has been repulsed."

Everyone in the room felt like celebrating.

"Brandy all round at the next good news!" said Heinrich.

The War Office was transmitting the new positions, serially, through Albert's receiver. Brigade-headquarters were calling up at the other telephone.

"Hand out the brandy, sir," said Albert. "We are advancing towards Ferrol, and the Coruña road is now open."

"Villaverde has been retaken."

"We are advancing on Quemada and Garalito!"

Part Three

THE PEASANTS

I. The Peasants

1

MAGNIN ran into Vargas in the Air Ministry at Valencia. He was much the same as he had found him at Madrid on the night after Medellin. The Ministers were new, those on active service were wearing uniforms, Franco had failed to take Madrid, the people's army was beginning to take shape. But the war was still the same war, and however many others had found either death or salvation in it, neither Vargas nor Magnin had changed much. As at Madrid, Vargas had just called for a whisky and cigarettes; as at Madrid, both their faces wore expressions of deep gloom.

"Malaga has fallen, Magnin," Vargas said.

Magnin was not surprised. He had not imagined that the Republicans would be able to hold their smashed centre line against the Italians and Germans. A week ago Garcia had said to him:

"I expect everything from the centre and nothing from the minor fronts. Malaga has been a second Toledo."

"The number of refugees is extraordinary, Magnin."

"Yes, more than a hundred thousand in flight! Terrible."

Above them, in the centre of that great room in which a rich merchant had lived, was a stuffed eagle supporting a chandelier.

"With Italian planes chasing them, and lorries. If the lorries can be stopped, they'll get to Almeria."

Eyes and moustache registering equal despondency, Magnin made a movement which seemed to say: when do we start?

"Madrid is the place for our best planes, Magnin, I know." (The fascists had launched a big offensive on the Jarama front.)

"We need two big bombers for the Malaga road. We've got practically no pursuit planes here."

"But we've got to find someone for Teruel, too. Nobody in the Column knows Teruel as well as you. I want you . . ." He went on in Spanish. "Not to choose the most risky, but

the most useful work. You for Teruel, Sembrano for Malaga.
He's here.

"You know," he added, "Teruel hasn't any pursuit planes,
either."

For two months now, the International Air Force had been
fighting on the Mediterranean front: the Balearics, Andalusia,
Teruel. The suicidal flights of the "Pelican period" were a
thing of the past. In the air twice a day, and spending a sub-
stantial proportion of their time in hospital, the squadron had
supported the International Brigade all through the battle of
Teruel, fighting, doing repairs, photographing the results of
their bombing while they fought.

The airmen lived in an abandoned château surrounded by
orange groves, near a secret landing-ground. During one engagement they had scored hits on Teruel station and the
enemy headquarters despite the anti-aircraft batteries, and an
enlarged photo of the explosion was pinned on the wall of
their mess-room. Magnin and his pilots knew every inch of
the front by instinct now.

"At dawn?" Magnin asked.

They began to study maps.

Jaime and Scali, Gardet and Pol, Attignies, Saïdi, the mechanic from one of the international contingents, and Karlitch
were drinking *manzanilla* in the town.

Behind them, on the other side of the café windows, was a
miniature fair, complete with lottery-wheels, candy-stalls and
shooting-galleries. They could hear the music from inside. It
was the children's gala-day. The shooting-galleries had attracted the machine-gunners, who were breaking pipes and
knocking down pasteboard pigs to their hearts' content; that
was where they had found Karlitch, surrounded by admirers.
It was the children, rather than the shooting-galleries, who
had brought Gardet and Saïdi there. They had spent all their
money handing out cakes. Gardet loved children much as
Slade loved animals, to offset his own dourness; in Saïdi they
evoked his own childishness, and his Moslem compassion.

"The Americans are fine," Pol said.

The first American volunteer pilots had just arrived.

"What I like," said Gardet, "is that they don't think that
they are saving democracy every time they leave the ground."

"And they've shown the other money-grubbers where they
get off," said Attignies.

He loathed all mercenaries, instinctively.

"But as for the new commandant," Pol went on, "he's just the local brand of bloody fool."

It was the first time that the Spanish commandant appointed to share the command of the aerodrome with Magnin had been difficult to work under.

"Cut it out!" Attignies said. "Nobody expects a bed of roses. It'll come right in time. Sembrano is coming back. Let's do our jobs, that's all that matters. The Bréguets have got a fine Spanish captain, anyway."

"Fighting modern planes week after week, handicapped like that, needs a bit of patience!"

"It's a curious thing," Scali said; "there's no other country with a sense of dignity and 'style' like this one. Take a peasant, or a journalist, or an intellectual and give him a job. He may do it well or badly, but he'll nearly always do it with a 'style' which could give points to any other country in Europe. This commandant hasn't any style. And when a Spaniard loses that, he's lost everything."

"I saw what you mean at the Alhambra last night," said Karlitch. "A dancer came on the stage pretty much in the nude. Right close. Could almost touch her. And a drunk *miliciano* ran up and took her in his arms. Got quite a hand for it. Then the *miliciano* turned round with his eyes closed and his hands clenched tight. As if she had given him her beauty when he had her in his arms, and it was there in his hands still. And he turned to the audience and threw her beauty in their faces. Contemptuously. Marvellously done. And only possible here."

His French had got much worse. Leader of an irregular unit, always dapper, he seemed to have just left a bathroom where the eau de Cologne had been replaced by camphor. He removed his peaked captain's cap, and Scali saw the familiar crest of stiff, black hair.

"What I like about this show is that I'm learning something," Pol said. "Seriously! But the commandant's a swine, all right."

"That's no way to talk of a commandant," Karlitch burst out.

He had let his moustache grow; his face was less childish, harder, and Scali could see something of the ex-Wrangel cadet coming to the fore again.

Pol shrugged his shoulders. Then, with raised finger emphasizing the words:

"I repeat, he's the *local* brand of bloody fool."

This can lead to trouble, Attignies thought.

"What made you join?" he asked Saïdi.

The latter raised an absurdly youthful finger as he answered. "When I heard that the Moors were fighting for Franco, I told my socialist section: 'We must do something. Otherwise what will our fellow-workers think of the Arabs?' "

"I can see lights," Jaime said, fiddling with a piece of wire. He made aeroplanes out of wire, with controls that worked. And the airmen pulled them to bits, playing with them.

He had been "seeing lights" every day for a month now. At first his friends used to look in the direction to which he pointed; but they always found, not lights, but only another disappointment. Scali and Jaime were sitting next to each other, with the others opposite.

"Well," Karlitch said, "we've taken Albarracin. One of the big-shot fascists was there. Quite young: perhaps twenty. He was hiding. When we first went there, all we could find was two old women. The boy had denounced maybe fifty of us. And others who hadn't even anything to do with us. All shot."

"Nothing worse than those young pups," Scali said.

"One of the old women says to us: 'No, there's nobody else, only my other nephew . . .' They were his aunts. Then, the next thing that happens, a boy comes out wearing socks and a hat," Karlitch made a circular gesture round his head to indicate a sailor-hat, ". . . and a sailor-suit and kid's shorts. 'You see,' said the old hags, 'there he is!' It was the little bastard we were after. They had dressed him up in the kid's clothes to make us . . ."

"The lights are going round," Jaime said. He had taken off his black glasses.

Karlitch laughed, the same laugh which had got on Scali's nerves before, in August.

"We shot him."

They all knew that Karlitch had twice rescued wounded comrades under fire. And that he'd be killed sooner or later. His passion was to serve others, and it was a quality which he expected to find also in those who served under him. The first time he had found some of his wounded tortured by the Moors, he had himself given their officers the *coup de grâce*. His contradictory character worried Scali and Attignies. The others thought Karlitch a little mad; Saïdi was not so sure about it.

Scali remembered Karlitch's arrival. He was wearing magnificent riding-boots, and had started to have them cleaned by the first boot-black he met. But polishing a pair of Cossack top-boots is by no means the same thing as polishing a pair of shoes, and the thirty fellow-officers in the bus they were sharing had had to wait for half an hour while Karlitch fumed and fretted, drumming his fingers on the table, waiting for the final gloss to be given to the second boot.

"The lights are stopping," Jaime said.

This continual renewal of hope provoked an atmosphere of intolerable strain each time that it occurred. The fact that Jaime was half-ashamed of being blind, and his consequent attempts at facetiousness, made it worse. One day he had promised them oysters, which he imagined he could dig up by means of some crazy plan. And the first ones to arrive (Scali and he were the last) had found a note at the café: *"On second thought we shan't be coming*—The Oysters!"

"Do you like this life?" Attignies asked Karlitch.

"When my father died (I've got three brothers) I was doing my military service, but even then my father said: 'I want three of them to be happy; the other one—must fight his way through.' "

Scali was once more coming up against the thing that had been worrying him for the past two months: what those who cared to analyze people's motives for fighting referred to as "the veterans." Scali liked natural fighters, mistrusted professional ones and loathed "veterans." Karlitch's case was clear enough, but what of the others? And there were thousands of that kind on Franco's side.

"I'm hoping to get into the tank corps," the machine-gunner went on.

Tank corps, air force, machine-guns—were German mercenaries of the sixteenth century going to reappear in Europe?

"What is the most frightening war experience you can remember?"

He wanted to ask what had aroused his horror and pity as well; but it was no good being too subtle.

"Most frightening? All of it, at first."

"And afterwards?"

"I don't know."

"Do you see the lights?" Jaime asked.

"Wait!" Karlitch went on. "There's one thing that I'm really scared of. Men who have been hanged. You, too?"

"I've never seen any."

"You're lucky. There's something terrifying about it. When a thing like that happens, you see, it's natural enough if there's blood. But men who have been hanged aren't natural. When there's no blood, it's not natural. And it's when things aren't natural that you get scared."

For twenty years now Scali had been hearing talk about "the human ideal" and had puzzled over it. Metaphysics! Now they were up against the spectacle of men engaged in a life-and-death struggle, a fine show it was making! Scali was completely unable to sort out his ideas. There was courage, generosity—and there was the physiological side. There were the revolutionaries—and there were the masses. There was politics —and ethics. "I like to know which of them I'm talking about," Alvear had said.

"The lights have started to move again," Jaime said.

Scali sat up straight, with his mouth open and both fists on the table, pushing the wire aeroplanes away from him. Gardet had taken Jaime by the shoulders, and they were both looking out through the café window at the big electric bulbs on the wooden horses which had just begun to revolve once more.

Gone completely crazy, whistling like linnets, Jaime and his friends, with Magnin in another car, were on their way up to the aerodrome to report for duty—for Malaga. An enemy squadron was shelling the harbour from four miles out to sea. Valencia was obscured beneath a fine drizzle which dripped gently from the oranges. For the children's fête-day the syndicates had decided to organize a huge procession. The children's delegations, when consulted, had asked if their favourite characters from the animated cartoons could be represented. The syndicates had accordingly constructed enormous cardboard models of Mickey Mouse, Felix the Cat, Donald Duck (preceded, nevertheless, by a Don Quixote and a Sancho Panza). Of the thousands of children who had come in from all over the province for the fête, which was in aid of the refugee-children from Madrid, many were without shelter. Their course completed, the triumphal chariots stood abandoned on the outer boulevard. Over a mile and a half or more the head-lights of the motor cars revealed the talking animal denizens of the modern fairy-land, the world in which those who are killed all come back to life. Small children with nowhere to go for shelter had taken refuge on the bases of the cardboard effigies, between the legs of the mice and cats. The enemy squadron went on shelling the port; and in time with the explosions, while Don Quixote kept his nocturnal vigil over them, trembling in the rain, the animals nodded their heads above the sleeping children.

Attignies was Sembrano's bomber. The crews of the two planes had been mixed up: in his machine were Pol, the mechanic, and Attignies. Sembrano had brought his second pilot with him, a Basque named Reyes. At their southernmost aerodrome they had found some bombs that they had had to change, and a degree of confusion worthy of Toledo. Nearing Malaga, the exodus one hundred and fifty thousand strong, sprawling along the coast road; then, beyond, the fascist cruisers trailing their smoke-clouds through the brilliant morning light as they made for Almeria; finally, the first of the combined Italian and Spanish motorized columns. Seen from the planes, it looked as if it must overtake the exodus within a few hours. Attignies and Sembrano had exchanged glances and come down as low as possible. There was nothing left of the column afterwards.

To speed his return, Sembrano opened his throttle wide and turned out to sea.

When Attignies looked round, the mechanic was rubbing his hands, which were covered with oil from the bomb-releasing controls. Attignies looked at the sky in front again, full of round clusters of cumulus cloud reminding him of the animated cartoons; eighteen enemy pursuit planes—overdue— were approaching in two groups. And still more behind, probably.

Their bullets came through the front gun-turret.

Sembrano felt a ferocious cudgel-blow on his right arm, which went limp. He turned to the second pilot: "Catch hold of the stick!" Reyes was holding not the stick but his stomach, with both hands. But for the belt which held him up, he would have fallen on top of Attignies, who lay prone behind his seat, with one foot a mass of blood. Now that the enemy fighter was behind their plane, it would probably fire on them from above. There was no possible protection. Faced with that number of enemies, the five Republican fighters had to cover the escape of the other heavy bomber, which was in a better position to put up a fight. The holes in the fuselage were like shell-holes: the Italians were using big quick-firers. Was the tail-gunner wounded?

As Sembrano turned to look, the starboard engine caught his eye: it was alight. Sembrano cut it out; all his machine-gunners had stopped firing now. The plane was losing height every second. Attignies was bending over Reyes, who was down off his seat and calling repeatedly for something to drink. "A stomach-wound," thought Sembrano. A new enemy on-slaught swept over the plane, only hitting the right wing. Sembrano was piloting with his feet and his left arm. Blood was trickling gently down his cheek; he had probably been hit in the head, too, but he felt no pain. The plane sank lower and lower. Behind, Malaga; beneath, the sea. Just the other side of a strip of sand ten yards wide, a reef of rocks.

Parachutes were out of the question. The enemy fighter was following, and their machine was already too low. To climb was impossible; the elevator, probably torn by the explosive bullets, scarcely answered the controls. The water was so near now that the lower gunner drew in his projecting turret and lay down within the fuselage above; his legs, too, were covered with blood. Reyes had closed his eyes and was talking Basque. The wounded men were no longer watching the enemy fighter, from which only the scattered final bullets reached them now; they were watching the sea. Several of them could not swim—if swimming were possible with an explosive bullet in one's foot, arm or stomach. They were more than half a mile from the shore, and a hundred feet above the sea; beneath them, twelve or fourteen feet of water. The enemy fighter returned, opening fire with every gun again; the bullets wove a pattern of red streaks like a spider's web round their plane. Beneath Sembrano the clear calm morning waves threw back the sun-light complacently; the best thing was to shut one's eyes and let the plane drop slowly down, until . . . Suddenly he no-ticed Pol's face, alarmed, blood-stained, but still to all appear-ances jubilant. The bullets' red flashes surrounded the blood-soaked fuselage, in which Attignies was now bending over Reyes who was down off his seat and seemed to be *in extremis:* Pol's face, the only one of which Sembrano could get a full view, was also streaming wet; but in the smooth cheeks of the fat, vivacious Jew burned such a desire for life that the pilot made a last effort to use his right arm. The arm had disap-peared. With all the strength of his legs and left arm he pulled the plane's nose up.

Pol had lowered the wheels and now began to take them
in again; the body of the plane glided along the surface of the
water like a flying-boat; for a moment it slowed up, then
plunged deeper into the waves and capsized. They struggled
against the water which came floating into the plane, like so
many drowned cats. It stopped short of what was now the
roof of the body. Pol threw himself against the door, tried to
open it in the normal way, downwards; failed, realized that
now that they were upside down he ought to look for the
handle at the top; but the door had been jammed by an explosive bullet. Sembrano, having righted himself in the overturned
plane after seeing the pilot's cabin tilt over in front of him,
was looking for his arm in the water like a dog running after
his tail; the blood from his wound was making a bright red
stain in the already reddened water in the cabin, but his arm
was not in its right place. The lower gunner had forced a
way through one of the main panels of his turret, which had
come open during the somersault. Sembrano, Attignies, Pol
and he succeeded in getting out and at last found themselves
facing the endless stream of the exodus, with the upper halves
of their bodies in the open air and their legs in the water.

Attignies was shouting as he propped himself against the
machine. But the waves drowned his voice. Maybe the peasants
saw him beckoning to them as they fled but that was all. And
Attignies knew that each member of a crowd believes that an
appeal for help is meant for his neighbour. A peasant was
walking along the beach. Attignies crawled as far as the sand:
"Come and help them!" he shouted as soon as he was within
earshot. "Can't swim," the other answered. "It's not deep."
The peasant stood there. When he saw Attignies close beside
him, out of the water, he said at last: "I've got a family." And
moved away. It may have been true; and what help was to be
expected from a man who would leave that headlong flight to
wait patiently for the fascists? Perhaps he was suspicious; Attignies' fair and strongly moulded head looked too much like
the Malaga peasant's conception of a German pilot. In the
east, the Republican planes were just disappearing over the
tops of the mountains. "Let's hope that they'll send a car for
us . . ."

Pol and Sembrano had got all the wounded out, and had
carried them to the beach.

A group of *milicianos* broke off from the surging mass of

fugitives. Poised on the roadside embankment, and as a result much taller than the crowd, they seemed more in keeping with the rocks and heavy banks of cloud than with living things; as though nothing which did not join in the stampede could be alive. Their eyes fixed on the plane, which was burning itself out and sending short flames out of the waves that hid the colour of the wing bands, they dominated the rush of jutting shoulders and upraised hands like keepers of some legendary vigil. Between their legs, wide splayed to resist the sea-wind, the heads flowed past like dead leaves. At last they began moving down towards Attignies. "Help the wounded!" They waded out to the plane, step by step, impeded by the water. The last man stopped and took Attignies' arm on his shoulder.

"D'you know where there's a telephone?" Attignies asked him.

"Yes."

The *miliciano* belonged to the village trainband; without artillery and without machine-guns, they were going to attempt to defend their homes of rubble against the Italian motorized columns. On the road, in tacit sympathy with them, one hundred and fifty thousand unarmed citizens out of the two hundred thousand inhabitants of Malaga were flying till their last breath from "the liberator of Spain."

They stopped half way up the bank. "People who say bullet-wounds don't hurt can have this one!" thought Attignies; and the sea-water did not improve matters. Above the embankment, the bent figures were still retreating westwards; some walking, some running. In front of many mouths a fist held up an ill-defined object, as if all were playing on some silent bugle; they were eating. Some short, thick, vegetable; celery, perhaps.

"There's a field of them," said the *miliciano*. An old woman came down the bank, shrieking; went up to Attignies and held out a bottle. "The poor things, poor little lads!" She saw the others below, withdrew her bottle before Attignies had taken it, and went on down as quickly as she could, shouting the same words again and again.

Attignies trudged up the slope, leaning on the *miliciano*. Women went running past, stopped, started to scream when they saw the wounded airmen and still smouldering plane, and ran on.

"The Sunday promenade," reflected Attignies bitterly, as he

reached the road. Against the background of the noise of the flight, punctuated by the pulsing of the sea, another sound, and one which Attignies recognized, was growing more insistent every second: an enemy pursuit plane. The crowd scattered; they had already been bombed and machine-gunned.

It was making straight for the big bomber, where the last flames were dying into the sea. The *milicianos* were already carrying the wounded away; they would reach the road before the enemy plane arrived. They did their best to make the crowd lie down, but nobody heard them. On Sembrano's instructions, the *milicianos* laid the wounded at the foot of a little wall. The plane came down very low, circling over the multi-seater, which had its wheels sticking into the air and glowing sparks all over it like a chicken on a spit. A photograph was no doubt taken, and the plane flew away again. "Don't forget the lorries' wheels are sticking in the air, as well!"

A cart was passing. Attignies stopped it, and left the *miliciano's* shoulder. A peasant girl gave up her place for him, went and squatted between an old woman's legs. The cart started off again. There were five peasants in it. Nobody had asked any questions, and Attignies had not said a word: the whole world, just then, was moving in the same direction.

The *miliciano* walked beside the cart. About half a mile farther on, the road swerved away from the sea. Fires had been lighted in the fields; fires from which, as from those who sat or lay motionless round them, emanated the same sense of hideous suffering as from the flight itself. Between the fields, the unresisting mass of homeless humanity continued the forlorn migration to Almeria. The various vehicles began to get into a hopeless jam. The cart stuck.

"Is it far now?" Attignies asked.

"Nearly two miles," replied the *miliciano*.

A peasant passed them on a donkey; leaving the road all the time and slipping through gaps, the donkeys were getting along much faster.

"Lend me your donkey. I'll give him back at the post office in the village. It's for a wounded airman."

The peasant got off without a word, and took Attignies' place in the cart.

A young man and girl, students no doubt—they were rather smartly dressed—without baggage, passed the donkey. They were holding hands. Attignies realized that until then he had

seen no one except poor people in the crowd; a few artisans,
but mostly peasants. And all with Mexican blankets on their
backs. No talking: shouts, or silence.

The road entered a tunnel.

Attignies looked for his electric torch. No good taking it
out of that soaking wet pocket. Countless little lights—lamps
of all kinds, matches, torches, flares, were flashing into life
and dying out, yellow or reddish; others remained alight,
throwing out a halo, on both sides of the stream of humanity,
beasts and carts. Protected against aeroplanes, a huge cara-
vanserai of nomads had come into subterranean existence there,
between the two far-away blue discs of daylight. A rout of
shadows capered here and there around the torches and
hurricane-lamps, their heads and shoulders momentarily sil-
houetted, legs veiled in darkness. And the rumbling of carts
through the rock was like an underground river, flowing
through a silence so profound that it had imposed itself even
on the animals.

Attignies felt half stifled in the tunnel. Did the heat come
from the closely packed crowd or from the fever growing in
his blood? He must get to the telephone, yes, he must get to
the telephone. But perhaps he had died on the way there,
perhaps the cart and donkey were figments of an unexpectedly
gentle dissolution? A moment ago he had been in the water;
now he was stealing into this fast-closed world in the bowels
of the earth. An awareness more complete than the perceptions
of normal life was leading him from the blood-drenched plane
he had just left to this suffocating tunnel; everything that his
life had meant became a series of futile memories merged in
a vast, desolating torpor; the points of lights became so many
deep-sea fishes in the hot darkness, and the political commissar
was wafted, motionless and imponderable, far beyond the con-
fines of death, across a mighty river of sleep.

The daylight was getting nearer; blazing out suddenly as
the road turned a corner, it vivified his body as if its rays had
been ice-cold. He was amazed to find everything still there,
the telephone obsession, his throbbing foot, the donkey between his legs. Now that he had survived both the battle in
the air and the crash, he felt the shadows giving place once
more to the mystery of life. Once more the tawny soil of
Spain rose up around the flood of fugitives, as far as the
Mediterranean, with black goats standing on the rocks.

Its cohesion sorely tried, the crowd surged around the first

village, leaving innumerable evidences of its passage round the
first houses, as the ebb-tide reveals a beach littered with pebbles and débris. A motley of costumes, with weapons jutting
out here and there, was penned between the walls like a herd
within a corral. The exodus was becoming less like an irre-
sistible avalanche: it was just a mob, now.

Thanks to the *miliciano,* Attignies, still on his donkey,
managed to reach the telephone. The wires had been cut.

When the wounded had been laid out in a row beneath the
wall, Pol asked the *miliciano* where he could find lorries. "At
the farms; but there's no petrol!" He had run to the nearest
farm, and found a lorry with an empty tank. Coming back
with a bucket, still at a run, he had managed to drain off
some of the petrol which remained in the plane's undamaged
tank. He had made his way back to the farm, keeping the
bucket level, compelled to make slow progress on the fringe
of the incessant stream of peasants, and expecting every moment the arrival of the lorries which were certainly following
those which he had destroyed that morning. He tried to start
the engine; the magneto had been put out of action.

He ran to the second farm. Imagining that Attignies would
be hampered by the prevailing confusion, Sembrano was counting on their finding a lorry rather than on one being sent. In
that country-house-like farm, bare of furniture, where the
earthenware, in a mixed Spanish and Moorish style, and the
pseudo-romantic frescos with their painted parrots seemed to
await impending incineration, the muffled murmur of the
fleeing mob became more ominously suggestive of the enemy's
arrival. This time Sembrano came with him, using his left
arm to support the right arm which had been shattered by a
Spanish machine-gunner. When they found the lorry, Sembrano lifted the hood; the gas-line had been cut. The lorries
had been systematically put out of action in order to prevent
their being used by the fascists. Sembrano drew back from
the hood and straightened himself, mouth open and eyes half-
closed like a picture of Voltaire after assassination; then
staggered on like a groggy boxer towards the next farm, mouth
still gaping.

In the middle of a field, he heard someone shout his name;
the Spanish machine-gunner, plump and rotund as a rosy-
cheeked apple, still smeared with blood, was leaping and hop-

ping over the ground towards him. Attignies had brought back
a lorry. Republican pursuit planes had notified the hospital.
Sembrano and Pol put the wounded on the floor and the seat
at the back; the machine-gunner stayed with them.

A doctor, the chief of the Canadian blood-transfusion
service, had come also.

Since their plane crashed, not one of the airmen had mentioned the arrival of the fascists; and no doubt each of them,
like Attignies, had constantly before him that picture of the
motorized column bombed outside Malaga.

Overloaded in front, the car seemed empty behind; every
half-mile it was stopped by *milicianos* who wanted to put
women on board, but saw the wounded as they stepped on the
running-board, and got off again. At first the crowd had
thought that the Committees were in flight; then, seeing
wounded piled inside each seemingly empty car, they had
begun to watch them passing with looks of sad solicitude.
Reyes' breath was rattling in his throat. "We'll try transfu-
sions," the doctor said to Attignies, "but I haven't much hope."
So many men lay stretched beside the road that it was impossible to distinguish the wounded from those who were asleep. A
number of women lay across the road itself; the doctor got out
and spoke to them; they stood up, let the car pass without a
word, and lay down to wait for the next one.

An old man, all nerves and sinews, with the strongly gnarled
features peculiar to aged peasants, was calling for help. He
carried a child only a few months old in the crook of his left
arm. There were plenty of equally pitiful cases along that
road. But perhaps a young child appeals to human sympathy
more poignantly than anything else. The doctor had the car
stopped, despite the desperate condition of Reyes. It was impossible to take the peasant inside. He settled himself down on
a fender, still with the child in his left arm; but he found
nothing to hold on to. From his place on the other fender
Pol was able to hold on to the door handle with his right hand;
his left hand he stretched across to the peasant, who gripped
it firmly. The driver was obliged to sit bolt upright in his seat
as the two hands met in front of the windshield.

Attignies and the doctor could not take their eyes off them.
In theatre or cinema love-scenes invariably made the doctor
feel like an eavesdropper. And it was the same here; there
was something about this working man from another land
gripping the wrist of the old Andalusian peasant, while a whole

populace in flight surged around them, which made him ill at ease. He made an effort not to look at them. Yet something fundamental in him remained linked to those hands—that same part of him which had caused the driver to stop the car a moment before, that which recognized maternity, childhood and death even in their most incongruous aspects.

"Halt!" shouted a *miliciano*. The driver did not slow down. The *miliciano* aimed his rifle at the car. "Wounded airmen!" the driver shouted. The man sprang on to the running-board.

"Stop, blast you!"

"I tell you they're wounded airmen, you bloody fool! Haven't you any eyes?"

Some more amenities, missed by those inside, were exchanged between the men. The *miliciano* fired; the driver toppled forward over the wheel. The car all but crashed into a tree. The *miliciano* jammed on the brake, jumped down, and made off along the road.

An anarchist soldier with a red-and-black cap and a sword at his side jumped on to the lorry. "Why did that imbecile stop you?"

"I haven't any idea," Attignies answered.

The anarchist jumped to the ground and ran after the *miliciano*. Both of them disappeared behind the trees, dark forms against the sunlight. The car was stranded. None of the wounded could drive. Suddenly the anarchist reappeared, like an actor entering abruptly from the wings; his sword was red. He crossed to the lorry, laid the dead driver by the roadside, took his seat and drove off without a word. Ten minutes later he turned round, showing the bloodstained sword.

"Swine. Enemy of the people. No more trouble from him!"

Sembrano shrugged his shoulders; he was utterly weary of death. Offended, the anarchist turned away.

Thereafter he ostentatiously refrained from looking at the men in the car, driving with elaborate care, even to the point of trying to minimize the jolting.

"Nice guy, isn't he?" Pol said in French, his face only a few inches away from the red-and-black *képi*. "You got to come to Spain to find that sort. When he's finished sulking, I suppose he'll tell us all about it."

Attignies glanced at the anarchist's face, set and scowling, behind the hands linked across the windshield.

At last they reached the hospital.

An empty hospital, but still littered with surgical instru-

ments and bandages—vestiges of the suffering it had har-
boured. The empty hollows in the unmade, often bloodstained,
beds were such a vivid reminder of the sentient beings who
had occupied them only a short while before, that it seemed
as if not living or dying men had been lying in them but dis-
embodied wounds—blood doing duty for an arm, a head, a
leg. The steady, unwinking glare of the electric lights seemed
to weigh on the room, giving it an air of unreality; the white
expanse of beds and walls might almost have been the figment
of a dream, but for the brutal realism of the bloodstains and,
here and there, a body. Three cases too serious to be moved
lay waiting for the fascists, their revolvers beside them.

There was nothing for those men to do but wait for death;
whether from their own hands or from their enemies', unless
the relieving aeroplanes turned up in time. They silently
studied the new arrivals: Pol with the fuzzy hair, Sembrano
with the projecting underlip, and the others in such agony that
all personal traits were blotted out. And the ward seemed to
grow vibrant with the fellowship that links the victims of a
great disaster.

2

Guadalajara

FORTY thousand Italians in completely mechanized units, with
tanks and aeroplanes, had broken through the Republican
front at Villaviciosa. Their plan of campaign was to work
down the valleys of the Ingria and the Tajuna, take Guadalajara, and Alcala de Henares, and link up with Franco's South-
ern army, checked at Aranda, thus completely cutting off
Madrid.

Flushed with their victory at Malaga, the Italians had
found fewer than five thousand men in front of them. But at
Malaga the *milicianos* had fought no better than at Toledo;
here they were fighting as they had fought at Madrid. On the
eleventh the Spaniards, the Poles, the Germans, the Franco-
Belgians, and the Garibaldi contingent from the First Brigade
—one against eight—checked the flood of Italians from both
sides of the Saragossa and Brihuega roads.

As the first pale rays of daylight slid under the heavy snowclouds, shells began to smash into the copses and the open

woodland from which the German Edgar André Battalion and the new volunteers hastily sent forward were operating. Uprooted by a single shell, entire olive-trees were flung into the air, zooming up to the snow-laden clouds and coming down like rockets on the surrounding branches with a noise of rustling paper.

The first wave of Italians arrived. "Comrades," said a political commissar, "in ten minutes the fate of the Republic will be decided." Every man in the heavy machine-gun section stood to his gun, withdrawing its breech-bolt just before he died. The Republicans managed to construct a line of defence despite the fire, and to protect their flanks.

Sometimes the fascist shells failed to explode.

The commissar appointed to the new company stood up:

"Hurrah for the munition-workers shot at Milan for sabotage!"

They all stood up, the munition-workers among them a little skeptically; they knew that in any case shells do not always explode.

Then came the fascist tanks.

But the International Column and the dynamite-squads had got used to tanks at the battle of the Jarama. When the tanks reached a stretch of open country, the Germans fell back among the trees and refused to budge. The tanks had machine-guns, but so had they; vainly the tanks slunk up and down in front of the compact wall of trees, like monstrous dogs, and now and again a small oak was projected violently skywards.

From the battered wood, the machine-guns of the Flemish contingent mowed down the lines of advancing fascists. "As long as we've the stuff to go on pumping out like this, we're all right," bawled the corps-commander amid the thunder of artillery and rifle-fire, the intense drumming of machine-guns, the detonations of explosive bullets, the high-pitched screeching of shells from the tanks and the sinister drone of the aeroplanes which found the clouds were hanging too low to allow them to emerge.

In the evening the Italians attacked with flame-throwers, which met with no more success than the tanks.

On the twelfth, the Italian shock-troops attacked again, meeting the brigades of the Fifth Corps: Manuel's, and the French and German. When the day ended, the Italians were concentrated on a narrow strip of ground, with their commu-

nications blocked. Their heavy artillery and their rations were
no longer reaching the front, and snow was beginning to fall.
The road was still in danger; but the Italian army not less so.

On the thirteenth, the snow ceased and men died from the
cold.

During the night the Spanish brigade from Madrid arrived
as reinforcements, together with a fresh draft from the International Column and the Ximenez carabineers. The Republicans were only outnumbered by two to one, now. The
International units came into the firing-line equipped, if not
well armed; but meanwhile, Manuel's men and the Lister
Brigade moving up on the other side of the road were wearing
light canvas shoes. Never during their three months at the
front together had Siry and Maringaud (now in the Franco-
Belgian battalion) felt so close to the Spaniards as on that
glacial March evening when the people's army marched
steadily towards the shell-shaken horizon, marching through
the night in their ragged sandals until the snow came. When,
at times, one gun quickened its rate of fire, a dozen others
took up the challenge, like the dogs in the Guadalajara farms,
in other days. The louder the noise of the guns grew, the
closer the men huddled against each other.

On the fourteenth, Manuel and the Fifth Corps attacked
and captured Trijueque. The enemy's other flank was protected by the Ibarra Palace, where there were submachine-guns
behind every window; it was being attacked since two o'clock
in the afternoon by the Franco-Belgians and the Garibaldi
contingent.

Sixty per cent of the Garibaldi contingent were more than
forty-five years of age.

From the wood they could see nothing of the low, flat
palace now except short flames, glimpsed through the dusk
and the snow which had begun again. The firing was slacken-
ing; they could distinguish separate shots again. And a mighty
voice, transcending the human voice as artillery predominates
over rifle-fire, began to boom out in Italian:

*"Comrades, workers and peasants from Italy, why are you
fighting against us? The noise that will cut off this loud-speaker
from your ears means death. Will you die to prevent the
workers and peasants of Spain from living a life of freedom?
You have been misled. We . . ."*

The voice of the Republican loud-speaker was lost in the
thunder of unleashed guns and grenades. Four-cornered, like

a gasoline-tank lying flat, larger than the lorry which carried it, it was almost alone behind the screen of trees. Abandoned, but living because it spoke. With a range of more than a mile and speaking very slowly so that the words were clear, the stentorian voice blared out like the last trumpet through the empty, darkening forest, the bullet-shattered branches and the interminable snow.

"Comrades, those of you who are prisoners with us will tell you that the 'Red scum' welcomed them with open arms, arms still bleeding from the wounds which you have inflicted . . ."

A fascist patrol was advancing through the snow in the part of the wood dominated by the loud-speaker. Another burst of firing; one of the fascists fell.

"Put your hands up," came a shout in Italian, during a second of silence.

"Cease fire, you dumb bastards," the officer shouted back. "It's us!"

"Put your hands up!"

"I tell you it's us!"

"We know that. Put up your hands!"

"Put up your own."

"We shall count three, then fire."

The patrol was beginning to realize that the Italians who were answering them were on the enemy side.

"One. Surrender."

"Never."

"Two. Surrender."

The patrol threw down their arms.

The Garibaldi contingent were attacking the palace from one side, the Franco-Belgians from the other. A rocket soared above the wood, showing up black branches against the driving snow. A tree with low, serried branches seemed to jump into the air. As it fell to earth far away with a noise of snapping wood, Siry saw five of his comrades run, four of them fall, the head of the man on his right disappear, and bullets ploughing the ground on all sides. The outstretched hand of a man who was pointing at something was bleeding as he drew it back. Even before he realized that now that the tree had disappeared he was under fire from one of the windows of the Ibarra Palace, Siry was off at top speed, contracting his back muscles to stop the bullets from penetrating. Common sense suddenly returning, he flung himself flat on his stomach in front of a lieutenant who raised himself from his prone position and immediately fell back with a surprised groan: "A—ah!" "What is the matter with him?" said Siry, half to himself. "Wounded?" "Dead," a voice answered.

Siry and the others had got as far as the wall of the palace; but the considerable gap made by the demolition of the tree was drawing the fire from twenty windows, each furnished with submachine-guns. The soldiers began to retire, crawling back, pressed to the ground, as if they had all been hit in the stomach.

There was one man dragging another along who was wriggling like a cockchafer; moving back slowly, with a look of terror on his face, but refusing to abandon his friend. His head pillowed on his left arm, Siry could hear through the incessant detonations of artillery, rifles, machine-guns and explosive bullets, the almost imperceptible ticking of his watch; as long as he heard that sound he was still alive. He had a confused feeling of something discreditable to be hidden, reminiscent of his fear of the keeper, in former days, when he was filching pears. At last he reached cover, at the same time as the wounded man and his rescuer.

Maringaud was within ten yards of the wall protecting the palace: one could throw hand-grenades from there. In the darkness and the snow the enemy shots, coming from the ground level and from every window, crackled like flames above the crest of the wall. Firing, firing away at the red flashes and the detonations, Maringaud felt more at ease. Someone bent forward behind him; it was the Captain. "Don't make such a row: it gives away your position." One of the Internationals was hanging with both hands from the palace wall; dead no doubt. Maringaud went on firing; on his right some of the others were advancing, through the din of submachine-guns, grenades, the shouting and the shells. Another rocket soared through the trees, lighting up the grenades bursting convulsively, branches and a bodiless arm with outstretched fingers. Maringaud's rifle was burning hot. He laid it on the snow and began to throw the grenades which a wounded comrade handed to him. Another man was opening and shutting his mouth like a suffocating fish. Three more were firing. Two yards to go: he was close up to the wall now, with his grenades; between his lips a cigarette which he imagined he was smoking.

"What in hell are they playing at on the left?" a voice shouted imperiously through the snow. "Quicken your fire!"

"They're dead," another voice answered.

The bravest of the fascists were trying to defend the wall, and it seemed to their crack shots that they had lost their aim, for the Garibaldi contingent and the Franco-Belgians, maddened alike by battle lust and the snow, hurled themselves frenziedly against the wall and kept standing there for several seconds after they had been hit. Gusts of shrill, eerie shouting burst suddenly from the palace and the wood, but there was a momentary silence when, in the light of a rocket, the fascists and the riff-raff gathered from the remotest corners of Sicily saw the grey-moustached veterans of the Garibaldi contingent charging down upon them through the blue-lit snow. Then the racket began again. Once more—whether it was that the attackers had reached the wall, or that that brief, inexplicable hush which sometimes falls on public gatherings or crowded cafés occurs in war as well—the furious din of the explosions seemed suddenly to be borne aloft with the whirling snowflakes which a fierce wind was flinging back into the black sky. And then (the loud-speaker had been waiting for this lull) the fascists, the Garibaldi unit and the Franco-Belgians heard a stentorian voice.

Listen, comrades! It's not true, what we were told. It's Angelo speaking. For one thing they've got tanks; I've seen them. And guns! And Generals! A General questioned us. They don't shoot you, not a bit of it! It's Angelo, your comrade Angelo, speaking. We've been taken in; we're being used as cannon-fodder, all of us! Come over, boys; this is the side for us!

Siry was back at the wall, listening. The Garibaldi contingent were listening. Maringaud and the Franco-Belgians were guessing what was meant. Every fascist submachine-gun in the palace replied. The wind had slackened and the snow was falling again, heavily, impartially.

From the corner of the wall where he was standing Siry could see under the trees in the distance some little houses. Those on the right were held by the Republicans, those on the left by the fascists. And sounding faint after the loud-speaker, like the wails of wounded men, the voices of some of last night's prisoners, who had joined the Garibaldi unit, came to him through the snowflakes.

"Carlo, Carlo, don't play the damned fool, don't stay with

them. It's me, Guido. You needn't be afraid, I'll fix everything."

"Lousy bastards, dirty traitors!"

An order; a ripple of fire from the submachine-guns.

"Bruno, they're our comrades, don't fire!"

The tumult rose and fell as though the tide of battle flowed
and ebbed with the great wind churning up the flurries of
the blizzard. Maringaud flung his last hand-grenade and
picked up his rifle. It was instantly wrenched from his hand,
and simultaneously his three companions were swept away in
a sheet of flame. He ran to the wall, pressed himself against
it, and picked up the rifle of the soldier who was clinging
with both hands to the stones.

It stopped snowing.

There was a sudden silence again, as if the elements were
stronger than the war, as if the peace which fell from the
winter sky, no longer muffled by the snowflakes, had imposed
itself upon the battle.

The moon had just appeared through a great rift in the
clouds and for the first time the snow, blue till now in the
glare of the rockets, showed up white. To the rear of the
foremost International units, across a maze of little dividing
walls at different levels, the Poles were attacking with cold
steel. Not in a body, but split up into small groups, protected
by the low walls half buried in the snow. The Franco-Belgians
and the Garibaldi contingent could hardly see them. But when
the bayonet attack was over they could distinctly hear their
fire coming nearer, as the almost invisible ranks whose firing
line was stubbornly progressing, amid the wild clangour of
detonations and explosions, as an underground attack might
have advanced, through a huge, soft veil of tiny snowflakes
poised in the moonlight, scaled the towering slopes of snow
like some strange cavalcade of superhuman warriors sent by
the gods to earth.

In the distance, Siry heard the unintelligible staccato ut-
terances of a Spanish loud-speaker through which old Barca,
Manuel's and Garcia's friend, was talking.

Suddenly Siry and Maringaud, and the Franco-Belgians,
and the Garibaldi unit fighting next to them, wondered if
they were going mad; from the palace a song that they knew
well came floating down. The Column was attacking from
three sides, and other units might have reached the interior
of the palace while they had been checked at the wall; but

they all remembered the singing of the *Internationale* at the battle of Jarama by the fascists who later assailed their trenches. "Throw down your arms first!" they shouted. There was no reply: the bombardment was still going on, the intensity of the firing was diminishing, snow was streaming down more heavily again. Yet just visible across the blizzard, the windows of the palace were empty of red flashes; and the singing was going on. In French or Italian? Impossible to distinguish a single word. They were no longer being fired at. And the loud-speaker shouted through the lopped trees, in Spanish: "Cease fire. The Ibarra Palace has been captured."

3

The next evening, Levant front

THE aerodrome telephone had been fixed up in a sentry-box. Holding the receiver to his ear, Magnin was watching the *Canard* land, outlined by the dust-laden rays of the setting sun.

"Headquarters speaking. Have you got two machines ready to go up?"

"Yes."

In use every day against Teruel, repaired with bad spare parts, the machines had become as unreliable as at Talavera. The breakdown squad were constantly busy with the carburetors.

"Commandant Garcia is sending you a peasant from up north of Albaracin who came through the fascist lines last night. It seems that there's a landing-ground for planes next to his village. And lots of them there. No underground shelters."

"I don't believe in their underground shelters. Any more than in our own. I said so in my report yesterday. Our bombing of the aerodrome on the Saragossa road was a failure simply because the planes are hidden in fields used as secret landing-grounds; not because they were in underground shelters."

"We are sending you the peasant. Decide whether the scheme is feasible, and call us back."

"Hullo!"

"Hullo?"

"Has the peasant got anybody to vouch for him?"

"The commandant. And his syndicate, I believe."

Half an hour later the peasant arrived, escorted by an N.C.O. from headquarters. Magnin took his arm and began pacing the field with him. The planes were finishing their test-flights in the fading light.

Dusk was descending on the sea and the flying ground, a wide, open expanse stretching as far as the hills, bathed in the peace of evening. Where had Magnin seen that face before? Everywhere; every Spanish dwarf had it. But this man was strongly built, and taller than he.

"You crossed the lines to warn us. We must all thank you for that."

The peasant smiled, a gentle hunchback's smile.

"Where are the planes?"

"They're in the wood." The peasant raised his forefinger. "In the wood." He looked at the wide glades between the olive-trees where the Republican planes were hidden. "In glades like that, just the same. But much deeper hidden, because it's a real wood."

"What's the flying-ground like?"

"Where they fly up into the air?"

"Yes."

"Not like this."

Magnin took out his notebook. The peasant drew a picture of the field.

"Very narrow?"

"Not wide. But the soldiers are working hard on it. They are going to make it larger."

"Which way does it face?"

The peasant shut his eyes and turned from side to side.

"It faces to the east wind."

"H'm . . . I see. Then the wood is on the west side of the field? You're certain?"

"Absolutely sure."

Magnin glanced at the wind-cone above the olive-trees. The wind was coming from the west. On a small aerodrome, however, aeroplanes take off into the wind. If the wind was blowing from the same direction at Teruel, the planes there would have to take off with the wind behind them, if attacked.

"Do you remember where the wind was yesterday?"

"North-west. It looked like rain was coming."

So the planes were certain to be still there. If the wind stayed the same, everything would be just right.

"How many planes?"

The peasant had a spur-like "quiff" in the middle of his forehead; he reminded Magnin of a macaw. Now he raised his forefinger again.

"I counted—my counting, you understand—six little ones. And some of the others managed to make a count, too. They don't all say the same; they say there are at least as many big ones. At least. Perhaps more."

Magnin thought for a minute. He took out his map, but, as he supposed, the peasant could not read.

"It's something quite new for me. But take me up in your contraption, and I'll show you. I'll take you straight there."

Magnin understood why Garcia had vouched for the peasant.

"Have you ever been up before?"

"No."

"You won't get panicky?"

He did not quite understand.

"You won't be afraid?"

He thought it over.

"No."

"You'll recognize the field all right?"

"I've lived twenty-eight years in the village. And I've worked in towns, too. You find me the Saragossa road and I'll find you the field. Without any trouble at all."

Magnin sent the peasant to the château and telephoned headquarters again.

"It seems that there are about ten enemy machines, or thereabouts. . . .

"It would obviously be best to attack at dawn; but to-morrow morning I shall have two transport machines and no fighters; all the fighters are at Guadalajara. I know the district pretty well, and the stake is a considerable one. There are nearly always clouds over there just now. . . . My idea therefore is to phone Sarion for a weather report at five in the morning, and, if the sky is at all overcast, make a start."

"Colonel Vargas will leave it to you to decide. If you should go, he would place Captain Moros' plane at your disposal. Don't forget that there may be pursuit planes at Sarion."

"Good. Thanks . . . Ah! another thing. Starting at night is all very well, but there are no ground-lights. Have you any beacons?"

"No."

"You are sure?"

"I'm being asked for them all day long."

"What about the Ministry?"

"Same thing."

"Oh. Lorries, then?"

"All in use."

"Right. I'll see what I can fix up myself."

He telephoned to the War Ministry; the same answer.

So he would have to take off at night from a small unlighted landing ground. With cars on three sides, it might be all right. But the lorries had still to be found.

Magnin took his own car and started off, in the dark now, for the nearest village Committee.

Requisitioned objects of all kinds were piled up on the floor: sewing-machines, pictures, springs, beds and a mass of harness, among which the projecting handles of tools caught the light of the lamps standing on a table at the far end of the room. Magnin was reminded of the organized chaos of an auction room. The peasants filed one by one past the table. Someone in charge approached Magnin.

"I need some cars," said the latter, giving him his hand.

The peasant delegate raised his arms discouragingly, but said nothing. Magnin knew these village delegates well; seldom young, earnest, shrewd (half their time was spent in defending the Committee against uninvited assistance) and almost always efficient.

"It's like this," Magnin said. "We have made a new aerodrome. There are no beacons yet, I mean no lights for take-offs and landings at night. There's only one thing to do: mark out a small area with motor headlights. The Ministry haven't any lorries. Staff headquarters haven't any lorries. You have. You must lend them to me for tonight."

"I ought to have a dozen and I've got five, three of which are only light ones. How do you expect me to lend them? If it was a question of one, perhaps . . ."

"One's no good. If our aeroplanes get to Teruel, they'll stop the fascists. If not, it's the fascists who will get there and the militia who will be wiped out. You understand. That's why lorries are wanted, light ones or otherwise. It is a question of life or death for our comrades up there. Listen now, what are they used for?"

"Nothing so important as that! Only, you see, we aren't

allowed to lend them without drivers, and the drivers have done a fifteen-hour day and . . ."

"If they want to sleep in them, I don't mind. I can have them driven by mechanics from the aerodrome. I'll talk to them if you want me to, and I'm sure they'll agree; and they'll agree if you explain to them yourself what is at stake."

"What time do you want them?"

"Four o'clock tomorrow morning."

The delegate discussed the situation with two others behind the table with the paraffin lamps, then came back.

"We'll do what we can. I promise you three, more if possible."

Magnin went on through the darkness from one village to another, from rooms littered with every kind of object to large whitewashed ones where delegates and peasants in black blouses cast a tracery of shadows on the walls: through squares coloured like stage sets, more and more deserted, where the café lights and the few gas jets still burning threw large iridescent reflections onto the violet domes of the secularized churches. The villages possessed twenty-three vehicles of various kinds. He had been promised nine of them.

It was half-past two in the morning, when he passed through the first village again on his return. In the half-light which outlined the façade of the house occupied by the Committee there were men carrying sacks, one behind the other, as if they were coaling a ship; they were crossing the road to enter the town hall, and Magnin's chauffeur had to stop. One of them passed close in front of the hood bending under the weight of a side of beef.

"What are they?" Magnin asked a peasant sitting on his doorstep.

"The volunteers."

"What volunteers?"

"The food volunteers. Transport volunteers have been called for. Our lorries have gone to the flying ground, to help Madrid."

When Magnin got back to the aerodrome, the first cars were arriving. By half-past four, twelve large and six light lorries were there, with drivers. Several had brought hurricane lamps, on the off chance.

"Isn't there any other job we could do?"

One of the volunteers was muttering vituperations, without anybody quite knowing why.

He allotted them places, and gave them instructions not to switch on their headlights until they heard the engines of the planes, and returned to the château.

Vargas was waiting for him.

"Magnin, Garcia says that there are more than fifteen machines in that field."

"All the better."

"No: because in that case they are for Madrid. You know an attack on Guadalajara started the day before yesterday. They broke through at Villaviciosa; we're holding them round Brihuega. They're trying to take Arganda."

"Who are 'they?' "

"Four Italian mechanised divisions, with tanks, planes and everything!"

From the sixth to the twentieth of the previous month, in the bloodiest battle of the war, the German high command had attempted to capture Arganda from the south.

"I'll start at dawn," Vargas said.

"See you soon," Magnin replied, touching the wooden butt of his revolver.

It was five o'clock, and the chill which precedes dawn had descended. Magnin wanted coffee. In front of the lime-washed château, blue in the darkness, his car was lighting up one of the orchards where vague forms, members of the Column waiting to start, could be seen roaming among the trees, picking the dew-drenched oranges that glimmered pale as hoar-frost. At the end of the field, the lorries waited in the gloom.

During the fall-in, Magnin explained their objective to the commanders of the planes who would give the orders when the machines were in flight. He made sure that all the machine-gunners had their gloves. Behind the lorry which had lit up the oranges and which was deputed to keep the planes in touch with each other until the last possible moment, the crews were crossing the field still fragrant with the scents of night; they were impeded by their flying-kits, like young dogs on the leash.

Slender wings barely perceptible against the sky, the aeroplanes waited. Dazzled by the unaccustomed lights, discouraged rather than roused by the wind which flung back in their faces the icy water with which they had sprinkled themselves, the men trudged along in silence. In the cold with which night-flights begin, each man knows that he is taking his life in his hands.

With pocket torches to help them, the mechanics had begun their work. The engines of the first plane were warming up. At the far end of the field, two headlights cut suddenly through the wall of darkness.

Two more: the lorries had heard the engines of the planes. Magnin could just make out the hills in the distance, and high above him, the nose of a large machine; then the wing of another plane, above the bluish sheen of a revolving propeller. Two more lights came on from the lorries marking one of the boundaries of the field. Behind were the tangerine-woods; and in the same direction, Teruel. In the distance, near the cemetery and among the frozen mountain torrents, an International Brigade was awaiting the attack, with the anarchists whose cloaks made them seem almost like Mexicans.

Fires were being kindled with dried oranges. Their sputtering red flames were drowned by the blaze from the headlights, but the wind wafted their bitter smell across the field, in intermittent smoke-like gusts. One by one, the lights were coming on. Magnin remembered the peasant with a skinned side of beef on his back, and all the volunteers loading the depot as if it were a ship. They were coming on now on all three sides at once, linked by the orange fires with the cloaks moving to and fro around them. For a moment the planes were silent and the individual engines of the eighteen lorries from the villages could be heard running. In the vast central mass of darkness unpenetrated by the beams of light, the hidden planes, whose engines suddenly all began to roar at once, seemed to represent the contribution of the collective peasantry of Spain that night to the protection of Guadalajara.

Magnin was the last to leave. The three planes from Teruel circled over the field, looking for each other's navigation lights before getting into formation. Beneath them, the trapezium-shaped flying-ground, quite small now, was merging into the trackless immensity of night which to Magnin seemed converging on the humble orange fires. The three transport planes were veering round. Magnin switched on his pocket-torch and checked the peasant's sketch against a map. A biting draught was sweeping in through the opening in the turret underneath the body. "In five minutes I shall have to put on my gloves: no good trying to use a pencil." The three planes were in formation. Magnin headed for Teruel. With the wind still carrying the smell of the burning oranges from the field, and the interior of the plane still in darkness, the rising sun showed up the merry, ruddy features of the gunner in the lower turret.

"Hullo, chief!"

Magnin could not take his eyes off the laughter-widened mouth, with the broken teeth, so oddly pink in the first rays of the rising sun. It was getting lighter in the plane. Down on the ground it was still dark. The planes were approaching the first barrier of mountains through the uncertain light; below, vague frontiers like primitive maps were beginning to be discernible. "Unless their machines are in the air, we're arriving absolutely at the right moment." Magnin could just distinguish some farm roofs now: day was breaking on the earth below.

Magnin had done so much fighting on this Teruel front that jutted southwards in a narrow strip like the Malay peninsula, that he knew it all by heart and kept his bearings unconsciously.

Machine-gunners and mechanics, nervous as usual before going into action, stopped looking at Teruel and began furtively to eye the peasant. Their covert glances saw a macaw-like tuft of hair kept obstinately lowered among the flying-helmets, or, for a moment, a terrified face with the teeth gnawing the lips.

The enemy batteries were not firing; the planes were sheltered by the clouds. Down on the ground, it was probably quite light. On the right Magnin could see the *Canard Déchâiné* commanded by Gardet; on the left Captain Moros' Spanish bombing plane; both were slightly behind him, linked to the *Marat* like two arms to a body, keeping their formation in the vast peaceful spread of sky, between the sun and the sea of clouds. Every time a flock of birds passed beneath the machine, the peasant signed to them with his finger. One after another, the curved black humps of the mountains round Teruel were left behind them; and on their right, sparkling white beneath the winter sun, brighter than the duskier white of the clouds beneath, was the huge mass which the airmen called the "snow-mountain." Magnin had grown used now to the primordial peace of that high world so aloof from man's restless strivings; but this time the world of men still imposed itself even up there. The impassivity of the sea of clouds could not dominate those aeroplanes flying wing to wing through the air together against their common enemy; united in their present comradeship, and in the face of the perils ambushed all round them in the peaceful sky, no less united: could not overshadow those men ready, one and all, to die for something higher than themselves, comrades whose compasses were set upon the same fateful course. Teruel would no doubt be visible beneath the clouds. But Magnin preferred to keep above them, in order not to give the alarm. "We shall be going lower in a minute," he shouted in the peasant's ear; he felt that the latter was wondering how he was to guide them when he could see nothing.

Elongated patches followed one after another until the bright steep crest-line of the Pyrenees showed up, like dark lakes in the snow gliding towards them. Once more, they could only wait.

The planes began to turn, with the steady, menacing persistence of war-machines. Now they were over the enemy lines.

At last a grey stain seemed to spread through the clouds. Roofs appeared through it, now on one edge of the stain and now on the other, like goldfish motionless against a moving background; then veins became paths, but still only two-dimensional. More roofs and an enormous pale circle: the bull-ring. And immediately, yellow and red in the leaden light, a vast shell of roofs filled the hole in the clouds. Magnin gripped the peasant by the shoulder:

"Teruel."

He failed to understand.

"That's Teruel!" Magnin bawled in his ear.

The town was growing bigger through the grey hole, isolated among the clouds which billowed away to the horizon, set in the midst of its countryside, river and railway-lines, growing clearer every minute.

"Is *that* Teruel? Is *that* Teruel?"

Shaking his mane of hair, the peasant was staring at the confused, scarred map beneath him.

Pale in the early light, the Saragossa road stood out from the darker background of the fields, to the north of the cemetery which the Republican army was attacking. Sure of his position, Magnin mounted above the clouds again immediately.

Keeping a straight course, the planes followed the Saragossa road which they could not see. The peasant's village was twenty-five miles away, a little to the right. The other aerodrome, unsuccessfully bombarded on the previous day, was half as far. They were probably flying over it now. Magnin was calculating the distance they had to go by seconds. Unless they found the second field very quickly, the alarm might be given and they would have on top of them not only the enemy chasers from both Saragossa and Calamocita and the hidden aerodrome, but those from this one too, if there were any there, barring their return. The clouds were their only protection. Twenty miles from Teruel, twenty-two, twenty-four, twenty-five: the plane dived.

The battle seemed already to have begun with their entry into the white cloud-mist. Magnin had his eye on the altimeter. There were no more hills now on that part of the front. But were there pursuit planes waiting beneath the cloudbank? The peasant had his nose glued to the window. The thick line of the road began to appear, painted on a pale background of mist; then the red houses of the village, staining the clouds like dried bloodstains on a bandage. No pursuit planes or anti-aircraft batteries yet. But to the east of the village were several long fields, all bordered on the same side by small woods.

No time to turn. They were all straining forward, peering. The plane flew over the church. They were taking a line parallel to the main street. Magnin took the peasant by the shoulder again and pointed out the roofs flashing by beneath them, bunched together like a herd of cattle. His mouth half-open, and tears zigzagging down his cheeks, one by one, the peasant was straining every nerve to see where they were. He could recognize nothing.

"The church!" Magnin shouted. "The main street! The Saragossa road!"

The peasant recognized them when Magnin pointed them out, but could not get his bearings. His chin was quivering convulsively beneath his stolid, tear-stained cheeks.

There was only one thing to do: to approach at an angle from which things would look familiar to him.

The earth rushed violently up towards the plane, swaying from right to left as if it had lost its balance, sweeping from its path a flight of panicked birds. Magnin was down to within a hundred feet of the ground.

The *Canard* and the Spanish plane followed in line.

The ground was flat. Magnin had nothing serious to fear from the ground defences; as for the small-calibre quick firers, if there was a battery protecting the aerodrome, it would be unable to fire so low. He nearly ordered the machine-gunners to open fire, but was afraid of unnerving the peasant. Skimming the ground, their angle of vision was that of a racing motorcar as they approached the woods. The cattle scattered frantically beneath them. The peasant peered in all directions as if his life depended on it. He seized Magnin by the middle of his flying-suit and pointed at something.

"What? Where?"

Magnin tore off his flying helmet.

"There!"

"What, for Christ's sake!"

The peasant was pushing him to the left with all his strength, as if Magnin were the plane, and pointing at a black and yellow hoarding advertising vermouth, dabbing at the mica window first in one place then in another.

"Which one?"

Six hundred yards beyond were four patches of trees. The peasant was still pushing him to the left. The clump of trees farthest to the left.

"Is that it?"

Magnin stared wildly. Eyelids fluttering, the peasant was screaming incoherently.

"Is that it?"

The peasant nodded head and shoulders in assent, without moving his outstretched arm. At that very moment a bright circle of light sprang to life at the edge of the wood, showing up against the dark background of leaves. It was a revolving propeller. An enemy chaser was coming out into the open.

The bomber turned round. He had seen it, too. Too late to drop bombs, and they were too low. The forward machine-gunner, who might have fired, had seen nothing.

"Open fire on the wood!" Magnin bellowed to the man in the lower turret, at that instant catching sight of a big bomber out in the open near the wood.

The gunner worked his pedals to swing the pit on the right line, and fired. The chaser was already hidden from their field of vision by the trees.

But Gardet had realized that these unrehearsed tactics would require a maximum of vigilance if they were to come off. He had taken charge of the forward gun of the *Canard* some minutes before, and was keeping his eyes glued to the *Marat*. He caught sight of the gleaming propeller against the dark green background of the wood; almost immediately he saw the firing from the *Marat's* lower gun; muttered: "Just a minute, now!" and opened fire.

His tracer bullets showed the whereabouts of the Fiat to Scali, who was handling the *Canard's* lower gun. He had given up bombing for machine-gunning as a concession to the urgency of the problems which now confronted him; passivity was no longer endurable. In the rear turret, Mireaux was prevented from firing by the tail. But Moros' plane was able to bring all three guns to bear.

Rising and banking, Magnin saw the propeller of the enemy plane cease turning as he passed over it again. A group of men were pushing the bomber under the trees. At that very minute, from somewhere inside the wood, the fascists would be telephoning to the other aerodromes. The *Marat* was rising in spirals, in order to drop its bombs from a height sufficient to prevent the risk of itself being brought down by them. But the spiral would have to be wider if the bomber was to have time to aim, and Darras time to make sure of passing right over the wood. Once must be enough, thought Magnin. The wood made a very good target. And if that was where the gasoline tank was, as was probable, the whole lot would go up. He went over to the bomber, wishing it was Attignies there.

"Let all the bombs go!"

The plane banked twice to give a clear view of the objective. At twelve hundred feet it ceased climbing and came straight over the wood at full speed, machine-guns firing. The bombers would have time to base their aims on the height. Huddled up near the mechanic, the peasant was trying not to get in the way. The mechanic, with both hands on the releasing-controls, was watching for a signal from the bomber's uplifted hand, as the latter saw the wood move into focus in his sighting gear.

All three hands fell together.

Magnin had to bank at right-angles to see the result. The other two machines followed suit, until there seemed to be a whole chain of tilted planes. A heavy black smoke that they all recognized was beginning to billow from the wood: gasoline. It rose in abrupt, intermittent swirls, as though subterreanean reservoirs had been ignited beneath that peaceful little wood, to all appearances no different from any other in the grey light of early morning. A group of about a dozen men ran out from the trees—then, a few seconds later, a body of about a hundred; both at the same panic-stricken scamper. Driven back over the fields by the wind, the smoke was beginning to spread out into the majestic mushroom shape which gasoline fires take on. The enemy pursuit planes were certainly in the air by now. The bomber was taking photographs, peering through the view-finder as he had peered through the sights a moment earlier; the mechanic was wiping his hands, oily from the releasing-controls; the peasant was drumming the soles of his feet against the side of the cabin-wall, half to express his joy, half on account of the cold. His big nose was crimson from being pressed against the mica.

The plane re-entered the clouds and made for Valencia.

As soon as Magnin came out above them again and could see farther ahead he realized that things were going badly for them.

The clouds were breaking up. Beyond Teruel an immense rift revealed twenty miles of earth and sky.

To get back without leaving the clouds would have meant a wide detour over the fascist lines—and there too, the clouds might break up very quickly.

Their sole remaining hope lay in the Sarion chaser arriving before the enemy ones.

Delighted with their success and particularly anxious to survive that day, Magnin was counting the minutes. If nothing appeared before he counted up to twenty . . .

They were going out into open sky without a cloud in it.

One after another, one, two, three, four, five, six, seven enemy planes came out of the clouds. The Republican pursuit planes were single-seaters with low wings which could not be mistaken for Heinkels. Alertly, Magnin lowered his glasses and told the three planes to close in on each other. "If we had decent guns we might take on even that lot," he thought. But he still had the old Lewis models, uncoupled. "800 rounds a minute $\times$ 3 guns = 2,400. Each Heinkel 1,800 rounds $\times$ 4 = 7,200." He knew that well enough, but it gave him a curious satisfaction to repeat it to himself.

The fascists were bearing down on the three bombing planes. They were keeping to the left, planning to begin by attacking one bomber alone. Not a Republican chaser in the sky.

Beneath the planes, the quails were passing on their annual migration.

Gardet's plane was on the left.

Pujol, piloting Gardet's plane, had just had chewing-gum handed round by Saïdi by way of celebration. Pujol lived up to the best Leclerc tradition. Shaved on one side of his face only (the result of a romantic vow), his gardener's straw hat trimmed with scarlet feathers on his head again, now that the bombing was over, twenty-four years old, beak-nosed, and wearing an F.A.I. scarf (though he was not a member of that party), he fitted in perfectly with the standard fascist conception of a "Red bandit." But for one or two socks wrapped round flying-helmets, and Gardet's little rifle, the appearance of the others was quite normal. While maintaining with discreet but firm authority the order indispensable to military efficiency, Gardet welcomed any picturesque touches such as his own wooden rifle; even Magnin was willing to countenance eccentricities which did not interfere with something essential, particularly when he felt that there was a fetish element involved.

Gardet understood the Germans' plan, too. He saw that Magnin was having the other two planes come down below him, so as to combine the fire of all the guns when the *Canard* was attacked. He glanced round at his own guns, took charge of the forward turret himself, thought once more how miserably inadequate a Lewis was, and turned his turret to face the Heinkels which were looming above the sights.

One or two bullets whizzed past.

"Don't get worried!" Gardet shouted: "there'll be plenty more!"

Pujol's flight was twisting, S-shaped. This was his first experience of a frontal attack by a chaser, at full speed; and he felt the natural bitterness of a pilot flying a slow, heavy machine attacked by fast planes. The Republican Pelicans knew that the best of their own fighters would have brought the enemy down without difficulty and, as always before an engagement, there was not a man who could quite forget the void beneath him.

Getting ready to fire, Scali suddenly saw on his left one of their large bombs: it had stuck while the others were released.

"There they come!"

Magnin had judged his distances well: the Heinkels were unable to surround the *Canard*. Two above, two below, three to the side, they grew so large that the pilots' flying-helmets could be seen.

The *Canard* shook all over as its three guns opened fire

together. For ten seconds there was an unearthly din, with the noise of wood snapping as the enemy bullets struck it, and a whole network of tracer bullets.

Gardet saw one of the Heinkels attacking from underneath fall headlong. Either Scali or the guns of the other two planes had made a hit. He was conscious of the void again. Mireaux was leaving the rear turret, his mouth half-open; one of his arms hung limply and from it blood was pouring into the cockpit like water from the nozzle of a watering-can. Scali came up out of his under-turret and lay down. One of his shoes seemed to have split open.

"Make a ligature!" Gardet bawled. He threw the first-aid outfit to Mireaux as if it were a match-box, and sprang down into the lower turret. Saïdi had taken over his own gun and the bomber had replaced Mireaux. The pilots did not seem to have been touched.

The Heinkels were coming back.

None underneath this time. Those which tried to attack zooming up from below were caught by the fire from the *Canard's* pit gun and all six guns of the *Marat* and Moros' plane, whose criss-crossing tracers formed a network of red streaks beneath the *Canard*. The companion of the Heinkel which had been shot down had soared above them. Pujol was travelling all out, each corkscrew twist flatter than the last.

Once again came the tracer bullets, the rattle, the sound of splintering wood. Silently, Saïdi left the rear turret. Propped on his elbows, he lay face downwards above Scali, beside whom Mireaux was lying. "If they have the nerve just to stick on to our tail and follow instead of passing us . . ." thought Gardet. The holes made by the enemy bullets shone like little flames where the bright light came through from outside into the half-light within. The port engine stopped. The *Marat* and the Spanish plane closed in round the *Canard*. Pujol thrust his blood-stained head out of his cabin, still wearing the feather-decked gardener's hat.

"They're beating it!"

The Heinkels were withdrawing. Gardet reached for his field-glasses; the Republican chasers were arriving from the south.

He sprang out of his turret, opened the first-aid box, untouched by the others, and put tourniquets on Mireaux and Scali. Mireaux had three bullets in the left arm and one in the shoulder (simultaneous hits), and Scali an explosive bullet in the foot. Saïdi had a bullet in his right thigh, but was not in great pain.

Gardet went over to the pilot's cabin. The plane was flying tilted at an angle of 30°, kept in the air by the one engine. Langlois, the second pilot, pointed to the revolution counter: 1,450 instead of 1,800. Soon the plane would only have its height to rely on. And the snow-covered mountain was close in front of them. From a house below, smoke was rising peacefully, absolutely vertically.

Bleeding, but not badly hit, Pujol could feel the contact of the stick welded to his body, identified with it, as the others felt their wounds. The counter dropped from 1,200 to 1,100.

Underneath them lay the spurs of the snow mountain. Landing there meant plunging headlong into the ravines, like a drunken wasp dashing itself to pieces against a wall. A broad undulating expanse of snow lay beyond. And what underneath?

They went into a cloud, a zone of snowy whiteness; the floor of the fuselage was patterned with red footprints. Pujol was trying to rise above the cloud. Actually, their unchecked fall brought them out below it. They were only 60 yards from the mountain. The earth was rushing towards them; how would these soft curves treat them . . . ? They wanted desperately to come through alive, now that they had brought off the bombing successfully and escaped the machine-guns.

"The bomb!" Gardet shouted.

If it failed to dislodge itself this time, they would all be blown sky high. Saïdi wrenched at both handles of the releasing mechanism, tugging them frantically downwards. The bomb fell, and the snow engulfed them as though the earth had been flung up against the plane by its fall.

Pujol sprang from his seat, suddenly open to the sky. Deaf? No, it must be the silence of the mountains after the noise of the crash, for he could hear a crow cawing, the shouts. Blood was trickling gently down his face and punching red holes in the snow in front of his shoes. His cheeks felt warm. He had nothing but his hands with which to wipe away the blood that was blinding him—through which he had a confused view of a black heap of metal loud with cries; the fantastic, inextricably fused tangle characteristic of wrecked aeroplanes.

Magnin and Moros had been able to get back. Headquarters had telephoned to the aerodrome to say that the wounded had been taken to a little hospital in Mora. The planes would have to be overhauled and would not fly again till the following day. Magnin had already left after giving the necessary orders. An ambulance would follow.

"One killed, two badly wounded, all the others slightly wounded," the officer on duty had said over the phone.

He did not know the names of the wounded or the dead man. He had not yet heard the result of the bombing.

Magnin's car was speeding along between interminable orange-groves. Ringed here and there with cypress trees, the orange-groves went on mile after mile, with the ruined fortresses of Sagunto in the background, Christian fortifications built upon Roman ones, Roman fortifications upon Carthaginian: war . . . Above them the snows on the Teruel mountains shimmered, poised in the cloudless air.

Oaks replaced the orange-trees: the mountains were beginning. Magnin phoned headquarters again. There had been sixteen planes at the peasant's aerodrome. They had all been burnt.

The hospital at Mora was in a school. No sign of any airmen. There was another hospital in the village hall: no sign there either. The local Popular Front committee advised Magnin to phone to Linares. A call for a doctor had come from there, for some wounded. Magnin set off for the telephone with one of the Popular Front delegates, through streets of blue, pink and green houses with wooden balconies, and past bridges with pointed arches dwarfed into insignificance beneath the ruins of castles straight from the ballads of chivalry.

The postmaster was an old militant socialist. His little boy was sitting on the telegraph-table.

"He wants to be an airman, too!"

There were bullet-marks on the walls.

"My predecessor belonged to the C.N.T.," said the postmaster. "The day the rebellion started, he was telegraphing to Madrid all the time. The fascists didn't know that, but they killed him just the same: those are the bullets."

At last Linares answered. No, the airmen were not there. They had come down near a little hamlet called Valdelinares. Higher up, in the snow.

What village would he have to call now? "Higher up, in the snow!" But the friendly tone in which the answers were given made Magnin feel more than ever that this was the real Spain which surrounded him, as though in each hospital, in each committee, in each post office a peasant was waiting with comradely greetings. At last there was a ring. The postmaster lifted the receiver; Valdelinares was answering. He listened, then turned round.

"One of the airmen can walk. He has gone to fetch him."

The little boy no longer dared to move. A cat's shadow flitted across the window.

The postmaster handed Magnin the antiquated receiver, from which came a muffled voice.

"Hullo! Who is that?"

"Magnin speaking. That's Pujol, isn't it?"

"Yes."

'Who has been killed?"

"Saïdi."

"And the wounded?"

"Gardet, badly: eyes in danger. Taillefer, left leg broken in three places, Mireaux, four bullets in the arm. Scali, an explosive bullet in the foot. Langlois and I will be all right."

"Can anyone walk?"

"All the way down?"

"Yes."

"No, nobody."

"Or ride down on mules?"

"Langlois and I. Perhaps Scali, with help; but I'm not sure."

"How are you being looked after?"

"The sooner we get down, the better. They're doing all they can, but . . ."

"Are there any stretchers?"

"Not here. Wait, the doctor's saying something."

He could hear the doctor's voice.

"Hullo!" Magnin said. "Can all the wounded be moved?"

"Yes—if you have stretchers."

Magnin questioned the postmaster. He didn't know. Perhaps there were stretchers at the hospital. But certainly not six. Magnin picked up the receiver again.

"Can you fix up litters with branches, straps and mattresses?"

"Well . . . I think so."

"I'm bringing what I can in the way of stretchers. Get them on to making the litters right away, and start down. I am waiting here for an ambulance. It will come up as far as it can."

"What about the body?"

"Bring everything down. Hallo! Hallo! And you might tell the men that sixteen enemy planes were destroyed. Don't forget."

The journey through the streets began again; past the brightly coloured houses, the square and its fountains, the steeply pitched bridges and the sharp cobbles, still shining after the showers which had fallen that morning from the low clouds. There were two stretchers in all and they were tied on to the roof of the car.

"Won't that be too high to go through the gate?"

At last, Magnin left for Linares.

From now on, he was in contact with the very soul of Spain. Passing through a village of houses with open balustrade-fronted lofts, the car came to a gorge where the spreading horns of a fighting bull showed dimly outlined on the grey sky. A dark, primitive hostility seemed rising from the soil, on which these un-European villages had left their scars; a hostility intensified for Magnin by the way the rocks continually reminded him, in between glances at his watch, of their pitilessness towards the wounded airmen. Nowhere to land; nothing but rocks, trees and fields terraced like steps. Every time the car ran down a slope Magnin imagined the plane sinking down towards that merciless ground.

Linares has a wall round it. Children were sitting on the ramparts, on either side of the gate. At the inn, where the ground floor was jammed full of carts with their shafts sticking up in the air, there were mules waiting. At the Committee there was one doctor, who had come up from the valley, and fifteen or twenty young men. They stared curiously at the tall stranger with the drooping moustache who wore the uniform of the Spanish Air Force.

"We don't need all those bearers," said Magnin.

"They all insist on coming," said the delegate.

"Right. What about the ambulance?"

The delegate phoned Mora; it hadn't arrived yet. Their carts drawn up in a semicircle around them, the mule-drivers were sitting in the courtyard eating from the communal pot, in this case an enormous inverted bell. It was full of bubbling olive oil, and covered with soot, which hid the inscription on it. Above the doorway was engraved: 1614.

At last the caravan got underway.

"How long will it take to get there?"

"Four hours. You'll meet them coming down."

Magnin was walking two hundred yards ahead, his burly
silhouette—uniform cap and leather coat—clear-cut against
the mountainside. There was hardly any mud, only stones to
impede progress. Behind him came the doctor on a mule;
farther behind, the stretcher-bearers wearing jerseys and
Basque berets (the local costumes were kept for fête-days and
old age); in the distance, mules and stretchers.

Soon there were no more bulls or fields; nothing but rocks,
the rocks of Spain, that sparkle red and yellow in the sun, but
now were pale beneath the overcast sky, with shadows lurking
in the huge clefts. They fell away in two or three precipitous
tiers from the snow on the skyline right down to the bottom of
the valley. Pebbles fell over the edge of the path as they
walked, clattering down from rock to rock until the silence of
the gorge engulfed them. It seemed to be engulfing the noise
of a mountain-stream they were leaving behind them. After
more than an hour the valley down which Linares could still
be seen came to an end. The moment they rounded the spur
of the mountain which separated them from it, Magnin could
no longer hear the noise of the water. The track went behind
a sheer wall of rock which overhung it in places. At the point
where it changed direction was an apple-tree, outlined against
the sky; in the centre of a minute field, recalling a Japanese
landscape. Its apples had not been picked. Strewn on the
ground, they formed a thick ring round it, which merged
gradually into grass again. This apple-tree was the only living
thing among the rocks, living with the mute ageless indifference of endlessly reincarnated plant-life.

Magnin could feel the fatigue growing steadily in his shoulders and leg-muscles as he climbed. Gradually the feeling of
effort invaded his whole body, driving everything else from
his mind. By now the litters would be making their way down
these same precipitous paths, with their load of shattered arms
and broken legs. His eyes wandered from the short stretch
of path visible in front to the snow-clad peaks fretting the
white clouds, and each new effort brought home to him with
vivid intensity the comradeship that bound him to his leader.

The Linares peasants, who had not seen any of the wounded
yet, followed him in silence, keeping him stern and dignified
company. He was thinking about the lorries from the villages.

He had been climbing for at least two hours when the path
which they had been following round the face of a spur of the
mountain came to an end. The track now led through snow,

up a new gorge, towards the higher and much less rugged part
of the mountains that the aeroplanes had seen rising beside
the other when they left for Teruel. From here, on the moun-
tain-streams were frozen. Where the path changed direction
again a Saracen warrior was waiting, like the apple-tree lower
down, black against the background of sky, and foreshortened
like a statue on a high pedestal seen from below. The horse
was a mule, and the Saracen was Pujol, complete with flying-
helmet. He turned round, his profile thrown into relief like a
carving, and shattered the intense silence with a shout. "There's
Magnin!"

Two long legs hanging straight and stiff on either side of a
tiny donkey, and a tuft of hair sticking up out of a bandage
like a badger's crest came over the skyline: the second pilot,
Langlois. As Magnin clasped Pujol's hand he saw that his
leather coat was so coated with congealed blood below the
belt that it looked almost like crocodile-skin. What wound
could have stained the leather with blood like that? There was
a whole network of trickles across the chest, down which the
blood had spurted so copiously that it could still be smelt.

"It's Gardet's coat," Pujol said. Craning his neck, he was
looking round for Gardet; without stirrups he could not rise
from the saddle. But the stretchers had not yet come into view
over the skyline.

Magnin was still staring at the leather coat. Pujol had already started to tell his story.

Langlois, slightly wounded in the head, had been able to
drag himself clear, limping on one foot; the other was sprained.
Saïdi and Scali were lying among the splintered ruins of the
tapering box which had been the fuselage. Beneath the dome
of the overturned lower turret was Mireaux, his limbs sticking
out from under the boss, the top of which was grinding into
his broken shoulder like an engraving of one of the ancient
tortures; right in among the wreckage, was the bomber, lying
flat. Obsessed by the ever-present danger of fire, all those who
were able were shouting for help, their cries echoing through
the mountain stillness.

Pujol and Langlois had freed Scali and Saïdi. Then Pujol
had begun to disentangle the bomber, while Langlois tried to
lift the turret which was crushing Mireaux. At last he managed

to tip it over, with a fresh crash of steel and mica which startled the wounded lying in the snow, then died away.

Gardet had seen a hut and went off towards it, supporting his broken jaw with the butt of his revolver (he did not dare to use his hand; blood was pouring from it). A peasant who had seen him in the distance had taken to his heels. The hut was nearly a mile away, empty except for a horse; it eyed him, hesitated, and began to whinny. "My face must be a god-awful mess," Gardet thought. "Still, a living, unrequisitioned horse must mean that we're in Republican territory . . ." The hut was warm after the snow outside, and he felt a desire to lie down and sleep. Nobody came. Gardet picked up a shovel that was in a corner, with one hand; it would help to get Saïdi out when he got back to the plane, and it would help him to walk. He was finding it difficult to see clearly, except just at his feet. His upper eyelids were swelling. He found his way back by following the trail of blood in the snow, and his foot-prints, blurred and elongated at the spots where he had fallen.

As he walked he remembered how a third of the *Canard* was constructed with old parts from a machine, paid for out of a joint international proletarian subscription, which had been brought down on the Sierra: the *Commune de Paris*.

Just as he reached the plane, a little boy approached Pujol. "If we're among fascists, we're done for," the pilot was think-ing. Where were the revolvers? Machine-guns don't lend them-selves to suicide.

"Which are you, here?" Pujol asked. "Reds or Franco?"

The boy—a sly-looking brat with ears that stuck out and a parting right on the top of his head—looked at him without answering. Pujol began to realize how extraordinary he must look. He had put on his red-feathered hat again, uncon-sciously, and was still wearing it; his face was only shaved on one side; and the blood was trickling down over his white overalls.

"Which is it, tell me!"

He moved towards the boy, who backed away from him. Threats would do no good. And there was no chewing-gum left.

"Republicans or fascists?"

They could hear the noise of water in the distance, and the cawing of rooks in flight above them.

"There's all sorts here," the boy answered, looking at the plane: "Republicans and fascists."

"What about the syndicate?" Gardet shouted.

Pujol had an inspiration.

"Which is the most important? The U.G.T.? The C.N.T.? Or the Catholics?"

Gardet was walking towards Mireaux, on the boy's right, and the boy could only see his back with the little wooden rifle slung across it.

"The U.G.T.," the child said at last, with a smile.

Gardet turned round. His face was still supported by the revolver-butt, and had been slashed wide open from ear to ear. The lower part of the nose was hanging down, and the blood, which was now flowing quietly after its first violent uprush, was congealing on the leather flying-coat which Gardet wore outside his overalls. The lad gave a shriek and fled, scuttling sideways like a cat.

Gardet helped Mireaux to gather his spread-eagled limbs together and got him into a kneeling position. When he leaned forward his face began to burn, and he tried to keep his head erect as he helped him up.

"We are on our own ground!" Pujol said.

"Completely disfigured this time," Gardet said. "Did you see how the kid beat it, then?"

"You've had the hell of a slash!"

"Nothing left."

"Some men are coming."

Some peasants were making for them now at last, led by the one who had run away when he saw Gardet. Now that he was no longer alone he had found the courage to return. The explosion of the bomb had brought out the whole village, and the boldest of them was approaching.

"Frente Popular!" Pujol shouted, hurling his red-feathered hat into the middle of the heap of twisted steel.

The peasants started to run. They seemed to have guessed that the crashed plane was one of theirs, for they were practically unarmed; perhaps one of them had caught sight of the red wing-bands while the plane was still in the air. Gardet saw the reflecting-mirror hanging still in place amid the jumble of joists and wire, in front of Pujol's seat. "If I look, I shall kill myself."

When the peasants were near enough to see the pile of frayed and twisted steel, the battered engines, the propeller folded in two like an arm and the bodies lying in the snow, they stopped. Gardet went towards them. They stood waiting

in a bunch, absolutely still, as if they were awaiting some catastrophe. The women were wearing black scarves round their
heads. "Look out!" said the peasant leading them; he had
noticed that Gardet's broken jaw was supported by a revolver.
Reverting instinctively to their former habits at the sight of
blood, the women began to cross themselves. Then, looking
towards the bodies in the snow rather than at Gardet and
Pujol, who had also started to walk towards them, one of the
peasants raised his clenched fist; and one after another, all
saluted with their fists the wrecked plane and the bodies which
they imagined to be those of dead men.

"There's no need for all that," Gardet muttered. Then, in
Spanish: "Give us a hand."

They returned to the other wounded. Directly the peasants
realized that only one of the bodies in the snow was dead, they
began to bustle round them with clumsy affection.

"Wait a minute!"

Gardet began to organize things. Pujol was showing great
activity, but nobody was obeying him. Gardet was in command, not because he was the actual commander but in virtue
of his face-wound. "If Death were to arrive on the scene, he'd
have just everybody fetching and carrying for him!" he
thought. Somebody must go for a doctor. A long way; but it
can't be helped. Moving Scali, Mireaux and the bomber was
going to be difficult; but they are used to broken legs in the
mountains. Pujol and Langlois could walk. Himself, too, if it
came to the worst.

They started the journey down to the village, a little group
of men and women dwarfed by the snow. Before losing consciousness Gardet tried to look once more at the mirror. It had
been smashed to pieces when the plane crashed; there was no
mirror in the wreckage.

Magnin could see the first improvised stretcher coming into
view. Four peasants were shouldering it. Four others followed
close behind. They were carrying the bomber.

He looked more like a case of long-standing tuberculosis
than a man with a broken leg. The deep-cut furrows in his
face increased the tensity of expression in the eyes to the
maximum, transmuting the small, squat, nondescript soldier's
head with the little moustache into a romantic mask.

Mireaux came next. He had changed, too, but in another
way. In his case pain had brought back the look of childhood.

"It was snowing when we started down!" he said when Magnin shook his hand. "A damn queer show!" He smiled and closed his eyes again.

Magnin went on, with the bearers from Linares following. It must be Gardet in the next litter; a dressing covered almost the entire face. Only the eyelids could be seen; swollen to bursting point, pale mauve in colour, and swollen till they almost met, between the flying-helmet and the flat bandage. The nose underneath seemed to have disappeared. Seeing that Magnin wanted to say something, the front two bearers lowered their end to the ground before the others, and for a moment the body lay aslant, the very symbol of battle.

Direct contact with him was impossible. Both Gardet's hands were under the blanket. Between the lids of the left eye, Magnin thought he could distinguish a faint line.

"Can you see?"

"Not too well. Just about see you, old chap!"

Magnin felt an impulse to take him in his arms and hug him.

"Anything we can do?"

"Tell the old woman to stop fussing round with that soup! And listen, when do we reach the hospital?"

"You'll get to the ambulance in an hour and a half. Hospital this evening."

The stretcher got underway again, with half Valdelinares behind it. As Scali's stretcher went past Magnin, an old woman with a black handkerchief over her hair approached with a cup and gave him some soup. She was carrying a basket containing a thermos and a Japanese cup, her pride, no doubt. Magnin pictured the rim of the cup slipped beneath the turned-up bandage on Gardet's face.

"Better not to give any to the man who's wounded in the face," he said to her.

"It was the only chicken in the village," she answered gravely.

"Even so!"

"You see my boy is at the front, too . . ."

Magnin watched the rest of the peasants and stretchers go past, with the coffin bringing up the rear. It had taken less time to make than the stretchers: a matter of habit . . . The peasants had tied one of the twisted machine-guns—from the plane—onto the lid.

The bearers changed over every twenty-five minutes, but

without putting the stretchers down. Magnin was amazed at
the contrast between the women's appearance of extreme poverty and the thermos flasks that several were carrying in their
baskets. One of them approached him, pointing at Mireaux:

"How old is he?"

"Twenty-seven."

She had been following the stretcher for some minutes with
a confused idea of being helpful, but also with a precise and
gentle tenderness in her movements, a way of propping up
the shoulders of the wounded man whenever the bearers had
to choose their footing carefully over a steep stretch, in which
Magnin recognized the imperishable maternal instinct.

The valley was taking them steadily down. On one side the
expanse of snow rose until it met a bleak and timeless waste
of sky; on the other, dreary-looking clouds were gliding past
the peaks.

The men were maintaining an unbroken silence. Once more
a woman approached Magnin.

"What are they, the foreigners?"

"One Belgian. One Italian. The rest are French."

"Are they the International Brigade?"

"No, but they're the same thing."

"The one who is . . . "

She pointed vaguely towards his face.

"French," Magnin said.

"Is the dead one French, too?"

"No, Arab."

"An Arab? Who'd have thought of it! An Arab—my word!"
She went off to spread the news.

Magnin moved up from the rear of the procession to Scali's
stretcher; he was the only one who could do anything except
lie flat. In front of him, the path led down in even zigzags to
a small frozen stream where Langlois was waiting. Pujol had
moved farther back. On the far side of the water the path
turned at right-angles. The stretchers were about two hundred
yards apart. Langlois, their outlandish advance-guard with
the bristling mane of hair, was more than half a mile away, a
ghostlike figure on his donkey, through the mist which was
beginning to rise from the valley. Behind Scali and Magnin
there was only the coffin. The stretchers were crossing the
stream one by one: seen from the side, the cortège was spreading out along the huge wall of the mountain with its vertical
shadows.

"You see," Scali said, "I used to . . ."

Magnin cut him short:

"Look at that! What a picture!"

Scali did not pursue his story. No doubt it would have got on Magnin's nerves as much as his comparison of what they could see in a picture got on Scali's.

In the days of the First Republic a Spaniard courting his sister, who neither encouraged nor discouraged his advances, had taken her once to his country house in Murcia. The house was a fantastic product of the end of the eighteenth century, with cream-coloured columns against a background of orange walls, stucco decorations flecked with tulips, and box hedges in the garden tracing a palm-like motif beneath the garnet-red roses. One of its former owners had built a miniature shadow-theatre, holding thirty people; the magic lantern was already working when they entered, and the silhouettes were visible on the minute screen. The Spaniard had been successful; she had slept with him that night. Scali had been jealous of that supremely fanciful tribute.

As he approached the mountain-stream below, he thought of the four loggias, gold and salmon-pink, which he had never seen. A house full of floral designs, with plaster busts between the dark leaves of the orange-trees. His stretcher crossed the stream and turned the corner. The bulls came into view again opposite. The Spain of his youth—love, make-believe, and misery! Now Spain was that twisted machine-gun on an Arab's coffin and birds numbed with cold crying in the ravines.

The mules in front were vanishing round another corner, following the original direction again. The new line of descent led straight to Linares: Magnin recognized the apple-tree.

What forest was that on which the rain was beating down, on the far side of the rock, where the path turned? Magnin coaxed his mule to a trot, went past all the others, and arrived at the turning. No rain; it was the sound of the streams which the cliff wall had screened from him, as a rock wall hides a landscape, and which could not be heard from the other slope. The sound was rising from Linares, as though the ambulances and the new lease of life which lay before them were sending up this insistent rustling, as of a high wind on leaves, from the far depths of the valley. Night had not fallen yet, but the light was failing. Like an equestrian statue, Magnin was sitting askew on his saddleless mule, gazing at the little apple-tree

standing surrounded by its dead fruit. Langlois' bristling crest
of bloodstained hair came into view in front of the branches.
In the silence suddenly grown murmurous with the sound of
rippling water, the ring of decaying fruit seemed to typify the
passage from life to death that not only was the doom of men
but was an immutable law of the universe. Magnin's eyes
wandered from the tree to the ageless ravines. One after another, the stretchers were going past. The branches reached
forward on either side over the swaying stretchers, as above
Langlois' head; above the corpse-like smile of Taillefer, the
childlike face of Mireaux, Gardet's flat bandage and Scali's
lacerated lips; above each bloodstained body gently borne
along by comrades' hands. The coffin went by, with its machine-gun twisted like the branch of a tree. Magnin moved on
again.

Without his quite knowing why, the deep gorges into which
they now were plunging, as if into the bowels of earth, seemed
imbued with the same agelessness as the trees. He thought of
the quarries in which prisoners were left to die in former days.
But that shattered leg which the muscles barely held together,
that sagging arm, that obliterated face, that machine-gun on a
coffin, all these were the results of risks voluntarily accepted,
sought after. The solemn, primitive march of that line of
stretchers had something as compelling about it as the pale
rocks that merged into the lowering sky, something as fundamental as the apples scattered on the ground. Birds of prey
were crying again, close beneath the clouds. How many years
had he to live? Twenty?

"What made the Arab airman join in?"

One of the women was approaching him again, accompanied by two others.

Up above the birds were wheeling through the air with
rigid wings, like so many aeroplanes.

"Can they really give people new noses now?"

The path widened steadily as the valley approached Linares;
the peasants were walking beside the stretchers now. The
black-clothed women, scarves on their heads and baskets on
their arms, were still bustling around the wounded, moving
from one to another. The men were keeping pace with the
stretchers, without ever getting in front of them, walking
abreast of each other, holding themselves with the stiff erect-
ness of those who have been carrying a weight on their shoulders. At each change-over, the new bearers abandoned their

stiff walk as they took up the shafts with affectionate care,
moving off again to the accompaniment of the grunts which
tell of physical effort, as if anxious to mask the betrayal of
their emotions which their solicitude denoted. Their attention
concentrated on the stones which obstructed the path, thinking
only of the necessity not to jolt the stretchers, they moved
steadily forward, slowly up a little on the steeper inclines. And
the steady rhythm of their tread over the long, pain-burdened
journey seemed to fill the vast ravine, down which the last
cries still came floating from the birds above, with a solemn
beat like a funeral drum. But it was not death which haunted
the mountains at that moment; it was triumphant human will.

They were beginning to be able to make out Linares at the
bottom of the valley, and the stretchers were drawing closer
together; the coffin was level with Scali. The machine-gun had
been tied on where a wreath would normally have been laid;
the whole procession recalled a funeral as precisely as that
twisted machine-gun recalled the wreaths which it replaced
Near the Saragossa road down below, round the fascist
planes, the fires of black wood were still burning in the fading
light. They would never reach Guadalajara. And all that long
line of black-clothed peasants, the women with their hair hidden beneath the scarves which they had worn from time immemorial, seemed to have more of the character of an austere
triumphal progress than a relief party bringing home wounded
men.

The gradient was easy now. Leaving the path, the stretchers
spread out across the grass, and the hill men scattered out
fan-wise. Children were running up from Linares; a hundred
yards from the stretchers they moved aside, let them pass,
and followed on behind. The road followed the fortifications
up to the gate; its cobbles, set edgewise, were more slippery
than the mountain-path.

The whole town was massed behind the battlements. Night
had not yet fallen, but there was little daylight left. Though
there had been no rain, the cobbles were moist and shining
and the bearers picked their way carefully. In the houses
which projected above the battlements lamps were glimmering.

The bomber still headed the line. The women on the battlements looked at him gravely, but without surprise; only the
face of the wounded man appeared above the blanket, and it
showed no sign of injury. Scali and Mireaux likewise. Langlois
gave them a shock; with a bleeding bandage round his head,

and toes sticking into the air (he had removed the shoe from
his sprained foot), he looked like Don Quixote. Was this how
war in the air ended, war in its most romantic form? The atmosphere grew tenser when Pujol went past; there was still
light enough for observant eyes to see the large bloodstains
on his leather coat. When Gardet arrived a hush so profound
fell upon the crowd that the noise of the distant mountain-
torrents suddenly became audible.

All the other wounded could see; and all, even the bomber,
had made an effort to smile when they saw the crowd. Gardet
did not look at them; he was alive, but that was all. From the
battlements the crowd could make out the thick coffin behind
him. Covered with a blanket up to his chin, and with the bandage under his flying-helmet lying so flat that it was impossible
that there could be any nose beneath it, this stretcher was the
visible incarnation of the peasants' immemorial conception of
war. And nobody had forced him to fight. For a moment they
hesitated; not knowing what to do, but determined to make
some gesture. Then, as at Valdelinares, they silently raised
their clenched fists.

It had begun to drizzle. The last stretchers, the peasants
from the mountains, and the last mules were advancing between the vast background of rocky landscape over which
dark rainclouds were massing, and the hundreds of peasants
standing motionless with raised fists. The women were weep-
ing quietly, and the procession seemed to be fleeing from the
eerie silence of the mountains, its noise of clattering hoofs and
clogs linking the everlasting clamour of the vultures with the
muffled sound of sobbing.

The ambulance left.

Through the driver's communicating-window Scali could
see square patches of the night-bound countryside. Here and
there a section of the ramparts of Sagunto showed up, and
cypresses, black and massive in the misty moonlight (that
selfsame mist which favoured night-bombing raids); ghostly
white houses, emblematic of peace; sheen of oranges in their
dark groves. Shakespearian orchards, Italian cypresses . . .
"On such a night as this, Jessica . . ." Yes, there still was
happiness in the world. On the stretcher above him the bomber
was groaning at every jolt.

There was no room for thoughts in Mireaux' brain. He was

in a high fever, fancied himself struggling to keep afloat in scalding water.

The bomber was thinking of his leg.

Gardet was thinking of his face. Gardet had been a great lover.

Magnin was listening to Vargas over the telephone.

"It's the decisive battle, Magnin. Bring everything you can, as best you can."

"The controls of the *Marat's* rudder are pretty well smashed."

"Do what you can."

4

Guadalajara, March 18th

THE Italians were counter-attacking towards Brihuega. If they broke through there they would take the entire Republican forces in the rear. It would mean Guadalajara threatened again, the centre army cut off from Madrid, the town left more or less defenceless, the Dimitroff, Thaelmann, Garibaldi, André-Marty and Sixth of February battalions deprived of their line of retreat. The advantages of the capture of Trijueque and Ibarra would be wiped out.

The Thaelmann and Edgar André battalions threw themselves into the fray again.

The Dimitroff battalion (Croats, Bulgars, Roumanians, Serbs, with representatives from all the Balkan States, and Yugoslav students from Paris) felt when facing the fascists that they were facing the murderers of their own people. They had spent twenty-four hours screaming curses at the Italian tanks from under cover of their woods, as they had done on the Jarama front, had captured half a mile of ground, and had been forced to give it up in a furious rage for the sake of keeping the line straight, had slept huddled together like flies in groups of four or five as a protection against the cold —such was the battalion that was attacking now under the bursting shrapnel. One of the section leaders, a Montenegrin, was running towards the rear shrieking: "Look after the line and don't bother about me, you bastards!" He was supporting his broken left arm with his right when an explosive bullet sent his head whirling in a flurry of snow.

It had started to snow again, and all along the front the advancing men, with their heads held low and their stomach muscles steeled in expectation of wounds, felt the shrapnel flying around them as thickly as the falling snowflakes.

In the Thaelmann battalion only two remarks were heard just now: "Where's the grub?" and "You can't expect to have a war without casualties."

The political delegate from the machine-gun corps, delirious from a stomach-wound, kept crying out: "Send our tanks! Send our tanks!"

The battalion had just repulsed its eleventh attack since the beginning of the battle. The trees still had their trunks, but no more branches.

"This isn't war!" yelled Siry to the Franco-Belgians; it's just a dose of clap that's going on forever!" And he would start to imitate the spluttering rat-tat-tat of the machine-guns.

The rifles were starting to burn their hands.

In Manuel's command, Pepe's men had 750 rounds left for a machine-gun which fired 600 a minute. Half of it was distributed to the best shots. At the sight of the obsolete rifles the recruits wept with exasperation and dismay. "Bring the machine-gun here," the section-leader shouted. When the smoke of the first shell had drifted away he lay dead at the very spot he had just pointed to. But the ammunition arrived, together with a few extra rifles.

At last a shout rolled down from the woods and plains above Brihuega, audible despite the bombardment which had just started again; it was taken up in the olive groves and the low walls along which the Republicans seemed embedded like insects, and in the devastated farms and fields. The horizon seemed to be expanding under the shattering detonations from all the fascist batteries; the Republican tanks were coming into action.

They were attacking along the whole front, more than fifty abreast, from one end to the other of the horizon, which was blotted out at intervals as blizzards swept across it.

The men who had been snatching a few moments of uneasy sleep under the frozen olive-trees, and those who had been plunged in the coma of utter exhaustion and had awakened stiff as boards, started to run behind the last tanks of which now and then they lost sight in flurries of snow.

In the Fifth Corps the commander of No. 1 Company was the first to be killed.

A few moments later one of the Republican tanks went up in flames, lighting with an uncanny blue effulgence the white-swathed battlefield and the snowflakes hanging in the air above it.

Caught by a cross-fire from enemy machine-guns, pressed flat to the ground behind the tree-stumps, the men began scooping up the snow with their cartridge-clips and peaked caps—had they used their bayonets they would have had to expose themselves—settled down into the cavities, standing up for a moment to launch their bombs, and ducking down again as the machine-guns swept their line. Of six volunteers who were trying to carry back the wounded Captain, four fell. The International companies on either flank could hear only the explosive bullets bursting behind them and now and then a voice shouting, "Getting on all right, boys?" and others answering, "Not so bad. What about you?"—and meanwhile, less loudly, all over the battlefield a pitiful chorus of cries for help.

At three o'clock, however, through sheer fatigue the men were getting drowsy, and they were dreading the prospect of a night out in the snow. Hot coffee was handed round again. Under the heavy cowls their heads were full of memories of the Madrid trenches where they used to loose off a casual shot or two during meals, where the brighter spirits had tamed mice and, as they waited for the shells to land, the married men had gazed in silence at the photographs of their children. And they remembered, too, the Jarama front, where they had joined in an attack behind the fascist tanks when these had run out of ammunition, and men had come up shouting wildly for urine to cool the barrels of the machine-guns.

"No tank without bullets, no bullet without a tank," Pepe shouted, pleased with his slogan, to his men as they advanced. On his right, the Fifth Corps, too, was steadily advancing across a hail of bullets. The Internationals were shouting, "If they get me, there's a pack of American cigarettes in my right-hand pocket!" or "I'll have to miss the semi-finals this year, damn it, thanks to those damned fascists!" And they advanced behind a barrage of artillery fire brilliantly directed by a Spanish officer. Even the pacifists from the first-aid units, with bombs in their hands and no armlets, were attacking the tanks so as to be able to carry away their wounded.

A few voices started the *International,* drowned at once by a furious roar from the Spaniards and a short, shrill yell from the International Brigade: "Forward!"

"The fascists are not being supported by their planes," one of the officers from the Air General Staff remarked.

The clouds were only two hundred feet up, and more snow was threatening.

"They're on the far side of the Sierra," Sembrano replied. "It's most unlikely that they'll get across it today."

His arm was in a sling and he could not fly his plane. The Italian troops were between the Republicans and the Sierra.

Vargas made no comment.

"Obviously," one of the officers observed, "if we go up, we risk losing every machine we've got; it only needs the wind to freshen to a gale. No military authority would take the risk for such a catastrophe."

Vargas called for the orderly officer.

"Those machines they have at Teruel could get round the Sierra even in this weather," Sembrano said.

"I doubt if there are any left," Vargas replied.

The orderly officer went to the telephone, "Hullo, Alcalá! Send us at once every plane you can muster to Aerodrome 17 at Guadalajara. Hullo, Aerodrome 21? Send us every plane you have to Aerodrome 17 at Guadalajara. Hullo, Sarion? Send us every plane you have to Aerodrome 17 at Guadalajara."

"If we lose this battle," Vargas said, "we lose everything. After all, we are only accountable to the Spanish people for our air force. For the fascists, it's not so simple. . . . Anyhow, let's risk it!"

For the first time in many months he put on his flying helmet again.

The recruits were attacking. The recruits' battalion, composed of men who had not yet been attached to any of the International companies, consisted chiefly of volunteers from distant countries recently arrived: Greeks, Jews, Syrians, North Americans, Cubans, Canadians, Irishmen, South Americans, Mexicans and a few Chinese. They had started by blazing away without any system; men who do not feel the need to make a noise in their first battle are rare. At the first shock of encounter many had imagined that they were wounded, because they had been told that just at first wounds did not hurt. Some had diagnosed the swish of the first bullets as the noise of "Spanish birds." Hampered by their helmets, the peaks and neck-flaps of which jogged them each time they fired, unnerved by the grisly aspect of the dead, dumbfounded by the sight of the first casualties, they had awaited the order to advance with the same forced smile on every face. Then they had heard a muffled clamour indicating that the Edgar André battalion on their right was coming out onto open ground; and they had rushed forward behind the tanks with their hand-grenades.

On the extreme left, an extraordinarily mobile machine-gun attack had left Manuel's battalions numb with surprise, until the Moorish cavalry, armed with Lewis guns, had charged down on their trenches. Those who were having their first experience of such methods of attack were on the point of running away. But Manuel had surrounded his recruits with Pepe's *dinamiteros,* who knew very well that cavalry in motion are unable to take proper aim, and that they themselves were under cover. They met the first charge with hand-grenades.

Then, entrenching themselves close behind a barricade of dead horses, and aided now by the recruits—who had understood what was expected of them and were firing at the cavalry as they tried to rally—they started to crawl under the horses so as to pick up the fallen Lewis guns. Only the peasant recruits remained behind, eager enough to fight the men, but hating to kill such fine horses. Standing behind a tank, Gartner was urging them on by word and gesture, taking care, however, not to spread his gestures beyond the shelter of the turret.

All along the front the stretcher-bearers' hands were turning red.

Then, as if miraculously it had squeezed through between the white snow on the ground and the dingy snowclouds overhead, the first Republican plane appeared.

And after it, one by one, quaint and ungainly, like wounded soldiers, came the old planes which had not seen service since the first month of the war, the little machines of the *señoritos,* the transport planes, the mail planes, the Contact Patrol machines, Leclerc's old "Orion" and the practice planes; and the Spanish troops greeted them with half-hearted smiles such as their feelings at the moment may well have inspired.

Emissaries of an aerial apocalypse, they bore down on the

Italian machine-guns, skimming the snow; and at that moment
the battalions of the People's Army which had been waiting to
advance received the order.

Despite the lowering sky and the menace of the snow, they
came on, three by three at first, then squadron by squadron,
bumping against the clouds like birds beating their wings
against a ceiling, and swooping down again; filling all the far-
flung field of battle raging from horizon to horizon with a
roar that ruffled the snow upon the ground and the thin
shrouds of snow above the dead; spanning the bleak desolation
of the steppes drearier even than the forest's gloom—on they
came, eighty Republican planes in battle formation, like an
invading host.

Below, the Republican troops were advancing, wrapped in
great-coats and wearing on their heads peaked cowls like the
Moors'. Across the battle-wrack, between the broken lines in
headlong flight before the planes, Magnin had a brief glimpse
of a vibrating road which gradually resolved itself into an
Italian motorized column. As the wind was blowing from the
Republican lines, Magnin could not make out, from the
"Orion," whether the column was fleeing from the cowls, from
the tanks scattered across the trackless plain, or whether it was
being driven before the wind, like the endless ranks of clouds,
borne on the ceaseless flux of all things below.

And yet he had never felt so keyed up in a battle; it was as
if the clouds and columns had been the expression of one and
the same mysterious will, as if guns and gale and fascism were
all attacking him together; as if the grey, lightless world
around him were conspiring to cut him off from victory. A
huge cloud, so thick that it gave the pilots the impression they
were going blind, plunged on to the light planes, the wings of
which were getting tipped with snow and beginning to shudder
under the furious impact of the flakes that poured upon them.
It hid the earth and sky from them, penning them in on every
side, making the planes, creaking and grinding in their struggle
against the elements, seem motionless in a moving world. Taking his bearings from a dark grey patch, Magnin saw the
"Orion" turning at almost 180°. The compass jammed, the
instruments showing the horizontal were smashed. Cold
though it was, Darras took off his helmet and bent over the
altimeter, which too had smashed, his hair as white as everything around the plane—perhaps they were diving earthwards

at 150 miles an hour, and they were less than 1200 feet up!

No, they were emerging from the top of the cloud.

Between the layer of ragged clouds dissolving onto the earth and the second layer of clouds stretched out above like some frozen Arctic sea, all the Republican Air Force was advancing in line.

Darras tried to shake his wings to get rid of the snow.

"The bombs! For God's sake, be careful!"

But there was little carefulness in the way he dived again.

"A fight in the snow—that'll be exciting!" Magnin murmured to himself. With his planes scattered to all the winds of Spain, and his comrades scattered—but not in vain—in all its graveyards, all that he lived for now was this incredible "Orion," furiously buffeted by the blizzard, and the ramshackle planes beside it tossing like dead leaves upon the gale.

Those clean-cut ranks of hooded figures below the seething cloud-bank were recovering not only the Italian positions of the previous day, but the spirit of a bygone epoch. Magnin knew well what he was watching now as, like a crazy lift, the "Orion" jerked him up and down: it was the birth-pangs of war.

Campesino was issuing from his forest, the Garibaldi and Franco-Belgian units were streaming down behind the Dombrovsky battalion, the Carabinieri surging up along the Tajuma. From one end of the front to the other, machine-gunners changing the barrels of their guns and standing up, stung by the heated metal, were being mowed down. Tanks were advancing all along the line; first-aid parties running backwards and forwards behind them, gathering endless harvests of wounded in their blankets. One Republican tank, with half its caterpillar-wheels hanging over a gully, stood gaunt and derelict against the low grey sky. Karlitch, at last a Section-leader in the Tank Corps, was advancing, firing ceaselessly on the enemy anti-tank units—mere shadows of eyeless, crouching men armed with hand-grenades.

Passing over Teruel, Magnin had had a glimpse of the walls of huge estates, with their bulls, lethargic or unruly, scattered among the mountains which the war had claimed. And here, too, he had a glimpse, half blurred by the snowflakes, of the little stone walls which the Internationals and Madrid brigades were attacking below him, and they brought to his mind the new-built, squat stone walls which he had seen at Teruel and in the South, still insecure among the giant relics of the past. And he remembered the fallow land which the goitrous agricultural labourers were not allowed to cultivate. Those infuriated peasants fighting beneath him were struggling to raise those little walls, the first condition of their dignity. And Magnin now discerned, across the chaos of the dreams that had obsessed him during the last few months, something beyond the range of town-dwellers' preoccupations, something simple, clear and fundamental as childbirth, joy and pain and death: the age-old struggle of the tillers of the soil against their hereditary landlords.

When for the fifth time the "Orion" and its draggled squadron swept across the battlefield, the Republican machines had come down below the clouds and were attacking in front of the line of cowls. Hardly any fascist planes had put in an appearance. The Republican tanks, in a formation as orderly as a parade in Red Square, were attacking, forming up, and attacking again and again. An evening mist, red with the flashes of bursting bombs, was creeping up, and already the convents and churches of Brihuega, down in a hollow, were all but swallowed up in it. The horseshoe curve of the Republican Army closing in on the town was etched against the mist in a red flare of explosions. At each end of the horseshoe gushes of flame were pouring from the batteries, like bonfires kindled to counteract the snow which had set in again. Once the two ends met it would mean an Italian retreat along the whole Guadalajara front.

Ahead of the empty space between them, strip-signals were being laid out on the ground. But the mist was swallowing up everything now; it was impossible to make out a uniform. If darkness saved the Italians, they would counter-attack on Trijueque.

The "Orion" lurched drunkenly through the air—all its bombs had been released and it was taking no further part in the fight—but it still held its course above the battlefield, buffeted, struggling against the darkness closing in upon the destinies of Spain, just as night had fallen—how long ago that seemed!—on Marcelino's homing flight. The long, dense line of the military planes was veering at less than two hundred yards' distance from the battle. They, too, could see nothing, and they, too, were loath to leave the sky above the battlefield. And still the mist came flooding up from the Tajuma valley.

In the dusk the desperate struggle of the volunteers went on, the ordeal that was to make or mar the fortunes of the Republican Army. And the planes which perhaps had won the battle were hovering near, not on the look-out for an opening for attack, but watching and waiting for the Spanish victory. Spellbound in the gathering dusk, they had forgotten the perils of return to lightless aerodromes.

Flying over the gap between the tips of the horseshoe, Magnin saw beneath him one of the Horca roads, which widened out at that point and was lined with abandoned lorries. He dived and skimmed the ground as he had done with the peasant on the Teruel aerodrome; and while the Republican troops, mistaking his identity, were riddling his wings with bullets, he recognized the strip-signals laid out there; they were those of Mera, the anarchist, of Campesino and the Carabinieri.

5

LAST spasmodic bursts of gunfire were rumbling in the distance. His lines established, Manuel, followed by his dog, was going round the village to get hold of some lorries. He had adopted a magnificent—ex-fascist—wolfhound, and it had been wounded four times. The more he felt cut off from men, the more he loved animals: bulls, army horses, wolfhounds, fighting cocks. The Italians had abandoned a number of lorries, and while waiting for their official distribution each commander of a unit tried to get hold of as many as he could (shrewdly maintaining that if they waited until Campesino arrived there would not be one left). The lorries were garaged for the time being in whatever buildings were large enough to house them: churches, village halls, or barns. In the village occupied by the Carabinieri they were in the church. But Manuel had been warned that Ximenes was there with the same intentions as himself.

The church was a lofty red-stone building, its stucco palms badly chipped by bullets. The slanted shafts of daylight which came through the cathedral-like vaulting fell on the débris of chairs smashed to matchwood, and the lorries lined up in order in the centre of the nave.

A *miliciano* guarding the church accompanied Manuel and Gartner.

"Have you seen the Colonel?" Gartner asked.

"He's over there, behind the lorries."

"That's bad, he'll have already pinched them."

Manuel's eyes were not yet used to the darkness; vaguely he seemed to see a mass of tangled gold quivering in the shadows above the porch like a bouquet of flames pinned to the wall. A band of angels, a medley of projecting wings and feet, around the pipes of an oddly shaped organ. Manuel noticed a spiral staircase and went up it, anxious for a clearer view.

The *miliciano* followed him. Gartner remained below, as if to guard the lorries, with the dog at his heel.

"How is it this has remained intact?" Manuel asked the *miliciano*.

"It's the Revolutionary Artistic Committee, as they call it. Some fellows came along and told the local committee: 'That organ and the choir, they've got to be preserved.' Quite right, they were, a lot of work went into it. So they took the necessary steps."

"What about the Italians?"

"There wasn't much fighting here."

Just recently an anarchist had used the torch with which he was about to set fire to a chapel to trace a huge black arrow above Cervantes' tomb, pointing to the Crucifix which had been left intact, and had written on it: "Cervantes has saved you."

"How do *you* feel about that?" Manuel asked.

"Well, the man who made those sculptures loved his job. I've never been one for destroying things. Priests of course I don't hold with. But I've nothing against churches. My idea is that they should be turned into theatres; they're nice to look at and you can hear well."

Manuel remembered the *milicianos* he had questioned with Ximenes on the Tagus front. He scanned the nave closely, and finally discerned, beside a pillar, a shaved, downy pate like a duckling's head, shining in the gloom. Manuel knew that Ximenes appreciated music. He looked at the old man's white halo with affection, smiled as if he were meditating a practical joke, and seated himself at the keyboard.

He began to play the first piece of sacred music which came into his head—the Palestrina *Kyrie*.

Essentially the music of devotion, the notes echoed down the empty nave, stiff and severe as Gothic draperies; quite out of keeping with war, but all too much in tune with death.

Despite the chairs smashed to atoms, and the lorries, and the war, the voice of the next world was claiming the church for its own again. And Manuel was moved, not by the melody but by his memories. The *miliciano* was gaping in amazement at the Lieutenant-Colonel who had taken to playing "hymns"!

"Well, that's all right, the old contraption's still all right," he said when Manuel had ceased playing.

Manuel climbed down from the stool and began stroking his dog, which had tactfully refrained from barking. He went on stroking it; he had nothing in his right hand now. Gartner was waiting for him at the bottom of the staircase. Near the lorries, big black stains covered the flagstones. Manuel had long since stopped wondering what liquid accounted for such stains.

"That *Kyrie* is a marvellous thing," he said with emotion, "and I was thinking of something else while I was playing it. I have finished with music . . . You saw that there was a whole pile of Chopin on the piano in our quarters last week —all the best things. I looked through them, but it all seemed to belong to another life."

"Perhaps it was too late—or too early."

"Perhaps . . . but I don't think so. I think another life started for me with the war—as definitely as the first time I slept with a woman. War purifies you."

"There's a lot could be said about that."

At last they found the Colonel, who was supervising the testing of the engines.

"So it's you, my son, who've been playing the music of Heaven for me? Thank you. You did it with that in mind, I think."

"It gave me pleasure to do it."

Ximenes was looking at him.

"You'll be a general before you're thirty-five, Manuel."

"I am a Spaniard of the sixteenth century," Manuel said, with the grave smile which drew down the corners of his mouth.

"But, tell me, you aren't a professional musician—how the devil did you learn to play the organ?"

"It was the result of a piece of blackmail. The padre who was supposed to teach me Latin used to confine his efforts to the first hour out of every two, the second being free for me to do whatever I liked. But at first what I liked became what he liked. He used to stick an ivory needle (a great luxury in those days) into an old-fashioned, second-hand gramophone

he had picked up, with a horn like a convolvulus, and play
Verdi. I got to know *L'Africaine* by heart. Later on, I insisted
on having lessons in tactics. (You hear that, Colonel!) He
pointed out that he was neither competent nor disposed to
teach such a subject. But he brought me an old shoe-box full
of soldiers cut out in cardboard."

There were soldiers going past them now, on stretchers,
rolled in blankets, living and dead.

"Then the Palestrina records appeared. He was a shrewd
old chap. To escape being pestered about tactics, he used to
ply the ivory needle on poor old Palestrina. It was a great
success. I gave up tactics and clamoured for organ lessons. I
was a good pianist already."

"Well, my son, it seems there are some priests who aren't
such bad lots," the old man said ironically.

Manuel skilfully switched the conversation to his lorries,
but he had hardly started when Ximenes cut him short.

"It's no good trying to wangle things. Until definite orders
arrive, those lorries are sacred."

"So it seems. We found them in a church. But your Carabinieri have got light lorries."

Ximenes chuckled, closing one eye in the old way.

"Nothing doing! You'll be a general by the time you're
thirty, but you won't get my lorries. I haven't got enough, anyway. Let's go and hunt for some more."

"In the Sierra I told a militia-girl she had lovely hair—and
I asked her to give me one, and she sent me to hell. You're as
mean as she was!"

"Get me a screw-spanner, and—let's drop the subject."

They set off; before they had got to Brihuega they had already found three lorries each. The drivers brought by Gartner
and Ximenes' men climbed into the drivers' seats and followed
on after them.

"This is a nice little jaunt," Manuel said. "Quite an Andalusian wedding-party."

"Kilometre 88!" a messenger shouted to them.

Victory was in the air.

In the square at Brihuega, in front of the military headquarters, which all the senior officers were expected to visit
in the course of the mornings, Garcia and Magnin were listening to a talkative old windbag wearing an elaborate cravat,
who had not shaved for days, and whose general appearance
suggested that he had just emerged from a cellar.

"When they decided to kick us out," he was saying, "they tidied up the place. But they forgot to take down the wires we'd used to hang our trousers on. And the new guides hadn't a notion what to say about those wires. All except one. One of the lads he was; quite an artist in his way."

He made a gesture of combing out long, "artistic" hair.

"He used to do sketches, write poetry, and so on. Yes he was a real artist. That's what he used to tell the tourists from the Toledo Alcazar: 'Ladies and gentlemen, that famous warrior, the Cid, was naturally a very busy man. But when he had finished all his work, giving orders and writing and making expeditions, he used to come to this room. All alone. And then what do you suppose he used to do, by way of taking a rest? Hang on to this wire and swing.' "

"He used to be a guide at the Guadalajara Palace, that comrade," Garcia said to Manuel and Ximenes; "and before that at Toledo."

He was an old man with side-whiskers like rabbits' paws and the face and mannerisms of a professional actor, the sort that can only exist in a world of make-believe. "I was one for queer things, too," he continued, "before I lost my first wife. I've travelled all over the world, used to be with a circus. Whenever there was something worth seeing, that was what I made for. But now with all this business . . ."

He extended a thumb in the direction of Guadalajara, where the wind beneath the lowering clouds reeked of a charnel-house, and towards which the Italian prisoners were going.

"I've been mixed up with all that, those cardinals, and even the Grecos, and the tourists and all the rest of it, for twenty-five years. And now after six months of war . . ."

He was still pointing towards the south-west—Guadalajara, Madrid, Toledo—as though he were unconcernedly brushing flies away.

An officer came and spoke to Manuel, who gave the dog a resounding smack on the back and shouted: "Kilometre 90! They're abandoning all their material."

"Do you wish to hear, Señor?" the guide went on.

He shrugged his shoulders and continued, as though summing up the experiences of a lifetime.

"Stones . . . old stones, that's all. Now if you go farther south you'll find things that are worth while—Roman remains! More than thirty years before Christ! Thirty years B.C.

—that's talking, eh? Sagunto is a fine place. Or give me the new districts of Barcelona. But all these old buildings! Just stones, if you ask me, like war."

Some Moors were going past, with the Italian prisoners.

"The longer you fight, the nearer you get to the real heart of Spain," Garcia said. "But in my case, the harder I work, the further away I get. I spent the morning questioning Moorish prisoners. There were only a few here, but still there were some. There are some everywhere. Magnin, do you remember Vargas saying to me: 'There are only twelve thousand Moors?' Right. Well, as a matter of fact, there are a considerable number of Moors from French territory here. At the present moment the real Islam, Islam considered as a spiritual unity, is more or less in Mussolini's hands. The French and English still nominally govern North Africa, but Italy controls the religious side. And the immediate result is that here in Brihuega we are capturing Moorish and Italian prisoners. There's unrest in French Morocco and Libya, unrest in Palestine, Egypt, promises from Franco to restore the Cordoba mosque to the followers of Mahomet . . ."

Garcia loved talking; and the others liked listening to him. They read nothing, except well-censored papers, and Garcia's information was good. But both Manuel and Ximenes remembered that they had their lorries to think of.

From the doorway of the house where he had taken refuge during the Italian occupation a woman was calling to the guide.

"We are waiting for Azaña to tackle the job now," he was saying to Garcia. "What will he do? That's something we just don't know." Pointing up at the low clouds he suddenly dropped the mysterious tone which he had till now assumed and said with complete indifference, "Nothing. He will do nothing. There's nothing can be done. Franco sticks at nothing, of course. But apart from him, it doesn't matter if it is Azaña or Caballero, the U.G.T. or the C.N.T., or you; now that I've come out of my cellar I shall serve customers and guide fools, and I shall die in Guadalajara serving customers and guiding fools."

The woman called to him again and he left them.

"He's a quaint bird, all right," Magnin said.

"In the most ferocious civil war there are always plenty of people who take no interest in it," Garcia replied.

"Do you know, Magnin," he continued, "after eight months

of war there's something still remains a bit of a mystery to me
—the exact moment when a man decides to pick up a rifle?"

"Our friend Barca used to do some hard thinking on that
point," Manuel said.

The wolfhound barked approvingly.

"On people's fundamental reasons for fighting, yes. But
what interests me is the actual spark that sets them off. It
seems as if fighting, the apocalypse, and hope, are baits used
by war to catch men. After all, syphilis starts with love. Pug-
nacity forms part of the play-acting which almost every man
indulges in, and it leads men into war just as almost every sort
of play-acting leads us right into life. Yes, the war is only
starting now."

The same thought had occurred to Magnin in the "Orion,"
and probably to many others too. This conversation reminded
him of his talk with Garcia and Vargas on the night after
Medellin; and he felt once again that the International Air
Force was dead.

"We're going to have Japan in the picture very soon,"
Garcia said. "An empire almost as big as the British Empire is
being created over there."

"Think of what Europe was when we were twenty, and
look at it now," Magnin said.

Manuel, Gartner and Ximenes started off again in quest of
lorries; Garcia took Magnin's arm.

"What about Scali?" he asked.

"Explosive bullet in the foot at Teruel. He'll lose his foot."

"What were his politics?"

"H'm well—more and more anarchist, more and more
Sorelian, almost anti-communist."

"It's not communism that he is opposed to, it's the Communist Party."

"Tell me, *commandante,* what do *you* think of communists?"

So that's not finished yet, Garcia thought.

"My friend Guernico," he answered, "says: 'They have all
the virtues of action and no others.' But action is what matters just at present."

His voice went lower, as always when he was recounting an
unpleasant experience.

"I went to see the Italian prisoners this morning. There was
one of them, an oldish man, blubbering like a baby. I asked
him what was the matter, but he just cried and cried. At last

he said 'I've got seven children—what's going to happen to them?' In the end I realized that he was convinced that we intended shooting the prisoners. I explained that we had no such intention, and at last he brought himself to believe me. Then suddenly he went frantic, jumped onto the bench and started yelling out a speech—just a few bits like: 'We have been tricked in Italy,' and so on. Then he yelled: 'Down with Mussolini!' Didn't cause any great stir. He began again. And the other prisoners took it up: 'To hell with him!' but like a chorus singing with closed lips, and looking with scared eyes towards the doors. And yet they were safe with us.

"It wasn't fear of the police which was weighing on them, Magnin; nor even personal fear of Mussolini. It was the Fascist Party. And it has been the same with us. At the beginning of the war loyal falangists died shouting, 'Long live Spain!' but later it was 'Long live the falangists!' Are you sure that among your airmen the type of communist who at first died shouting 'Long live the Proletariat!' or 'Long live Communism!' doesn't shout today, in the same circumstances: 'Long live the Party!'?

"They won't have much more shouting to do, anyway, for they are nearly all either in hospital or under the ground. Perhaps it's all a matter of personal feelings. Attignies would probably shout: 'Long live the Party!' The others, something else.

"The word 'party' is misleading, in any case. It is most difficult to group together under one label a mass of people united by the same vote, and parties whose ultimate roots go down into the deep, irrational mainsprings of human nature. The age of parties is beginning, my friend."

All the same, mused Magnin, Garcia assured me that the U.S.S.R. would never intervene. He is interesting, but not infallible. The Major was tightening his grasp on his arm, which he still held.

"Don't let us exaggerate our victory. This battle is no Battle of the Marne. But it's a victory, all the same. There were more unemployed here than Blackshirts, that's why I arranged for the propaganda by loud-speakers, which you will remember. Still, we were fighting actual fascist units. We should regard this patch of ground with due deference, my friend, for it is our Valmy. The two real Parties have come up against each other here for the first time."

Some officers were coming out of their headquarters, clapping each other on the back.

"Kilometre 92!" they were shouting to each other.

"Have you been through Ibarra?" Magnin asked Garcia.

"Yes, but only during the fighting."

"The whole place is full of bowls of rice. *Riz au lait*, it seems; which the Garibaldi units kept on asking for—they hate Spanish oil—and which they at last managed to have made for them. Then the rice in the bowls got covered with snow. Just like the first casualties. They dug them out of the snow to bury them; and every one of those dead faces looked happy; smiles on their lips, the smiles of satisfied stomachs."

"Life's a queer business," Garcia said.

Magnin was thinking of the peasants. He was by no means as much at home with abstract thinking as was Garcia. But his flying experience had given his mind a purely physical flexibility which at times made up for lack of depth. The peasants obsessed him: the one Garcia had sent him, those whom he had asked for lorries in the villages, the ones who had accompanied the wounded down from the mountains, and those whom he had seen fighting below him the day before.

"What about the peasants?" was all he said.

"Before leaving Guadalajara, I had a coffee and *anis* (still without sugar). The inn-keeper was having the paper read to him by his little daughter—she knew how to read. Either Franco will do what we are doing, wherever he wins, or he'll embark on an endless guerrilla war. Christ's triumph was only won through Constantine; Napoleon was completely crushed at Waterloo, but the essential points of French liberty defied suppression. One of the things that worries me most is seeing how in every war each side adopts the characteristics of the enemy, whether they wish it or not."

The guide was behind Garcia, who had not heard him return. He raised his forefinger and screwed up his eyes, and an enigmatic look gave the face an air of refinement despite his drunkard's nose.

"The deadliest enemy of man, gentlemen, is the forest. It is stronger than we are, stronger than the Republic, stronger than the Revolution, stronger than the war . . . If man ceased to struggle against it, Europe would be covered with forests in less than sixty years. It would be here in the street,

in the devastated houses, branches growing out of windows
—pianos tangled up with the roots. Yes, gentlemen, that's a
fact!"

Some soldiers had entered the gutted houses and were picking out tunes on the pianos with one finger.

"Kilometre 93!" a voice shouted from a window.

More prisoners were crossing the square.

"The bunch of bastards!" said the guide. "Why couldn't
they stay at home?"

He lowered his eyes, and caught sight of his new shoes.

"Still, I've got them to thank for these shoes, you know.
My word, haven't they just left some stuff behind them! But
some of them are quite good scouts, though. Hey you, sing
us something!" He waved his arm to the men who were passing near him. One of the prisoners shouted something that
he could not understand.

"What did he say?"

"The unhappy do not sing," Garcia translated.

"Then sing about your troubles, you fool," the guide replied
in Spanish.

The prisoners were getting farther away; he followed them
with his eyes.

"Never mind, old fellow, it'll all come right one day!"

In the distance, the sound of an accordion was coming
from the Garibaldi battalion.

"Yes, how little it all matters! At Guadalajara I look after
a garden. The lizards come . . . When I was in India with
the circus I learnt a Hindu tune. I whistle it, and the lizards
run onto my face. You've only got to close your eyes—and
know the tune. And now, what? War, prisoners, and death.
And when it's all over, I shall stretch myself out as usual on
the bench and whistle, and the lizards will crawl over my
face."

"I shall look forward to seeing that," Magnin said, tugging
at his moustache.

The guide looked at him, raised his finger again, and said:

"Nobody understands that, Monsieur, nobody." Then, pointing at the door from which he had been summoned: "Not
even my second wife."

"Kilometre 94!" shouted a second messenger.

6

As SOON as the requisition order for the Italian lorries came
in from headquarters, Manuel had left Ximenes. He walked
back to the place where his Brigade was quartered, with the
wolfhound trotting composedly beside him, while Gartner
busied himself returning the lorries that had been scrounged
before the battle.

The soldiers were wandering about Brihuega, empty-handed
and unwontedly at a loose end. The main street with its pink
and yellow houses, austere churches and huge convents, was
so full of rubbish, so many shattered houses had disgorged
their furniture into the roadway, and the whole street was so
closely linked up with the war that, now there was a cessation
of hostilities, it seemed unreal, preposterous as the tombs and
temples of an extinct race, and the soldiers roaming it now
without their rifles had the lost look of civilian unemployed.

Some streets, however, seemed unscathed by war. Garcia
had told Manuel how at Jaipur in India all the house-fronts
are painted in sham perspective and how each house wears in
front of it, like a mask, its pink façade. Many of the Brihuega
streets brought to mind a city not of mud but of the dead;
death was lurking behind the windows that stood half open
on the cheerless sky and the gay house-fronts that recalled
siesta and the holiday season.

It seemed to Manuel that he heard the plash of fountains
everywhere. A thaw had set in. Water was gushing from the
stone corbels and along the gutters, fraying into little rivulets
between the pointed cobble-stones so typical of old Spain and
tumbling over them with the sound of miniature mountain-
torrents, amid the pictures, scraps of furniture, pots and pans,
and miscellaneous wreckage in the street. Not an animal had
stayed in Brihuega; but now, like homeless cats, the *milicianos*
were to be seen prowling from one street to another, in the
desolation murmurous with running water.

As Manuel approached the centre of the town another
sound mingled with the plash of water, in a counterpoint of
limpid harmonies—the notes of a piano. The front wall of a
house he was passing had collapsed into the street, leaving all
the dwelling-rooms open to the sky; in one of them a *miliciano*

was picking out the notes of a popular song with one finger. Manuel listened attentively; now across the water-music of the street he could make out the sounds of three pianos. Nothing like the *International*. The tunes were those of sentimental refrains, but played so slowly that they might have been in homage to the infinite pathos of the slopes, strewn with derelict lorries, that rose from Brihuega towards the livid sky.

Manuel had told Gartner that he had given up music, but he suddenly realized that what he needed most at this moment —alone in the street of a conquered town—was to hear some music. He had no desire to play, himself, and he wanted to remain alone. There were two gramophones in the Brigade mess-room. He had discarded the records which he had carried about with him in the early days of the war, but the big gramophone cabinet was well stocked. Gartner was a German.

He found some Beethoven symphonies and the *Adieux*. He was no more than a half-hearted admirer of Beethoven, but that made no difference. Taking the smaller gramophone into his room, he set it going. Now that the tension of his will relaxed, the past came into its own. He remembered his exact gesture when he had handed his revolver to Alba. Perhaps, as Ximenes said, he had found the life he was meant for. He was born to war, born to the responsibility of death. Like the sleepwalker who wakes up suddenly on the edge of a roof, he felt the dying cadence of the music bringing home to him the terrible precariousness of his mental foothold; any false step might land him in—a shambles! Another memory crossed his mind—of a blind beggar he had seen in Madrid on the night of Carabanchel. Manuel had been with the Chief of Police, in his car, when suddenly the headlights had lit up a blind man's outstretched fingers, magnifying their form, against the steep upward slope of the Gran Via, to a prodigious size, showing them humped and gnarled against the cobbles, criss-crossed by the pavements, and momentarily effaced by the few cars which the war had not driven from the streets—long, groping hands, long as the hands of Fate.

"Kilometre 95! Kilometre 95!" men were shouting in all parts of the town, always with the same intonation.

He felt the seething life around him charged with portents, as though some blind destiny lay in wait for him behind those lowering cloudbanks which the guns no longer racked. The wolfhound was listening, lying full length like the dogs in bas-reliefs. Some day there would be peace. And he, Manuel, would become another man, someone he could not visualize as yet; just as the soldier he had become could no more visualize the Manuel who once had bought a little car to go skiing in the Sierra.

Most likely it was the same with all those others moving through the streets, and the same with the men he could hear strumming their favourite tunes on pianos open to the public gaze—the men whose heavy pointed cowls had led the battle yesterday. Once it had been deliberate contemplation that had taught Manuel about himself; now it fell to chance to snatch him from the activities of the moment and force his mind upon his past. And, like himself, like all those others, drained of her blood, Spain, too, was growing conscious of herself—as in the hour of death, suddenly, a man takes stock of all his life. . . . But war may be discovered only once in a lifetime; life, many times.

As the strands of melody took form, interwoven with his past, they conveyed to him the self-same message that the dim sky, those ageless fields and that town which had stopped the Moors might, too, have given him. For the first time Manuel was hearing the voice of that which is more awe-inspiring even than the blood of men, more enigmatic even than their presence on the earth—the infinite possibilities of their destiny. And he felt that this new consciousness within him was linked up with the sounds of running water in the street and the footfalls of the prisoners, profound and permanent as the beating of his heart.

Bantam Modern Classics

☐ SY4018   APE AND ESSENCE   Aldous Huxley   75¢

☐ SY4014   MADELEINE   André Gide   75¢

☐ SY4012   DESERT OF LOVE   François Mauriac   75¢

☐ NY4058   THE TIME OF THE ASSASSINS
           Godfrey Blunden   95¢

☐ NY4010   GOODBYE, COLUMBUS   Philip Roth   95¢

☐ NY4054   DEMIAN   Hermann Hesse   95¢

☐ NY4009   ALL THE KING'S MEN   Robert Penn Warren   95¢

☐ QY4013   MAN'S HOPE   André Malraux $1.25

☐ QY4006   THE LAST TEMPTATION OF CHRIST
           Nikos Kazantzakis $1.25

☐ NY4089   LADY CHATTERLEY'S LOVER   D. H. Lawrence   95¢

☐ SY4074   ZAZIE   Raymond Queneau   75¢

☐ NY4090   EYELESS IN GAZA   Aldous Huxley   95¢

☐ NY4008   DARKNESS AT NOON   Arthur Koestler   95¢

Available wherever paperbacks are sold

BANTAM WORLD DRAMA

Introducing a new library of living theater—from Euripides to Osborne. This series contains authoritative editions as well as fresh modern translations of the classics and important contemporary plays including the latest experiments of the avant-garde. Many of the plays contain introductions and commentaries by leading critics and scholars.